# SEVEN CHARACTERS IN SEARCH OF AN AUTHOR

Shaila Van Sickle
in collaboration with Doreen Mehs

Shaila Van Sickle
in collaboration with Doreen Mehs


ISBN 978-0-615-65932-9
Library of Congress Control Number:  2012916661


Editor: Elizabeth A. Green
Book and cover design: Lisa Snider Atchison


Printed in the U.S.A.

## To Doreen

❧

If not for my longtime friend and colleague Doreen Mehs, this book would never have been written.

After we both retired from teaching, she told me she would be enlarging her flock of sheep during her retirement and then chided me for not having a post-retirement plan of my own.

"What about that mystery novel you claimed you were going to write back in the 1970s?" she asked.

"I'll write it if you'll help," I replied. She said she would.

For several years we plotted and revised the story, reading aloud what the other had written and then trading rewrites. Sadly, Doreen developed vascular dementia before we were done. Even when she could no longer type or follow the printed lines as I read aloud, she remained an excellent listener with an uncanny memory of our characters and their doings. She could still suggest better words or phrases and catch contradictions in the story.

After her death in May 2009, I put the manuscript aside for many months before I could return to it. I'm pleased to pay tribute to our friendship and love of teaching with this book and I know she'd be happy to see it in other readers' hands.

## Cast of Characters

**Main Characters**
**Walt Asher,** president, Southwestern College
**Erica Ebenezer,** professor of geology, task force co-chair
**Toni Hexton,** associate professor of journalism, task force co-chair
**Jim Scoop,** chief of college security and public safety

**Task Force Members**
**Sarah Jennings,** chair of fine arts department
**Jeff Miles,** public relations director
**Lloyd Reasoner,** professor of philosophy
**Steve Scott,** library director

**Academic Awards**
**Frederick Burns,** fictional president of Canyon College
**Stanley Johnson,** CEO, North America Mystery Writers Association
**Mary Sheepherder,** fictional student at Canyon College
**Geoffrey Thompson,** fictional student at Canyon College

**Supporting Characters**
**Taylor Anderson,** professor of art
**Joe Blake,** physical plant director
**Edith Tansley Coyle,** pseudonym used by author of award-winning book
**Bill Ebenezer,** freelance writer & Erica's husband
**Richard Frankel,** professor of English, mystery buff
**Betty Frost,** editor of student newspaper
**Jonathan Gill,** assistant professor of political science
**Jolene Gonzales,** physical plant staff; Jake Henderson's neighbor
**Ruby Hall,** Walt Asher's secretary
**Bill Hamill,** vice-president of faculty
**Jake Henderson,** former professor of history at Southwestern College
**Billy Bob Jenkins,** (aka B.B.) senior security officer
**Sheila Mays,** retired professor of physical education
**Melinda Merry,** computer center staff member
**Florencio Ordoñez,** Albuquerque police officer
**Lois Pidgin,** professor of sociology, chair of faculty senate
**Charlie Roanhorse,** recent Southwestern College graduate
**Sally Sanchez,** vice-president of student services
**Jane Snow,** professor of psychology

# SATURDAY AND SUNDAY, SEPTEMBER 3 AND 4

*The beginning of another academic year at Southwestern College in New Mexico. The college president is confronted by a problem in need of a quick solution.*

Journalism professor Toni Hexton returned home on the first Saturday night in September to the insistent ringing of her phone. She dropped her camping gear on the porch, scrabbled around in her purse for her house key, and wrestled it into the balky lock. Switching on her living room light, she heard a click signaling the end of a telephone message.

She was ready to fall into bed, but the late night call worried her. She stuffed the contents of her duffel into the washer and hung her sleeping bag to air while she replayed the messages that had piled up during her two-week absence. Most were from students begging her to save them a spot in her senior seminar. Three were from her mother. Toni had told her she'd be away between mid-August and early September, teaching a geology field camp with her good friend and colleague, Erica Ebenezer. As usual, her mother hadn't listened.

The last four messages all came from a most unlikely source. Three times Toni heard Walt Asher, Southwestern College's president, asking her to return his call immediately. The fourth time, his voice, despite his apology, sounded curt. "Sorry to call you so often and so late. There's been a crisis on campus I need to talk to you about, but it can wait until tomorrow. If you're not home by now, you must be exhausted. It's after eleven, and I'm turning in, so don't call me back. Just be at my office at eight tomorrow morning."

Toni set her alarm clock, took her first hot shower in weeks, and crawled into bed. She tried not to worry about the president's phone calls—unsuccessfully."

At 7:00 the next morning Toni, fighting off a fierce headache, was on the road for her forty-five minute drive to the college.

She was tired. Trailing after long-legged Erica and a group of sturdy students several miles every day was hard work, and sleep had eluded her until shortly before her alarm went off.

Still sleepy and out of sorts, Toni ticked off her resentments. One, the twice-weekly aerobic exercise classes she'd attended all summer long hadn't made her nearly as fit as her athletic friend Erica. Two, she hadn't enjoyed yesterday's long drive chauffeuring chatty students in a college van on rutty mountain roads. Three, she wondered why she'd expected camping out in the mountains of Colorado to be more like a vacation than work or that she could teach students more about scientific writing than Erica could. Four, she resented feeling like a junior high kid being summoned to the principal's office. Five, she had turned 45 yesterday and nobody, not even her own mother, had wished her a happy birthday.

What was so urgent that Walt needed to meet with her on Sunday morning anyway? Why couldn't he just tell her what the crisis was? And what part could she have played in it? She revisited all the possibilities that had occurred to her during the night. Most of her transgressions were too trivial to have come to the attention of the president. She had failed a student for plagiarism last spring. Her "F" kept him from graduating and elicited an angry protest from his wealthy parents, but the president and two vice-presidents had stood behind her.

Toni longed for just one quiet day before encountering clamoring students, meeting with colleagues—debating about such crucial issues as whether Introduction to News Writing should be offered during the first or second semester—and wrangling over times when whatever committees she'd agreed to be on for the coming year could meet. She needed a day to buy groceries, prepare classes, and read twenty geology field journals.

As Toni dropped down from the mesa top toward the village of Cottonwood, she passed Erica's restored 1880s farmhouse. Glancing at the driveway, she saw Erica's old green Forest Service truck idling. She made a sharp left and, pulling up next to the truck, shouted, "Are you on your way to Asher's office?"

"Yeah. You too? Do you know what the president wants to see us about? He called here yesterday afternoon but wouldn't tell Bill what was so urgent that he's violating his no-work-on-Sundays prohibition."

"Hop in with me. No need for us both to drive."

"Thanks. Here, I have something for you. It's one day late, and awfully crumpled, but I couldn't find it when we were packing up yesterday morning," Erica said, handing Toni a sheet of paper.

Next to a dot at the very top of a hand-drawn chart of the geologic ages, from Cambrian through Jurassic to Holocene, Erica had written, "From the point of view of a geologist, 45 is very young! And even from my point of view as your 55-year-old friend, you're relatively young."

"Well, I don't feel it. I feel decidedly creaky and middle-aged. You may be ten years older than I am, but you walk like the basketball player you were in college. And I bet you don't even have any sore muscles this morning! I suppose your athletic career began in elementary school?"

"Oh, yes," laughed Erica. "No one in my first grade class could outlast me in rope-jumping contests."

As Toni backed out of Erica's driveway, feeling lots better with Erica's birthday greeting in hand, she changed the subject. "Walt called me four times yesterday. He finally left a terse message close to midnight. I'd been looking forward to a soft bed and a long sleep. Instead, I stayed awake wondering how I'd misbehaved. If Walt has commanded an audience with you too, he's probably heard about something awful we did at field camp."

"Maybe," said Erica, shrugging as she fastened her seat belt. "More likely, it's something we *didn't* do. I'm sure we ignored at least one of the endless *official guidelines* for taking students off campus."

Erica's snidely emphasized words jolted Toni into remembering their second night out. Two students had wandered away from their campsite shortly after supper and hadn't returned until the following morning. "Do you suppose Walt heard about Jeb and Sam's trying to view the eclipse from the top of Engineer Mountain?" asked Toni.

"How? Unless somebody called home on a cell phone, there's no way Walt could have learned they'd been stranded all night. Jeb and Sam wouldn't tell. They were too embarrassed. They wouldn't have admitted they weren't the mountain men they claimed to be. And the rest of the students won't complain. They were pissed. Especially when the two guys walked into camp and asked why breakfast wasn't ready yet in the midst of our search-and-rescue preparations."

"I still feel guilty though. I was the one who said the best view of the eclipse would occur shortly after ten-thirty on top of the mountain."

"Except for being chilly, they returned none the worse for wear. That's one crisis we can cross off the list. We'll find out what Walt's crisis is soon enough," said Erica, as Toni turned into Center Hall's parking lot. "Uh oh, there's his Jeep, but it isn't alone. I think I recognize Bill Hamill's car."

"And Sally Sanchez's new VW, too," said Toni. "If the other cars belong to more of the high muckety-mucks we must be suspected of breaking every rule in the book. Oh, well, let's go face the firing squad."

Toni and Erica were silent as they climbed the two flights of stairs to the president's office suite. They hesitated before the open door of the conference room. The president and six members of his administrative cabinet, a group he often referred to as his teammates, confronted them. Seated clockwise around a large oval table flanking him were three vice-presidents—of faculty, students, and finance—and three directors—of the physical plant, the library, and athletics.

Glancing at the expectant faces, Erica blurted out, "Are you all here for an execution?"

"Nothing quite as ominous as that." Asher smiled. "After my calls yesterday, I realized I should have explained the reason for this morning's meeting. But it's a long story and I didn't know where to begin. I certainly didn't mean to make you think you were in trouble. I should have told you both that we're hoping you *have* done something, something good," said Walt. "Get yourselves some coffee and I'll tell you why we think you may be the answer to our prayers."

Toni looked quizzical. Erica looked skeptical.

After they had poured themselves some coffee and sat down at the conference table, Asher opened a manila folder. Ceremoniously, he withdrew a newspaper clipping. He pushed it across the table, turning it around so that it faced Toni and Erica.

A minute later, Joe Blake, the physical plant director, asked, "Does that look familiar?"

Vice-President of Student Affairs Sally Sanchez leaned forward, hoping to see signs of recognition. Clearly disappointed, she asked. "You've never heard of a competition sponsored by NAMWA?"

"No," said Toni, bending over the clipping, "and I've never even heard of the North American Mystery Writers Association."

Erica circled one paragraph with a finger and began to read aloud: "The winning contestant will not only win fifty thousand dollars but will be able to present five hundred thousand dollars to the institution that provides the setting for the prize-winning novel." She guffawed, then slowly realized she was the only one laughing. "Is this some kind of joke?"

"Far from it," replied Walt. "The winner of NAMWA's contest will be guaranteed publication and a handsome advance and will also add a cool half million to Southwestern College's coffers. There's a problem though. That's why we've asked you to meet with us this morning. NAMWA knows the winner selected Southwestern for the novel's setting. They sent me a copy of the manuscript. I had no trouble recognizing our school. Before we can thank the author for our good fortune, we have to produce the author—or authors. Through a major snafu, the people at NAMWA can't *find* the author. They're expecting us to do that for them. We'd hate to see our local winner lose out. And of course we'd hate to see Southwestern forfeit quite a windfall, which we'll do unless the author materializes. The awards will pass to the runner-up and some other college or university. We certainly don't want that to happen."

It seemed to both Toni and Erica that the eyes of Asher and the members of his cabinet were focused on them, daring the two women not to let them down. The president voiced their common hope. "You two are our best bet."

"You thought the two of us had written a mystery?" asked Erica, cocking one eyebrow in disbelief.

"That's not so far fetched," said Bill Hamill, vice-president of faculty affairs. "You've collaborated on quite a few things over the years. Why not a book?"

"But why us?" asked Toni.

"First, it sounds like the kind of thing you two might have done for a lark," explained Fred Parker, the athletic director. He addressed Erica, whose support of the women's basketball and volleyball teams over many years made her one of his favorite faculty members. "In all the time I've known you, I've never known you to be at a loss for words."

Walt looked directly at Toni. "You were a reporter before you came here to teach journalism, and as I understand it, journalists write. What could be more natural than for you to write a book? At Friday's faculty meeting, you and Erica were still off in the mountains. When we asked the faculty whether anyone were guilty, they all said no."

"You should be honored." Sally Sanchez chuckled. "Your colleagues were quick to point to you as the most likely culprits."

"Several of your friends revealed your membership in a heretofore secret society," added Steve Scott, the library director, "some kind of club that trades mysteries."

"Even though we do swap mysteries with some of our low-brow

colleagues, we're not guilty of writing any mystery book," said Toni.

"Alone or together," added Erica.

There was an awkward silence before Bill Hamill spoke up. "As long as we're gathered here, Walt, I suggest we get another sweet roll, refill our coffee cups, and cue Toni and Erica in on the problem we hoped they could solve for us. Not every faculty member attended last Friday's meeting. Maybe someone else who was absent wrote the book. Or maybe, someone who was there kept silent for some strange reason. Knowing the faculty better than we do, you two might be able to suggest someone we've overlooked."

"I'm not sure about that, but now that you've gotten us up and out so early, you should at least satisfy our curiosity. Why *hasn't* the author come forward?" asked Erica. "If *we'd* written a book and won a contest, you can bet we'd have identified ourselves."

"The problem, as I said earlier, is that NAMWA hasn't been able to notify the winner of the contest," answered Asher. "Let me begin at the beginning. I received a telephone call a week ago from a Stanley Johnson, the CEO of NAMWA, in Toronto. He was able to figure out that *Academic Awards*—that's the title of the winning novel—takes place on a campus clearly modeled on Southwestern College. Someone named Edith Tansley Coyle wrote it. The only trouble was that Johnson and his staff couldn't locate an address or phone number for Ms. Coyle. It seems that a temporary secretary had somehow lost or tossed the submission letter accompanying the manuscript. Luckily for us, Johnson could identify the college—small colleges in Northwest New Mexico being fairly rare. He quickly equated the book's Canyon College with Southwestern. He was sure that as Southwestern's president I'd be able to solve his mystery about the book's author.

"I couldn't. But, figuring that Edith Tansley Coyle must be a pseudonym, I told him I was sure I could quickly produce the author. I was wrong, of course.

"Johnson is impatient. He wants to publicize the award and showcase the winning author along with the lucky school at NAMWA's annual meeting on October fifth. I had a hard time persuading him to give me a few days to question the faculty. Getting the word out to everyone before last Friday's meeting would have been impossible. We all," Walt said, looking around the table at his fellow administrators, "fully expected someone to come forward then, claim the prize, and apologize for murdering a college president, albeit a fictional one. I would happily forgive the writer for doing in my counterpart, especially since he, or she, has procured the single biggest gift this institution has ever gotten and done so without trivializing the school. My wife, whose two passions are quilting and whodunits, says that's rare in academic mysteries." He paused. "When we had to search for clues about the author, Erica, your name came up."

"I understand why you thought of Toni. She's the writer. But why me?" demanded Erica.

"It's your own fault," responded Asher, grinning. "Consider Ms. Coyle's initials. You may not know it, but you've become notorious for your work orders. I'm told they all end with 'etcetera, etcetera, etcetera' and 'call me for details'."

"I'm trying to make a point. What's wrong with a phone call, or better yet, a face-to-face chat? Jeesh, we're drowning in paperwork. Those e-t-c's are my protest against environmental waste and bureaucratic inefficiency."

"They also happen to be the initials of Edith Tansley Coyle!" replied Bill.

"Purely coincidental," said Erica, shrugging.

"I can see why you thought of us," said Toni. "We've collaborated on courses, but never on a book. I wish we had. But I'm afraid you'll have to look elsewhere for the guilty party."

"Toni, I apologize for calling you so late last night. And, Erica, I didn't know how to explain to your husband in twenty-five words or less why I needed to see you this morning. Thanks to both of you for coming in on such short notice." Erica and Toni rose from their seats and headed for the door.

"Again, I'm sorry to have disturbed your Sunday," said the president, pushing his chair back in time to get up and open the door for them.

Dejected, he sighed as the two women left. "There goes the easy solution to our mystery. We'd all pinned our hopes on Ebenezer and Hexton. They certainly could have written the book. It pokes fun at lots of academic peccadilloes. I could imagine the two of them chortling as they skewered their colleagues."

"And some of us as well, I suspect," said Bill.

Sally spoke up. "From what you've told us about the book, the author must be someone thoroughly familiar with Southwestern College."

"Oh, yes, collectively we're all mocked. But my wife, who as I said, reads lots of these things, assures me that the cast of characters in *Academic Awards* is a fairly generic bunch. You won't be able to find yourselves. "

"That may be true of the rest of us," said Steve. "But I'm worried about you. From your account, Walt, the fictional president doesn't *sound* generic. In many ways, he's a dead ringer for you, uhm—pun unintended. Until we can prove otherwise, we'll be remiss unless we consider the possibility that the book could be meant as a threat."

"That seems unlikely," replied Walt. "I'd rather consider what could be done with five-hundred thousand dollars than worry about a very slim possibility."

The president, knowing the proper administrative response to problems, large or small, brought the meeting to a close. "Since we're at the end of our rope, I'll form a task force to look for our missing benefactor."

☺

Not everyone expected a day of rest on Sunday. Jim Scoop, chief of security and public safety, had called his staff together for a briefing at 7:30 P.M. Jim, a six-footer with abundant black hair kept under control by frequent haircuts, wore the suit that served as his uniform. The four full-time officers arrived together. After a Sunday spent on the town's municipal golf course or in their yards, they were glad to be out of *their* uniforms, dark blue slacks and shirts.

Billy Bob Jenkins, wearing pressed khakis, had risen to the rank of senior officer from humble beginnings as the college's first night watchman. His dual name, as well as his accent, marked him as a rural boy. (He preferred to be called B.B.) He was as fine an officer as any Jim had known during his twenty-year career in the military. Jim had been able to hire Ben Jackson and Nick Delmari when Dr. Asher had brought him in to beef up campus security. Ben and Nick had at first resented Jim's professionalism. Now that they had been at Southwestern for five years, he no longer had to remind them of the gap between themselves and the students. Johnny Burke, a recent Southwestern graduate and a brand new recruit, had served as an officer-in-training during his final two years at the college.

Ben and Nick were laughing as they followed B.B. and Johnny into Jim's office. Johnny was recounting the latest campus flak. Since many things the faculty did seemed inexplicable, Ben and Nick were not surprised that someone had written a murder mystery but had disappeared without claiming credit for it.

"I suppose," said Billy Bob, who had long ago given up trying to figure the faculty out, "we'll have to find the perpetrator."

"Of the book, or the murder?" asked Nick. "I wouldn't mind reading the book."

"Especially on company time," added Ben.

Jim waited until the four officers had taken their seats and then said, "I'm sure I'll be talking to Dr. Asher soon and I'll find out what's going on. I suspect this will be a problem for him and the faculty, not us, B.B. We can go about our usual business. As you know, the number of assaults on campus increased last year."

"Isn't that why there were so many new lights installed this summer?" asked Ben.

"Yes," replied Jim. "But the job isn't complete. Parts of the river walk are still too dark, especially where it borders the edge of the creek. We'll need to patrol there more often until we can get more lights.

"On a more positive note, let's hope for an uneventful new year. It's especially important during these first weeks for all of you to provide a friendly, but visible presence on campus. Smile and be patient. You'll be asked lots of questions. The parents seem surprised that the faculty and staff aren't lined up, Wal-Mart like, as official greeters. Since they see you outside and in uniform, they'll approach you, and not *just* for directions. Nick and Ben, I'd like you to work from noon to midnight this week. Don't worry, you'll be paid overtime. The new part-time officer I've hired will be taking an evening shift next week.

"B.B., I'll see you tomorrow morning. Johnny, you know the routine. And congratulations on finishing the certification course in Farmington. The main difference from when you were a student is that you'll have a new uniform. It's hanging there behind the door. Take it home tonight."

Billy Bob turned towards Johnny and said, "You'll really be able to impress the co-eds now."

"I've got a girlfriend," said Johnny. "I don't think she'd like that."

Jim addressed Johnny. "Shine your shoes before you come into my office again." The young man stuck out his left foot and looked guiltily at his dusty shoe.

Jim, sorry that he'd embarrassed his new recruit, softened his tone. "Why don't you begin the day in the bookstore and then circle around to the health center and the library before checking on the dormitories?"

Johnny spoke up. "Maybe the students will take me more seriously now that I'm a full-time officer. There were quite a few I wish I could have arrested last year."

"Oh, we don't go in for many arrests. Sally Sanchez takes care of major behavior problems and minor criminal activities. We deal with the students initially, but Dr. Sanchez follows up after we send her our reports. Occasionally, I will call in backup from the Cottonwood police force. But only for potential violence or when a crowd starts to gather."

The office emptied and Jim was left alone. He listened to the messages that had piled up over the weekend. He could put off answering most of them until tomorrow, but not President Asher's. He was surprised, though, that Walt should be doing school business on a Sunday.

"Good evening, Walt. Jim Scoop here. ... Yes, I could meet you tomorrow morning. Sometime before you get tied up with parents and students? ... Nine-thirty is no problem. Especially if you'll tell me when we can expect the new river walk lights and..."

Walt interrupted. "They're on back order and the company doesn't consider *that* a crisis. Right now, I must confess, I'm more worried about another crisis. I don't suppose you've heard about our missing author."

Jim said he had, but he didn't reveal his sense that it hardly deserved to be called a crisis. The tone of Walt's voice showed that the president thought it did. "Strange," thought Jim to himself after Walt hung up. "The president is usually unflappable. I wonder why he sounds so worried."

*Meetings, meetings, and more meetings.*

In the way of all institutions, the first Monday of a new year began with meetings.

Sally Sanchez had scheduled an early morning meeting for freshmen advisors in the Student Affairs Office at 7 A.M.

At 6:55 Cheryl Gray, the housing director, entered the conference room followed by Jill Smith, the registrar, and Dr. Arnold Greenberg, faculty coordinator of freshman advising. He stood by the door, peering expectantly into the hallway. "I hope the coffee will be here soon." He sounded plaintive.

"It's coming," replied Sally's secretary.

Pastries, coffee and fourteen faculty advisors arrived simultaneously. Wasting no time, Sally called the meeting to order. She and Cheryl were well into their morning's agendas when Franz Lattermitz, professor of German, making his usual late entrance, spotted Erica. He thundered at her. "What are you doing here? I thought you'd be long gone now that you've become a famous author!"

"Rumor, pure rumor," she replied.

Cheryl pointedly ignored the interruption. Franz interrupted her again as she described how the refurbishing of several dormitories should improve student civility.

"Will that guarantee that the students won't make a, how do you say it, graffiti wall out of the corridors?" he asked.

Cheryl glared at Franz. "Nothing," she said, "guarantees student behavior…but in housing we've learned to hope…and be vigilant."

Hiding her impatience, Sally quickly turned the meeting over to the registrar. She ran down the list of what advisors should say to their advisees. "You'll need to tell them more than once that scheduling all their classes between 10:00 and 2:00 isn't possible and that we don't expect them to take *all* the college's required courses the first semester. Also, correct any bits of misinformation they've gleaned from who knows where."

When Sally next yielded to Arnold, Erica groaned inwardly, anticipating his distinctive monotone and tendency to say again what had already been said. Sure enough, his preamble was ample—and repetitive.

Erica burst out, "Arnold, are you going to review the *whole* cotton-picking list for us? I think you can assume that we *can* read."

"I'm not so sure of that, especially after all the changes this faculty was foolish enough to adopt last year."

"Sheesh. I hope you can speed read!" Erica snapped.

He couldn't. Forty-five minutes later, Sally ended the meeting. Erica was the first to hustle out the door.

@

Melinda Merry arrived ten minutes early for the first computer center meeting with the new director, Dr. José Martinez. She liked José. He asked questions and listened to the answers. He'd taken the staff's suggestions for improvements seriously and never once flaunted his years of experience in Silicon Valley. He was so easy to talk to that she'd told him more than she'd intended: not only how much she liked her work, but also how dissatisfied she was with her status—and her pay. She hoped she hadn't complained too much. At any rate, he'd ended their private conference with high praise for the manual she'd written for faculty and staff.

Howie, who had served as the computer center's assistant director for the last two years, arrived next. A hardware wizard, he had no people skills. Melinda had been relieved that he hadn't even applied to be promoted to director.

Frowning, she watched Becky and Alan walk in together. Stereotypical computer nerds, they were as eager as a couple of puppies. Their recent computer science degrees rankled almost as much as their salaries. Until José arrived and negotiated a long overdue raise for her with the president, they made more than Melinda did.

Promptly at 8 A.M., José arrived, wearing neatly pressed slacks, sports shirt, and bolo tie. He called the meeting to order. "I am delighted to be here at SWC, back home in New Mexico, and working with you all. Are the student computer labs ready to go? Have faculty and staff signed up for your training sessions, Melinda?"

The youngsters answered in tandem. "Yes, Dr. Martinez, all ready. We'll be training the student monitors tomorrow before classes begin on Wednesday."

"I'm meeting with all the new staff people this week," said Melinda. "Only two faculty members haven't responded to my invitation to go over our system."

José, glancing at his list, continued, "Registration set?"

"Yep, all ready to go." Melinda hid her irritation at Becky's youthful and unprofessional "yep," but she couldn't keep from cringing outwardly when Alan answered, "We're set to jet. Bring on the kiddies."

"We do have a problem," said Howie. "We're having trouble with our third server. Our supplier said it's going to be days before he can send us the parts we need." Becky turned to Alan, and raised an eyebrow. In response, he covered his mouth with a hand, tapped his lips, and yawned. Melinda bristled. *Just like young people,* she thought, *bored when they're not the center of attention.*

"Why the delay?" asked José.

"This is Cottonwood. We're a long way from Silicon Valley."

"I'll gladly trade some delays for the rat race I just left," replied José. "If complaints get vicious, refer the complainers to me."

☺

Joe Blake, director of the physical plant, waited impatiently to start his 8 A.M. meeting. As usual, George, head custodian, and Wally, shop superintendent, were late.

At five after the hour, Ed, head of transportation services, was muttering in the general direction of the clock he was staring at, "You should see the vans that came back from a geology trip late Saturday night. Mud splattered to the rooftops... I don't know why they have to wander dirt roads like that."

Just then Wally and George walked in. Ever congenial and unaware that he was being censured, Wally shook his head and laughed. "You keep the college cars cleaner than my mother-in-law keeps her kitchen. If you had your way, Ed, you wouldn't allow any of your precious vehicles out of the garage! You sound like the Texas tourist who complained about the ruins at Mesa Verde being so far from the highway."

As the two latecomers took their seats, Joe spoke brusquely. "All right, we're all here. Before classes begin on Wednesday, I'm hoping we can cross off everything on this list," he said, raising a ratty clipboard that held a stack of assorted-sized notes.

Before he could continue, Joyce, his secretary, entered the room, setting a large platter with warm cinnamon rolls and a neatly typed sheet of paper in front of him. Looking around the table, she broke into a big smile. "Here, I baked these this morning. They should improve everybody's mood on this Labor Day."

Joyce's offering and words were greeted with smiles and appreciative comments as the platter made its way around the table. Joe thanked Joyce and signaled for her to take a seat. Turning towards Bobby, the young carpenter he'd hired in mid-August, he said, "I think I explained to you that we *always* work on Labor Day." The young man nodded.

Joe continued, "We're not alone at Southwestern. Many colleges these days begin on or sometimes *before* the holiday that's supposed to honor workmen." Joyce looked up at her boss with a mock frown. He hastily added, "or work*women*." Joyce grinned her approval. "By now, most of us have come to think having a longer Christmas vacation is a good trade-off."

Joe examined the sheet Joyce had given him. "Some of you, it looks like, could use more hours in the day, or a helping hand." Joe examined his list again. "For those of you who're done, or nearly done, it would help if you could spare one of your guys for a day or two."

He turned to Wally and asked, "Are the dorms ready?"

"Almost. We finished painting corridors in Marley on Thursday. I went by this morning and the new paint smell is gone. But our Albuquerque supplier sent us twenty-five faucets instead of twenty-five showerheads. When I finally reached someone at the warehouse, she said she *thought* she could get someone else to get the showerheads to us by Friday. Unless we're willing to make the kids go without showers until then, I need to send someone to Albuquerque today. But that's going to leave me short-handed here on campus."

Joe sighed. "Send one of your boys. Friday's too late."

George reported that with four new custodians to train, he needed his whole crew to get the gym and the auditorium cleaned and the classrooms set up.

Joe addressed Bobby again. "Have you been able to install all the custom bookcases Mr. Scott ordered for the library?"

"No way, sir. I would have finished the job, but after I'd stained the shelves and begun mounting them, Mr. Scott changed his mind. I can't finish remounting the shelves all by myself tomorrow. Scott sounded awfully upset when he thought I might still be hammering away once classes start."

"Don't worry about Scott. I saw him late Friday afternoon. He asked who you were and said he was afraid he'd sounded angry with you. He also said he appreciated your craftsmanship and we'd be lucky to keep you. So, congratulations, young man. That guy's a real perfectionist, stingy with praise. I'll see if I can get you some help."

Ed looked up. Hesitantly, he admitted that most of the campus vans and cars were ready. "I suppose I could send you one of my mechanics for a day or two."

"If you can teach an auto mechanic new tricks, Bobby, I'll send Ed's man to the library this morning," said Joe.

"Thanks, I sure can use some help."

Joe turned to his secretary. "Have I left anything out, Joyce?"

"No, Mr. Blake," she answered as he signaled to the rest of the crew that the meeting was over. "I have a question though. What should I say to President Asher the next time he calls about the bulbs that keep burning out in his office?"

Reacting as if in concert to Joe's dismissal, his staff pushed their chairs back, rose, and quickly made for the exit—all except George who reached across the table to grab the last cinnamon roll before hastening to catch up with the others.

In the hubbub of their departure no one heard Joe answer Joyce's question. "There's something fishy about that lamp. It's brand new. I'll give his secretary a whole box full of spare bulbs. Ruby can put in a new one every morning if the president's damn lamp keeps going on the fritz every night."

℮

Walt Asher sat in his office, alone. He stared, unseeing, out his window. The questions NAMWA's Stanley Johnson had fired at him Friday night after the faculty meeting had been haunting the college president all weekend.

Walt could still hear Johnson asking, "What do you mean, you can't find Edith Tansley Coyle? Do you realize half a million dollars is at stake?"

Yesterday morning he'd hoped Erica and Toni would admit to being Edith Tansley Coyle. This morning, when he woke long before his alarm went off, he was sickened at the prospect of a $500,000 windfall slipping away.

He had never been quite as sure as the other members of his cabinet that the two women would prove to have written *Academic Awards*.

He couldn't imagine their taking the time to collaborate on a mystery story. Nor could he fathom why two academics who had published in their own fields would take the time to enter a mystery-writing competition.

Now on Monday morning, shortly after 9:30, he was impatiently awaiting the arrival of Jim Scoop, his chief security officer.

Yesterday, Walt, having already violated his vow to keep Sunday free from campus affairs, reread *Academic Awards* much more carefully than he had the first time. He found the book interesting, not just because it had won a huge award for Southwestern but also because its author had portrayed college life in general so well, and Southwestern College so accurately. Only an insider would have furnished the fictional president's office with theology, philosophy, archaeology, and history books—and tennis trophies.

Waiting for Jim, he straightened his tie, one of twenty similar ones that made up what his wife called his uniform—grey flannel slacks, white or light blue shirt, rep tie, and navy blue or dark grey blazer.

When Ruby ushered Jim into his office, Walt motioned to a chair at the small round table where he met visitors. The table was his wife Annette's idea. Much less intimidating than having to face him across a desk, she'd claimed. She was right—as she so often was. Walt was less sure she was right about the necessity of telling Jim about the book and its murder scene. However, reluctant as he was to admit it either then or now, he had found the murder scene eerie and disturbing.

"Sorry to ask you to come in on such short notice, but Annette made me promise to fill you in on the campus's recent mystery."

"I've heard something about that. Sounds like good news for the college. Is there a problem?"

"From my point of view, the biggest problem is that we haven't yet located the author who wrote the prize-winning mystery. And until or unless we do, we stand to forfeit a sum of money sizable enough to bolster our endowment, to say nothing of the positive publicity for Southwestern College."

"How much money are you talking about?"

"Fifty thousand for the winner of the mystery-writing contest and half a million dollars for the college."

"Whew, no small pickings."

"*I'm* worried about the money. My good wife is more worried about what's *in* the book. Tell me what you've heard, and then I'll fill you in on the rest."

"Not much," answered Jim. "Until students arrive on campus, the rumor mill doesn't swirl around my operation. What I do know is that you're reputed to have been immortalized in a book that no one claims to have written. What in particular bothers Annette?"

"Let's see if I can explain. I took the manuscript the North American Mystery Writers Association had sent me home Friday evening. Annette read the book on Saturday. At first she enjoyed it and didn't see anything especially ominous. She did wonder who could have written it. She also wondered why anyone competing for a prize would have used a pseudonym.

"Let me backtrack a bit. The company thought they'd be awarding the prize for a best first mystery to someone here at Southwestern named Edith Tansley Coyle. Johnson, the CEO, didn't know what Annette did: that there's never been anyone here by that name. By Sunday morning, however, Annette decided that writing under a false name hides evil intentions. She's convinced the author wants to stay hidden for reasons injurious to my health."

"What led her to that conclusion?"

"The fact that President Frederick Burns—my fictional counterpart—gets done in. I tried to persuade her that in a murder mystery there has to be a murder victim."

From the way that Walt spoke, along with his half-hearted attempt at a laugh, Jim suspected the president wasn't entirely ready to dismiss the murder as a laughing matter.

Walt continued, "Who makes a better corpse in a mystery story taking place at a college than its president?"

"Any chance that whoever wrote the book isn't staying hidden on purpose?" asked Jim. "Isn't it more likely that for some reason the author simply doesn't know about the prize?"

"That's what I'd like to think. However, there's been so much talk on campus, Annette believes the winner must have an insidious motive for not coming forward. Like you, the cabinet and I have assumed the author hasn't heard the good news. That would be the best-case scenario. At any rate, I promised Annette I'd talk with you. At least," said Walt, "she didn't insist I request a body guard. I'm sorry to get you involved, Jim."

"Now that you've told me this much, you've aroused my curiosity. Tell me more about the book and its presidential murder. Then you can assure Annette that the local constabulary is looking out for your safety.

"Why don't you start with Friday's faculty meeting? That I did hear about. I understand your announcement about the mysterious mystery book made quite a splash."

"It did. But unfortunately it didn't produce what we hoped it would: Edith Tansley Coyle coming out of the woodwork." Walt paused. "Are you sure you want me to describe the faculty meeting?"

"Yes. If the author *is* dangling a carrot just out of reach, or as Annette suspects, is up to no good, he—or she—could have been at the faculty meeting. So I'd like to know what was said."

"Fair enough, I'll take the stand and you can act the part of Perry Mason. The meeting began with a whole series of innocuous announcements—various vice-presidents and directors showing faculty how students feel sitting in *their* classes and only pretending to be interested in information they feel no need to know. Then new faculty and staff members were introduced. Next, the registrar took an unconscionable amount of time promising that registration would go smoothly. I took the podium last. I'm sure everyone expected the meeting to end with the usual presidential drill: I'd express high hopes for the students, praise the faculty and the fine staff, and, like the registrar, I would promise that *this* would surely be Southwestern's finest year.

"For once, I was eager to have the final say. I was confident, as I told NAMWA's skeptical, impatient Stanley Johnson, that someone was bound to claim—or admit—to having written the book. When no one did, I even professed myself willing to forgive the mysterious author for having murdered a college president. My remarks were met with mild but perplexed interest at first, then amusement, but no admissions. Gradually, a general consensus emerged about who might be guilty. Toni Hexton and Erica Ebenezer, according to their colleagues, could have done it. They had the means, the motive, and the opportunity. They're mystery fans. They're friends. They spend a lot of time together. As the clincher, they're known to have perpetrated several elaborate practical jokes."

The president paused and then resumed his account. "With nothing else to go on, I agreed with the cabinet that we should talk with the two women before pursuing other possibilities. Since they weren't yet back from a geology field camp, we couldn't get in touch with them until late Saturday night."

"Must have been frustrating."

"It was. Very. And when we did talk with them yesterday morning, we reached another dead end. Toni and Erica weren't guilty—despite our fondest hopes. We decided to tackle our problem by creating a task force. And since they've been here a long time, know the faculty well, and are avid mystery readers, we decided to give them one of their own to solve. They agreed this morning to chair the task force."

"I trust Annette's wrong about the book's being a threat. But it could, couldn't it, provide clues as to who the writer might be?"

"It certainly could. The book lets us narrow the field. After rereading *Academic Awards*—that's its amusing and appropriate title—it's obvious that a faculty member who's teaching now or who retired recently, must have written it. Campus intrigue and campus politics are delightfully portrayed."

"How specific is *Academic Awards* to Southwestern?" asked Jim.

"Except for the setting, not very. In the novel, Southwestern becomes Canyon College. Our buildings, our plaza, our roads, our river are all clearly recognizable. The characters, however, don't resemble anyone working at Southwestern. The president's office is clearly modeled on mine, but otherwise the book's president is not much like me. Nor does the plot bear any resemblance to anything that's happened here. It hinges on a young male student who becomes enamored with an older female student."

"That kind of thing happens though, doesn't it?"

"Yes, but in the book the older student is Native American. The young Anglo student goes to court asking to change his name to one that sounds Navajo."

Jim raised his eyebrows. "That happens in the book?"

"Oh, yes. In a very funny scene, as a matter of fact. Geoffrey Thompson wants to become Flatfoot Becay. The female judge, Florence *Begay*, before whom he appears, is, unfortunately for him, Navajo. She lectures poor Geoffrey on culture snatching and his getting it wrong anyway. Becay, with a "c" instead of a "g," is *not*, she tells him, a Navajo name. He argues that a young Indian friend honored him with the Indian name of Flatfoot and that he purposefully chose a variation of Begay. He angers the judge. She shows her irritation, addresses him as sonny, and calls him hopelessly naïve. She heaps scorn on wannabe Indians like poor Geoffrey. She tells him to forget his fantasy, go back to his home in Wisconsin after graduation, and do something useful with his life."

"What's Geoffrey's motive for killing Canyon College's president?

Sounds like the judge would be the target of his anger, not the president. She's the one who turned down his request."

"I'm no psychologist, but I'm impressed with how the author shows Geoffrey snapping after the court scene. His parents are due in that night. He's afraid of them, his father especially. Mr. Thompson is some kind of professional, a lawyer, I think. Geoffrey's gotten it into his head that if he had a different name, his father wouldn't intimidate him, and his socialite mother would quit trying to cover over his ineptness. The humiliation at the hands of the judge brings back echoes of countless childhood humiliations—especially at the hands of his father, but also from classmates.

"Even though he's a senior ready to graduate, he's a very young senior—without social savvy. It's no wonder that Mary Sheepherder became the woman of his dreams. The author made her very appealing. She and Geoffrey were enrolled in the same senior seminar. The instructor assigned the students to pair up. Seeing that no one else was going to volunteer to work with Geoffrey, softhearted Mary asked him to be her partner. *She* didn't treat him as a nerd. From then on the die was cast.

"On a Friday in the study room where they're working, Geoffrey overhears her making a call to a garage. She's disconsolate when she learns she can't pick up her car that afternoon to take her two children to a family gathering. Geoffrey offers to drive them home, even though it's more than a hundred miles away. Her relatives take him in for the weekend so that he won't have to make two trips.

"Alberto, Mary's son, sees him barefoot, points to his flat feet, and calls him by what Geoffrey comes to believe his rightful name. From that moment on, he feels destined to take the place of the husband she never mentions and who, he learns from one of her brothers, departed before Alberto was born. Mary misreads Geoffrey's devotion. She thinks he's warmed by kindness. He's so much younger than any of her many siblings that it never occurs to her that he sees himself as more than a fellow student. She's genuinely happy to see the lonely young man relaxing with her extended family, and pleased that he's carried his weight and done good work on their joint biology project. And of course she's grateful to him for driving her home."

"All very interesting, but I still don't understand how the president of the college comes into the story," said Jim.

"The president turns out to be Geoffrey's rival..."

"That," said Jim, chuckling, "undercuts any parallels between you and the book's murder victim."

"President Frederick Burns' hustling of a student is not what upset Annette. However, it's several resemblances that scare her: Burns' scholarly interests, his love of tennis, even the arrangement of the furniture in his office. By last evening she had concluded that the book is meant to be a threat. And she insisted I inform you about the danger I'm supposedly in."

Walt's tone of voice, and his staring at some spot in the middle distance above Jim's head, made Jim realize that Walt was not immune to Annette's uneasiness. Avoiding Jim's eyes, Walt resumed his summary.

"After the trip to Red Mesa, and the best weekend of his life, Geoffrey begins to follow Mary around. I liked the title the author gives the chapter describing Geoffrey and Mary's week after they return from Arizona. 'Everywhere that Mary went…'"

"The author sounds more playful than threatening."

"Thank you, Jim. I'll try that line on Annette. Perhaps it will lessen her fears." Walt leaned back in his chair looking, for the first time, totally relaxed. "Now that you mention it, it's the obvious sense of play that makes me eager to meet the author of *Academic Awards*."

"Let's hope that will happen soon."

Walt held his wrist up and glanced at his watch. "I'm not scheduled to address the parents and the new students for another hour. If you've got the time, I'll tell you more about the adventures of Geoffrey, Mary, and Frederick Burns."

"I've got the time. Besides, you've got me hooked."

"One of the places Mary goes is Burns' office during final exam week. Burns is to give Mary, Canyon College's top graduate, a special commendation at graduation and he wants to find out more about her for his speech. Burns asks Mary to come to his office. When Geoffrey sees her climbing the stairs to the president's wing, he follows her. He doesn't know what transpires in the president's office, but with as few antennas as he has, he *has* heard the campus scuttlebutt about the president's notorious flirting. Lurking by the water fountain outside the president's office, Geoffrey sees Burns walk to the door with Mary, pat her on the arm, and whisper something inaudible as they say goodbye.

"Geoffrey goes crazy with jealousy. The next day, he barges into Burns' office and accuses him of trying to steal his girl. Burns treats him even more condescendingly than the judge did. Like the judge,

Burns calls Geoffrey sonny and tells him the girl is too old and too mature to be interested in a kid. Geoffrey goes berserk, spots a tennis trophy, grabs it and throws it at Burns. The trophy hits Burns squarely in the face. He falls, Geoffrey panics, and runs out of the room after unconsciously and repeatedly stabbing the president with a letter opener he sees on Burns' desk.

"Later that day, during dinner with his parents—another funny scene—Geoffrey is simply numb and barely responds to them. They don't seem to notice, because he's been a vague presence in their lives for many years. His father pontificates about all the possibilities in store for a college graduate. His mother muses about the social connections he'll now be able to establish." Dropping his voice, Walt said, "I suspect the same kind of scene is reenacted all too regularly on graduation day. Students exhorted to change the world by graduation speakers in the morning are subject to their family's less grandiose expectations in the evening."

Ruby poked her head around the door, "Sorry to interrupt, sir, but Mr. Johnson is on the phone. Can you talk to him now?"

Walt nodded, and, holding the receiver at arms length, rifled through the stack of loose pages sitting in the middle of the blotter on his desk. Extracting two sections from the manuscript, he handed them to Jim. "These are the other passages that spooked Annette. See what you make of them while I talk to Stanley Johnson."

Jim enjoyed the description of what should have been a celebratory dinner but which was, in fact, an awkward effort at communication. The author described Geoffrey looking uninterested and vacant as his parents plowed cheerily ahead, envisioning their son's working in his uncle's posh men's clothing store, "Just while you wait to choose between law or business school." Geoffrey's mind, Walter Mitty-like, drifts away from the words he's heard every vacation for the last four years. He remembers Burns laughing at him, but he doesn't remember much about his own response. He remembers holding the tennis trophy, but not hurling it at Burns. It never occurs to Geoffrey that he might have seriously hurt the man until the next day when the graduation ceremony is delayed, with everyone waiting for the president to arrive.

Jim found the psychological analysis of a desperately shy youngster eager to become his own man engrossing. In fact, so engrossing that he didn't hear Walt hang up.

"Sorry for the interruption. Especially since it was Stanley Johnson from Toronto—again. He can't believe we haven't identified our prizewinner. He's given me an ultimatum. The prize will revert to the runner-up if we can't produce an author soon. I did persuade him to give us more time in lieu of the fact that classes don't begin until the middle of the week and that some faculty won't set foot on campus until then."

"How long is he giving us?" asked Jim.

"He's granted a reprieve until a week from today, September twelfth. I'm trusting the task force will have been successful by then."

"If you'll get a copy of the whole manuscript to me, I'd like to read it for myself. I'll let you know whether I agree with Annette in reading the book as a threat."

"Thanks, she'll like knowing you're taking this whole business seriously."

@

Jim left the president's office bemused. Surely Annette Asher was overreacting. What possible harm could there be in a book by an academic? Especially one that must have been written for a lark? His interest aroused, he'd enjoy looking for clues. Furthermore, he sensed that his willingness to get involved in the hunt was taking pressure off Walt.

Jim walked slowly towards his office. He stopped and sat on one of the stone benches in the old flagstone plaza between Center Hall and Cottonwood Creek. Leafy cottonwoods encircled the plaza. They shaded the area in spring, summer, and fall. Even when students, staff members, and faculty crisscrossed the plaza going about their business, or when they congregated there, the place was always a serene oasis. An ancient Moorish tiled fountain dated from when this place had been an original Spanish hacienda. A gnarled juniper grew beside a little waterfall bringing water into the plaza. This tree, with its thick half-dead trunk, rose to the sky at nearly a forty-five degree angle. One large horizontal branch, very much alive, supported many vertical branches. Jim noticed the red-winged blackbirds alternately sitting on the horizontal branch over the waterfall and dropping down to frolic in the shallow pool at the bottom of the falls. As usual, Jim found the soft sounds of falls, fountain, and birds soothing.

Jim was eager to see how the author would describe his favorite place on campus. From what Walt had told him, the book's descriptions were accurate. He hoped they showed an appreciation for this particular part of northwestern New Mexico with its living link to the old Jesuit school that was part of the college's past.

After reading the murder scene, Jim understood why Annette, and Walt too, had found it disturbing. The scene depicted a great deal of anger and hate. *If* news of the award had in fact reached the pseudonymous author, it *was* strange that he or she had not appeared.

Jim returned to his office. He heard the phone ring and his secretary's answer as he passed her desk. "Hello....Yes, Mr. Ordoñez, Mr. Scoop is right here."

Jim hurried into his office. "Hello, friend, it's been a long time."

"Too long. Are you free tonight? I'm in Farmington, practically next door. Could you join me for supper?"

"Yes, but what brings you to Farmington?"

"A two-day conference on violence in the schools. Right now everyone else is scarfing down pastries and drinking coffee, so I've snuck away to call you."

"You don't have to attend a mandatory banquet?"

"I doubt anyone will be taking attendance. I'm more than happy to skip it. The keynote speaker won't be there either. Her plane didn't get off the ground in Boston this morning, because of a fortuitous act of the gods—a thunderstorm, or an inundation of pigeons, or some such thing. She won't arrive in time to enjoy this evening's generic banquet fare. Her address has been rescheduled for eight-thirty. So, I'll be free between five and eight."

"What about meeting at the Red Lobster at five-fifteen?"

"Great. We've got a lot of catching up to do."

"To say nothing of indulging in a basketful of the Lobster's melt-in-your-mouth biscuits!"

☙

Toni and Erica met at the front door of Center Hall a few minutes before noon. As they walked up the stairs to the third floor, Erica said, "Southwestern might not have the reputation of being a publish-or-perish place, but I think Walt is penalizing us for not having written some silly book! I wish he'd never asked us to chair this task force."

"You could have just said no," said Toni, laughing.

"I notice you didn't say no either. Maybe we can dispense with our task quickly."

"Let's hope so. Task forces, unlike committees, are meant to be short-lived. By the way, do you know who else Walt commandeered?"

"No," answered Erica, "but he did say there will be six of us."

"That's capital!" replied Toni, "Six characters in search of an author."

"Huh?"

"You un-liberally educated scientists," said Toni, laughing. "That's the title of a famous play by Pirandello," she said as she opened the door into the president's private meeting room. Sarah Jennings and Lloyd Reasoner were already seated at its oversized conference table. Sarah successfully chaired Fine Arts, the most contentious department on campus. Lloyd perennially served as parliamentarian of the faculty senate. Between them, Sarah and Lloyd knew everyone, remembered everything, and had a wealth of information about the college.

Sarah, adding several packets of cream to her coffee, looked up and said, "This will have to do for my daily latte."

Lloyd, ready to take his first bite of sandwich, raised his free hand in a gesture of greeting. "I understand you two get to share the honor of heading up this task force of Walt's."

"We'll be glad to turn the honor over to you, Lloyd," said Erica.

"No thanks. One of the perks of being near retirement is not having to chair anything ever again."

While Toni and Erica surveyed the makings for sandwiches, Jeff Miles, Southwestern's first-ever public relations director, and Steve Scott joined the others.

Erica, building her sandwich, grumbled, "I thought this was supposed to be a *faculty* task force."

Toni directed an admonitory "shh" in her friend's direction, and then whispered, making sure that her comment would be muffled by the conversation of the other four, "It's obvious why Walt chose Jeff."

"Yeah," responded Erica, "Finding the author will make a great PR story for Southwestern. But why Scott?" Not giving Toni time to respond, she answered her own question. "I suppose we *can* use a sleuthing librarian, especially one with a previous career in military intelligence."

Toni carried her sandwich and a bottle of water back to the table. She felt like chiding Erica for her oft-expressed suspicion of administrators until she remembered that it was Erica who publicly defended Steve Scott for replacing the faculty's beloved wooden card catalogs with a computerized system.

At this point, the president entered.

"Thank you all for coming on such short notice. And thank you even more for agreeing to take on this task. I'm trusting you'll be more successful than the cabinet and I were at ferreting out who has won NAMWA's contest. Surely, someone will be overjoyed at learning their book has won fifty thousand dollars."

Walt paused, and then continued. "With luck, the contest winner will come forward to acknowledge authorship, and your task will be over. I'll be sending out a general announcement today explaining that my office is still looking for the college's unknown benefactor. I'm not saying anything about your involvement, on the off chance that whoever wrote *Academic Awards* doesn't want to be found and might resent being sought.

"Two of the cabinet's three prime suspects aren't around. Art Professor Taylor Anderson seems to have disappeared from the face of the earth. As I'm sure you all know, he was very angry when we didn't offer a full-time position to his wife."

"And a good thing that was," interrupted Sarah. "Stephanie Anderson was difficult enough as a part-timer. I hate to think how imperious she would have become with a full-time appointment!"

Walt resumed. "Sixteen months ago I had several run-ins with an older Indian student, Charlie Roanhorse. Bill Hamill persuaded me—reluctantly, I might add—to put him on our list. He *is* articulate, he majored in English, and he aspires to be a writer. I thought he was asking for special privileges for Native Americans. To me, that smacked of discrimination. Charlie didn't see it that way.

"Our final candidate is Dr. Snow, from the psychology department. I suppose you know she is teaching this year with a terminal contract."

"About time," said Lloyd. "She's a perfect illustration of the pitfalls of tenure."

"I didn't know Dr. Snow was fired," put in Jeff. "My wife, who started college here at Southwestern, took an introductory psych course from her. Irene thought she was an excellent teacher."

"She *was*," explained Sarah, turning towards Jeff, "until recently. Even when her advanced courses started to deteriorate, she kept on wowing freshmen in introductory classes. It's not surprising, Jeff, that your wife liked her."

"Sadly," said Walt, "I would be surprised if we're not seeing the early stages of Alzheimer's. Jane is becoming increasingly irrational."

Lloyd added, "She's been talking about her unfair treatment, especially after the grievance committee didn't support her. They concluded she was terminated with cause."

"Even those who might have been sympathetic," continued the president, "see why she had to be let go. That her bread-and-butter course has remained popular contributes to her unrealistic view of herself." Walt addressed Jeff. "Sometime ask Sarah to tell you what Dr. Snow did that gave us cause to dismiss her."

Walt glanced at each of the group in turn. "My charge is for you to give Taylor Anderson, Charlie Roanhorse, and Jane Snow a very close look. Since Toni and Erica disappointed us, those three are the only candidates we have. We hope the six of you, with more access to faculty opinion and intrigue, may be able to add to our short list. It would really be a shame if Southwestern loses out on the prize—and the positive publicity it will bring. The people at NAMWA are impatient for us to locate the author."

With that comment, Walt rose and left the room. Sarah was the first to break the silence. "Isn't it typical that an institution of higher education should have to appoint a committee to find out who wrote a book about it!"

Erica looked down at her watch. "It's almost one. I hate to schedule another meeting for today, but we don't have much time to produce President Asher's author. Could you all reconvene in the mineralogy lab a few minutes after five?"

Lloyd and Steve nodded, Jeff said "sure" between bites, and Sarah shrugged.

"Wait a minute. I'd like to know what the rest of you think of the cabinet's candidates," said Toni. "*None* seem very likely."

"I agree," said Erica. "Taylor Anderson's too self-preoccupied, Charlie Roanhorse is bright—he graduated with honors last spring—but I can't see him putting in the energy to write a book, and, if I may be un-PC, Jane Snow's too crazy. By five, maybe we can come up with some other possibilities to add to the president's list." Erica looked around the table. "Is there anything else?"

"Yes," said Steve. "Shouldn't we all read *Academic Awards?*" Addressing Erica, he asked, "Can you get a copy for each of us?"

She hesitated. "I'll try. I'm sure Walt hasn't shown the manuscript to anyone but his wife."

"And Bill Hamill," inserted Toni. "He and Walt both agreed that whoever wrote the book clearly had Southwestern in mind."

Steve nodded. "There's no doubt of that. NAMWA's Johnson had figured that out before he got in touch with President Asher."

"I understand why Walt would be reluctant to have the manuscript leave his hands," said Toni. "Until a book has gone to press, manuscripts are not for general distribution."

Erica bristled. "Well, if Walt wants us to do the task he's given us, he'll have to let us have copies of the book. Steve's right. We each need to read it—that's a more likely place to find clues than guessing why one of our colleagues wants to remain incognito." She stood up. "I'll get the copies somehow. If possible, by the time we meet this afternoon."

☙

Shortly before 5:00 that afternoon the task force reassembled, with Sarah, Lloyd, Jeff, Steve, and Toni taking seats at one of the narrow tables in the geology lab. Toni, the first to arrive, suppressed a smile as she noticed how characteristically the others entered the room and chose their seats. Jeff sauntered in clutching a donut in one hand, a large mug of coffee in the other, and a stenographer's pad tucked under his arm. He walked over to peer at a geological cross-section map of the Grand Canyon before sitting down. Steve, heading directly to the table, gave a cursory glance at the rock specimens in floor-to-ceiling glass display cases. He squared his spring-bound clipboard neatly in front of him before opening its cover and extracting one of the two pens aligned under the clip. Sarah marched in and grimaced as she pulled a bulging appointment book out of an even larger, more bulging straw bag. Lloyd automatically switched on the overhead lights, though they weren't necessary. He fingered the spiral bound set of index cards visible at the top of one of his corduroy coat pockets and then, pulling the jacket aside, he began tapping each of the pens and pencils emerging from his shirt pocket.

Exactly at five, Erica breezed into the room and wheeled a tall lab stool to the head of the table. Perching on its seat, she spoke breathlessly, "If it's okay with you, I'll do whatever presiding needs to be done and Toni will act as secretary." Nods all around. "I think Steve was right this morning when he suggested we need to read the book carefully before approaching any suspects. I've talked with Walt. Ruby will make each of us a copy—providing we show it to no one, no matter how much we're questioned. Until someone admits authoring the book, Walt wants us to keep quiet about what's *in* it."

Lloyd asked, "May I ask why?"

Erica shrugged her shoulders. "You heard him this morning. He seems awfully nervous," she answered. "I don't see any harm in playing the game by his rules. And as Toni explained, publishers are given to secrecy about upcoming works."

Sarah chimed in, "I find the prospect of reading a book tonight rather enticing. It makes me feel like a kid being told I can eat my dessert even if I don't finish my spinach."

Toni sighed. "I just hope the book will be as interesting as the late-night movie I was going to treat myself to."

"It should be fun to read," said Jeff. "We may learn all sorts of things about our president."

"Even if *Academic Awards* isn't great literature, I suspect we'll be engrossed looking for parallels and clues," said Toni. "Erica, you might as well adjourn the meeting now, and send us home with our homework."

"Sorry, can't do that. We'll have to prolong this first Monday—which, God knows, is always the longest day of the school year—a little longer. Ruby will be bringing us our copies soon. She's making them now. While we wait, I think we should review Walt's suspects and add to the cabinet's list if we can."

Erica, looking at her morning's notes, summarized the cabinet's reasons for suspecting Anderson, Roanhorse, and Snow. "They were all disappointed if not royally miffed about something last year. Because Taylor Anderson and Charlie Roanhorse are no longer around, they might not have heard of the award. If Jane did hear of it—she must have—and if she wrote *Academic Awards,* she'll be delighted to keep everyone dangling.

"Let's make sure we've got our facts straight," continued Erica. "One, Taylor resigned in a huff when his wife wasn't given a permanent position. He then tried, unsuccessfully, to rescind his resignation."

"Leaving," interrupted Sarah, "one holy mess in his office."

Erica held up a second finger. "While Walt doesn't seem to think Charlie's a very good candidate, they were at odds over a number of sensitive issues."

"I played on a soccer team with Charlie last year, and several of us hung around together after our games," said Jeff. "If he was angry about his run-ins with Dr. Asher, he didn't show it. I knew he'd met with the president. He really felt Southwestern should be doing more to acclimate the Indian students to college. He also asked me a lot of questions about my job. He was hoping to find one like mine that entails writing, but he wasn't having much luck. He didn't bring up his own writing until we were walking home together one night. After he told me he's had several articles and stories published, I asked to see them. That guy can write. I think he could be our missing author."

Erica looked towards Toni. "Do you agree? You must know Charlie pretty well."

"He took one of my classes his last semester. He was so focused on graduating and finding a job that I can't believe he'd have taken the time to write a whole book, but I do agree with Jeff that he's certainly capable of writing one. So I guess we should keep him in the hopper for now," said Toni.

"Jane Snow seems unlikely, but let's not dismiss her just yet," continued Erica. "If not certifiably crazy, she acts like she is. She was incensed when she received a terminal contract. She was even more incensed when the faculty grievance committee dismissed her case last spring. She's erratic and who knows what she'll say. From what I hear, she's been saying lots to anyone she's been able to corner. I can't see her sustaining the effort to write a whole book, though."

"Oh, I'm not so sure she couldn't," said Sarah. "I remember when she was hired. The psychology department raved about her. She evidently showed unusual promise in graduate school. As Steve said this noon, resentment can drive people to do all kinds of unexpected things."

"Somebody was obviously driven to write a whole cotton-picking book," said Erica. "That's no small task. I don't think we should dismiss any of the possible candidates until we talk to them. Our first task is to talk to each of them directly. We should be able to track Charlie down pretty easily, but I'm not so sure about Taylor." Erica paused before looking at her fellow task force members and asking, "In the couple of hours since lunch, have any of you come up with other names to add to the list?"

Lloyd spoke up immediately. "I'm really surprised that the president didn't include Jonathan Gill in his list."

"The international studies prof?" asked Jeff.

"Yes."

"Why wouldn't he have revealed himself last Friday?" Jeff asked.

"He might have kept quiet if his aim was to make the administration squirm," replied Lloyd.

"Does he want to make them squirm? I thought he was happy here. Even somebody as out of the faculty loop as I am has heard that he's made quite a splash in just six years," said Steve.

Lloyd spoke up. "He has, certainly among the students. They flock to his courses. He's engaging and energetic. But Bill Hamill worries about Gill's summer abroad courses. I know Gill has argued with the vice-president more than once."

"Well," said Sarah, "if we're going to put everyone who's ever argued with an administrator on our list, we'll have a very long list indeed. Jonathan regularly rants about something at almost every faculty meeting. That leads me to think he doesn't easily let go of his grudges."

"Jonathan has quarreled with Vice-President Hamill over academic freedom ever since he came to Southwestern," added Lloyd. "Bill objects to the interviews Gill sets up for his students with political dissidents on his summer abroad courses."

Toni spoke up. "Understandable, given his field. He *is* excitable. At the beginning of the fall term last year, he told me he was getting in contact with the American Civil Liberties Union. When I asked him why, he just shrugged. I'd be surprised if it didn't have to do with those summer courses."

"Okay, Toni," said Erica, "you know him better than any of us. Why don't you approach him? He wouldn't lie if asked a direct question, would he?"

"I'm sure he wouldn't. He relishes debates, but he's not sneaky. Besides, he would be the first person to admit to having done our president in vicariously. I'm willing to talk with him, but I bet he'll soon convince me he didn't do it."

"Hmm," said Steve. "His name didn't even come up when the cabinet was pondering who our reluctant benefactor might be."

Lloyd spread the fingers of his right hand over his upper lip. "We should let Toni interview him. He's young enough to resent being told what he can and can't do. His summer abroad courses have been immensely popular and he's always seemed excited about them. I was surprised when he cancelled this year's trip. If the cancellation wasn't Jonathan's idea, he just might have whipped off the book as a payback."

"Has anything bad actually happened on one of his trips?" Jeff asked.

Before Erica could answer, there was a knock on the door. Ruby came in, pulling a library cart holding six stacks of photocopies.

"Thanks, Ruby. Sorry you had to stay so late."

"The president said you'd need these right away."

After the door closed behind Ruby, Toni answered Jeff's question. "No, I haven't heard of problems on any of Gill's trips."

"It's well known, however," said Steve, "that Jonathan Gill has a short fuse."

Lloyd added, "I like the young man. He's prickly. Though he's not a product of the sixties, he is quick to spot real or imagined violations of academic freedom. I can see him putting a lot of energy into making a protest of some sort."

"I wonder whether Jonathan has had much time for extracurricular writing," mused Sarah slyly. "I've heard lots of grumbling about Gill from young faculty women—and secretaries. Seems they resent his trekking off to Farmington and Durango instead of looking in his own backyard for social life. I understand there's a steadily growing office pool that'll go to the first woman on campus Jonathan asks out. No matter how peeved he was, I doubt he'd spend his spare time writing a novel!"

"I agree," said Toni, "but I'll tackle Jonathan, especially since we seem to be short of candidates. It's just possible he may be enjoying watching the administrators stew. I'll figure out some non-committal way to start him talking about the book."

"All right. Gill is one possibility," said Erica, "Any others?"

"What about Lois Pidgin?" asked Jeff. "When she was elected president of the Senate last spring, I interviewed her. Her sarcasm about the administration oozed through statements she tried to keep neutral. Her main beef seems to be that the administrators aren't nearly as concerned about faculty governance as she is."

"She's right, of course," laughed Toni.

Jeff smiled and shrugged his shoulders. "I've heard jokes about the inordinate amount of time she spends on faculty governance…"

"Obviously a non-essential, trivial pursuit," said Erica.

Jeff resumed, "She's certainly verbal enough."

Toni agreed. "She's got the appropriate sense of play for pulling off a light-hearted book. And she'd enjoy making fun of the highest muckety-mucks. As I understand it," she said, looking towards Lloyd, "Lois knew the cabinet was not especially pleased when she was elected by acclamation."

He nodded. "I just don't see her as the author. She's dogged about stating her case, but I've never known her to carry grudges from one crisis to the next. Besides she once told me she didn't like reading fiction. We'll be wasting our time interviewing her."

Erica glanced at Jeff before saying, "So we scratch Lois, at least for now." He nodded in agreement.

"What about Richard Frankel?" asked Steve.

Toni sounded incredulous. "Duckhead?"

"People in his department call him that and they dismiss him as a tiresome buffoon. But I've often wondered," said Lloyd, "if he's quite the buffoon his colleagues think he is."

"I can't think of a better word to describe Frankel," replied Toni. "Richard absolutely refuses to write his own letters or reports. Whenever he has to send a letter or submit a report, he expects a secretary to turn his very sketchy draft into something presentable. That may be just laziness, because he prides himself on how quickly he can write for publication."

"Then how come he out-publishes everyone else in the English department?" challenged Lloyd.

"Do you know what he publishes?" retorted Toni. "Mostly a slew of book reviews and jacket blurbs for a minor publisher. Rumor has it that he only reads the books he's sent if they're mysteries."

"He teaches a course on mysteries, doesn't he?" asked Steve. "Isn't his 'History of the Mystery' being offered this fall for the third or fourth time?"

Toni frowned and said, "Being a mystery lover doesn't mean he can write one."

Erica intervened, "Frankel may have a higher opinion of himself than you do, Toni."

"I think he envisions himself as the next Dick Francis," added Steve. "We may dismiss mysteries as the fast food of literature, but he doesn't. He was certainly angry when I told him he'd have to go to Barnes and Noble for the current bestsellers. He's chastised my staff—repeatedly—for having only the nineteenth century stand-bys, Poe, Conan-Doyle, and Collins."

Toni thought a moment before agreeing to withdraw her objections. "It can't hurt to talk to him. But I'm still willing to bet he's not our man."

"Frankel and I have been here a long time. I can't think of anyone less aware of what's going on outside his own department," said Sarah. "I doubt he even knows he's the butt of half the faculty jokes on this campus."

Steve spoke hesitantly. "You all make him sound like a long shot indeed. Nevertheless, I think we shouldn't rule him out until Lloyd talks to him."

"I'll interview him, but don't expect me to be enthusiastic about it," said Lloyd. "The only thing I've ever heard him talk about is the literary merit of the whodunit. He even claims that *Hamlet* is more mystery than tragedy."

"I wonder," reflected Steve. "Remember being in grade school and saying dreadful things about the kid least able to defend himself? My friends and I used to laugh openly at our class dunce. We thought he was too dumb to know he was being tormented. It turned out we were wrong. He was not dumb. And he was much more observant than we gave him credit for. You may have heard of the child psychologist who is beloved by talk show hosts. He's made a reputation—and a fortune—urging the world not to overlook outcasts and misfits. *Our* class dunce grew up to become *Dr.* Earnest McFlanigan.

"From what the president has told the cabinet about *Academic Awards*," continued Steve, "the English faculty gets more than their fair share of ribbing. In ridiculing them, Frankel may be paying them back for ridiculing him."

Erica looked around the room. "We've added two suspects to Walt's list. Anybody else you can think of?"

No one spoke up.

"Steve," asked Erica, "will you track Taylor Anderson down?"

"Yes, I'll be glad to."

"Sarah, you've known Jane Snow for a long time, haven't you? Will you talk to her?"

"Yes, although I can't say I'll be *glad* to."

"Toni, journalism is over there with lit and creative writing. Perhaps one of his profs could tell you where Charlie Roanhorse went after he graduated. Will you ask around?"

Before Toni could reply, Jeff intervened. "I can locate Charlie. And I'd like to get in touch with him. I hope he *does* turn out to be our author. Fifty K would let him write full time, which is what he wants to do."

"Good, that's everyone then. Lloyd will talk to Frankel; Toni, you'll see Jonathan Gill; Sarah, you get the privilege of interviewing crazy Jane, and Steve, your job may be the hardest. Taylor Anderson seems to be incommunicado. Since we've crossed Lois off the list, you've left me without anyone to interview."

"Don't worry," said Sarah, "when we get stuck or threatened, we'll hand everything back to you."

Sarah's words served to adjourn the meeting. Everyone gathered their belongings and, like a roomful of students anticipating the end of a class hour, shifted in their seats, eager to be gone. Erica concluded, "I hate to schedule another meeting this Friday but," pointing to the schedules she'd collected at the noon meeting, "Fridays and Mondays at five are the only times all of us are free. We'll meet again this Friday unless someone confesses, in which case we'll not only earn Walt's undying gratitude but we can also call our search off. Otherwise, see you Friday, same place, same time."

☉

Pulling into adjacent parking spaces beside the Red Lobster in Farmington at 5:10, Jim Scoop and Florencio Ordoñez got out of their cars simultaneously.

After being seated, they asked—and answered—a whole series of questions. Jim learned that Florencio's youngest, one of six, would be entering the University of New Mexico as a freshman on Wednesday, that his wife's ill mother would be moving in with them now that they were empty nesters, and that he'd been promoted during the summer into a private office with a window. Florencio learned that Jim and his former wife could at last speak civilly with each other now that their two children were grown, that he was enjoying his womanless years so much he'd decided to settle down into a happy bachelorhood, and that he was still ridiculously content with his job at Southwestern. He did, however, have a favor to ask. Could Florencio find a way for Jim to send his newest recruit down to Albuquerque for one of his training sessions?

"I could do that. There are still a few slots open for my next class. But won't you be short-handed?"

"No, I don't think so. Southwestern has been lucky," replied Jim. "For the past several years I've been able to hire three retired police officers who live in the area to work part-time. Two of them have told me they'd welcome more hours, and I'm sure the college president will approve of the extra expense." He paused. "Now, tell me about this conference. Is violence in the schools really getting worse, or has the tragedy at Columbine High School in Colorado alerted us to the possibility of violence where we haven't expected it?"

"Yes," said Florencio, "in answer to both your questions. We've always known that inner city schools have more than their share of fights and malicious vandalism. But no one is safe from violence. It's spreading into so-called safe places. Some violent acts are undoubtedly copycat crimes. At the same time, adolescent psychology seems to be changing."

"We see that at Southwestern. There's certainly a maddening sense of entitlement these days. I can't believe how quickly—and often—college students express their outrage over any criticism of their behavior. Southwestern's vice-president of student affairs—a great lady, incidentally—often asks me to back her up in reiterating the negative consequences of what they've done."

"Does it work?"

"Sometimes. Often enough, at least, that we keep trying. I suspect the violence and crime we see at Southwestern doesn't compare with what goes on in urban areas."

"I used to think that was true. I envisioned small town schools and all college campuses as oases. But these days, reports from colleges are pretty grim. Urban schools have no campuses to speak of, and are located in areas that shut down at night, when nearby factories and shops are closed and the sidewalks empty."

"You make me glad Southwestern is in Cottonwood!"

"How many students are enrolled at Southwestern?" asked Florencio.

"Just under a thousand."

"You're unlikely to have the criminal activity of bigger colleges and universities. But any community of a thousand or more isn't completely exempt."

"You're right. Last year, we had a series of assaults. The whole campus is being relit because of that. And no term goes by without destruction of school property and a few fights that get out of hand. So far, I guess we've been lucky."

"How much of your luck is due to the fact that you can suspend the most unruly students?"

Jim shrugged and threw his hands up in the air.

Florencio, suddenly somber, said, "I may laugh about the food I'm missing tonight, but the problem the conference is addressing is real. School violence is increasing, at all levels. No one involved in education can afford to be complacent, even you, Jim, at your little, idyllic college. Actually, I'm here to conduct a workshop tomorrow morning for school counselors and principals, including those at elementary and middle schools."

"Elementary schools?" asked Jim, incredulous.

"Oh, yes, unfortunately. You should see the stash of stuff I've collected, all confiscated from kids 11 years old and younger: mostly razors, knives, and dirty pictures, but one loaded gun, and even the makings of a car bomb. All this in addition to lots of threatening notes."

"Wow, I had no idea. That's spooky. I suppose it's legal to haul in those things?"

Florencio nodded. "What's even spookier is wondering how many children would have used those weapons if we hadn't confiscated them. Luckily, schools have rules prohibiting weapons on site so it *is* legal to confiscate them."

"I can see reacting *after* an incident," said Jim, "but what can you tell people to look for *before* violence erupts?"

Florencio laughed. "Come hear my talk tomorrow, and you'll find out."

Serious, Jim replied. "I can't, but why don't you give me a summary in a hundred words or less?"

"I can't be that brief, but I can outline the case studies I'll be presenting."

Jim listened, fascinated. Maybe Annette Asher had been right to warn her husband, and maybe Walt had been right to be nervous. After all, notorious attacks had occurred on college campuses. Jim didn't remember the details, but he did remember hearing about a professor being shot and killed in broad daylight going up the steps into Sproul Hall on the Berkeley campus of the University of California.

Subdued, Jim remained quiet when Florencio finished talking.

After a long, awkward silence, Florencio said, "My friend, you look worried."

"I am."

"What gives? Something rotten up your way?"

"Rotten, probably not. But disturbing, yes. Listening to you makes me wonder whether I'm treating a possible threat less seriously than I should."

"My advice is not to dismiss any threat cavalierly until you're sure it no longer exists. If you'll tolerate a bit more of my preaching, I'll explain some ideas I discussed with a mischief loving friend from my high school days," said Florencio, fishing a warm biscuit from the basket in the middle of the table. "We met at a mutual friend's house in Las Cruces last summer. He was as shocked to discover I'd become a policeman as I was to learn he'd become a school superintendent. Later, Carl Kiefer evidently read about my meeting with Albuquerque administrators on violence in the schools. A month ago he called from Farmington, inviting me to be one of the speakers at his fall conference.

"Carl maintains that teachers are constitutionally averse to the idea of anticipating trouble. They've been indoctrinated into thinking it's wrong to prejudge or label young people. Consequently, they squelch their suspicions. And that, I believe, can be dangerous."

Jim leaned forward, and, shoving his plate aside, put both elbows on the table. "Time for a confession. I may be downplaying a potentially suspicious activity too. Until I listened to you, I felt justified in doing so, partly because the suspicions weren't mine."

Jim explained, recounting his morning's conversation with the president and his own reactions to Annette Asher's fears.

"There's a good chance," replied Florencio, shrugging his shoulders and laughing, "that Southwestern College's missing author may appear from some cockamamie academic jaunt, the college may get its half million dollars, and the writer his or her fifty grand. But until those things happen, act as if Southwestern is on a sort of orange alert on the off chance that the author is either vicious enough or unbalanced enough to be lying in wait for an opportunity to strike. After all, we've both seen our share of professional types who only *seem* to function normally."

"True." It was Jim's turn to laugh. "I'm not sure whether I've come across more examples of unhinged people in the service or during my two years among would-be philosophers at graduate school. I've been lulled into complacency at Southwestern."

Florencio insisted on paying the bill. While waiting for change, he said, "I'll be glad to get your young officer licensed—that is, if he's had some experience shooting."

"Oh, I'm sure you'll find Johnny a good shot. He's been hunting all his life."

As the two friends threaded their way out of the crowded restaurant, Jim sighed. "I resent needing to have my officers armed. Yet many colleges and universities have gone that route in the last decade or two. I hate to think it's necessary."

"I'm afraid it is. As much as you may dislike having all your security officers licensed to carry, it's probably a good idea. In the words of an old cliché, better safe than sorry."

*Steve Scott gets the lowdown on Taylor Anderson and tracks him down.*

When Steve walked into the library on Tuesday morning, he was amused to hear Sarah Jennings arguing with Margie, the reference librarian. "I didn't ask you to put the *Music History Encyclopedia* on reserve *last week* because I knew at *that* time that the library only had the second edition. I was waiting until the library's copy of the *third* edition arrived to put in my request."

Margie's face fell as Sarah's voice rose. "Didn't you inform me *yesterday* that the third edition was delivered just that morning? *That* is the edition that needs to be on reserve for my students, not the second edition!"

Steve directed an assuring smile in Margie's direction and then asked Sarah if she could spare him a few minutes when she was through at the front desk.

Five minutes later, Sarah entered his office sputtering. "That is one stubborn lady. Why would I want the second edition on reserve when the third is finally out!"

Steve thought to himself that Margie didn't have a corner on stubbornness. Aloud, he appealed to Sarah's good humor. "Librarians are sticklers for details. It's a requirement of our profession."

"And so it should be," said Sarah, her scowl beginning to evaporate.

"We don't really expect everyone to adhere to our policy. But if we don't set an August fifteenth deadline for reserve requests, we'll be deluged the first week of school."

"I know, I know," said Sarah, now grinning broadly. She dumped a pile of assorted books and sheet music, along with her bulging purse, on one of the two chairs facing Steve's desk and plunked down in the other. "Sorry to be so huffy. Sometimes I think we drown in rules and regulations. What did you want to talk to me about?"

"Before I ask you for an insider's tips on my assigned suspect," said Steve, "tell me, did you persuade Margie to break the rules for you?" Sarah nodded. "Good. I thought you would. Now I have a request for you. Could you review what happened last spring when Taylor Anderson resigned and then tried to say he hadn't meant it? I want to be familiar with his story."

"He'll certainly expect you to be," said Sarah. "It wouldn't occur to him that everyone hadn't followed every detail of the Anderson saga. I'll try to be brief. The story is really more Stephanie's than his."

"Oh?" Scott raised his eyebrows as Sarah continued. "Taylor is nothing if not loyal. He sees Stephanie as she sees herself—God's gift to the art world.

"It all began when Stephanie offered herself to the college as an artist-in-residence with a full-time salary. She made her offer in a long memo directly to the president. She fully expected that Asher, on behalf of the college, would be delighted. It didn't dawn on her that the president does not hire people. He shmoozes with the college's benefactors.

"Asher turned her offer down—on his behalf, *and* ours.

"Without a by-your-leave, Stephanie walked away from her classes. Ever supportive, Taylor resigned. He couldn't believe that I wouldn't rush to his and Stephanie's defense. And he was astonished that the president was letting them both go with only a polite thank you and good-bye. He waited for apologies and supplications that never came."

"Has the art department been allowed to hire replacements for them both?" asked Steve.

"For Taylor, yes. There were almost fifty applications for his full-time slot. Not surprising, really. Lots of artists have settled in the Four Corners area. Getting a chance for regular, salaried work in art is rare—and welcome. We've already hired an accomplished weaver to take over Stephanie's weaving classes, and we've got a lead on a jewelry maker for winter term."

"Did the students object to having other instructors?"

"Not much. There were very few complaints. Most students were glad to see the last of Stephanie. She never understood that a small undergraduate college is not an art academy and that we *want* to encourage hobbyists. She had no time for anybody who wasn't serious enough to major in art. You know who her father is, don't you?" Sarah paused when Steve didn't answer. "Ernest diAngelo."

"The sculptor?"

"Yes. He's rather famous in the Philadelphia area."

"In D.C. too. At least he was a couple of decades ago. To enter half the shopping centers built in the '70s you had to wend your way past diAngelo's squat, climb-on-able critters swarming with *squealing* children."

"I understand diAngelo is doing more graceful, abstract stuff now. But it was those critters that inspired his daughter. She spent a number of years sculpting imitative miniatures. When she wasn't successful at that, she tried her hand first at painting, then charcoal."

"When did she become a weaver, *and* a jewelry maker? Seems to me she's pretty gutsy to try her hand at so many different kinds of art."

"Yes, Stephanie's gutsy, all right."

"From what I've heard, her weavings and jewelry sell well."

"They do. She finally found her niche, not in her father's Philadelphia but out here where the bright blue skies are not cloudy all day. Taylor brought his new wife with him when he came west to teach in Prescott, Arizona. By that time, she'd given up on art. Instead, she started marketing her husband's drawings. I even bought one."

"We have three in the library and I've seen others around campus."

"Oh, Stephanie became quite the entrepreneur. First here with us. Then she branched out and persuaded regional gift shops to stock cards with Taylor's black-and-white drawings. Her biggest coup was getting them into the Grand Canyon's gift shops. She was nearing 40, childless, and no longer soliciting orders in person. She was bored. She joined a weekend weaving commune in Farmington, and drove up to Fort Lewis to take a jewelry class from Ben Nighthorse Campbell— before he went into politics.

"The prices an Anderson weaving or piece of jewelry sold for skyrocketed. We felt fortunate when she started teaching for us. It didn't take her long to disabuse us about our good fortune. She scorned her colleagues and ignored her students. We were lucky we *didn't* have a position she was qualified for!"

"Since Taylor resigned because of the insult to his wife, are there any sore spots I need to skirt?" asked Steve.

"That's a good question. I don't trust armchair psychiatry. Yet when I try to figure the Andersons out, I invariably engage in it. I think Stephanie has never quite forgiven Taylor for getting the kind of encouragement from her father that she badly wanted—and didn't get. Since she couldn't show off her art, she was glad to show off her very own artist. Taylor was teaching art at Drexel when she met him. Daddy had gone to a faculty art show there and came home praising

Taylor's drawings. The very next day, according to rumor, she went to see the show and immediately introduced herself to Taylor. Her flattery and being the daughter of a famous sculptor were evidently a winning combination. I can't help wondering if Taylor ever resents having such a successful wife."

"Would I be cynical to suggest that money may trump resentment? I've given up trying to analyze marriages; all but my own seem mysterious." *Steve Scott was not*, thought Sarah, *all military formality*. She no longer minded that his few minutes promised to stretch into a good half hour.

Steve continued, "Since Stephanie has been showered with critical acclaim for her artwork, and is doing well selling it, why did she even *want* a full-time teaching position?"

"I'm not sure, but I have a theory. Once, I was invited to the Andersons' for dinner when her father was visiting. I've never forgotten the look on her face when he questioned whether she was imitating Ben Campbell's jewelry and then said she had the *domestic* crafts in her genes: after all, her grandmother had sewn the quilts she'd slept under as a child. Think about how Stephanie must have felt. No artist wants to be called an imitator and few think of themselves as *mere* craftsmen. Her weavings, like her father's sculptures, are grandiose. They demand attention. They're honored as works of art. But not by him!"

"I'm getting the picture," said Steve. "She offers herself to Southwestern and we turn her down. That insult must seem like an echo of her father's dismissive attitude."

"That's certainly my reading," responded Sarah. "However mysterious you find their marriage, at least Taylor took umbrage on his wife's behalf. He is very protective, and very defensive. After all, she made money for him too. He puts her on a pedestal even though her father doesn't. I suspect he's too timid and still too much in awe of diAngelo as a sculptor to reproach his father-in-law, but he *can* accuse the college of foul play."

☙

After Sarah left, Steve compared what she had told him about the Andersons with his own sense of them. He'd seen them on campus, and he and his wife had had a few brief conversations with them during intermissions at concerts in Durango. Taylor was a big bear of a man, with sagging jowls, a mane of unruly silver hair, and perpetually hunched shoulders. He wore muted colors—grays, beiges, tans, and an occasional brown heather. He was monochromatic in both personality and dress. Stephanie, on the other hand, draped herself in voluminous colorful flowing capes. Four or five exotic birds or animals would descend, pyramid-like, on gold wires from her ears. The top of her head, with its neatly wound braid intertwined with a multi-colored strip of Guatemalan fabric, was on a level with her husband's shoulders. Steve imagined Taylor developing his slouch from years of leaning down to talk to her. She was barely five feet, and then only in the high-heeled sandals she wore all year. She commanded attention, Steve realized, less by talking herself, than by waiting for others to talk to her.

Sarah had given Steve the name of the part-timer, Angelica Trujillo, who had filled in when Stephanie had walked off the job last February. Since Sarah said Ms. Trujillo also taught classes at San Juan College, Steve hunted for her in the Farmington directory. He found a page full of Trujillos, but no Angelicas. Dialing the number of the second A Trujillo, he lucked out. She was at home. Unluckily, she had no idea where the Andersons were now.

Steve thanked her and was about to hang up, when Angelica said, "Oh, I just put two and two together. I remember overhearing one of Stephanie's protégés, a member of the class I inherited, say she'd found a place to live for the summer. Sandy Holman—I think that was the girl's name—bragged that all she'd have to do was take care of a spoiled cat and prevent any would-be burglars from stealing a large art collection. I'll bet the cat and the art belong to the Andersons."

Steve found Sandy at her parents' home in Durango. He introduced himself and then repeated the story he'd fabricated for Ms. Trujillo. "I want to get in touch with Professor Anderson to tell him that the two interlibrary loan books he ordered months ago finally arrived. I need to know whether he wants me to send them back or send them on to him."

Sandy sounded embarrassed. "Gee, Dr. Scott, I'm sure he'll appreciate that, but the Andersons told me not give their address to *anyone*."

"I think Dr. Anderson won't mind your telling me. He scrawled *urgent* on the top of his interlibrary loan request."

Sandy hesitated before replying, "They might be in Philly visiting her father."

"And if they're not, do you know where else they might have gone?"

"Gee, somewhere abroad I think."

Steve, swallowing his exasperation with Sandy's vocabulary and her vagueness, was relieved when she came up with a useful suggestion. "I'm going to be house-sitting again this fall. I think I saw a forwarding address somewhere. I guess it'd be okay to give it to you. I'm going to be moving back into their house tomorrow."

"Could I get in touch with you at the Andersons' house then?"

"Yeah, but don't call before six o'clock. I'm not sure when I'll get in."

Steve only half listened to Sandy's litany of her full afternoon schedule. "I've got to gas up my car here in Durango, then go by the Southwestern bookstore before it closes and then pick up the cat from the vet's. You won't tell on me, will you? The Andersons would freak out if they knew I'd boarded their precious Picasso, the cat, that is. Not their Picasso original! I needed a break. From the damn cat—and all their artwork. It's everywhere, you know. On every shelf and every wall. It wore me out to have to look at it all the time."

*And it's wearing me out to listen to you, young lady*, thought Steve.

Sandy took a quick breath before continuing, "Besides, I wanted to see my folks." That sounded like the last line of a dull play. But she added a memorable conclusion that more than made up for her hesitations and digressions: "My folks' idea of art is everything I've ever drawn or painted since junior high. They've even framed it all. You know what? It looks pretty good after a summer spent in the midst of all the Andersons' pricey stuff."

@

Jeff Miles had left yesterday's task force meeting elated. He liked intrigue. He liked hunting for information, and he looked forward to getting in touch with Charlie. Most of all, he liked imagining the press release he could write. It would be picked up all over the country! Boy, would he like to be the one to unravel the mystery! Especially if he could prove his fellow committee members wrong in their assumption that a mere student couldn't have written *Academic Awards*.

By the time students arrived, the campus was buzzing. That the students should have learned about the book and its missing author so soon surprised and dismayed Dr. Asher. But Jeff was still close enough to his own years as a student to know that college campuses harbor few secrets.

The news about the book and its author-in-hiding had started making its rounds before last Friday's faculty meeting was even over. Jeff, sitting in the last row of the auditorium along with several other staff members, was aware that the two students who delivered refreshments to last Friday's faculty meeting overheard the president's plea for the writers of *Academic Awards* to come forward. They wouldn't have kept such juicy, interesting information to themselves. Protecting a secret within a small group was hard enough, but the sheer size of a college community made keeping a secret almost impossible. Before the first day of classes, students were asking when the book would be published, when they could get copies, and whether any of *their* professors had been suitably lampooned. Most of the faculty and staff were amused and curious. A few hoped they would appear in the book. A few feared they might.

One of the young campus cops had confided to Jeff that Jim Scoop was mighty nervous. He'd started to tell Jeff about the increased patrols, and then thought better of it. Jeff guessed that Ben was talking when he'd been told not to.

Walking home late Tuesday afternoon, Jeff felt he'd finally come of age. When he first arrived at Southwestern, he had felt isolated. Being young and in an office by himself made him almost as invisible as the missing author. He'd gradually learned that many of the older faculty thought the college could do without public relations. What was wrong, they grumbled, with assigning an English or journalism professor to keep on writing the alumni newsletter and sending out an occasional story to regional newspapers? New faculty members, more attuned to the importance of image, resented his salary and his airy office. Both were larger than theirs. Southwestern's only journalist, Toni Hexton, who'd spent years practicing what she taught, appreciated and understood his work. She had always treated him as an equal. She had invited him to talk in her classes and to mentor some of her students. She'd immediately welcomed him to the task force. As he neared the house he was renting from the college, his spirits fell. The little box was one in a row of similar squat bungalows referred to as the "Habitat for Impoverished Instructors."

Today, Jeff did not look forward to going home to his wife. He tried to erase the sadness that accompanied his recognition of the decline of their marriage—made at the University of New Mexico, if not in heaven. He and Irene had married the day she graduated, a grand celebration attended by their families and assorted high school and college friends. Jeff had started working on a master's degree in public relations. With his scholarship came a plum internship in the president's office. The university hired Irene too, as secretary to the women's athletic department and manager of the gymnastics squad until their first child, Mary, was born. Margaret arrived a year and a half after Mary. By then, Jeff had earned his master's degree and become assistant director of the school's public relations office. When Southwestern College offered him a job three years later, Irene was again pregnant. Her determination to have her children quickly—unlike her parents whose nine children spanned twenty-four years—had originally seemed a good idea. Now with three children under six, it was hard to see past diapers and bottles and squabbles and a houseful of scattered plastic toys.

Still, the girls were cute and loving, and accepted their father unconditionally. Today, they would greet him with smiles and hugs. Irene wouldn't. She would be put out that he hadn't gotten home anywhere near their agreed-upon dinner hour of 5:30. He'd tried to call her in the afternoon to tell her he'd be late and to go ahead and feed the girls. But each time he called the line was busy. For a woman who complained about no time for herself, she spent an inordinate amount of time talking on the phone.

Jeff barely paid attention to the children's chatter during dinner. Irene herself was gloomy and silent. Jeff was thinking of who might be able to help him locate Charlie with part of his mind and wondering what had happened to the lively girl he'd married with another part. He could see *why* life in a small New Mexican town where her husband had little recognition and she had none must seem uneventful. Especially after years of being the mainstay on UNM's gymnastics team and the lead jazz dancer in most of the university's musical productions. Yet he couldn't help wishing she showed some interest in the events of *his* life. He decided on his way home that he'd swear her to secrecy—no gossip at the morning coffee klatches—and talk over his latest assignment. He'd like an ear, and he hoped that the puzzle would perk her up. At one time, she would have been eager to hear all the particulars.

Jeff felt guilty when he begged off giving the girls their baths. He felt even guiltier for excusing himself from reading them a story, a nightly chore he usually treasured. Irene shrugged indifferently and didn't even ask what business he had to take care of that was so urgent he had to do it at home.

"Well, at least you will do the dishes, won't you?" she asked, tromping out of the kitchen and pushing the girls ahead of her without waiting for his assent.

As Jeff cleared the table, he heard the sounds of giggles and splashing water. He was tempted to leave the house for a fast walk around the block when the sounds ceased. Mary, Margaret, and Tish had become quiet. Irene had begun singing to them. He could picture her toweling the girls dry and starting in on a song whose last lines she never could remember: "Stair by stair, to castles in the air, I climb my stairway of dreams…mmm…" Jeff's guilt and anger melted away. He listened to his wife's lovely voice. Gently, he loaded the dishwasher, washed off the table and the counters, and vowed to be more compassionate in the future.

He walked to his desk tucked into one corner of the living room, and looked in the telephone directory for Sherry Littlefield's number. She was chairman of the English Department and might know where Charlie had gone after he graduated from Southwestern fifteen months ago.

She answered the phone on its first ring.

"Say, Sherry, have you got a few minutes to talk to me about one of your recent graduates?"

"Is this a story for the next alumni bulletin?"

"Yes. I'm doing a series on students who've graduated in the last decade," he replied, silently thanking Sherry for giving him an excuse for his questions. "I'd like to interview Charlie Roanhorse, but I don't know how to reach him. The alumni office has no address for him."

"Matt Leslie might. Wait a sec, I can give you his number. It's easy to remember: 747-1234."

"Charlie took several creative writing classes from Matt, didn't he?"

"Yes, and some independent studies too. I only had Charlie in one class. I'd have paid him to take more. He's every teacher's ideal student."

"That's quite a compliment. That would be a great way to start my story. May I quote you? … Thanks. Before I call Leslie, what else can you tell me about Charlie?"

"As I said, I loved having him in class. Being a few years older than most of the other students made a lot of difference. His comments and questions would get the whole class talking, something I couldn't always do. But he never lorded it over the other students. His exams and papers were superb. I actually looked forward to reading them. I'd read his work last—after I'd graded everybody else's. Otherwise, A's would have been very scarce." Sherry paused. "You do know, don't you, that several of his stories and feature articles were published?"

"Yes, he showed me a couple. I was surprised he didn't apply to graduate school."

"I'm not. He had no patience for lots of what passes for scholarship in literature these days. Professor Leslie encouraged him to stick to writing. He thinks Charlie's one of the few who has a chance of making it as a writer."

If that's so, thought Jeff, the committee is making a mistake to discount him as our author. Jeff could see him tossing off a light-hearted murder mystery.

"Anyway," Sherry continued, "I'm sure Matt Leslie will be able to help you get in touch with Charlie."

Jeff thanked Sherry and called Professor Leslie. He was home and more than willing to sing Charlie's praises. Although he wasn't sure exactly where Charlie was, he thought he could lead Jeff in the right direction.

"I've heard he's working in Arizona near the Mexican border. I don't remember where. He started out doing grunt work for some travel agency. Then they discovered he spoke Spanish fluently. In addition to making the arrangements for trips, he began to drive the vans and serve as a guide. But I hope he won't have to do that for long. He's brilliant. He *should* be teaching, or better yet, writing."

*Well,* thought Jeff, *maybe he is.* Aloud he said, "He'll have more time for writing if he *isn't* teaching. As far as I can tell, you English profs spend so much time grading papers that you don't have much time for your own work."

Leslie chuckled. "Charlie said he needed a job to support his writing habit. That's why he thought he'd found an ideal job. After putting in two or three seven-day weeks, he gets a whole week off from his travel gig. Living out in the back of nowhere, he has uninterrupted stretches of time to write."

Trying not to sound as excited as he felt, Jeff asked, "If you don't know where he is, do you know the name of the agency he's working for? I'd like to talk to him firsthand."

"Sorry, I can't help you there."

Jeff thanked Leslie and went out to the garage to hunt for a map of Arizona. He found a stack of grimy, torn, and folded state maps held together by two large rubber bands in the trunk of their second-hand Subaru.

Right now he was eager to look for towns along Arizona's southern border. He wanted to talk with Charlie—face to face. He'd had enough telephoning and if Charlie wanted not to be found, he'd be forewarned by a phone call. If Leslie was right, and Charlie was living and working somewhere near the Mexican border, there weren't many choices. The only possible towns were Nogales, Sierra Vista, Bisbee, and Douglas in the east, and Yuma, Somerton, and San Luis in the west.

ⓒ

Steve spent the rest of the morning, after pumping Sarah for information about Taylor Anderson and walking around the library, double-checking to make sure the staff had everything in order for tomorrow's onslaught of students. Seeing Johnny putting the last of the bookcases in place in the entryway, he was reminded that he'd been awfully brusque with the young man. "Looks good, son," he said. "Sorry my change of mind made so much extra work for you."

Back in his office, Steve located the Andersons' address in last year's faculty directory, grabbed his sandwich and keys and headed for his car. Believing that people's homes revealed a great deal about them, he was curious to see the Andersons' house.

Their house, not surprisingly, was in Cottonwood's only upscale neighborhood. After finding himself on Tamarisk Terrace twice and Juniper Junction at least four times before he found Piñon Point, Steve cursed the developer enamored of alliteration and twisting streets.

Steve pulled his car to the curb across from number 11. He was startled to see an old Chevy turn into the driveway. The dusty car was filled with boxes. The bicycle riding upright on its roof looked more expensive than the car. A young man in jeans and a white T-shirt straightened up from an apparent attempt to dislodge a suitcase wedged behind the driver's seat when Steve approached. His face broke into a welcoming grin. "Hey, Dr. Scott, what are you doing here?"

"I might ask *you* the same thing. You used to work in the library, didn't you?"

"Yeah, for a couple of years before I went back home to Indiana to finish up at I.U."

"What's brought you here now?" asked Steve.

"Grad school. I got a full scholarship in economics to UC-Santa Barbara. Cottonwood isn't very much of a detour between Blooming-ton, Indiana, and Santa Barbara, California. I've come to see my fiancé, Sandy Holman. She's housesitting for the Andersons. She's not expect-ing me, so she'll be surprised to find me here this afternoon."

After an awkward moment, Steve retrieved a name for the young man. While watching him carry his suitcase to the front steps, Steve said, "Tom, Sandy's not going to get here until tonight."

Tom looked puzzled. Steve explained how he knew Sandy's sched-ule and why he'd gotten in touch with her.

Tom fished a key from his pocket and proudly held it up. "I still have this key Sandy gave me in June. I know three or four places the Andersons might have left a forwarding address. I guess I could try to find it for you. I don't think Sandy would mind."

Steve thought it would have been more appropriate for Tom to ask whether the Andersons would mind, but not wanting to jinx getting the information he was after, he said nothing.

Steve gratefully followed his fortuitous host into the house. Tom leaned over to pick up a week's worth of mail that had been inserted through a slot in the front door and lay scattered on top of a cobalt blue rug. Steve peered into the living room, noting that the wall facing him was a deep red and almost completely filled with paintings from floor to ceiling. Sandy was right. He'd already seen enough to know he, too, would grow crazy in these surroundings.

Handing Steve an envelope, Tom said. "I don't think I'll need to look around. This letter to Sandy from the Andersons has a return ad-dress."

"Thanks," said Steve, looking at the address and the postmark. "If Stephanie and Taylor mailed this from Philadelphia, I should be able to reach them there. Thank Sandy for me. I won't need to be calling her tonight. By the way, Tom, congratulations, on your engagement *and* your scholarship."

℗

Steve Scott spent the rest of the afternoon alternating between playing librarian and playing detective. Despite a few piles of books still stacked on the floor in front of partly empty shelves, he trusted the library would be ready for business tomorrow.

Arriving home shortly before six, Steve found a note from Marni, his wife, reminding him that she'd be home late from a League of Women Voters meeting in Farmington. He'd been glad of the extra hour for a leisurely drink and the chance to call the diAngelos in Philadelphia, where it was already past dinnertime.

His luck held. Stephanie's mother answered the phone. She didn't share Sandy's reluctance to give out her daughter's whereabouts. "Stephanie and Taylor left for Spain several days ago. You can reach them there at…" said Mrs. diAngelo, interrupting herself, "What a peculiar number, but I'm sure I've copied it correctly. It's two, seven nine, zero five one, zero five three."

@

After eating dinner late, Steve and Marni watched an hour of CNN news before calling it a night. Steve set his alarm for 1 A.M. so he could call the Andersons at a respectable 9 A.M. in Spain. Unless, of course, they had already acquired the late night-late morning hours enjoyed by the Spanish.

Steve slipped downstairs to place his call. The phone rang with the faint tinny sound typical of overseas connections.

Bingo, the voice that finally answered was unmistakably Taylor's.

"Taylor Anderson? This is Steve Scott calling from Cottonwood."

"Steve! How'd you track me down? Nothing's happened to Picasso, has it?" It took Steve only a minute to realize that Taylor was talking about his cat.

"No, nothing like that. I've called with what may be good news."

"From *Southwestern*? I don't associate the college with good news."

There was an awkward silence before Steve said, "You must enjoy having time for your drawing and sketching."

"I'm not doing much of either just now." Steve involuntarily leaned forward as if to encourage a confession. His hopes were immediately dashed.

"What I *am* enjoying," said Taylor, "besides being away from Southwestern and Cottonwood is working again in oils after a long hiatus."

Steve was sure he'd reached a dead-end, but just in case, he forced himself to ask one more question.

"I don't suppose you're trying a completely different medium— writing, for instance?"

"*Writing*? Me? Stephanie takes care of all our correspondence. The only time I use a pen is to sign checks. Why do you ask?" Taylor sounded suspicious.

Without specifying whom he meant by "we," Steve continued, "We hoped you might have written a book featuring Southwestern."

"If I had, everyone at the college would know about it and they wouldn't be too happy about it either. Still I don't understand why you're calling me. I haven't written a book. I have *no* intention of writing a book. But now that you've gotten me on the phone, what made you go to the trouble of contacting me?"

"The college needs to identify a so-far anonymous author. We need to find him—or her. For our sake as well as the writer's. Quite a bit of money is at stake, not just for the prize winner but also the college." Sure now that Taylor had not written *Academic Awards*, Steve was reluctant to mention how great Southwestern's share of the prize would be.

Taylor's voice rose. "I wouldn't, as you should know, do a damn thing for Southwestern. The college owes Stephanie and me our jobs back, to say the least." Taylor paused. "But tell me again, what made you contact me?"

"Several of us are interviewing people who aren't on campus this term and therefore haven't heard all the hullabaloo about the winning book and the half million dollars Southwestern stands to receive—*if* we can produce the author. I hoped you'd be our man."

"Your hopes are in vain. Surely, you and everyone there must know I'd be the last person to buy a meal ticket for Southwestern after what they did to Stephanie and me," grumbled Taylor.

"But," said Steve, trying to sound playful, "you might have enjoyed exposing the school to a little ridicule. As an artist, you're an observer. The book is filled with funny, on-target observations of academic life."

"Southwestern doesn't deserve just a *little* ridicule. Any observations I'd have made would be far from funny! You can tell Walt Asher for me—and I assume that's whose bidding you're doing—that I'm not happy to hear from Southwestern. We are," continued Taylor, lapsing into royal-speak, "happy to be a continent and a half away from Cottonwood."

While Steve was trying to think of a way to end the conversation, Taylor hung up.

WEDNESDAY, SEPTEMBER 7

*Jeff locates Charlie Roanhorse, Sarah interviews Jane Snow, and Lloyd is served sherry and monomania by Richard Frankel.*

Wednesday morning Jeff got up early enough to eat breakfast by himself. He was uneasy. He and Irene hadn't said good night. She'd slept huddled on her side of the bed. When he'd reached out to touch her shoulder, she'd pulled away from him.

He was glad to be preoccupied. The whiff of danger from someone who didn't want to be found seemed manageable—unlike his home life.

And so, as he walked to his office, he focused on remembering the times he'd spent with Charlie. He saw the two of them sitting in a back booth of Cottonwood's only bar, relaxed after a soccer game, enjoying a beer and rambling conversation. Jeff had said he envied Charlie his unusual last name. "Oh," Charlie had responded, "You won't think Roanhorse is so unusual once half my cousins and brothers and sisters start showing up. Southwestern will be crawling with Roanhorses in a few years."

Jeff was delighted to discover Charlie was right. From the registrar's office he learned that a Berniece Roanhorse was a freshman living on campus in Española Hall. On Wednesdays she would be attending a nine o'clock history class and an eleven o'clock psychology class. That meant, thought Jeff, she might be in her room now. Luck was with him. A sleepy-voiced roommate, obviously unhappy to be awakened, told him to hang on a minute.

After a long pause, Berniece answered. She thought it was neat that her cousin was going to be the subject of a lead article. Jeff promised to send her a copy of the alumni magazine with his story about Charlie. After his lie last night, Jeff felt obligated to write the series. Besides, he'd decided it was a good idea. Berniece told him that Charlie was living in an old VW van somewhere between Bisbee and Douglas, that he had no telephone, but that Jeff could probably leave a message for Charlie with the company he was working for.

"Do you know what his company is called?"

"No, but I'm pretty sure it's named for a famous Indian. I *think* it's either in Bisbee or Douglas, but I'm not sure which."

Since he always waffled between using "Indian" and "Native American," Jeff was glad to hear Berniece use the shorter term. He was also amused that she didn't know the name of the famous Indian. Her information, though vague, should make it easy to find the right agency.

After telling Berniece that he and Charlie had become friends when they played on a soccer team together, Jeff invited her to drop by his office sometime. "I will," said Bernice. A note of pride crept into her voice when she added, "I play soccer, too. I'm trying out for the girl's team this afternoon."

"That's great. Charlie would like that. And good luck," said Jeff. "I hope you make the team. I'll come watch you play sometime."

While Jeff was looking up the names of travel companies on the Internet, he was thinking of the times Charlie had scoffed at the Indian wannabees. He would have ridiculed a character wanting to change his name to Flatfoot *Becay*. Especially one ignorant or inattentive enough to substitute the un-Navajo *Becay* for the common Navajo name *Begay*. Not only that, but the young man's motive for murder came with his discovery that the fictional president laughed at Geoffrey for thinking himself a suitable suitor for Mary Sheepherder, a thirty-something Navajo student.

Jeff found Menendez Travel listed in the yellow pages for Douglas, Bisbee, and Sierra Vista. He laughed aloud at seeing its un-PC email address, <getgeronimo@theriver.com>.

When Jeff phoned the travel office, a very nice lady agreed the Geronimo email address *was* embarrassing. She assured him that no offense had been intended. Their headquarters were originally on Mule Pass Creek. Nevertheless they were in the process of changing their e-mail address. And yes, she knew Charlie. The owner of the travel company, who identified herself as Becky, spent several minutes praising Charlie and his work for the travel agency.

"Look," Jeff said, "I'm going to be coming down your way on some school business." He grinned to himself, thinking that although he was not exactly lying, Becky could hardly imagine the kind of school business sending him to southern Arizona. "Charlie and I were buddies at Southwestern and I'd hate not to see him while I'm in the area."

Becky told Jeff that he could drop by the office the next day. The travel agency was on the main road and easy to find. Charlie's place wasn't. She'd draw Jeff a map. Without directions, he'd never locate Charlie's trailer.

Jeff called Erica to explain that he was going to make a quick trip south. "I've told my secretary I'm going away to do a series of interviews with recent graduates. I usually clear any off-campus business with Dr. Asher. Do you think I should tell him I'm going to Bisbee and why?"

"No. I'll tell him you're going off-campus on task force business. And thanks a lot, Jeff. That's a long drive."

"I know, but I've always liked driving," he said. "Bisbee's not far from the Mexican border. I *think* I'll be back in time for Friday's meeting. I hope I can announce that I've solved our mystery."

Jeff handed his secretary the draft of the recruiting brochure he'd been working on, made sure she knew how to insert text around pictures and graphics, and told her that the admissions people were expecting the finished product the next afternoon.

He went home, packed, and informed an uninterested Irene he'd be away for two or three days. She groused a little bit about the unfairness of his being sent off without some warning, but he sensed that she wouldn't mind his being gone any more than he minded going. He'd enjoy seeing Charlie. And if he discovered that Charlie had written the award-winning book, *that* would count as one of the most satisfying things he'd ever done.

@

Sarah Jennings was not a procrastinator. She had little sympathy for people who put off until tomorrow what could be done today. Until today that is—when faced with the prospect of meeting Jane Snow before she'd had her second cup of tea. She'd heard the litany of Jane's woes too many times. Sarah doubted that Jane could stay focused long enough to have written even one chapter of *Academic Awards,* but in order to be absolutely sure, she needed to let Jane talk...and talk...and talk.

After Jane had rattled off a list of reasons why it would be better to meet at some distant time in the future than anytime soon—as if she were unique in having classes to prepare, students to see, books to put on reserve, and files to reorganize—Jane suggested meeting Sarah the next morning at 7:00.

Sarah quailed. She didn't look forward to spending an hour with Jane at any time of day. Trying to keep Jane on track was not the way she would have chosen to start the first day of a new term. But her eight o'clock would give her a good excuse to cut the interview short if Jane rambled as she usually did.

When Sarah arrived the next morning, Jane was standing with her back to the door, looking out the window. "Here, Sarah. Look at those damn kids, smooching in the bushes in broad daylight."

Sarah couldn't resist the temptation to be perverse. "It isn't broad daylight yet."

Reluctantly, Jane pulled herself away from the window. Sitting down behind her desk, she swept aside a tower of piled papers. They fell to the floor.

Sarah leaned forward to pick them up.

"Never mind," said Jane. "I'll pick them up later. I need to go through them anyway. She pointed to a sign centered on the bulletin board behind her: An orderly desk reveals a sick mind.

"That's my motto. Disorder inspires me. I suppose," she continued, looking not at Sarah but somewhere in the middle distance, "musicians don't much like chaos. Too disharmonious." *Except Bartok*, thought Sarah.

Jane didn't give Sarah a chance to explain why she'd asked for this morning's meeting. "Last year was hell, Sarah. Too bad students can't get fired. That girl who caused me so much grief, Annie Trostle, is in graduate school, you know. To get a *teaching* certificate," said Jane, oozing scorn. "*Third grade* is what she wants to teach, when I'd spent hours getting her a full ride to graduate school in psychology!"

"Well," said Sarah, amused but not surprised that Jane had taken the lead in the conversation, "God knows good elementary teachers are sorely needed."

Jane paid no attention to Sarah's comment as she barreled ahead. "You know what's worse. Annie took her husband's name, and didn't keep her own."

"Some feminists argue that keeping a father's name is as bad as taking a husband's," replied Sarah.

Once again, ignoring Sarah's comment, Jane continued, "What a ninny. She's a throwback. To say nothing of the damage she did me!"

For a woman in her 50s, Sarah thought, Jane adopted the demeanor of a furious 10-year-old.

"Has the psychology department heard from Annie since she graduated?"

"*I* haven't and *I* don't want to," Jane yelled in reply.

She continued, speaking softly and haltingly while shuffling and reshuffling a stack of index cards. "I did write the education department at her graduate school warning them that she's a troublemaker. I thought I owed them that. No one responded, but I suppose they won't until something happens."

Jane began drumming her fingers on her desk. "Why someone as smart as Annie wants to teach on an Indian reservation, I can't imagine."

"Admirable," thought Sarah to herself. She had a hard time swallowing the retort she'd have liked to make. Instead, she asked, "Annie's from Gallup, isn't she?"

Jane nodded.

"Didn't she come here with a high-school friend who was a Native American?"

Again, Jane nodded. "Yes, Doris Begay. They roomed together all four years. I don't know why Annie didn't try to broaden her horizons."

Just like the name of the judge in the book, thought Sarah. Coincidence, or were the odds of Jane's having written *Academic Awards* increasing?

"Doris," continued Jane, "doesn't sound Indian. I bet I'm as much Indian as she is. My mother once told me that she suspected *her* great grandfather was Cherokee, but no one in the family would admit it. Mother grew up in Lawton, Oklahoma, you know. Even though it's no shame to be part Cherokee—half the people from Oklahoma are. Annie thought Doris was wonderful. But I don't capitalize on my Indianness the way Doris did. Sometimes I think Annie herself is a wannabe Indian."

"Oops," thought Sarah, another echo. Aloud, she said, "I saw Doris and Annie together quite a bit. You probably know Doris majored in music. She was quite an accomplished flutist."

Sarah could see that Jane was losing interest in the conversation when it veered away from her. Unable to squelch her disapproval, Sarah needled Jane. "Doris has many Indian features, with her lovely dark complexion and shiny black hair. I would never have known that you're part Indian," said Sarah, looking at Jane's mousy blond hair and pale face, marred by blotches and wrinkles. "Doris must be at least half Indian and you're, what, one-eighth?"

Jane shifted in her chair. "Oh, so you're taking her side, are you?"

Sarah was about to protest, but Jane was off again.

"Not many college students have the potential Annie has. She's wasting it. She's bright. She can think, she can write. If she wanted, I could have gotten her into Stanford or UCLA. There was nothing I wasn't prepared to do to help her get ahead. For years, she conned me, always acting as if she were grateful for my time. Without my help, she'd never have gotten a paper accepted by the APA national convention."

Sarah remembered the fuss that had arisen when Annie called foul after Jane submitted the girl's senior project to an annual psychology conference.

"I gave that child a once-in-a-lifetime opportunity that no other undergraduate has ever had…"

"Aren't many academic conferences beginning to showcase work by undergraduate students these days? I know Erica has co-authored papers with her students and shared the podium with them at conferences."

"Erica *Ebenezer*?" Jane pronounced Erica's last name as if she needed to be sure which of many Ericas Sarah was talking about. "Let's get back on track," snarled Jane. "Let me tell you the whole story of my dealings with Annie Trostle."

Inwardly, Sarah groaned. Outwardly, she fought to maintain an interested expression.

"Annie's senior project was about the over-diagnosis of attention deficit disorder in young children. You know what A.D.D. is, don't you?"

Sarah nodded. Was it possible that Jane saw no connection between Annie's topic and her desire to become an elementary teacher?

As if she had never been over this ground with Sarah before, Jane went on. "Annie's senior seminar paper was superlative. I planned to talk with her about it during exam week in December, but she'd unaccountably left early.

"So I submitted her damn paper for her. And it got accepted. Was she pleased? No! She balked, she complained. For no good reason!

"With Annie I'd let down my guard. I usually keep my distance from students. But we became friendly—at her instigation, I might add. She would come into my office to talk over what she was reading. I was totally shocked when she objected to my having submitted her paper for her. After all, I was doing her a big favor."

Sarah felt slightly guilty to be encouraging Jane. "It's a treat to have a student like that, isn't it?"

"It wasn't a treat to have a student like Annie! She betrayed me!"

Jane continued, "She shows no appreciation for all I've done for her." Sarah noticed Jane's lapse into the present tense. Obviously, what had happened months earlier was ever-present in Jane's mind.

Jane dropped her stack of index cards and got abruptly to her feet. So softly that Sarah had to strain to hear her words, Jane snarled. "I could strangle that girl." Then, ignoring Sarah completely, she turned around to the bulletin board behind her and started yanking out thumbtacks. A hodgepodge of overlapping notes, cartoons, postcards, notices, and even the prominently displayed sign equating good minds and messy desks drifted to the floor.

Jane's frenetic activity amazed Sarah. Jane, oblivious that anyone was in the room with her, bent her head in the direction of the mess, and began to stamp her feet and whimper. She sounded more animal than human.

Sarah rose quickly, walked toward Jane, and firmly placed a hand on her shoulder. Jane responded by wiggling and shuddering to avoid Sarah's grasp. She crumpled to the floor.

Just as Sarah was thinking that she ought to call for help, Jane sat up

She looked bewildered for a moment, then, quite calmly and with no sign of distress, said, "I must have slipped."

"You did. I was worried."

"Oh, you needn't worry. I have a mild case of narcolepsy. Every once in a while, I black out. My last episode was so long ago I thought I'd outgrown it. Though they say you never do. But that's not what you came to see me about, is it?" Jane dusted herself off and went back to her chair as if nothing had happened. "Give me a minute to get back into the real world. What were we talking about?"

Sarah doubted that Jane spent much time in the *real* world. "We were discussing Annie Trostle and her objecting after you submitted her paper. When did you say you sent it in to the psychology conference?"

If Jane registered the question, she ignored it.

Shaking her head slowly back and forth, Jane put her elbows on her desk and rested her chin on her knuckles. "Annie had the gall to call me on the carpet for sending her stuff off. Why, I could have introduced her to important people, and launched her career. You'd have thought I committed a major crime by signing her name." Jane's voice rose indignantly. "She wasn't here; I had to sign for her. She'd already left campus. She went home to Momma and Poppa and that scruffy, pimply kid she was engaged to."

"Annie must have been shocked," said Sarah, "when she got the notice that her paper had been accepted and that she'd be expected to deliver it in person."

"Anyone in their right mind would have been overjoyed."

"That's all water under the bridge now, isn't it?" asked Sarah. Jane's confrontation with Annie's parents at graduation was grist for the gossip mill. Sarah had heard five or six different accounts of what had happened on graduation day.

Jane exploded. "No! Our esteemed president still faults me—for being unprofessional or some such nonsense. When I finally found Annie, her *husband*, and her parents, they were taking pictures of Annie in her cap and gown, holding up her diploma. I tried to talk to the Trostles. They turned their backs on me. So I followed them, and of course I had to talk louder and louder when they began walking faster and faster."

This lady does have a certain sense of style, thought Sarah, as Jane's voice rose with indignation. "Finally, they looked me right in the face and said I was lucky their daughter had decided not to sue *me* for forging her name!"

Sarah felt more saddened than irritated at Jane Snow's inability to see herself. No doubt she would become the brunt of jokes for years after she left Southwestern and Cottonwood.

Sarah's interest in the interview had waned. She had no appetite for collecting Jane stories—even for the task force. But she couldn't leave without questioning Jane directly about *Academic Awards*.

"I see," said Sarah, staring at the cards that Jane was shuffling, "that you…"

"I always take notes on index cards. I love reorganizing my ideas," said Jane, interrupting and becoming calm with the change of topic. "I like to spread everything out in front of me."

"Why do you use different colored cards?"

"Oh, to make it easier to sort out my ideas. I'm very sensitive to colors."

"Do you write often?" asked Sarah, wanting to be able to report that she'd left no question unasked.

"I'm always writing. Sometimes I work at home, at other times here on campus."

"What are you working on now?"

"I'm thinking of writing a beginning psych text. Most introductory textbooks are rather awful."

That was one insight Sarah could agree with. "The same thing is true in music, too. Have you ever written anything outside your field?"

Jane looked up, surprised. Sarah took advantage of the momentary silence to continue, "I wondered if you could be the person who's written the book featuring Southwestern. That's what I came to talk about."

"Hah, that book sure has this place in a twit. My hat's off to the author, but I wouldn't waste *my* time writing a mystery novel."

☺

Lloyd Reasoner had not even considered interviewing Richard Frankel for his book on the cultural significance of leisure activities from Plato to Pinker. Lloyd considered Frankel a very dark horse indeed. However, he realized that his research would give him a good excuse to question Richard.

When Lloyd called early Wednesday morning, Richard had been delighted to be sought out, but disappointed that Lloyd couldn't join him for lunch. As a second choice, he invited Lloyd to his house for sherry and a discussion of mystery books that afternoon between 3:00 and 4:00.

"I understand that you've been a mystery fan for a long time?" Lloyd asked as Richard ushered him into his study.

"My father first introduced me to Sherlock Holmes way back when I was a young whippersnapper. And I devoured Wilkie Collins when I was in high school."

Richard Frankel was a large man, with unruly gray hair and bushy eyebrows. Except for the neatly displayed guns in a glass-fronted cabinet behind his desk, the room was as unkempt as he was. He had to remove a stack of magazines and old newspapers from a wooden rocking chair to offer Lloyd a seat. "I wasn't expecting you quite so soon. I'm just cleaning this Ruger. Let me reassemble it. Then we can talk. There, that does it."

Stuffing a dirty chamois cloth into the pocket of his trousers,

Richard shoved aside an overflowing ashtray. He then opened the right-hand drawer of his desk and casually tossed the gun inside. He sat down and faced Lloyd.

"If I understood you," said Richard, "You've come to learn more about my favorite subject."

"That's right. For the second edition of my book on leisure activity as a philosophical pursuit. It's due out early next year."

"Congratulations."

"Thank you. I've always thought that how people spend their so-called free time is a barometer of their values. Libraries circulate mysteries faster than any other type of book."

"I didn't know that, but I'm not surprised. Ever since Collins' *The Woman in White* and *The Moonstone* were published in the 1860s, mysteries have been enormously popular."

"Since I don't read that kind of literature myself, I'd like to hear your explanation of their appeal."

Lloyd pulled out a notepad and took notes as Richard began talking. When he finally finished, Lloyd, pretending idle curiosity, asked, "Have you ever tried your hand at writing a mystery?"

"No, I've imagined numerous plots and devious villains, but I've been too busy with scholarly writing to delve into fiction."

From what he'd heard of Richard's academic writing—mostly jacket blurbs for books put out by little-known publishing houses and reviews in obscure journals—Lloyd doubted whether Richard's writing could be called scholarly.

"I'm glad you're becoming interested in an overlooked genre. You should become acquainted with Tey if you don't know her works. She and Dorothy Sayers are two or three cuts above better-known authors such as Agatha Christie and Rex Stout. Tey can hold her own as a historiographer, too. She's especially good at depicting the world of work of her characters—something Dick Francis also does superbly. Sayers introduces the kind of analysis of character that will lead to the plethora of psychological portraits made so popular by Ruth Rendall, P.D. James, and Elizabeth George."

Lloyd, recognizing no names but Christie's and Stout's, looked blank.

Richard moved to his desk, heaped high with books. Barely visible on the table behind him were two computers, one of them turned on. (The screen saver must have been custom made: brightly colored covers of mystery classics sporting wings angled down the screen from top left to bottom right.) Pawing through the books, Richard picked up one by Charles Todd.

"Todd is relatively new. Interestingly, Charles Todd is not just a pseudonym used by one author, but by two people working together."

Hearing the word "pseudonym," Lloyd started paying closer attention to Richard's long monologue, but he soon decided it was just another detail, a coincidence he could ignore.

"Would you believe it, they're a mother and son? I can't imagine doing anything with my mother, much less collaborating on something as time intensive as writing a whole series of books. I haven't yet been successful in finding out more about them, but I'm on their track..."

Richard's meandering talk made it hard for Lloyd to keep alert. Unless he could redirect the conversation, Richard was certainly gearing up for a lecture. Lloyd feared a dissertation on the development of the modern mystery. He began to begrudge the time he'd scheduled for the drink and the chat.

"Excuse me, Richard," he interrupted. "These names don't mean a lot to me. I'd like to know whether you think mysteries appeal to the same people who bowl, follow sports, keep up with the latest TV sitcoms and talk shows, or whether, as I suspect, they appeal to a different audience."

Richard Frankel frowned, obviously unhappy to relinquish his control of the conversation. He resignedly pushed his chair back, came around to the front of his desk and lowered himself slowly into a dark red leather recliner while Lloyd sipped his sherry. It was very dry and very good. Using a skill he'd perfected during student presentations, he appeared to be paying attention.

"You may not know much about mysteries, but at least you think they're worthy of study," said Richard.

Lloyd remembered how indignant Richard had been that a course he'd taught three years in a row was denied permanent status in the curriculum despite its popularity. He'd fulminated at two different faculty meetings about the stupidity and cupidity of the curriculum committee's having endorsed "Politics, Business, and Pornography" while at the same time turning down his "History of the Mystery."

After almost two hours in Richard's smoke-filled study, and two too many glasses of sherry, Lloyd yearned to escape. He needed to clear his head of cigar fumes, his host's fury *and* his encyclopedic knowledge of mysteries.

After the long drinks' journey into evening, however, Lloyd was sure that Richard Frankel could be counted out. He was not known for his understanding of campus politics, and his grudge against President Asher was no greater than his grudge against the curriculum committee. If anything, his greatest grudge was directed at students who could watch mindless violence at 8 P.M. on television but found it tedious to follow a clever, convoluted plot in a book. Richard had little sense of humor and no sense of irony. This afternoon had convinced Lloyd that he saw other people only when they crossed him.

Lloyd tried to draw the visit to a conclusion by telling Richard that he concentrated on histories and autobiographies for his own leisure reading. He commented on how much he had enjoyed *Academic Awards,* attributing his enjoyment to its many humorous passages and ironic view of campus life. Realizing that he'd just let Richard know he'd read the manuscript, he wished he could have withdrawn his words. But then, also realizing that Richard paid sparse attention to topics not revolving around him, he doubted that his admission had even registered with his host.

At 5:45 Lloyd was trying to get out the door gracefully. "I can tell by the smells from the kitchen," he said, "that your dinner is almost ready. My evening constitutional will get me home just in time for mine." But a timely departure was not to be. Richard reached out to put a hand on Lloyd's arm and steered him back into the den.

Forty minutes later, Lloyd edged toward the door and held aloft the bundle of papers Richard had given him. "Thank you so much for talking with me and giving me these copies of your latest reviews." Lloyd trusted that Richard missed the irony behind his thanks.

*Jeff meets with Charlie; Ruby summons Jim to the president's office; Jim calls in at the newspaper office.*

Since Jeff Miles' Wednesday drive had been impeded by two local but heavy rainstorms on his way south, he decided to call it a day in Willcox. That left less than a hundred miles to drive the next morning. He could easily get to the Menendez Travel headquarters by 8:30 when Rebecca had promised to meet him and give him directions to Charlie's hideaway.

True to her word, she had a hand-drawn map ready as well as a note for Charlie. She warned him that there would be no numbers identifying the shacks and trailers scattered on the dusty dirt roads leading to Charlie's. After taking one wrong fork, he found himself at Charlie's trailer shortly after 10:00. There was no answer to his knock, but he figured Charlie had to be around. His truck was parked between two saguaro cactuses (or, should that be *cacti*, Jeff wondered before chiding himself for his habit of chasing word trails in the midst of other pursuits). Jeff walked around the truck. He found Charlie sitting at a faded grey picnic table, his hands resting immobile over the keys of a laptop computer. It took Charlie a full minute to realize he wasn't alone. He jumped up. "Hey, man, you scared me. What the hell are you doing down this way? And how did you find me?"

Jeff, not wanting to reveal his real reason for contacting Charlie, ignored Charlie's first question and in answer to the second, handed his friend Rebecca's map and note. Charlie glanced at the map, and, grinning, showed Jeff what Rebecca had written in block capitals: "This guy says you *will* want to see him. I hope so. He looks and sounds legit."

Charlie stood up slowly, flexed his fingers, arched his back, and then, taking a giant step towards Jeff, grabbed him by the shoulders and gave him a bear hug. "You're a sight for sore eyes. 'Specially mine. I've been staring at the same blank screen for almost an hour. Until you came along I had no excuse for taking a break. I can sure use one. I can even start paying you back for all the beers you bought me when you were pulling in the big money and I was a poor student."

One beer later—after all it was morning—and a walk along the arroyo where Charlie's trailer was perched, Charlie accepted Jeff's invitation to go into Bisbee for lunch. Getting away from Charlie's place was much easier than getting to it. All Jeff had to do was follow Charlie's truck. He didn't have to slow down each time he peered at Rebecca's map, looking for the landmarks she'd drawn: a house with boarded up windows, and a dip in the road where an old, once yellow camper top was turned upside down off to the right.

While waiting for their meals to be served, the two young men recalled their days playing soccer. Charlie told Jeff that shepherding Elderhostelers through Apache and Tarahumara country was a good job for him. He liked the drivers and guides he worked with. Most of his charges were experienced travelers who seldom complained and were interested in what they were seeing.

Just as Jeff was wondering how to find out what he'd come to find out, Charlie made it easy for him. He started talking about his current projects. "Getting one whole week off out of three more than makes up for working weekends. Man, I can't believe what an advantage that is. There's a chance I'll be able to finish my book by the end of the year."

"You willing to divulge what your book is about?"

"I guess so—to you. But normally I'm suspicious about people who talk about what they're *going* to do."

"Me too," said Jeff.

Charlie, suddenly serious, paused. "I don't know whether I told you, but I spent one summer with an uncle who'd moved to Gallup. I was 16; he was ten years older. He got me a job in the garage where he worked. He'd loved working on cars and trucks when he was a kid. He lived in the hills near Toadlena, halfway between Shiprock and Gallup. There wasn't anything he didn't know about the inside of a car. And there wasn't any car he couldn't fix. He was the star mechanic of the Chuska Mountains. When he wasn't working on cars and trucks people brought to him, he'd go all over the reservation in New Mexico and Arizona, a kind of itinerant car doctor. Anyway, the lure of a regular salary, regular hours, and the big town took him away from home. He was getting paid—and he was getting laid—but he wasn't happy. He wanted to go back home, but he thought he couldn't. When I decided to go to college, he told me I was crazy. 'You'll just get uppity,' he said, 'and you won't like it there. But you'll decide you've gotta live in that world anyway.' I've been haunted by those words ever since.

"At Southwestern, I found I wasn't alone in trying to belong in two worlds—and being desperately afraid I'd discover it was impossible. I can't tell you how many papers I wrote about the topic. My book takes off from where those papers began. I don't want to just whine, or tell heartrending stories, I want to illustrate and explain *why* it's so difficult to live simultaneously in two different worlds."

"Wasn't one of your papers published when you were still at Southwestern?"

"Yes. That was my lucky break. One of the editors of the UNM Press, a Miss Deirdre Duncan, read my article, and liked it—enough to track me down here. We've talked and written several times and she's still interested."

"That's wonderful, Charlie. Sounds as if publication is guaranteed."

"I won't count on getting in print until I've sent in my manuscript and Miss Duncan says it's a go."

Now seemed like a good time for Jeff to ask the question that brought him to Bisbee. "Didn't you tell me last spring that you'd written a short story on the same subject?"

"Just as an assignment for Professor Leslie's creative writing class."

"If I remember right, Matt Leslie didn't think of it as *just* an assignment. You told me he wanted you to submit the story to some regional magazines? Did you?"

"No. It seemed awfully unfinished and I didn't have time or energy to rewrite it. I did send it in to the school's literary mag. That was in the fall. The following winter term, I took a Southwest American Literature class and really admired the novelists we were reading." Charlie smiled ruefully. "For a short time, I had grandiose dreams of becoming the next Anaya or Silko. As much as I liked *their* books, I realized writing fiction was not for me. I like to weigh and probe and explain too much. And nothing kills fiction faster than analysis."

Jeff sighed, relinquishing his hopes of discovering the author of *Academic Awards* this morning. Inwardly, he realized he was as much disappointed for his own sake as for Charlie's. How he would have liked to announce that their missing author was not a faculty member but a former student. Except for Toni and Sarah, the other task force members hadn't considered Charlie a serious possibility.

"What *are* you writing?"

"Something that started as a feature article I thought I'd send in for the *Albuquerque Journal*'s Sunday magazine. Over the summer I must have interviewed fifty family members and friends. My little article has mushroomed into a whole book.

"What's most fun of all," he continued, with only a hint of a smile, "is that I'm breaking a rule I used to think was unbreakable. Despite what my English profs said about avoiding the first person pronoun, I've always enjoyed reading stuff by writers who do get in my face. My book is sprinkled with an 'I' on every other page. I'm not a central voice but I'm there all the time. I need the 'I.' I'm writing as an insider looking at what so many Indians have to do to maintain our traditions when we leave the reservation."

Charlie leaned forward, his eyes lighting up. "Even if we think we've left for good, few of us do. This job has been great for me, personally, but also because it's made me see that my subject is much broader than I knew."

"How?"

"My fellow drivers are all Mexican-Indians. They've become U.S. citizens—with dual licenses and U.S. addresses. They cross the border once or twice a month, going *south* with part of their earnings. And part of their hearts. That's not so different from what we Navajos do. We constantly switch between our two lives."

"That *is* an interesting angle for your topic. It's one I haven't seen before. I'll look forward to reading your book. I'll even buy a copy. I see why you're so excited. You've got a super topic, and it's certainly timely. Are you working on anything else?"

"Yeah. I've just finished a series on Cochise for the Douglas grade schools. They're being self-published in pamphlet form."

"You don't by any chance dabble in mysteries in your spare time?" asked Jeff, "I saw the collection of Hillermans in your trailer."

"Not mine. They came with the place. In fact, most of them are autographed. The guy I rented the trailer from has gone off to the Peace Corps for two years. He'd just retired from teaching junior high history. The Hillermans are his pride and joy, but he's got a whole stash of paperback mysteries in the bedroom. I don't even read 'em."

"You ever try your hand at writing a mystery?" Jeff's high hopes were gone, but he thought he ought to be thorough now that he was here.

"Me? No way."

"You sure?"

Charlie sounded a little miffed. "What is this, an interrogation?"

Jeff peered at his friend, disappointedly convinced that Charlie wasn't being coy or evasive. Then he laughed.

"I guess it *is* an interrogation. I've been hoping your answers to my questions about mysteries would have led to a confession…"

"On my part? Of what?"

"Oh, that you *had* written a mystery…Wait, let me finish. One that took place on a marginally fictionalized version of Southwestern College."

"Would I have been guilty of slander or libel if I had?"

"No," laughed Jeff. "There are a few parallels between the fictional president and Walt Asher, but nothing libelous. For a moment, I was afraid I'd been cast as the murderer. But that's because my name, Jeff, *sounds* like the name of the bloke who done it. But his name is fancier. It's spelled with a "g" and an "e" and an "o" and he's always called Geoffrey—never Geoff. So I'm in the clear.

"So are you, and I wish you weren't. Despite what I told your boss Rebecca, I'm not on any recruiting mission. Seeing you has made the trip worthwhile."

"Well thanks, buddy. But I can't believe Southwestern gave you time off midweek this early in the term."

"*If* you'd confessed to having written a book called *Academic Awards*, you'd have landed a big fat endowment for the college, to say nothing of fifty thousand dollars for yourself. And I'd have been the lucky guy who found you in your hideaway."

"That I would have liked—for both of us. But as I said, I didn't enjoy my one foray into fiction. Tell me more about this *mysterious* mystery which sent you on a wild goose chase."

Jeff explained that he and five others had been chosen to play detective, charged with finding out who had posed as Edith Tansley Coyle.

Charlie barraged Jeff with questions about the book and the intriguing case of the missing writer. "Sounds like an interesting little mystery itself."

"It is."

Charlie leaned his head back until it was touching the cracked leather of the high booth. "That's priceless. Six characters in search of an author?"

Jeff looked blank.

"I knew my lit major was good for something. I've stumped you.

Ever heard of Pirandello?"

Jeff shook his head.

"His most famous play is called *Six Characters in Search of an Author.*"

"Really? Great title. I must admit, half the fun of being on the president's task force is getting to know the other five characters he's appointed to find the author."

"Oh, who else besides you?"

"Toni Hexton, for one."

"She's hardly a character."

"No, Hexton's a straight shooter. But Dr. Ebenezer *is* quite a character. She's brusque. And she's funny. She says whatever she's thinking and doesn't kowtow to anyone. Sarah Jennings..."

"The chairman of Fine Arts?"

"Yeah. I thought she'd be intimidating, but she isn't. Neither is Steve Scott, from the library. He's kinda formal, more professorial than anyone else actually. The guy I can't figure out is Lloyd Reasoner."

"I took an ethics class from him. Interesting man. He believes in the Socratic method. He never asked *us* questions. He made us ask *him* questions. Believe me, there were some long, awkward silences at first while he waited us out."

Jeff leaned forward. "That's it! That's what bothers me about Reasoner. He always seems to be waiting for something, something he refuses to give us any hints about."

"This search of yours must be pretty urgent if you were allowed to drive all the way down here."

"It is. There's a deadline. If we can't produce our author soon the awards will go to the runner-up and someone else's school. I think Walt Asher has already spent that five-hundred grand several times over."

"Who else am I competing with?"

"Sorry, I can't tell you that. We've agreed to keep our suspects to ourselves on the principle that everyone's innocent until..."

Charlie interrupted. "Sorry I asked. Unfair question. I hope you find your writer quickly and that Southwestern gets its windfall. I'm sorry it wasn't me. But I guess I should thank you for thinking I might have done the dastardly deed."

Jeff refused an after-lunch beer. He'd decided to start for home this afternoon. Taking the freeways would be longer, but much faster. If he only stopped for gas, he could get to Cottonwood by 10:00 or 11:00 at the latest.

Charlie forgave him for barging in, thanked Jeff for the lunch, and they agreed to meet the next time Charlie drove north.

During Jeff's long drive back to Cottonwood, he thought about Charlie Roanhorse. He was more driven than he ever was as a student. Typical, thought Jeff. He'd also become more serious after getting his first full-time job at UNM.

Thinking about his life before Southwestern led Jeff to thinking about how his—and Irene's—lives had changed since they'd left Albuquerque. Irene had always said she wanted three children, and wanted them spaced close together. Maybe that was a mistake. Since the birth of Tish, Irene seemed drained and despondent a good deal of the time.

Driving along mile after mile of gently rolling, straw-colored hills unexpectedly interrupted by roadside signs warning of steep grades and strong winds struck Jeff as symbolic. Did something cataclysmic account for the distance gradually developing between him and Irene? He couldn't think of anything specific.

Better to think about who might have written *Academic Awards*. He'd pinned his hopes on Charlie. Well, maybe someone else at tomorrow's task force meeting would have been more successful than he'd been.

Jeff mentally reviewed the task force's suspects. From several publicity interviews with Taylor Anderson, Jeff was ready to rule him out. He was too entrenched in his world of art. Richard Frankel was even easier to dismiss. Jeff had the PR files with copies of his reviews and his one published article. After Monday's meeting, he'd read them all. Anyone who wrote either long, stilted sentences or short, grade-schoolish ones could not have written *Academic Awards*. Despite the title of his article, "Portraits of Famous Detectives," Frankel painted no verbal portraits. Instead, he got mired in a series of plot summaries. Could Jeff have been wrong about Jonathan Gill? He did have more energy than anyone he'd ever encountered. And what about Dr. Snow? If she had once been more competent than she was now, then she might well be their writer.

As Jeff approached Albuquerque, he became edgy. He didn't like being passed by pickups and semis weaving north through the construction on I-25. Once past the city, Jeff relaxed, enjoying a full moon and his supply of Carlos Nakai and Beatles tapes.

@

Thursday had not been a good day for Jim Scoop. It had begun with a frantic call from Ruby shortly after eight. She'd found a mess on Asher's desk and several missing items in her office. Most disturbing of all, Walt's treasured tennis trophy was also missing. When she didn't see it in its usual place of honor on the bookshelf behind his desk, she'd phoned Jim.

Ruby's message sent Jim dumping his second cup of coffee and hurrying to the presidential suite.

As soon as he arrived, Ruby led Jim past the reception area where her desk sat and into Walt's office. She first pointed to an overturned mug in the middle of a rectangular green blotter, and then to letters scattered higgledy-piggledy over the blotter and the bare desktop surrounding it. "I put those letters in a neat pile last evening," she explained, "for the president to sign when he comes in this morning."

Jim reached out to touch the brown stains that had seeped through many of the letters, leaving them and the blotter soggy and stained. "Tea, not coffee" he said, pulling a bag out of the mug. "Dry and cold. Whoever was in here, was here last night."

Jim handed Ruby the mug.

"How did anyone get in here?" she asked. "I checked around and locked up, as I always do," she said.

"Did you or Walt leave first yesterday afternoon?" asked Jim.

"He did. He had a meeting with the vice-presidents downstairs at four-thirty and said he'd go right home afterwards."

"Do you know when he'll be coming in this morning?"

"Not until nine or nine-thirty. He goes to Rotary breakfasts downtown most Thursdays."

"Good. That will give us some time to assess the damages before Walt returns."

Walking over to the bookshelf behind the president's desk, Ruby gestured to the empty corner where the tennis trophy had been. "You've seen the damage in here. Most of the other stuff that's missing is mine, not Walt's. I can't imagine why anyone would want to take any of it. It's not worth stealing."

Jim followed Ruby into her outer office. "Look," she said, picking up a shallow basket and a Southwestern College beer stein from a narrow side table between two visitors' chairs. Both containers were empty.

"I keep hard candies in the basket, and a handful of pens in the stein."

"I don't suppose you suspect any visitors of absconding with *all* the candy or *all* the pens?"

"No," laughed Ruby. "Once in awhile I see someone take more than one piece of candy or borrow a pen—and forget to return it. But I look around when I leave at night and I'm sure I'd have noticed if all the candies and all the pens were gone."

"Before Walt gets here, Ruby, I'd like you to look around carefully one more time to see if anything else is missing or has been moved."

"Okay." Ruby began opening her desk drawers one by one. Only when she opened the last one did she pause. Frowning and gesturing to the space behind the box of tissues she kept in the lower left-hand drawer, she pointed to a jumble of hard candies and pens. "The thief must have grabbed what was on the table, and then just dumped it in here."

"That's one mystery solved," said Jim. "The thief is messier than he is greedy."

"But what a strange thing to do," sighed Ruby.

"Agreed," replied Jim. "Most ordinary thieves aren't given to tampering with things, though, and then leaving them as evidence. The more I see the more I'm puzzled."

As Ruby was replacing the supplies on the side table, she saw something shiny on the floor. Leaning over, she picked up a pen almost hidden in the crevice between rug and wall. "This isn't one of mine," she said. "Oh, it's Walt's."

She stood up, holding the pen in her palm for Jim's inspection. Taking it out of her hand, he noticed that it was a classic burgundy Parker fountain pen. He read its inscription: "To Walter, from Dad, on your 16th birthday. Write well."

Jim, giving the pen back to Ruby, headed towards the outer door.

"Thanks for coming, Jim. I'll return this and clean up the mess on Walt's desk. But I hate to have to tell him his tennis trophy's gone."

"I'm afraid we're both going to have to tell him that someone has gained entry to his office after hours. Before I go, though, I'd like to check the closet."

"This *used* to be a closet," said Ruby, pushing against a partially open door sitting at right angles to the door into the hallway. "Now it's our storeroom as well."

Jim glanced at the printer and copy machine on the countertop.

Scanning the reams of paper and other supplies on a high shelf, he saw a messy pile of rags.

Ruby, following Jim's gaze, exclaimed, "I didn't put those there!"

Jim felt the rags gingerly. "Wait a minute. There's something hard inside." He unwrapped several layers of oily rags. "Well, well, well. The trophy's not missing after all."

"But it's dented badly," said Ruby. "It looks like it's been hit with a hammer!"

Jim examined several deep dents. "I'll send B.B. over right away to take this to our lab. We won't get any fingerprints from it, though. The whole trophy has been thoroughly wiped off," said Jim, running a hand lightly over the statuette. "Have Walt call me when he gets in," added Jim, shrugging his shoulders apologetically. "I'm afraid I'm going to ask you both to double and triple check your offices before you leave each afternoon, and then check again when you come in the next morning."

☺

Later that evening, Jim made his way over to the Student Union. As he passed the gym, several of the students outside the building greeted him. He returned their greetings absent-mindedly. Try as he might, he couldn't quit fretting about who had been in the presidential suite. Most of the damage was petty, more irritating than ominous. But attacking Walt's prized trophy with a hammer struck Jim as a danger signal. Whoever had been in his and Ruby's offices must have been there after the night custodian had made his rounds, or at least part of the mess would have been picked up. The intruder must have a key to the building, as well as two more for the doors into the office suite. Jim grimaced thinking how often campus keys ended up in the hands of people who shouldn't have them.

Taking a slight detour by Center Hall, he noted that the entire building was dark, including the windows in Walt's office.

The area outside the Student Union was crowded. Jim approached the almost empty snack bar intending to get a cup of coffee. But hearing many loud, angry-sounding voices coming from the open door across the hall from the snack bar, he hesitated. Unused to night patrol, it took him a minute to register that not all the students were outside. He was jumpy. There was no reason to expect that anything was wrong. It was only the staff of the college's newspaper, *The Southwesterner*, rushing to get the paper ready to distribute by Friday noon. He heard a raised voice that he recognized. Toni Hexton was appealing for one question at a time. No wonder, he thought as he stood by the door. Ms. Hexton was being bombarded by questions and given no time to answer any of them.

"What's the book got to do with Southwestern?"

"Who wrote it?"

"Is there really a humongus prize?"

"Who got murdered?"

Thinking Toni might welcome an interruption, Jim entered the room and walked towards her. Surprised, she glanced up.

"I need to talk with you for a moment," he said. "Away from all this clamor."

Toni looked gratefully at Jim, before addressing the students. "Excuse us for a minute. It shouldn't take long."

The students stared speculatively at Jim and then, curiosity written on their faces, back to Toni. "It's not newspaper business." Jim wondered if the students were as aware as he was of the blush rising from her neck to her cheeks. When she added, "It's just personal," the blush deepened. Jim had a hard time suppressing a smile.

Toni motioned for him to follow her into the glassed-in editor's office. "Thanks for rescuing me. Don't worry, we can be seen but not heard. I'm facing a real dilemma. The task force charge is supposed to be secret, but I have to tell these students *something*."

"I can see you're in an awkward position. Can't you tell them what Asher told the faculty last week? All that information must be common knowledge by now."

"That's true." Toni perked up. "I *can* tell them about the NAMWA contest and the money for the author and the college. Although I expect they already know that. I guess there'd be nothing wrong with also telling them President Asher thinks one of their professors may have written *Academic Awards*." She paused and laughed, "Erica Ebenezer or me, for instance."

"I'm sure the students will enjoy hearing *that*."

"The students view the college's search for an unknown, anonymous author as something funny to write home about. The president, understandably, doesn't want off-campus publicity about our mystery until it's solved, but as an advisor to the student newspaper staff, I must treat them as budding, professional journalists. I can't stifle their desire to cover a great story.

"But unless they bring up the possibility that the search for Edith

Tansley Coyle could entail danger as well as humor, you don't have to spell out that possibility, do you?" asked Jim.

"No. I'll hope the students continue to take the whole thing as a joke."

"And I'll hope they turn out to be right!"

"Well, then," replied Toni, "don't let them suspect you have anything to do with the search. If they think the police are concerned, they'll hunt for a criminal angle."

"I'm trying my best to appear uninvolved," said Jim, laughing. "But I'm afraid your friend Erica caught me in the act."

Now it was Toni's turn to laugh. "She did, she did. She told me she ran into you outside Walt's office on Monday, making off with a copy of the manuscript."

"She let me know she wasn't happy about that. I couldn't really blame her. In her eyes, I had no right to read, much less make a copy of the manuscript. She hadn't realized the president asked me to do some detecting of my own."

"When she thought about it, she told me she understood why Walt wants you involved. An incognito author's motives *have to be* suspicious. Most of us would happily come out of hiding for fifty thousand dollars! By the way, did she apologize? I think Erica's embarrassed for blowing up at you."

"Your friend Erica doesn't strike me as someone who embarrasses easily. And yes, I did get a very gracious apology. In a voice mail message. Back to your immediate problem. I think your students will stop hounding you if you let them guess which of their professors might not want to come forward to claim the prize, and why."

"Of course, that's what Walt, *and* you, *and* I, *and* my fellow task force members want to know also. But I do hate all this secrecy."

Jim frowned. "I know. But it's necessary. You don't have to mention that Walt has created a task force to search for the missing author. Nor that I'm increasing the number of security staff on duty at any one time until the author is found."

"So that's why you've assigned yourself night patrol duty?" asked Toni.

"Yes, that's why I'm here now, in uniform."

As Jim spoke, Toni thought what a nice smile he had. It involved his eyes as well as his mouth and undercut the formality of his appearance. She must remember to tell Erica that Jim Scoop was *not* a stuffed shirt.

"I'll go back and drown the students with so many details about the contest that they'll leave me alone," said Toni.

"You might assign someone to write the story. Who knows, an article in the paper might bring the author out of the woodwork." Jim turned and reached for the door. "I think someone wants to talk to you."

"Oh, that's our sports editor. He wasn't one of the kids pumping me for information."

Jim recognized the young man standing outside the door. "I know Eddy Spencer. I introduced myself to him at a basketball game last year. I told him how much I liked his articles. He does much more than list how many points each player scores or how many shots they block. Young Spencer has an engaging style. He does what even many professionals don't manage to do—make me feel as if I'm seeing a game for myself."

Toni tucked away another praiseworthy bit of information about Jim Scoop to pass on to Erica. Erica should applaud him for paying the kind of attention to students that Jim's comments revealed instead of calling him "Officer Snoopy."

"Eddy's a great kid—and a good writer. He deserves the scholarship he just learned about at this afternoon's honors convocation."

"Oh?" Jim looked quizzical.

"He's been selected as this year's most promising journalism student. That means a nice addition to his regular scholarship. I suspect he wants to thank me. He told me after the convocation that with the extra money, he'll be able to quit his Sunday job." Toni opened the door for them both. "And I want to thank you, Jim. You've been a great help. I was feeling uncomfortably cornered. I should have been pleased. For once, I didn't need to harangue the reporters about not asking enough follow-up questions to produce a good news story."

"I'll come back to see whether you get away unscathed after I've checked the rest of the building."

He and Toni walked out of the editor's cubicle together. "Ms. Hexton," blurted Eddy, holding up a sheath of notes and addressing Toni the minute she emerged, "I don't think I should write this story even though Betty assigned it to me a few days ago. I got the journalism award so I can't write an unbiased article. Betty told me to ask Neal O'Donald to take a picture of all the honors recipients. She didn't know I'd be getting the award he thought *he* had a good chance of getting."

"No, you can't assign Neal to take the photo," Toni sympathized. "Especially after Neal ran out of the convocation. By the way, did you understand what he was saying?"

"Yeah, he yelled that *he* should have gotten the journalism scholarship. I see why he expected it. His photographs have received honorable mentions in national competitions. No wonder he was miffed," said Eddy diffidently.

"Eddy," said Toni. "Don't be so modest. You're the best sports writer we've had in years." She looked over at Jim for confirmation. He smiled broadly and nodded. "Officer Scoop tells me he *always* reads the stories under your byline."

Toni said she'd ask Betty to reassign the story before addressing the newspaper staff and regaling them with minute, niggling details about NAMWA's contest. While the students' attention was focused on Toni, Jim left unnoticed.

When he returned half an hour later, a few of the students were chatting, but most were busily writing.

"Hi, Mr. Scoop," said Betty Frost, beaming at Jim.

"I see you're working for the newspaper again this year. As editor-in-chief no less."

"Yes sir, and *this* year I get paid."

"Congratulations. But I'm sorry you don't have time to work for us again. We miss you in the security office. I'm sure you'll do as good a job for the paper as you did for us."

"Thanks for that compliment, Mr. Scoop. The newspaper and my course load have kept me too busy to even stop by just to say hello."

Toni walked across the room and joined them. "With Betty on board this year, I expect things to run very smoothly."

"Wow! Another compliment! This is my day. Professor Hexton, I need your help. Take a look at this article."

"You two look as if you have plenty to do," said Jim, as he surveyed the room full of students busily working this late at night. They didn't, he thought, deserve to be stereotyped as spoiled and undisciplined. Of course, part of the hard work he was seeing must be attributed to the hard work of their advisor. "I'll just wander around a bit," said Jim to Toni, "I'd like to congratulate Eddy."

As Toni started reading the copy Betty handed her, Jim walked to where Eddy was hunched over several sheets of paper. To Jim's eyes, there were more crossed-out words and marginal insertions than original text. Eddy suddenly sat up, flexed his fingers, scrunched up the top sheet of paper and aimed it at a wastebasket in a far corner of the room. "Not easily satisfied, I see," said Jim, startling the young man, who'd been unaware of Jim's presence.

Without waiting for a reply, Jim asked, "When do we play Adams State, Fort Lewis, and St. Esteban? And what do you think our chances are of winning any of those games?"

Eddy turned completely around and, facing Jim, answered each of his questions. "We have a better than average team this year, with a new transfer quarterback. He's smart, and he can run and he can pass. The first game is against Adams State here on Friday; I don't think we have *any* chance against them. Saturday we play Fort Lewis in Durango. Then next Friday afternoon we play St. Esteban here. They're the only team we have a chance of beating. I wish we played them first. Of course, for Fort Lewis and Adams State, these games are just preseason scrimmages, while for us it's the beginning of our independent season."

"Thanks for the predictions. I didn't know we had a new quarter-back. I'll look forward to seeing him in action. I figured that we'd take St. Esteban, and lose the other two games, but with a good quarter-back, who knows?"

Jim decided this wasn't the time to congratulate Eddy. Having heard Toni and Eddy talking about the disgruntled photographer, Jim didn't want to provoke another outburst. He didn't want Neal, whom he wouldn't recognize, to overhear him praising Eddy. Jim moved quietly around the working students, inching his way to the front of the room.

Somewhere behind him and out of sight, Jim heard Toni saying to Betty, "If you run this, you had better edit it to about half its length or less. It's way too wordy as it is. It might be better to return it to the writer for major editing and run it next week."

Jim also heard Betty's reply and thought how much she'd matured into a confident young woman since the day when he'd first seen her. Three years earlier, as a freshman, she had been shy and almost tongue-tied. She would never have been relaxed enough then to give the pert reply to an adult she now gave to Toni Hexton. "That's what I hoped you'd say. Now I can share the blame with you when the writer gets upset with me."

As Betty turned back to her work, Toni and Jim found themselves facing each other. "I'll buy you a cup of coffee across the hall if you have time. I want to thank you again for running interference," said Toni.

"I'll be delighted to join you for coffee," replied Jim.

*Jim goes to Albuquerque; Toni corners Jonathan Gill; the task force reconvenes; Jeff gets free advice and dinner too.*

Jim finished his rounds quickly after visiting the newspaper office and having coffee with Toni Thursday night. He'd wanted to get some sleep before driving to Albuquerque to meet Florencio for dinner. He was back in his office by 9:00 on Friday morning. Lily, his secretary, reported that the officers on night duty had signed in, leaving no messages. He attacked the mail that had piled up during the past few days. Most were general mailings —memos on the proper ways to purchase airline tickets and request reimbursement for travel expenses, announcements, and an updated telephone directory for college employees, and trashable trivia. The only important piece of mail was from the financial office approving his revised budget. Two hours later his desk was empty. He could leave for Albuquerque with a clear conscience.

He stopped to tell Lily that he'd grab a bite to eat before driving to Albuquerque to pick up Johnny. "I'll be back Monday morning."

Jim walked across campus to the rock garden outside the snack bar. As he threaded his way through the crowded tables, he was pleased to see how many were occupied by a mix of faculty, staff, and students. He'd always thought the camaraderie signaled by that mixture was Southwestern's greatest strength—regardless of what his snobbish, urban sister thought. It still rankled that Sue had scoffed at his invitation to include Southwestern on the college tour she and her daughter made the summer before his niece's senior year in high school. Sue couldn't believe he expected *her* daughter to consider a school noted for nothing more than "sheep and serenity."

Jim found Billy Bob and Ben inside. They were both chowing down on the day's special—fried chicken smothered with green chili. Jim went to the counter and, with only a small tinge of regret, avoided temptation. He ordered a Caesar salad.

He joined his officers. He arched an eyebrow at the sight of a huge slice of apple pie and two glazed donuts sitting in the middle of the table. "B.B.," he asked, "don't you ever get tired of donuts?"

"Jim, Jim, Jim, when Ben puts ice cream on that pie, it will be more fattening than a half a dozen donuts. Do you see the size of that slice of pie? Do you realize what a charmer Ben's become? He's convinced these motherly ladies that he is continually starving. He gets the biggest and choicest portions of whatever he orders."

"Okay, eat your donuts in peace," shrugged Jim. "Now let's get serious. Billy Bob, you are in charge until tomorrow night. Be sure that Ben, Nick, and the three part-timers know where you are at all times. Their schedules are posted outside my door. I should return with Johnny late tomorrow afternoon. I'll give you a call when I get home."

Ben pushed his chair back. Looking slightly abashed, he asked, "May I be excused, sirs? I need to get some ice cream for my pie."

"Go ahead," said Billy Bob, as he watched the young man scurry away. "Jim, kidding aside, I didn't think that young man would last a year when you hired him five years ago! But you were right; he's turned into a good cop."

"I agree, and I'm glad to hear you eat your words—as well as your donuts."

@

Jim drove west on the local road that would bring him to US 550, which he still thought of by its former designation—State Road 44. Barely aware of the familiar scenery, he reviewed the mystery novel in his head. It was an odd novel. It described a violent, passionate murder, yet at the same time it placidly described the campus and its surroundings with an eye for detail that was extraordinary. It was also clearly and simply written. Academics, he thought, seldom write simply. They have been trained to write jargon-laden prose. Jim actually grinned, remembering the philosophy department at Vanderbilt. They were a very well educated group. He liked them. But they hadn't liked his unwillingness to spend time on what had come to seem unnecessarily arcane.

Nearing Cuba, he gazed approvingly at the big stands of piñon and juniper on the higher slopes. Turning south on US 550, he considered stopping for a cup of coffee. In an odd way, the old and somewhat dilapidated town was a comfortable little place. As usual, however, he decided that he could drive the eighty-five miles to Albuquerque without bad coffee.

Once past the town, he continued his ruminations about the mystery book and its unknown author. He'd found the Southwestern faculty refreshingly different from the hyper-specialized Vanderbilt graduate school professors. People like his sister would be surprised that any of them did publish, but they tended to write for general audiences, not a small cadre of other scholars. He had acquired a bird guide by the resident biologist/ornithologist when he first arrived in Cottonwood. It was clearly written, well illustrated, and full of interesting information. Certainly Erica's *Landforms of Northern New Mexico* was a wonderfully clear description of the formation of the landscape through geological time periods. Several faculty members, including Erica Ebenezer, would have been capable of writing *Academic Awards*.

Soon he'd left the high country around Cuba for the lower elevations. Yucca and prickly pear replaced piñon and juniper. Hills became arid, barren buttes. He liked the desert almost as much as the higher canyon country around the college, but he didn't like the new Indian casino or its billboards dotting the approach to Bernalillo. There he turned south onto I-25 for a straight shot into Albuquerque.

Jim's mind went back, unbidden, to the late-night intruder in Walt's office. Damn, I should have told B.B. to look for prints on all likely surfaces when he found none on the trophy. He shook his head and reprimanded himself for continuing to worry about past mistakes. Much better to think about his pleasant talk with Toni Hexton over coffee last evening. Something that wouldn't have happened if he hadn't taken on night shifts. He was definitely pleased that retrieving Johnny gave him a chance to visit with both Florencio and Roberto Gonzales. He'd called the young man earlier in the week on a whim and was delighted that Roberto would have time to meet him for breakfast on Saturday.

Jim had first met Roberto and his twin brother Rick when he arrived in Cottonwood, eleven years ago now. For a few months, he had casually spent time with the boys' widowed mother, Jolene, one of the first people to welcome him to SWC. It was hard to believe the gangly, shy youngster was now a second-year medical student at UNM after graduating with honors in chemistry at the university.

Jim drove directly to the Holiday Inn and checked in. He changed into "visiting-the-city" clothes and headed for The Quarters for a barbeque dinner with Florencio.

☙

Friday morning, Toni finally met Jonathan Gill, the popular young political science professor. He had promised to see her after his ten o'-clock class on Wednesday, but he hadn't shown up. After pacing the hallway outside his office for fifteen minutes, Toni had left him a note. At 11:40, he had called, unapologetic, and explained that he had stopped to talk with a student after class and forgotten about their appointment.

On Thursday, Jonathan *had been* in his office—as promised. But he was on the phone. He scrawled a few words on the back of an envelope, and pushed it in her direction: "Long distance. D.C. Same time Friday? Your office?"

Toni nodded and then, hoping to forestall another delay, mouthed, "See you tomorrow. It's urgent."

The next day Toni, not willing to waste time on small talk, addressed Jonathan before he was fully seated. "You didn't by any chance write *Academic Awards*, did you?"

"Heavens, no," Jonathan replied. "Why are you asking me?"

"Because I think you're clever enough and fluent enough to have done it. And you might have enjoyed producing a send-up of academia."

"Is that what the book is? When Asher told us about it last Friday, I was surprised about how serious he was. By the way, have you read it?"

Toni evaded the question. "I'm just one of the people assigned to hunt for the college's benefactor. As you heard at the faculty meeting, Southwestern stands to receive a half million dollars as soon as the author turns up and accepts his—or her—share of the prize money."

"I wouldn't mind having the dough. Tell me again, how much richer would I be if I *had* written the thing?"

"Fifty grand."

"Whew. Enough to pay off all my student loans." Jonathan smiled disarmingly. Toni could understand why her single, young female colleagues grumbled about Jonathan conducting his social life in Farmington and Durango. "If no one comes forward, I'd be happy to claim authorship." Jonathan leaned back in the chair, elbows akimbo and hands shoved into his pockets. "I'd even swallow my objections to benefitting Southwestern."

"Despite having your summer abroad class canceled?"

"You heard about that, did you? Now I remember, I got the number of the legal department of the American Association of University Professors from you, didn't I?"

"Yes, but I wasn't the only one you talked to. You weren't exactly quiet about your discontent."

"True. It's not in my nature to acquiesce quietly. So I screamed a little around here, and then I contacted both the AAUP and the ACLU. Both groups told me that if I pursued my complaint I should expect the wheels of justice to grind slowly. No one I talked to seemed surprised that Southwestern's administration should be so cautious. I guess we're no different from any place else."

"What reason *were* you given for having to cancel your class?"

"The first cause, I suspect, was a complaint from parents. David, the Johnsons' twenty-one-year-old son—whom they still consider a child—didn't ask permission to take the class or the trip. David didn't think he needed his parents' blessing. *They* did. When he informed Mom and Pop that he'd be studying in Israel instead of working at home in Topeka, all hell broke loose. The Johnsons couldn't get the young man to back down. So they passed the job over to Asher and Hamill and company. Our hypocritical administrators questioned the wisdom of taking a class to Israel—even though twelve students had already signed on for the course. Asher was waffling about whether to allow the trip even before the Albuquerque paper ran an editorial about how irresponsible it was for undergraduate colleges to send underage students abroad in these dangerous times. The editorial pushed Asher over the edge. He didn't object to its source even when I pointed out that it echoed—almost word-for-word—Dave's parents' written complaint! But it put the kibosh on my trip. So much for the college's commitment to travel abroad, experiential learning, and responsible journalism."

Toni waited a moment for Jonathan to calm down. She responded to his frown with a smile. "In the journalistic world, there's a dictum that bad publicity is better than no publicity at all."

"Too bad Asher and his cronies don't believe that."

"Were there any other objections to the trip? I remember hearing that your arranging for the students to interview Israeli and Palestinian activists was the proverbial straw that made everyone *very* nervous."

"Oh, that was only a convenient excuse for canceling the class. In their hearts, I don't think the administration cottons to having students go anywhere besides England and other safe places in Europe. Exposing students to the messy fight for truth and justice in the real world doesn't wash. *In loco parentis* is alive and well. Even at the dawn of the twenty-first century."

"Was it the prospect of a long delay that made you decide to drop your protest?"

"Not really. I got a better offer. Next summer, I'll be taking students abroad for the University of Maryland's summer overseas program. They do all the recruiting, and make all the arrangements. Less work and more money for me. Not a bad deal, huh?"

Jonathan looked so openly and innocently pleased that Toni stopped herself from asking, "What about justice and truth?"

@

At 5:00, Erica, believing that most committee work is best done before meetings and not in them, sounded impatient as she called the meeting to order. "No one, I presume, has hit the jackpot, or you would have called. But have any of you found a likely suspect?"

Steve Scott spoke up. "Wait, I don't think we should answer that question yet. I think each of us should explain what we learned, *as* we learned it. One of us may pick up on clues the interviewer overlooked. Unless the author is someone who didn't attend last week's faculty meeting, he—or she—denied authorship even when given the chance to confess and earn the president's undying gratitude. I suppose we have to believe your denials," Steve said, cocking an eyebrow first in Erica's direction and then Toni's. "But we may have been too quick to accept other people's."

"You two," said Lloyd Reasoner, laughing, "could have saved us a whole lot of trouble if you *had* written the book."

"Don't I wish we had," said Toni. "We'd be rich."

"And also at home by now," added Erica. "Sorry to interrupt you, Steve. Go on."

"There's a chance we've been conned into accepting denials from the people we've interviewed. They may have reasons for staying hidden. I doubt that Taylor Anderson is holding out because he doesn't want the college to get its half million. However, he could be our man. He might have relished fooling me as much as I'm sure he would relish dangling the carrot out of President Asher's reach. I'd like for you to listen to my account. You may detect an inconsistency or an outright lie that I didn't. And we may all be able to do the same for each other."

"As we said last time, it's hard to believe that any one of them could, or would, have written *Academic Awards*."

"You're right. Obviously, none of us elicited a confession. That doesn't mean all the people we interviewed are innocent," said Erica.

"So, on the dubious assumption that six heads are better than one, why don't you each give an account of your sleuthing efforts?"

"It'll be hard not to reveal our own views," said Toni.

"Ignore your journalistic training," replied Erica. "Emulate suspense writers instead. Save some of the *who's, what's, when's, where's,* and *why's* for the end of your reports."

She turned to Steve. "Will you begin by telling us about your interview with Taylor Anderson?"

"All right." Steve leaned back in his chair and hooked his thumbs behind his head. "Finding Taylor was not easy. When I reached him—in Spain—at 9:00 in the morning *his* time—he seemed delighted to learn that the president wants something he can't get. Whether Taylor's reaction is genuine or disingenuous I don't know.

"As you *do* know, Taylor resigned in a huff the day his wife Stephanie learned there would be no full-time tenure-track position for her. Several days later, he asked to withdraw his resignation. Asher and Vice-President Hamill refused his request. They, along with you, Sarah," continued Steve, looking in her direction, "must have found Taylor almost impossible to deal with."

Sarah Jennings, eager to justify her irritation with both Andersons, who between them had torpedoed many attempts to maintain a semblance of agreement among the nine prima donnas filling the art, music, and theater departments, explained, "Taylor himself has always been arrogant and pushy. You have no idea how that man's paints, sketches, uncleaned brushes, discarded sweaters, and half-drunk cans of Pepsi spilled out of his studio. Besides, he insisted that I schedule all his classes between ten and three…"

In the midst of Sarah's outburst, Steve unclasped his hands, and leaned slightly forward. "I think we're all aware that Taylor suffered from a case of colossal self-importance. And we understand why all of you in Fine Arts might have sighed good riddance. *He* should have understood that art and music need a cadre of part-timers for specialties that no *one* person could possibly teach. Stephanie was certainly out of line thinking there was a great demand for advanced weaving and jewelry-making classes."

Jeff Miles looked puzzled. "Why did Stephanie even want a full-time job? Her weavings bring in quite a bit, don't they? And I see Taylor's greeting cards for sale in every coffee house in Durango and Albuquerque."

"Oh," said Toni, "It's a matter of pride. Taylor thought he and Stephanie were God's gift to this college. I'll bet it never occurred to Taylor that Walt wouldn't try to talk him out of resigning."

"When I finally located him, I discovered another reason he wanted to take back his resignation," resumed Steve, "He's taught at Southwestern for nineteen years, not twenty."

"That means," put in Erica, turning towards Jeff, "he forfeits a sizable chunk of his pension."

"Taylor," added Sarah, "hates to find himself on the short end of any stick. Especially a financial one. I never got the sense he was driven to produce great art. He churned out those cards because he liked to make money. As his house here shows." Steve nodded vigorously. "He and Stephanie," continued Sarah, "were both looking forward to retiring on easy street. Most of us thought they'd go back East."

"From his description over the phone, they're in no hurry to return to the U.S.," said Steve. "They're luxuriating in Ibiza."

"Incidentally," interposed Erica, "how did you manage to find Taylor *there*? From what I heard last week, no one knew where he and Stephanie had gone."

With a straight face, Steve replied, "My CIA connections." Seeing that his fellow task force members didn't know whether or not to take him seriously, Steve smiled and shook his head. "All kidding aside, the Andersons were very secretive. No one on campus seemed to have the slightest idea where he might be. Including you, Sarah. I finally got a lead from Sandy, the student who's housesitting for them. I used the pretext that some interlibrary loan books he'd requested had arrived. However, when I went into his house, I saw why Taylor wouldn't leave it unguarded for long. In addition to their own art works, he and Stephanie have a couple of original Gormans, a sizable collection of Navajo rugs, Zuni fetishes, Santa Clara pottery, and a shelf full of Anasazi pots and potsherds."

"Undoubtedly illegal," muttered Erica.

"They also have a despicable cat, named Picasso." Steve held out his hand, palm down, revealing three long, red scratches. "I dropped by the house Tuesday. Sandy wasn't there, but her boyfriend, a former Southwestern student, had just driven up. I couldn't believe my luck. I recognized him and even remembered his first name. Tom had been one of the library's work-study students. Now he's on his way to graduate school. Incidentally, I'm sure the Andersons would be horrified to know that Sandy had given him a key to their house! My good luck held. Tom not only invited me in but he also ferreted out an address and an emergency phone number from a pile of notes by the phone.

"I thanked Tom for his help, and, several hours later, got up to call Taylor in the middle of the night. After some small talk—mostly concerning the damn cat—I asked him point blank if he'd written a book in which a college president was murdered. His answer was 'Don't I wish.' And when I told him more, I could almost *hear* the self-satisfied grin on his face. Taylor's anything but a forgiving man. He told me he didn't do it, but went on to say, almost chortling, 'but my hat's off to whoever did. Asher deserves to squirm.' When I told him how much money the author would stand to earn, he wasn't impressed. When I mentioned how much more the college would gain, he became very quiet. Taylor wasn't even curious about who might have written *Academic Awards*. He *did* seem to like the choice of murder victim, though."

"He seems like a long shot to me," said Erica.

"I hate to say it," said Sarah, "but I agree. If he'd written the book, he would have gloated."

"I'm sure he wouldn't have been at all embarrassed about killing off Walt Asher's counterpart," added Lloyd. "As I said earlier, I doubt Taylor's our culprit, but I don't think we can put him in the discard pile yet." He looked around the table. Erica shrugged. The others looked noncommittal.

"Steve, are you willing to keep working on Anderson?" asked Erica.

"Yes, but I don't know how much more information I can dig up."

"As long as we're not ready to write him off," said Erica, "every little bit may be useful. What with the stink he and Stephanie raised last spring and their threats about suing the college, I can't believe he'd have had time to write a book—even if he had the inclination."

"Spite and self-pity can be great motivators," commented Toni. "If he wrote *Academic Awards*, he'd surely have started it *after* all the uproar."

Sarah, doing what she always did when her interest was aroused, carefully removed her glasses and set them on the table. "Last spring, Taylor wasn't sketching, he wasn't painting, he wasn't meeting with students. Every minute he wasn't in class, he was at his computer. I *thought* he was inundating his lawyer with information he thought would damn President Asher, Southwestern College, and me. Maybe he was sublimating his anger into this novel. Artists are adept at creating imaginary worlds to get back at people who insult them." She paused before saying, "I'd like to take a look at his computer."

"And *what*," asked Steve, "can you find out that you don't already know?"

Lloyd groaned and laughed. "Maybe all you'll discover is a fine collection of porno sites."

Sarah ignored Lloyd and answered Steve's question. "Anything left on his computer will still be there. He departed in a huff, without even bothering to shut it down. I had to turn it off! It's still in the Fine Arts storage room."

"Wouldn't he have trashed everything?" asked Jeff.

"No, that's the point," answered Sarah. "He didn't. His last angry memo leapt out at me when I touched the mouse and the screen came back on. So I'm sure I can open other documents as well."

"That makes me uncomfortable," Toni said. "Taylor decided, I heard, to drop his suit when he found out a written resignation was watertight. Could he sue us if we went into his computer now?"

Jeff spoke up. "I don't think so. Didn't you get the recent notice from the computer center saying that we should *not* consider what we've written on campus confidential, that there might be times when they'd have to look at our files?"

Sarah sighed, audibly. "I don't usually read memoranda from the computer center. Their memos are too long, too technical, and too boring. I figure if I wander into cyberspace that's off limits to ordinary mortals, I'll be told what I shouldn't have done."

Smiles traveled around the table. "The rules committee is investigating whether the computer center has the right to invade our privacy," said Lloyd, solemnly, "no matter what the computer gurus say."

"Oh, for heaven's sakes," Sarah squawked. "All I'll do is look at his list of documents to see if there's anything suspicious. And if there is, I'll take a little peek. Taylor Anderson doesn't even own that computer any more. It belongs to the Fine Arts department. If he didn't erase his documents, he has no one to blame but himself. I've been remiss in not getting his desktop cleared before now. Especially since I've been intending to give that computer to his replacement."

"I think you're right, Sarah," said Steve. "If Taylor didn't choose to erase his files, I think we can assume they belong to the college."

Jeff agreed. "I believe you'll find that whatever you produce on college equipment and on college time is *not* private. There have been a couple of recent cases…"

"Go ahead then, Sarah," said Erica, "Look into Taylor's computer files and report back. Is that okay with everyone?"

Without waiting for confirmation and wanting to be conciliatory after her interruption, she turned to Jeff. "Okay, Jeff, what about your candidate? Incidentally, you deserve kudos for the long trip you took to interview Charlie Roanhorse."

"Let me review our reasons for thinking he might have written *Academic Awards* first. Then," pulling a stack of three by five index cards out of his pocket, Jeff said, "I'll go over my notes in chronological order.

"If you remember, Dr. Asher didn't include him in his short list. Vice-President Hamill wasn't ready to exclude him, though. That's because Charlie was outspokenly critical of some of the things the college did and didn't do for Indian students. He stood up to the president, and even asked for a meeting with the cabinet. Hamill knows how articulate he is and that he plans to become a writer. Charlie and I became good friends when we played some pick-up soccer together. Despite being encouraged to apply to grad schools, he decided to get a job that would let him live simply and write. Unlike Taylor Anderson, he'd consider fifty thousand dollars a fortune. He did find the ideal job. And even though it wasn't simple, I found Charlie. He wasn't trying to hide. He just didn't leave a clear trail.

"Anyway, early this week, I made it a point to wander into the faculty lounge several times. I'd plop down next to teachers who might have had Charlie in class. I asked if they knew what he's been doing since graduation. To top off my investigation, I'd work the conversation around to an article he'd written for the student newspaper that got picked up by Farmington's *Daily Times* and the *Durango Herald*."

"I remember the article you're talking about," said Lloyd. "Didn't Charlie pose as a visiting efficiency expert who had come to observe faculty at work?"

"I'm not sure you should have said *at work*, Lloyd," answered Sarah. "As I remember the article, which, by the way, was very clever and often right on target, Charlie chronicled how a typical professor spent his day. Working didn't play a major role. I especially liked his headline: 'To Teach or Not to Teach.' I don't know when I've laughed so hard."

Sarah turned towards Lloyd. "I wouldn't have thought *you* liked it, Lloyd. It ridiculed nitpicking parliamentary procedure. Didn't the article conclude with a question—something about why faculty members spend such an inordinate amount of time on academic politics when the stakes are so low?"

"I don't know when an article in a student weekly paper has caused such a furor," Toni added. "I got lots of calls from irate faculty. Along with a few congratulations."

"Give me credit," said Erica. "My call was congratulatory!"

"Half the faculty believe I run the newspaper like a class. But the editors assign articles, not me, and they decide which ones will be printed. I'm surprised at how many of my colleagues don't understand that while I can warn students about libel and slander, I can't forbid them to run an article. There wasn't even any reason to caution the editor about Charlie's story, though. It ridiculed faculty in general, not any specific Southwestern professor."

"We faculty are pretty thin-skinned," said Sarah. "I'm sure those the shoe fit felt targeted." Sarah shot Lloyd an amused, questioning look. "However, you must have been impressed that Charlie attributed his final quotation correctly."

He shrugged and smiled. "I was. Most people think Mark Twain must have said that, but he didn't. It was a Columbia University professor named Sayre. According to him, 'academic politics are so bitter' because the 'stakes are so low'." Lloyd looked directly at Toni. "*I* wasn't one of the people who called you to complain about the article. As a matter of fact, not only was I impressed with Charlie's finding the source for his last line, I found the whole article hilarious. And it *was* better written than most of the proposals faculty submit for a vote."

"That's why I thought I had the best chance of any of us to nab our author," said Jeff. "I've read some of Charlie's stuff. He's one helluva writer. The portrait of Canyon College in *Academic Awards* wasn't vindictive. Charlie isn't vindictive either. He'll fight for what he believes in, but he doesn't bear grudges. I didn't see him as much last spring as usual. He said he was too busy to go for a beer after some of our games. At the time, I didn't find that odd. He was working on his final senior paper. When we started wondering who might have the talent and time to write a book, Charlie came to mind—even before Bill Hamill suggested him.

"I finally located Charlie. We talked all morning. At his place, and then over lunch. Luckily, I tracked him down during his off week. He's working with an educational travel agency headquartered in Bisbee, Arizona, and he's gone quite a bit. His boss, Rebecca Owens, gave me directions to his trailer since he doesn't have a phone. I got to her through Charlie's cousin who's a student here. Incidentally, Rebecca thinks he walks—well, drives—on water.

"When I got around to the point of my visit, Charlie thanked us for considering him. He would like to have written the book, but he said over and over that he'd never make it writing fiction."

"Are you sure that wasn't a case of protesting too much?" asked Sarah.

Jeff kept shaking his head while Sarah kept on making a case for Charlie. "I remember when he first arrived. He was a little older and a lot more mature than most students. He became a spokesman for the Native Americans. Within a year, he had persuaded the cabinet to designate a room outfitted with easy chairs, desks, and lockers so that the Indian students, most of whom commute, wouldn't have to cart all their books and notebooks around with them all day. If Charlie Roanhorse could persuade the cabinet to spring for thousands of dollars to renovate a storage room in the basement of Old Main, I'm sure he could toss off a mystery. Besides, I noticed that Mary Sheepherder spends a lot of time in a commuters' common room in *Academic Awards*. The author could have been describing Charlie's lounge."

"That doesn't necessarily point the finger at Charlie, though," said Erica. "There's no doubt whoever wrote the book had this campus in mind. Anything else convince you to eliminate Charlie from suspicion, Jeff?"

"Mostly his attitude. During his weeks off, he's expanding on a project he started here as a student. He was writing about dual lives of Native Americans caught between the world of the reservation and the white world of work in cities and towns. Now he's broadening the story to include the Mexican tour drivers he's gotten to know. He's interviewed lots of people. He'll tell their stories, but not fictionally. He's written part of the book and found an editor at the University of New Mexico Press. The book may come out as early as next summer."

"I move we take Charlie Roanhorse off our list," said Steve.

Toni and Lloyd nodded in agreement.

"I'll give Charlie up—reluctantly," said Sarah. "He'd surely come forward to collect the reward if he'd earned it."

"It was a good lead, Jeff, and following it took some doing. Thanks again," said Erica before pausing and then looking around the table. "Maybe this is a good time to take a short break."

Lloyd was already on his feet. "I'll go get us all some coffee. That is, if everyone wants a cup."

"Decaf for me, please, Lloyd," said Steve.

"Ditto," said Sarah. "But if I'm going to drink coffee I better take a break now." She stood up and stretched, before marching, Sarah-like, out of the room.

Toni and Steve walked over to the window.

"These fall afternoons are the thing I like best about New Mexico," said Steve.

"I've got oodles of relatives in the East," answered Toni. "I've visited them in all four seasons. I couldn't believe the humidity."

"I suspect they complain about the dryness when they visit you."

"They sure do. A cousin my age never stopped complaining about her hair, her complexion, and needing *another* glass of water all day long."

Lloyd re-entered the room, balancing a tray with six mugs, a pile of stirrers, and packets of sugar and creamer. He accosted Erica, "Just how do you rate a mobile La Carte in the geology wing? Bribery? Or graft?"

Erica smiled broadly. "Pure economics. We scientists work our students harder than you humanists. Different labs, on a rotating basis, are open to the students until nine-thirty at night. La Carte does a brisk business until it closes around nine. I'll bet the food service wouldn't begin to make a profit in *your* hall in the evening."

Sarah entered the room during the interchange. Laughing, she said, "If it's just a matter of economics, Fine Arts could keep a vendor in business until midnight. I'll have to bring it up with my faculty. I'll cite your example, Erica."

"Okay, Sarah," continued Erica, when everyone was seated, "it's your turn. What did you learn from Jane Snow? I almost hate to ask how your interview went."

"Badly," responded Sarah. "At first Jane seemed amused that we suspected her, then irritated, and finally evasive.

"There's no doubt she's angry—at almost everybody and everything, but especially Hamill and Asher. I think a therapist would explain that she's sublimated her disappointment over not living up to her promise. She came to Southwestern with great recommendations and lots of self-confidence. Slowly it's become evident to her colleagues, and many of her students, that she shouldn't be teaching. Nevertheless, she's done a good job of squelching the evidence—at least, in her own mind."

"I thought psychologists had more self-knowledge than the rest of us," said Jeff.

"In my experience," responded Lloyd, "they have less. I've long suspected that studying rats doesn't lead to self-knowledge."

Sarah continued. "Jane didn't take to the daily grind of undergraduate teaching. When she was hired, getting tenure after seven years was almost automatic—unless you did something really outrageous. Until last year, she was arbitrary and cantankerous, but not outrageous. She still seems to think she has a case—even though the grievance committee told her she didn't. Her response to that has been to call the whole grievance committee tainted and their decision invalid. And if that weren't enough, she claims she's being denied academic freedom."

"Freedom to be an ass," said Erica under her breath.

"Is she really going to challenge the grievance committee at the next faculty meeting?" asked Steve. "I heard she was planning to."

Lloyd looked incredulous. "But it's a little late for a challenge!"

Sarah said, "Not according to Jane. On Wednesday morning, I heard her talk about events that happened years ago as if they were as present as things happening today."

"That's so," said Lloyd. "I remember when she protested the faculty's decision to require a psychology lab for majors. Her protest came long *after* her department had proposed the change and both the curriculum committee and the faculty had approved it."

"Even though the vote was ninety-nine to one," said Sarah. "As far as Jane's concerned, ninety-nine of us were wrong. I hope, Erica, you won't ask me to follow up on Jane. Talking with her is more discombobulating than playing leapfrog at a 5-year-old's birthday party."

Erica smiled. "If you're refusing to see her again, do you have any incriminating details to share?" asked Erica.

"I did find out that she gets by on three or four hours of sleep a night. As far as having time to write, you could count her in. Still, I seriously doubt that she could create anything coherent late at night when nothing else in her life is coherent."

"Wait," said Jeff. "It sounds like this dame is a more likely suspect than Charlie. Firing a tenured professor is pretty difficult, isn't it? I guess I'm the only person who hasn't heard why she was given a terminal contract, and I need to know about that before I count her out."

"Do you want my version—or Jane's?" asked Sarah.

Jeff grinned. "Sounds as if yours would be more trustworthy."

"She claims that one of the psychology department's best students and a former pet of hers—acted unethically.

"A week or so before graduation last year, Jane changed the A she'd originally given Annie Trostle to an F. When Annie received a copy of the change-of-grade form, she went directly to President Asher. He sided with Annie and then did something unheard of. He had the grade changed back to an A. The records office claims they notified Jane of his action. She claims they didn't.

"Jane was well aware of what an F would do to Annie's grade point. Therefore, she was stunned to hear Asher say *magna cum laude* after reading Annie's name as she walked across the stage at graduation. Even though I was sitting several rows behind Jane, I heard her gasp. If Dave Perkins, who sat next to her, hadn't pulled her back down in her seat, I think she would have marched onto the stage then and there. Instead, after the ceremony, she marched into the middle of a family photograph, and harangued Annie and her parents, loudly—and with obscenities."

"Why did Dr. Snow change the grade to an F in the first place?" asked Jeff.

"For a number of reasons. Let me count them. First, Jane recognized how extraordinarily good Annie's fall term senior seminar paper was. Second, that led Jane to decide it should be submitted to the national psychology conference held each March. Third, since Jane decided this during Christmas vacation *after* Annie had left campus, she sent the paper, along with a cover letter, to the APA. Fourth, she signed Annie's name to the letter she'd written herself."

"But that's illegal!" protested Jeff.

"Uh huh," replied Sarah. "A fact, however, that still eludes Jane. Her culpability gets worse and worse. She'd neglected to tell Annie she'd sent her paper in. In mid-January when Annie was notified that her paper had been accepted for presentation, she went directly to Jane. At which point, Jane congratulated Annie, and proudly showed off the letter she'd written—and signed.

"I can't believe how obtuse Jane Snow is. She seems to have no idea why Annie objected to what she'd done. She still can't understand why Annie wasn't willing to postpone her wedding in order to attend the conference. Jane was so indignant that she changed Annie's grade. And that brings me full circle to her shouting tirade after graduation."

"I heard," said Toni, "that Annie added insult to injury by deciding to become an elementary teacher rather than going on in psychology. Being repudiated by her prize pupil must have infuriated Jane."

Erica looked around the room. "Does that mean we shouldn't dismiss her yet? Walt's interference in her revenge—changing Annie's grade back to an A—must have been the final straw. Motive enough to…" Erica didn't need to finish her thought. The other five members of the task force agreed, with hesitant uhms and shrugs, to include Jane as a suspect, at least until more likely candidates emerged.

Erica addressed Toni. "Okay. Toni, it's your turn. What have we got against—or for—Jonathan Gill?"

"Jonathan certainly has ability and discipline," said Toni. "Furthermore, he's bright, he's articulate, and he has the gift of seeing us as we'd rather not be seen. Of course, he sees himself in a much better light than others do. Hmm, I'm a little bitter. Jonathan stood me up twice, before we finally connected." Trying to attribute his maddening ease to youth, rather than to unwarranted self-assurance, Toni downplayed her irritation as she described her conversation with him. "I asked Jonathan outright if he'd written *Academic Awards*."

"I suppose he said no," said Sarah.

Toni replied, "Quite definitively."

Steve asked, "But wouldn't he deny he'd written the book, if his aim were to embarrass the college?"

"Maybe," answered Toni. "But he seemed too comfortable while I was questioning him to be our author."

"He *could* be a good actor," said Steve.

"I doubt it," said Erica. "With Jonathan, what you see is what you get."

Lloyd arched his eyebrows as he glanced from Erica to Toni. "I think Jonathan has you both as snowed as he does most of the women in this place. No, let me finish," he said, as Erica started to protest. "Jonathan's office is across the hall from mine. I see him come and go many times every day. We both leave our doors open, and so I hear him even more than I see him. Gill's beginning, what, his sixth year here? The first year, he was finishing his dissertation. He went to class, but otherwise he wasn't around much. But since then, Prince Charming keeps more office hours than anyone. I can hear him, oozing charm from every pore. Being curious about my two-toned friend, I looked and I was right. Gill saves his honeyed tones for the women."

"And what's your evidence?" asked Erica.

"My eyes."

"Oh, you snooped?"

"Yes, but only long enough to support my hunch. It didn't take much doing. Jonathan brought in a small two-seater couch to replace the two chairs supplied by the college…"

Sarah chuckled. "I think two-seaters are usually called love seats."

"Anyway, I can see Gill's couch anytime I swivel my desk chair. Sure enough, every time Gill's voice is particularly smooth and smarmy, his visitor is female." Lloyd smiled, first in Erica's direction and then Toni's.

"Oh," huffed Toni, "I think Erica and I are old enough to be immune to his charms."

"Seriously," put in Steve, "I think you need to consider why Jonathan might have lied to you. I've seen enough young radicals to believe that *their* belief in some cause takes precedence over the need for honesty. If Jonathan wants to subvert the system…" Steve let his sentence hang, revealing his conservatism.

"I have some information about Jonathan Gill that we ought to be considering." Jeff, looking guilty, hesitated. "Some of it isn't public knowledge, though."

"If it's relevant," prodded Erica, "you need to tell us. Remember our agreement. What is said in this room stays in this room. As long as we're investigating our colleagues, we'll be suggesting lots of possibilities that will turn out to be impossible. So go ahead, Jeff."

Jeff continued. "Last spring I did a profile on Gill for the alumni magazine. After the interview, he said he counted on me to omit most of what he told me. He *did* let slip that he was on tenterhooks at the time we talked. He was up for early tenure."

"I didn't know that," said Sarah. "It would've been very unusual if he'd gotten it."

At the same time Lloyd said, "Not a wise thing to go for. If you get early tenure, you make yourself mighty unpopular. Everyone resents an early bloomer."

"Jonathan himself didn't ask for early tenure. Evidently, his department recommended him without his knowledge and he felt it would be bad form to tell them not to push him. But that's not my point. I don't think there's any way Jonathan would've had the time to write a book!"

"Why not?" asked Steve.

"During his first year here, he got two articles out. Parts of his dissertation, I think. Every single year, he's delivered papers at poli sci conventions. He is also advisor to the Political Science Club."

"And a good one," said Sarah. "Until Jonathan revitalized the club, they did nothing but have an annual bake sale. And now they sponsor a lecture series."

"A series that makes the townspeople nervous," added Lloyd. "They're afraid Southwestern has started training a bunch of liberal rabble-rousers."

"It's not just the townspeople," said Erica. "Remember the fuss last year when the Poli Sci Club invited two skinheads."

"Maybe I *was* naive to accept Gill's disclaimer so quickly," acknowledged Toni. "I remember how much he seemed to relish the controversy. Reporters from half the state's papers were camped out by Jonathan's office for several days, trying to get a statement from him. He kept telling them it was the students they should be talking to..."

"As if he hadn't instigated the invitation," said Lloyd under his breath.

Toni ignored the interruption. Her experience as newspaper advisor made her understand Jonathan's reluctance to act as spokesman for a student group. "I've always found Jonathan up front and frank about his activities and his criticisms. If he had a quarrel with Walt, he'd confront him directly. Jonathan made no secret of the fact that he'd approached the American Association of University Professors and the American Civil Liberties Union with a request to take his 'case'."

"Did they?" asked Erica.

"No, he withdrew his request before they even considered it." Toni smiled, remembering how quickly Jonathan had abandoned his show of righteous indignation. "He's signed on as a summer instructor for the University of Maryland. They have a very active overseas program, open to students from all over the country."

Toni turned towards Jeff, who was holding up last spring's issue of *Southwestern News and Notes*.

"This issue contains one of Jonathan's articles," he explained, eyeing one of his index cards. "It's not his only one. He's had several other articles published and a chapter of a book on Irish politics; he's been an officer of Amnesty International; he's conducted three summer classes abroad. He's bringing his dissertation up to date—at the University of Massachusetts' request. They publish one doctoral dissertation each year, and they chose his. I don't see how he could have done all that *and* written another book."

"You've almost convinced me," responded Steve. "Still, I'm not quite ready to take him off our list."

"I think we should. There's another reason to eliminate him," said Toni. "I was on that tenure and promotion committee when his name came up. I'd forgotten, but I read some of those papers and articles Jeff mentioned. He may be a free spirit, but he writes like a recent graduate student. Lots of buzz words, lots of convoluted, long sentences, and lots of qualifications."

"You're probably right, Toni. Jonathan may be another one of those people who has time to write because he gets by with very little sleep," said Steve. "I'd like to do for Jonathan what Sarah is going to do for Taylor. Only I don't want to look at what he's written, but what he's been reading. The librarians joke that Jonathan keeps more library books in his office than any three other professors put together. I want to find out what he borrowed the last twelve months."

"A clear invasion of privacy," growled Erica.

"We asked for it ourselves," said Lloyd, culling the pertinent information from his prodigious memory of everything the faculty had voted on during the last twenty-five years. "Don't you remember? The faculty asked the library staff to give us a list at the end of the year of all the books we'd checked out."

Sarah laughed irrepressibly. "I certainly do remember. The library started fining us for unreturned books! Talk of righteous indignation. We demanded your list since we couldn't separate our books from the library's books. It's no wonder we begin to think they're ours. The library allows us to keep them for a whole year—something I've always considered a mistake."

"Go ahead, then, Steve," said Erica, "we'll make our final decision on Gill after you let us know what you find out, but I agree with Toni. I bet you'll find that everything Jonathan reads is about politics. He isn't likely to spend much time on a little local murder, especially a fictional one."

Turning to Lloyd, she asked, "Well, how about our final candidate?"

"Let's see. Unlike Roanhorse and Gill, Frankel knows mysteries. He's been reading them since—in his words—he was a 'wee tad.' Detectives and their victims are his intimate friends."

"Good thing—he doesn't have any noticeable friends on the faculty," mumbled Erica.

Lloyd ignored Erica's comment. "Richard Frankel makes fine distinctions among authors, ranking them according to merits that mystery readers might appreciate more than I do. And he's inordinately proud of his name just because it's similar to some well known mystery writer's...I forget whose."

Erica shouted "Dick Francis" at the same time Toni looked up at the ceiling and murmured, "Richard Frankel—Dick Francis."

Lloyd continued, "Yeah, that's the name. Anyway, Richard spent a good ten minutes discoursing about his *serendipitous* name. He was so struck by the coincidence that he even wrote to Francis. He thinks he received a personal reply from the man. Richard showed it to me. It was so obviously *impersonal* that I'm certain it was a form letter.

"But I'm veering off track. His remarks, as well as his home office, gave me quite a few insights into the man. He hunts, and he is familiar with guns; in fact, he was in the midst of cleaning one when I came in."

"That must have struck you as strange," commented Steve.

"Just for a moment. But not really, not around here. Many of our faculty champ at the bit if they can't get a day off during the fall hunting season. Somehow I'd never thought of Frankel as an outdoor type before."

"Not too surprising," said Sarah, who, as usual, was a font of information about her colleagues. "He comes from an old Durango ranching family."

Lloyd continued, "Richard sounded pleased when I asked if he had written *Academic Awards,* but he told me that his *endeavors* were critical rather than creative." Lloyd's imitation of Frankel's pedantic speech elicited laughs. "He majestically waved a hand, pointing to a shelf full of books in new jackets. He took down one of them, opened its front cover and jabbed a finger at the words on the inside of the flap. 'Mine, all mine,' he said.

"While he waited, looking the part of a proud papa showing off his first born, I dutifully read his blurb."

"Was it masterful prose?" asked Sarah.

"I wouldn't call it masterful. But it was brief and clear."

"Brevity and clarity *do* have their place," commented Steve.

"So Richard said. He railed about how his English department colleagues don't appreciate the amount of work that goes into writing of this kind. 'Do you know,' he asked me, 'how difficult it is to write what appears on flyleafs?' He spent several minutes castigating his chairman for not counting his blurbs as professional development."

Erica scanned the faces of her fellow task force members. "How about Frankel? Do you think he's a viable candidate?"

"In some ways, no," responded Sarah. "He's tedious, he's bullheaded, and he can't see why we don't recognize that mysteries can be classics. But I think Steve has a point we shouldn't overlook. Richard Frankel's blurbs aren't, after all, too different from Taylor's greeting cards. The publishers, who don't share academia's concern for professional development, keep on asking him to write those things. And they do indicate a certain level of competence. There's something about Richard that makes me think we shouldn't eliminate him yet—in his reviews and advertising blurbs, he shows an ability to write straightforwardly when he wants to and to entice others to want to read more."

"But," asked Toni, "does he know half as much about campus life as he knows about fictional murders? From what I've seen of him, he's almost as out of touch about life here at Southwestern as Jane Snow. And Edith Tansley Coyle—whoever she is—seems attuned to college life in general and Southwestern in particular."

"If we need to cross-examine Richard further, I don't think I, or anyone else, will get more information out of him," said Lloyd. "He didn't seem to be hiding anything. He reveled in having an audience. He collared me like the ancient mariner. I didn't get home until almost seven o'clock."

Again, Erica looked around the room. "If I'm reading your expressions right, we all want to toss Richard Frankel out, but in the absence of a more likely possibility, we're not ready to."

Five nodding heads confirmed Erica's sense of the meeting.

"Look, it's after six," she said. "When shall we meet next?"

"Why do we need to meet at all until after someone has uncovered some damning evidence?" asked Lloyd.

Toni disagreed. "I think we do. Monday again? By then, we might think of somebody we've overlooked. I suggest we scrutinize the campus directory for additional candidates."

"Don't you think we've already combed the list of possibilities pretty thoroughly?" asked Erica.

"Yes, but over the weekend we might think of others to add to our list. Even without new information, the reports we've heard today may make us assign motive or means or opportunity to one of our current candidates."

"Okay, Toni. You may be right." Erica smiled at her friend. "You often are." She glanced around the table at the others. "Toni constantly tells me I'm too impetuous. To clear me of that charge, will you all look through your directories this weekend? We'll meet here again Monday. On the off chance that we might think of something—or someone—new. In all likelihood, it'll be a short meeting."

@

Jeff made no move to get up from the table when Erica adjourned the meeting. She turned from the doorway when she saw him slumped in his chair, head down. Walking back to the table, she tentatively tapped his shoulder.

"Hey, Jeff, I'm sorry we gave you such a hard time. Charlie *was* a good candidate even if Scott and Sarah didn't think so. You and Toni convinced me he could write circles around half our colleagues and you had good reason to think an observant student could have ferreted out so much info about the school."

"I confess I *was* very disappointed," said Jeff. "I tend to get prematurely committed to a particular angle whenever I go after a story. Anyway, I had a good visit with Charlie. I left some stuff from the admissions office at the high schools in Douglas and Bisbee, so the trip wasn't wasted. I wanted Charlie to have written *Academic Awards*, but he hadn't. With a book due to be published soon, he hopes to be launched on the writing career he's always dreamed of. I got over my disappointment by the time we said good-bye. That's not what's eating me."

"Oh?"

"My problem doesn't have anything to do with school."

"Want to talk?" Before he could say no, Erica continued, "I'm walking home this evening. I go right by your house."

"Yeah, I know. I've seen you. But," said Jeff, laughing, "I don't know if I can keep up with you. My wife sometimes watches you rush by. She says you walk faster than any woman she's ever seen." From the look in Jeff's eyes, Erica guessed where his problem lay. "Irene says she'd recognize a former jock anywhere. She's sure you must have been a college athlete."

"I was. Now I'm the oldest player on Southwestern's staff basketball team. We've even beaten younger and stronger undergraduates—once or twice."

Jeff waited while Erica gathered papers and pens and stuffed them in her briefcase. "Irene was quite an athlete herself, wasn't she?" asked Erica. "I remember reading about her New Mexico team winning the NCAA gymnastics championship two years running."

Jeff perked up. "That's how I met her. I interned with UNM's athletic department. I covered girls gymnastics and got to go to their out of town matches."

"Was that when you were working on your master's?"

"Yes."

"In communications?"

"The actual title of my degree," said Jeff, shrugging and looking embarrassed, "was Public Relations in Higher Education."

"Gad, I didn't know communications degrees could be so specialized."

"If I didn't learn anything else in grad school, I did learn that specialization is the name of the game these days. The sports teams all clamored for us freebies. We needed practice laying on the praise; the coaches wanted someone to get their teams mentioned in the media. For the big name sports we interns were just extras. When I wasn't assigned to cover basketball or football, I felt gypped at first. It was only later that I realized I was lucky. I didn't have one of the sports information staff guys looking over my shoulder and wanting credit for my stuff. One of the best pieces I wrote featured Irene. She was an incredible gymnast!"

"I'd say you were lucky. You got a wife out of your assignment!"

"If I can keep her," Jeff muttered too softly for Erica to hear.

"What did you say?"

"Sorry. I'm afraid I'm not very good company."

"Jeff, what's wrong? I've never seen you this way."

"So quiet, you mean?"

"More than that. So glum. You don't strike me as a moody person."

Jeff said nothing.

Erica reached out to touch his arm, and said softly, "I didn't know you and Irene were having problems."

"I didn't either, until recently."

Erica remembered that every time she'd seen Jeff with his family, his wife was shepherding three very young girls and looking hassled. "Your job involves many late meetings, and doing things such as rushing off to southern Arizona. Does she feel overwhelmed being left alone to cope with the kids so much?"

"Partly that," said Jeff. "But Irene seems to resent almost everything I'm doing these days, whether I'm at home or not. In fact, she objects so much that she took the girls and left for Albuquerque this morning."

"Oh, Jeff, I'm sorry."

"Thanks. I am too. Her mom's been sick for a long time. They talk on the phone almost every day. Irene's had friends and relatives checking in on her mother. All of a sudden Irene decided she had to go see her mother for herself."

"That's not necessarily a slam at you."

"It feels like one. Our three girls tire her mother out even when she feels good, so I can't imagine she'd want them around now."

"Look, since you're alone tonight, why not walk me home and stay for supper?"

"I don't want to put you to any trouble," said Jeff. "Irene left me some leftovers, and the stack of frozen pizzas in our fridge could feed a whole dormful of college students."

"I can guarantee that what Bill will have waiting will be better than leftovers or a pizza. I married a gourmet cook who has my slippers, the evening paper, and a scotch awaiting my return from campus."

"Mr. Ebenezer's a writer as well as a cook, isn't he?" asked Jeff, "He won't be expecting you to bring a stray home for supper, will he?"

"Bill has learned to expect the unexpected from me. I'm lucky. He writes—and cooks—at home. And he's a very fussy cook. He's such a perfectionist that he waits for me to appear to put the final touches on his concoctions. Unless your appetite is enormous, any dinner he makes will feed three, or four, or more."

"Well, thanks. I must admit I don't want to face another pepperoni pizza—and I'm no cook. Actually, I look forward to meeting your husband. I was assigned one of his books in a history class. It was much better than any of our other required texts!"

Jeff and Erica walked, companionably but silently, for another half block. Jeff paused before a small, recently mowed lawn in front of a house the mirror image of the one across the street, and duplicated in every fourth house they'd passed. On the lawn were an over-turned tricycle, a small hand lawnmower, a red wagon, and the evening paper.

"Here's my house. I'll put my notes inside and grab a jacket. It'll be cool after supper."

"Good, Bill will be glad to meet you—especially since you liked one of his books."

"Say, why didn't his name get thrown into the hopper as the phantom author?"

"Because he'd have had to keep it a big secret from me. He's no good at secrets. Besides, fiction isn't his thing. He teases Toni and me unmercifully about our taste in reading matter. He considers mysteries on a par with romance novels."

Jeff stopped at the bottom step of his minuscule front porch. He paused in embarrassment. "I'd invite you in, but the place is a mess."

Erica shrugged. "Don't worry. I'm not a neatnick."

Jeff opened the door and ushered her into the front room. Blocks and children's books had been stashed in one corner, a bottle half filled with some unappetizing orange liquid was making a ring on the week's *TV Guide* next to the TV set, and a half filled coffee cup sat next to a stack of magazines on the coffee table.

"Just a sec, I'll be with you."

Erica took advantage of Jeff's absence to glance at the magazines. In addition to a *Newsweek* and two *Christian Science Monitors* there were several copies of *Modern Dance* and *Ballet*.

Jeff came down the stairs two at a time, his jacket slung over one shoulder. Trying to put him at ease, Erica chattered on. "As long as dishes don't pile up—dishes are *my* responsibility—Bill and I live in what I like to think of as organized clutter. Bill writes in the living room. He has an enormous desk. I think it's oak, but I'm not sure. I haven't seen the top of it for years. Whatever books and articles and Internet printouts he's currently using—and he uses lots—end up piled on his desk, half the chairs in the room, and when he runs out of space, the floor."

"It's a good thing you didn't see our kitchen. It was my turn to do the dishes last night," Jeff confessed, "but we argued at supper, and instead of washing up, I went for a long bike ride. This morning, Irene served us cold cereal. She'd stacked last night's dirty dishes in the middle of the table."

"Sounds like she was trying to make a point."

"I know. She was. And I yelled at her. In front of the kids. I don't usually do that."

"None of us react well all the time, no matter how much we intend to." Erica cringed, hearing the echo of an aunt whose platitudes used to drive her crazy.

Jeff thawed as he sensed Erica's good will and sympathy. During the rest of their quarter mile walk to her house, he poured out the story of his and Irene's impasse.

"Irene plunked bowls down in front of the girls. They looked as baffled as I felt. Usually, they're pretty talkative, but not today. Even Tish—she's the youngest—didn't bang her spoon once. I was no help. I just sat there. Like a kid, I played with my cereal instead of eating it. All at once, Irene jumped up, and told me to call the preschool to tell them that Mary would be out for a couple of days visiting grandparents. That was the first I knew about her plans."

"It was probably the first she knew about them, too."

"I suppose so. Anyway, off she trounces upstairs and in a few minutes comes back down with a suitcase and a giant box of Pampers."

To herself, Erica thought, *Maybe she needs some pampering herself.*

"Here we are," she said, "come on in. I'll introduce you to Bill."

She yelled down the long hallway into the kitchen, "Hon, I've brought someone home for supper."

Bill, wearing an oversized apron and holding a wooden spoon in one hand and an oven mitt in the other, walked through the kitchen door.

"Hi, I'm Erica's *greater* half."

"Bill, this is Jeff. We've just come from our task force meeting. He's baching it tonight so I brought him home."

"Hi, Jeff. Sorry, I can't shake hands," said Bill, as he walked towards his wife, nuzzled the hair behind her ear, and planted a kiss on her cheek.

Bill turned to Jeff. "You must be the PR guy."

Jeff felt a pang of regret. Obviously very much in love and comfortable with each other, Erica and Bill made the prospect of becoming an old married couple look enviable.

Supper was delicious: a chicken pasta dish, Bill's freshly baked bread, and a salad made with vegetables from their garden.

After they had finished eating, Bill started to pull himself out of his chair. "How about some Palisade peaches for dessert?"

Erica jumped up, and gently putting her hand on Bill's shoulder, said, "Sit down, Bill. You made dinner. I'll do dessert."

As Erica walked to the kitchen, there was a moment of silence before Jeff turned to Bill. "Do you mind talking about what you're writing?"

"Not at all. I think most writers who pretend to mind are probably lying. There's nothing we like better than going on—and on."

Jeff laughed. Bill, he decided, was just as unpretentious as his wife.

"I'm putting together a book on rural courthouses."

"Putting?" asked Jeff.

"Yes, I'm not feigning modesty. *Putting* is the right word. I spent the summer photographing over a dozen courthouses. Before her field school began, Erica and I made a vacation of visiting every western Colorado town big enough to appear on motor vehicle maps. In some of the littler towns, the courthouses are no longer in use, at least not for their original purpose. There are some cases that get heard locally, mostly involving civil disputes. I think Erica became more interested in my courthouse project than I did. Of course, she sent me off in a new direction. She persuaded me to sit in on several trials. Now she's gone one step further and is trying to persuade me to make the book snazzier by including something about a few of the more unusual ones."

"Do you think she's right?"

It was Bill's turn to laugh. "She almost always is, though as a proper husband I have to protest a little."

Erica, returning with bowls of freshly sliced peaches in thick cream, heard her husband's last remark. "You have to admit, Bill, that the personal touch sells." She turned towards Jeff. "Wouldn't you like to read side-by-side descriptions of a present-day trial and one that took place in the old West?"

Jeff was spared the necessity of answering when Bill jumped up announcing that he'd fetch some hot cider and bring it out to the patio. Jeff sat contentedly, lulled by the sounds of grasshoppers and birds, and Erica's companionable silence.

The three sat silently enjoying their cider. After a few minutes,

Erica broke into Jeff's trance. "Okay, friend, it's time to talk. You've got a problem. Bill and I are great listeners, and, what's more, we're pretty damn good at solving problems."

"I doubt you can solve this one."

"Try us. We've been married for almost thirty years."

"And," said Bill, "contrary to present appearances, our lives haven't always been as smooth as they may look to you tonight. It's taken a long time, and some rather uncertain roller coaster rides, to get us where we are today."

"I'd certainly like to be where you are," replied Jeff, "when I get to be your age. Oops, sorry."

"Nothing to be sorry about, we have more than twenty years on you."

Erica chimed in. "Since I invited you here for cider and sympathy, it's time to give out with the sympathy…"

"Oh, you've already done that, and I do feel better."

"Good, but Bill's food and homemade cider will not keep you from stewing about you and Irene when you leave, will they?"

"No, I guess not." Jeff gave a deep sigh. "Okay, here goes. I hadn't fully realized it until recently, but our marriage has been sliding for a couple of years. We both seem to be drifting along in neutral. Irene is busy with the kids and I've been so occupied with my job I didn't notice that we weren't in gear anymore. We live in the same house, we know each other's routines…"

"And that's part of the problem, isn't it?" asked Bill. "Routine can be dull."

Jeff leaned forward, until he was almost perched on the slanted edge of the seat of a dilapidated Adirondack chair, its dark green paint flaking and peeling. "That's it! I feel dull around Irene. And I don't, you know, when I'm at the college—even when I get irked at some of the trivial stuff I do. And then I'm angry with Irene, and disappointed in her. I guess I've been blaming her for not making life at home exciting. There are moments when I enjoy the kids, especially if I get to be with them one at a time. That doesn't happen very often.

"Lately," Jeff continued, "there's always tension when both of us are with the girls. We used to enjoy being together with them. But since Tish came along—she's the youngest—Irene's almost always exhausted."

Erica and Bill let Jeff vent until he ran out of steam.

Bill glanced at Erica. "It seems to me Irene's problem is that the girls have become her entire life. Her days are nowhere as diverse as they had been. All she does now is take care of the girls, changing diapers, picking up toys, watching them play, and wondering why she doesn't feel fulfilled. You get to run across lots of people on your job, and your work is more varied."

"I hadn't thought of it that way," said Jeff.

"We only had one child," added Erica, "but she put a strain on our marriage when we first came to Southwestern. She was very young then. I had a full-time job and Bill was teaching a feature writing class. We prided ourselves for being wonderful parents—hah, talk about pride going before a fall! We'd arranged our schedules so that we could share child-tending duties. The sharing didn't work out so well with Bill trying to write at home. As long as he was around, Natalie kept interrupting him."

"And I," said Bill, "was getting grumpier and grumpier at not being able to write more than a sentence at a time."

"Grumpy? You were downright angry."

"But I didn't think I ought to be—and of course that made everything worse. Fortunately, Erica came up with a solution. We'd both give full attention to Natalie at supper and sometimes we'd even read her a bedtime story together. She loved that. Erica took complete charge of Natalie on Saturdays and Sundays, giving me two whole days of peace and quiet."

"Bill and I quit wondering what had happened to our 'ideal' marriage. I had to learn it was okay to take weekends off; teaching can suck up all your time if you're not careful. Even when Natalie didn't need so much supervision, she and I developed a routine. I took her to volleyball and basketball games for years. We explored the Four Corners area and went to Farmington or Durango to see lots of movies. I think we got close on all those drives. Sitting together in a car, not having to talk and not having to look at each other, was, as they say, a great bonding experience. Natalie would confide in me and ask my advice in a way she seldom did at home."

"And," said Bill, "those two days allowed me to regain my life as a writer. And I began appreciating my time alone with Natalie during the week."

"By the time Bill sold some articles and then two books, Natalie didn't need us to make her the center of our lives. Bill became a full-time writer and I didn't feel so torn between career and motherhood."

"With more than one child, though," said Bill, "your life is much more complex than ours was. Still, I suspect Irene would love to share more of her parenting duties. And she also needs time to pursue her own activities and interests."

"While you were getting your jacket," said Erica thoughtfully," I noticed modern dance and ballet magazines on your living room table. I trust they were Irene's and not yours?"

Jeff nodded.

"Could you arrange to give her a gift of time? Doing nothing but watching children, talking about children with other young mothers, and vegging out mentally and physically is not good for anyone, especially someone as active as Irene had been."

"I guess I thought since she's always loved children, she'd be happy just being with them." Jeff straightened up in the chair. "When she comes back from her visit, we'll talk and try to work out a schedule the way you did."

"I'd suggest you talk over a dinner—*out*," said Bill.

"Bring home some flowers, too," added Erica. "Incidentally, supermarket flowers are just as nice and much cheaper than a florist's."

"I'll do that!" responded Jeff.

"Has she ever played volleyball?" asked Erica, with a sudden gleam in her eye.

"Only a little. She spent all her time on gymnastics in college."

"My intramural team needs more players. I'll invite her to join us," said Erica.

Jeff stood up. "Thank you both. It's late and I need to be getting home. The food was wonderful—and so was your advice."

Bill rose and shook Jeff's hand. "If you find you need more of either, feel free to call."

Bill pointed Jeff to the sidewalk running around the side of the house from the patio. When he was out of earshot, Erica said, "He's a nice young man. I hope Irene will return from mama's in a receptive mood."

*Jim in Albuquerque.*

Jim woke up at 7 A.M. after a very pleasant, and rather late, evening with Florencio in The Quarters and went to the motel's modest fitness room for a quick workout.

He tuned out what passed as newsworthy from a blaring TV several feet above eye level. Instead, his mind wandered back over his conversation with Florencio. Jim had explained that President Asher mobilized a search to uncover the identity of the anonymous author of *Academic Awards* and that getting all his officers licensed to carry showed he was heeding Florencio's warnings. He thanked his friend for Johnny's crash training course, and then they analyzed the world's problems, even solving one or two of them.

Jim, sweating but relaxed, returned to his room, showered, and dressed. Fully refreshed, he walked the two blocks to the Pancake House to meet Roberto Gonzales at 8:00. Jim, a few minutes early, was halfway through his first cup of coffee when a tall, handsome, weary young man walked, zombie-like, into the restaurant. Jim smiled, seeing how hard Roberto was working to keep his eyes open. Spotting Jim, Roberto broke into a wide smile that quickly turned to laughter. The young medical student enveloped his old friend in a bear hug before sitting down.

"Sorry I'm late, Jim," he said.

Jim glanced at his watch. "It's only five after. You're not very late, Roberto. I suspect a med student doesn't get much sleep." Roberto nodded. Jim continued, "You look exhausted."

"That goes with the territory, I'm afraid. I drove straight from the hospital. I've been spending the last week there, observing all night in the emergency room. I've come *here* directly from my shift. I wouldn't have missed seeing you, so don't look as if you want to send me home. First food, then sleep."

"Are you still enjoying medical school as much as your mother tells me you are?" Jolene Gonzales had a right to be proud of her son, he thought, as the waitress interrupted their conversation to take Roberto's order. What a wonderful job she'd done bringing up her twin boys as a single mother. Jim had become an honorary uncle to the twins ever since he'd taken them to a spring training exhibition match when they were still in middle school.

Jim brought his attention back to Roberto, who, Jim realized, was answering his question. "Sure, on the whole, I'm glad to be in med school, but I can't say I always *enjoy* it. It's a grind—intellectually and physically. It's hard to believe it now, but someday I will be done."

"What are your plans for life after medical school?"

"The same as they've always been: go back home to open my own practice. I'm determined to achieve the goal I set for myself when Grandfather died of cancer."

Roberto leaned back into his chair and stretched. After giving a satisfied yawn, he asked, "Anything interesting happening in Cottonwood?"

Jim hesitated a second before deciding there was no reason not to tell Roberto about the college's newest preoccupation. Jim briefly explained the mystery of the mystery book.

"Wow, that's more excitement at the college than anything I can remember. But what are you doing here in Albuquerque?"

"Oh, I had some police business down here that gave me a chance to see my old friend Florencio—and you too, of course."

Jim and Roberto stopped talking when their waitress plopped two over-flowing plates on the table. They industriously spread butter and syrup on their pancakes and started eating.

Jim wished he could see the mystery as Roberto did. For him, the fact that the author hadn't come forward was ominous, not exciting. He'd tried to assure Walt that his wife's fears were groundless, but he had to admit, nebulous though they were, her fears echoed some of his. This short time away from campus was not providing the respite he'd hoped it would. He couldn't shake his anxiety about what might be happening to Walt and about whether the task force was stirring up a hornet's nest with their search for the elusive author.

"How's your brother doing this term?" Jim asked between bites—determined to shed his worrisome reflections during his short visit with Roberto.

"I don't see much of Rick even though we share an apartment. He's changed his major again. For the last time, I hope. He's on track to graduate with a degree in English, in June."

"Will he be playing baseball for UNM again this spring?"

"No, he's used up his eligibility." Roberto laughed. "Mom thinks that's a blessing, and so do I. He'll have no excuse to put off taking the senior seminar he needs to graduate. Studying was never as important to him as pitching. I guess we'd be more alike if we'd been identical twins. Rick and I've always had different priorities."

"Yes, I know," said Jim. "I've seen more of Rick than you in the last couple years since he spends summers in Cottonwood. From all reports, your brother has done a terrific job coaching youth baseball. You went to summer school so you could start medical school early. When you come home for a few days at Christmas, you don't have enough time to see anybody except your hundreds of uncles, aunts, and cousins. That's why I wanted to take you to breakfast and catch up on your life."

"Rick's a good guy. His coaching was all volunteer work. Mom told me he always got up early enough to do all sorts of things on our farm, and to help out some of our Silva and Gonzales relatives too. I didn't expect that since I always had the dickens of a time getting him out of bed when we were in high school.

"Rick's a talented pitcher," said Roberto, speaking softly. "I think for a while he was hoping for a shot at the big leagues. As long as he saw that as a possibility, he let baseball take an enormous toll on his academic performance. Even in his favorite course, creative writing, he only earned a C. I accused Rick of bragging that he was the only student who completed the course who didn't get at least a B. He excuses himself by saying he inherited Dad's good arm while I inherited Mom's brain. Rick's not short on brains, just on stick-to-itiveness. Mom has both. She took several courses at Southwestern, while she was working full time and raising two kids! And *she* earned A's in all of them."

"I'm not surprised. I knew she'd attended several classes, but I thought she was auditing them, not taking them for grades," responded Jim.

"When Rick finds something he wants to do," continued Jim, "I suspect he'll prove he's his mother's son. My two kids were as different as you and Rick. Barbara always did well in school, but I despaired of Dennis when he was in high school and college and only cared about hanging out with his friends. Turns out, I needn't have worried."

"What's he doing now?" asked Roberto. "I haven't seen him in years."

"He just finished law school. He's signed on for a two-year internship in Appalachia doing pro bono work. He's thriving and happy, and I couldn't be prouder."

Jim was amused watching his young friend thoroughly mopping up all the syrup on his plate with the last of his pancakes. When Roberto had finished, he pushed his plate away and looked up at Jim. "Do you mind if I ask you a question?" he hesitated. "Are you dating Mom these days?"

"We eat lunch together occasionally, but our get-togethers are not what either of us would call dating. With offices in the same building, we sometimes meet in the hall and take our sack lunches out to the plaza. She likes the place as much as I do. It's a treat listening to her stories. She knows more about northern New Mexico and its history than any guidebook to the area."

"No wonder," laughed Roberto. "We Silvas have lived in or around Cottonwood for five generations, six for Rick and me. Mom's really proud of the fact that our house is still on part of an old Spanish land grant. When Rick and I were kids, we used to get tired of her stories."

It was Jim's turn to laugh. "I remember. When I first came to Cottonwood, she gave me a wonderful old-timer's tour of the area, with you two in tow. You groaned and moaned and looked bored as only twelve-year-olds can. I loved our Sunday drives to Angel Peak, Chaco Canyon, Kennebec Pass, and all around the Four Corners. I especially appreciated her taking so much time to welcome a newcomer."

"And," said Roberto good-naturedly, "you paid her back by playing catch with us and taking us to college games."

"I didn't think of it as a payback. I got to play Saturday father, and that was fun for me. I missed my own two kids something fierce. Arranging summer visits and Christmas visits was never very satisfactory. Spending time with you two and Jolene filled a big gap in my life. She and I've remained good friends ever since."

"Ricardo and I thought you'd make a great dad. We used to try to figure out ways to make you two fall madly in love so you would become our father."

"Thank you," said Jim. "You'd have made great sons, too. But neither Jolene nor I was a candidate for romance at that time."

The waitress came around offering refills on coffee.

After she bustled away, Roberto hesitated and then asked, "You know about Jake Henderson, don't you?"

"Yes," replied Jim. "I saw quite a bit of Jake and his children when they were your neighbors. I know that the tractor accident that took your father's life happened about the same time that Jake's wife went completely over the edge." Roberto looked down at his plate, and Jim hurried to fill in the awkward silence. "I was aware of how much your mother and Jake helped each other out."

"Rick and I were older than the Henderson kids. We occasionally babysat for them after Mrs. Henderson went back East somewhere to be with her folks. That was long after Ricardo and I had given up on you and Mom."

"Sorry we disappointed you."

"When Jake and Mom started taking long walks and then asking us to watch the Henderson kids while they went out to dinner, we might have switched our allegiance if we hadn't dismissed him as out of the running. After all, he was a married man."

"Roberto, did you think Jolene and Jake were more than helpful neighbors? Adults can be friends, like your mom and I were, without being romantically involved."

"Rick and I were slow to think Mom and Jake wanted to be more than friends. As teenagers, Rick and I didn't dream that the movies and TV shows we'd seen had anything to do with us, and certainly nothing to do with our mother. After Jake and the kids left to join his wife in D.C., I don't think their names cropped up more than a few times." Roberto suddenly put his fork down and rested his elbows on the table. He spoke so softly that Jim had to strain to hear him. He sounded much younger than his twenty-three years. "If Rick and I hadn't wondered about how Mom and Jake felt about each other, and if there'd been *nothing* between the two of them, wouldn't you think we would have talked about the Hendersons more often than we did? It was as if none of us wanted to bring him into our house by saying his name."

The waitress, appearing at an opportune time, slapped a bill down on the table. "Y'all can pay at the cash register when you're through. It'll be faster that way." Jim ignored the rudeness *and* Roberto's question.

Roberto's mute plea to have his suspicions about his mother and Jake proved wrong—they probably weren't—gave Jim the second jolt of the morning. He shook his head ruefully. He would not have made Roberto and Ricardo a good father a decade ago, any more than he'd have made Jolene a good husband when he was still reeling from a divorce he hadn't expected and didn't want. He remembered what he'd told Florencio last night when once again pressed about his social life: "No entanglements for this committed bachelor, my friend. Couplehood has passed me by." He thought he'd meant what he said. Why then, could he hear Toni Hexton's voice asking, "Really? Are you so sure?"

Roberto had to fight to keep his eyes open during the rest of the meal.

Jim smiled at his young friend and picked up the check. "You need some sleep and I need to get back to Cottonwood."

ⓒ

As Jim made his way home, Toni was driving 26 miles to visit an old friend of her own.

She was more than twenty years younger than Sheila Mays, whose professional career put her in a very different world. Nevertheless, Toni had warmed to the woman immediately and come to rely on her, especially during her first year as a full-fledged academic.

Toni remembered how awkward and insecure she had felt upon arriving at Southwestern for her interview. Getting from the parking lot to the English/journalism department was an ordeal. She had to ask for directions three times. Then a frazzled secretary informed her that the department member assigned to shepherd her around campus was nowhere to be found. At that point a woman entered the departmental office. Overhearing the conversation, she raised both hands in mock horror. "That's not surprising, is it?" she said. "Professor Miller has a long history of not being where he's expected to be. I'll take her on a tour of the campus." Turning to Toni, she said, "Hi. I'm Sheila Mays."

Introductions done, she asked the secretary, "She can leave her things here in the office with you, can't she, Mary Ann?"

"Sure. They'll be behind my desk when you come back for the interview with the personnel committee."

Hesitantly, Toni handed Mary Ann her purse and briefcase. Working in chaotic, crowded newsrooms, she had learned to keep money, interview notes, and anything of value in sight at all times.

"We've got almost forty minutes," said Sheila, glancing at her watch as they headed out the door.

"As we walk around campus, I'll fill you in on some of Southwestern's odder practices—practices that are not, I think, unique to us. It's customary for selection committees to include one member from outside the department hiring a new faculty member—to keep the process honest, I suspect. In your case, I'm it. Come to think of it, it is unusual to go as far afield as the English/journalism department went in appointing me."

In answer to Toni's puzzled expression, Sheila explained. "I teach physical education courses, coach a few minor sports like archery and fencing, and run the school's intramural program." Sounding amused, she added, "In some schools PE instructors exist beyond the pale, unless they coach a major sport. I'm sure that's one of the reasons physical education departments all over the country are changing their name to Exercise Science, to counter that attitude."

Sheila continued to point out buildings, while describing the current battles among the faculty of various departments. Chuckling, she said, "For instance, the science people are arguing that their beginning courses should be full-year instead of one semester courses. The historians chime in, wanting to require year-long American, European, and world history courses. Then the sociologists argue that if both those changes were instituted, students would still be taking introductory classes into their junior year."

Toni let her companion's words wash over her without paying much attention. Subconsciously, she was more aware of the tall trees, the attractive campus, well-tended lawns, and meandering walkways. Tired from her drive and aware of how small a world she was applying to enter, she was assailed by doubts she thought she'd resolved. Did she really want to trade the competition she encountered in the newspaper world for an academic version of the same thing?

During the remainder of their tour, Sheila extolled Southwestern's virtues. Toni realized the twinkle in Sheila's eyes and the warmth in her voice showed affection for her colleagues and respect for Southwestern—however strange some of its customs might seem to a newcomer.

On the way back to the English/journalism department, Sheila pointed out signs reserving the front row of parking spaces for faculty and staff. With another laugh, she stressed the importance of displaying a much coveted "F" sticker and taking advantage of the special privilege it signified. "Otherwise, you'll be ticketed along with students hoping to usurp our rights."

Sheila, noticing that Toni was once again not sure how to take her advice, explained, "Don't get me wrong. On the whole, Southwestern has fewer class divisions between students and faculty than most colleges and universities. I think that's one of the things I most like about this place."

Sheila continued, "I've come to realize what a weather vane complaints about parking are. As long as students complain loudly about how much parking stickers cost—fifty dollars a year—and where they can park their cars more than any other issues, we're in for a calm year.

"I'm glad Professor Miller didn't show up. I'll give you many more reasons for why you'll like it here than he would have."

Without Sheila's introduction to Southwestern College, Toni later thought she might not have performed well in her interview. As they climbed the stairs to the departmental office, Sheila had warned her that some of the faculty might not welcome her right away if she ended up taking the job. "The campus is in kind of a hullabaloo right now. Some of the faculty think the college has grown up enough that it can now afford to hire only people with PhD's." *Great*, Toni thought, her doubts resurfacing, *I might as well drive back to Albuquerque right now.*

Sheila was quick to pick up on Toni's reactions. "Wait a minute. Luckily, cooler heads have prevailed. We're small enough and independent enough that we don't have to play the numbers game. Having a PhD isn't the only route to becoming a legitimate and good teacher. Southwestern, fortunately, has recognized that. As have most of the faculty. We've hired several respected faculty members because of their experience, *not* their degrees. For instance, the current political science chairman moved up the ranks from Las Cruces city councilman, to New Mexico Senator to U.S. Representative. The woman who teaches piano played with the Chicago Symphony for years until arthritis cut short her career.

"And," she'd turned to Toni, laughing, "There are others. I wouldn't be walking around campus with you today if the athletic director and the other physical education professors hadn't seen in me someone whose years of teaching high school physical education and coaching girls basketball were a reliable indication of my ability to teach and coach and contribute to their department.

"So remember that you have the qualifications we're looking for: firsthand experience as a practicing journalist as well as some graduate work. We'll want to hear about your work and how you can bring the lessons you learned in newsrooms to bear on your classrooms."

Sheila's candid remarks had allowed Toni to feel comfortable when faced with the whole staff. Instead of being put off by the tension within the department, she had focused on showcasing her strengths as a journalist. She was able to tell her interviewers she recognized both the difficulty and necessity of writing against deadlines, conducting fruitful interviews, and writing objectively even when you desperately do not want to and have trouble eliminating your own biases. And she had gotten the job, thanks in no small part to Sheila.

Over the next few years, Toni learned a great deal more about Sheila Mays—from others, not from her. While still in college, she had competed in the Olympics as a member of the U.S. fencing team. She was asked by Southwestern's biology department to teach kinesiology when the faculty member who had been teaching it resigned and his replacement was not prepared to teach the subject (an unusual sign of acceptance and respect from a "regular" academic department). There had been no intramural sports program before Sheila instigated it. Intramural games, played and refereed by the students, eventually involved almost half the students every term. The program was so successful that the college awarded Sheila its first outstanding service award. A few years later, she received the same honor from the state of New Mexico.

Now her friend lay in a hospital bed, recovering from hip surgery. Toni knew it was time to turn the tables and support Sheila.

"Hi Sheila, you're looking good for someone who just had surgery," Toni said as she entered the hospital room.

"Thanks, Toni. You brighten up this place," Sheila replied.

Toni chatted about the geology field trip with Erica and her students, and described her impatience with the usual endless meetings at the beginning of a new school year. When Sheila smiled wanly but said nothing, Toni tried switching gears, but Sheila's answers remained non-committal. The conversation faltered. Toni resorted to commenting about the weather.

Finally, Sheila's eyes lit up. She leaned forward and said, "That's what I miss most, being able to get out and stroll, or drive into the Colorado mountains, during my favorite season of the year. No hiking or driving for at least six weeks, the doctor says."

"I'll bet he outlawed fencing too," said Toni.

"Well," laughed Sheila, "I gave that up a decade ago. In fact, I almost gave it up when I was on my college's fencing team."

"Really?" asked Toni, glad to see Sheila perking up. "If I remember rightly, you were invited to audition for the U.S. Olympic team because of your collegiate triumphs."

"As the newest recruit I was assigned to room with the brashest, most unpleasant member of the team. Just before I dropped off to sleep, I heard a loud thump and automatically jumped out of bed and turned on a light. My roomie had her back to the wall and was loudly snoring. Then I saw what had made the noise. There was a small pistol lying on the floor by the head of her bed. She turned over, saw her gun on the floor, and told me what she would do to me if I told the coach. Next she told me *why* she carried a gun with her, even though she knew it was illegal. She recited a whole litany of endangering episodes she'd experienced when she became a college student—and a fencing champion. She topped that off by quipping, 'Have to travel, will carry gun.' And then she asked me if I didn't think it was better to be wrong than dead. As a shy, inexperienced freshman, I was scared to death. Believe me, I lost my enthusiasm for travel—and fencing—for the rest of that year."

Toni suddenly jumped out of her seat.

" 'Scuse me, Sheila, I'll be back in a jiff," she called back to her bewildered friend.

Toni ran down the hall to where she'd passed a public pay phone. Good luck, the phone book was intact. And even better luck, the regional directory listed a home phone number for Jim Scoop.

"*Damn*," she said to herself, when she heard his voice on an answering machine. How inconsiderate of him not to be there when she was finally ready to share some information she'd learned during yesterday afternoon's task force meeting.

"This is Toni Hexton. Nothing urgent. Call me at my office sometime Monday if you get a chance?"

Toni hung up. As she walked back to Sheila's room, she tried to stifle her disappointment that Jim had not been home.

*The plot thickens.*

On the second Monday of the fall term, Toni Hexton left her house in Ignacio at 8:25 A.M. As usual, she met almost no traffic on County Road 318. When she'd first moved up to Ignacio two years earlier, she thought she'd mind the forty-minute commute, but she didn't. It framed her days.

She loved the gently rolling hills and she never ceased to marvel at the golden outcroppings of rock visible as she rounded each curve. While letting her mind wander, examples of story leads occurred to her. They were much better than the ones she'd jotted down last night for her introductory news writing class. She would get to her office in plenty of time to add them to her notes for her ten o'clock class.

She drove into the parking lot nearest her office, not expecting to find any empty slots. She found one, right in the middle of the row reserved for faculty. She realized why a space was still miraculously vacant shortly after 9:00 on a Monday morning as she nudged her Subaru between two cars angled in opposite directions. Only after arduous effort did she manage to extricate herself, her keys, her purse, her briefcase, and a thermos through an impossibly narrow wedge between the driver's seat and the car door.

What she saw as she entered her office made her forget both her new examples and her irritation.

All four drawers of one file cabinet were wide open—and empty. Dismayed and still clutching keys, purse, briefcase, and thermos, Toni examined the rest of her ransacked office. File folders were stacked every which way on top of a two-drawer filing cabinet. Even though its lock had been forcibly opened, the drawers were shut. Except for a stray, unglued label, three paper clips, a favorite pen she'd given up as lost several years ago, and the bent lock, those drawers had also been emptied. She gazed around the room once more. Jumbled papers, files, letters, and books were scattered on every available surface.

She put keys and thermos on the windowsill. While looking for places to set her purse and briefcase, she noticed that the phone wasn't on her desk. Furious, she balanced her briefcase atop a mass of papers and files, dumped her purse on her desk chair as she moved it aside, dropped to her hands and knees, poked her head under the desk, and blindly reached towards the back wall. After two or three tries, she found the phone jack. Holding on to the cord, she twisted backwards and inched out of a second tight spot of the day.

As she uttered her third "damn," she finally located the phone. After unwinding its tangled cord, she hesitated for a minute, then dialed the security office.

"Lily, this is Toni Hexton. I need to speak with a security officer. Someone's broken into my office."

"Toni, that's terrible! Are you all right?"

"Yes, I'm fine. But my office is a mess."

"I'll patch you through to B.B. Hold on a sec."

"Ms. Hexton? Officer Jenkins here. What's happened? How can I help you?"

"My office has been ransacked. All my files and drawers have been emptied, and… and…"

Taking advantage of Toni's pause to catch her breath, Billy Bob said, "I'm nearby, ma'am. I'll be there in a jiff. You can show me the damage. Don't touch anything until I get there."

Pushing loose papers from a chair, she found a place to sit. She was still grasping the phone when Billy Bob knocked on the frame of the open door.

"You're not hurt, are you, Ms. Hexton?" asked Billy Bob. She shook her head. Billy Bob turned, motioning to Ben Jackson, whom he'd asked to accompany him. The two officers stepped into the office. At a signal from his boss, Ben closed the door behind them.

"You've brought the fingerprint kit, haven't you?"

"Yes, sir. It's all here."

"Are you sure you're okay, Ms. Hexton? You look pale."

"Yes. I'm just fine. But as you can see, my office isn't. If I look strange, it's because I'm shocked and angry. And dreading the job of re-filing all these papers. After you get whatever information you need, I'll straighten everything up and get back to work."

Billy Bob shook his head sympathetically. "I'm sorry. You can't do that. I called Chief Scoop on my way here. He wants everything left just as it is until he sees the damage for himself."

"But I've already moved a few things. I had to—or I couldn't have found the phone to call you."

"No harm done. We'll wait for Mr. Scoop. Look, you can't do anything here for a while. You're not missing a class, are you?" Toni shook her head. Billy Bob continued, "Why don't you go someplace where you can relax?"

"I brought a briefcase and thermos of coffee from home. I presume I can take *them* with me?"

"Certainly, ma'am." Billy Bob's politeness made Toni regret her caustic response to his suggestion.

"Maybe you should get a donut or something sweet to go with your coffee. Sugar is good for relieving shock."

"I'll do that. And thanks for coming so promptly."

Toni looked at her watch. She couldn't believe only twenty minutes had passed since she walked from her car to the office. "I guess it'll be good to get away from this mess for a little while."

"Ben and I'll lock up for you. Jim said he'd page me when he gets to campus. Until you hear from him, it might be best to keep quiet about the break-in. Have you talked to anyone else in your hallway?"

"No. I came straight into my office. I haven't seen anyone."

Absent-mindedly, Toni stuffed her keys in her purse, slung its strap over her shoulder, and began to walk out of the room. Billy Bob touched her elbow gently and politely handed her the briefcase and thermos.

An hour and a half later, after class, she returned to her office and found Jim waiting for her, along with Ben.

Jim greeted her. "Good morning, Toni. What a lousy way to start a week. You know Ben Jackson, don't you?"

Toni recognized Ben with a grin. "Yes, he came with Billy Bob this morning. Last winter Ben rescued me. He helped me dig my car out of an enormous snowdrift on one of the Thursday nights I stayed late with the newspaper staff. The blizzard that dumped at least a foot was bad enough. But the campus snow removers were worse. Their plow buried my car."

Toni looked away from Ben and faced Jim. "And yes, from my perspective, it *is* a lousy morning. I'll feel better when I can start cleaning up all this stuff. But Billy Bob said I should wait."

"You can start cleaning up now. We've looked all around, and taken both fingerprints and photographs. Do you have any idea yet whether anything is missing?"

"You're kidding! In all this mess?"

"I hate to make your task any harder. But I'm going to ask you to put things away very slowly. Look for any documents or letters that *aren't* here. And check your computer, too."

"I'm sure no intruder could get into my files. I used to be irked with the computer center people for insisting we have a password. Now I'm thankful!"

"Check anyway, just in case someone was savvy enough to circumvent your password. And pay special attention to whatever you kept in the file cabinet by your desk. By the looks of it, someone had to work hard to jimmy that lock."

"You think whoever broke in was hunting for something in particular?" asked Toni.

"Yes," answered Jim, "That's what it looks like."

Toni remained dubious. "To me, it looks like random vandalism."

"I don't think so. Anyone raising havoc just for the hell of it wouldn't have left your bookshelves intact."

Toni had been so concerned with the chaos that greeted her upon her arrival that she'd paid no attention to her bookshelves. Now, she saw that Jim was right. The books on the lower shelves hadn't been touched. But the books on the top shelf tilted precariously; below them, books lay on the floor amidst shards of tan and white stone.

"Hey, my favorite bookends. Erica's geology students presented them to me just last Wednesday. My reward for two hard weeks of work at their summer field school. I'll be sick if they've been destroyed. They were quite an improvement over the flimsy metal ones supplied by the college. They were made of some kind of sandstone whose name I can't remember."

"Metamorphic sandstone," said Jim, quietly and matter-of-factly.

"Uh huh." Toni arched her eyebrows. Jim Scoop was proving to be well informed about many things. She was amused at herself for wanting—now, of all times—to tell Erica to stop classifying Jim Scoop as a dumb cop.

While Jim and Toni were talking, Ben stepped gingerly over and around the papers on the floor. He leaned down, picked up a chiseled rectangle of striated white and tan rock. "Is this one of your bookends?" he asked, handing it to her. "I don't see the other one."

"That's probably what those pieces are from. One of the geology students brought the set of bookends to me last week all wrapped up. When she handed me the package, I didn't expect it to be so heavy, and I dropped it. One of the bookends broke. If it got thrown on the floor, my glue job might not have held up."

"If we find it in pieces, I'm a whiz with superglue," said Jim, smiling as he pulled a small notebook from his shirt pocket and began writing.

From years in newsrooms and classrooms, Toni had acquired the ability to read upside down. She watched as Jim printed, left-handedly but neatly: "MISSING ITEMS-RM 206, NEW MAIN." Next to a (1), he wrote 'sandstone bookend, probably broken.' Toni watched him make a vertical list of numerals from 2 to 10 below the 1.

It was Toni's turn to smile. "I hope I'm not going to be able to find nine more things destroyed or missing for you to put on that list!"

"If you come across anything you don't expect, no matter how insignificant it seems, call me. Make a list for yourself, but don't keep it here in the office."

Toni glanced quizzically at Jim.

"I know, this seems like overkill. But at this stage of our investigation, I don't want to leave any stone unturned." Jim grimaced. "No pun intended."

"Jim," replied Toni with asperity, "until I've finished re-filing all this stuff," pointing to the papers strewn about, "there's no way I'm going to know what is here and what isn't."

"True, but if you notice *any*thing peculiar, do get in touch—immediately."

While Jim pulled a business card out of his shirt pocket and handed it to Toni, she barked, "My whole office looks peculiar!"

"Agreed. It seems most likely that whoever did this was looking for something specific. As soon as you're sure something is missing and not just tossed about, let me know. Toni, I'll leave you to your task. But before I go, I'd like you to give me a detailed schedule for the rest of your day."

Toni frowned at Jim and said, "Oh my god, you sound like my big brother. Between his teasing and his over-protectiveness, he used to drive me nuts."

"Toni, protectiveness is part of my job description!"

A trace of a grin crossed Toni's face. "Sorting through all of *this* is not part of my job description. My schedule? It's simple. I'm meeting Erica for a quick lunch in the snack bar at twelve. Then I have classes at two and three, both in this building. In between lunch and my classes, I have office hours, though I'll probably snarl at anybody who wants to see me today."

Ben, beginning to feel like a third wheel, addressed Jim. "Mr. Scoop, should I take the fingerprint kit back to your office?"

"Yes, and thanks for your help. You can continue on your rounds now."

"I'll be leaving also, Toni, as soon as I jot down your schedule. When you're through here, I would appreciate your calling me if you go anywhere other than the cafeteria and your classes."

Toni half turned away from Jim. "Should I report to you when I go to the ladies room?"

Jim suppressed a smile. "No. I just don't want you wandering around campus for the rest of the day."

@

Toni was glad to have an excuse to leave her office to meet Erica for lunch. She saw Billy Bob turning the corner at the end of the hall-way and Ben talking to the departmental secretary, Mary Ann. Really, Jim was going overboard. She felt more stalked than protected.

As soon as she ran into Erica outside the Union Building, she launched into a description of her morning, starting with her parking problem. Erica quit laughing when she heard about the vandalism.

"Toni, is anything missing?" she asked as they placed their orders.

"You're the second person who's asked me that in the last hour. I don't know yet. I've just begun looking. If I finish sorting before I give up for the day—and that's a big *if*—I may find out if anything's been taken. As long as I have to look at every piece of paper, I decided I might as well re-organize. My way of naming files has turned out not to be nearly as sensible as I thought it was! I can't even imagine why I labeled some of the files as I did or what could possibly have been in them."

Erica, looking sympathetic between bites of a giant cheeseburger, said, "I almost think I prefer grading papers and attending meetings to filing."

Billy Bob and Ben passed by Toni and Erica with heavily laden trays and sat down two tables away. Billy Bob quickly got up, walked over, and addressed Toni, "How're you doing?"

"Better. Still pretty upset, though. That donut you suggested did seem to help. I've made *some* headway. Thanks for asking, and I hope you catch the s-o-b."

As Billy Bob returned to his lunch, Erica said, "B.B.'s a good guy.

He's hardly a typical cop."

Toni, smiling at hearing Erica echo her phrase, thought, *He's not the only one.* For some reason, she couldn't bring herself to voice her comment aloud. Erica continued, "Maybe you could ask B.B. to engage in a bit of police brutality when he catches the scoundrel."

"Or maybe I should just ask him to bring me the guy, along with a horsewhip! Frankly, I hope he's not enrolled in one of my classes this term."

"If the culprit is caught, I'm sure he—*or she*—will be disenrolled and expelled."

For the remainder of their lunch, Toni and Erica pondered why the task force was unearthing no claimants to fifty thousand dollars and the chance to win Walt Asher's eternal gratitude. As for their fellow committee members, they agreed in liking Sarah, appreciating Lloyd's wry humor, finding Steve less stiff than they'd expected, and finding Jeff's earnestness endearing.

Back in her office, Toni collected what she needed for her afternoon classes and then tackled the chaos. Just before she had to leave for her two o'clock, she realized she had reassembled only thirteen of last year's sixteen personnel committee files. Should she call Jim? Not yet, she decided, since the missing papers and files might yet show up.

On her way to class, Toni stopped in the journalism office. She did a double take when she noticed Billy Bob sitting in the chair beside the departmental secretary's desk. She addressed Mary Ann curtly. "I've had a hectic morning. If you're not too busy, could you run off thirty copies of this handout I need for my two o'clock class?"

Mary Ann, puzzled by Toni's unusual brusqueness, stood up slowly, and took the sheet Toni handed her. "Sure, no problem."

"Hello again, Ms. Hexton," Billy Bob said. "I'm on my way out. I just came by to invite my cousin Mary Ann and her husband for dinner on Saturday."

Billy Bob's warm smile and parting words made Toni regret her rudeness, for the second time that day. Like most of her faculty friends, she had moved often and far away from family. Being reminded of the rich social fabric connecting many of the non-teaching staff members at Southwestern made her feel petty.

After gathering the still warm photocopies from Mary Ann, Toni walked in with the stragglers for her two o'clock class. The hour passed slowly. She kept envisioning her cluttered office, and had to force herself to follow her notes and respond appropriately to students' comments and questions.

Toni did a slightly better job of forgetting her worries during her three o'clock class. For the first Monday of a new term, the students were uncharacteristically ready to go. In fact, they were eager. If Toni hadn't been preoccupied, wondering about the three missing files, she'd have been delighted with the class. The discussion was lively. The students challenged each other's interpretations. They even argued about style as well as ideas—something most classes noticed only after she'd hammered away about its importance for months.

As the students exited the classroom, Toni saw two campus police officers walking past. Her resentment resurfaced. Didn't they have other things to do today besides watching over her?

She started looking for the missing papers and files as soon as she returned to her office. She examined every loose piece of paper, two or even three times. Reluctantly, she called Jim. Frustrated about the theft—and being followed so closely—Toni spoke angrily. "I've called for two reasons: first, to let you know there *is* something missing, and second, to register a complaint."

"Okay, shoot," said Jim. "Tell me what's missing first."

"Three promotion and tenure files." Toni realized she needed to explain. "Last year I was a member of the college-wide PT committee. I'm embarrassed to say, I still have all the documents. I should have returned them to Vice-President Hamill at the end of the school year, but I didn't. I had sixteen folders. Now, three of them are missing."

"Do you know whose?"

"Do you think that's really important?" Hearing no answer from Jim, Toni continued. "Sorry I asked; you'll tell me everything's important, won't you?"

Jim chuckled. "That shouldn't surprise *you*. After all, we cops have lots in common with you journalists. We collect information indiscriminately, assuming that anything and everything *might* be important."

"Touché." Toni paused. "Just a minute and I can tell you whose files have been taken." Setting the phone down, Toni put the remaining folders back in alphabetical order and then scanned through them. "Interesting," she muttered, as much to herself as to Jim, "As far as I can tell at a quick glance, the thirteen files that are here *are* complete. But everything pertaining to Browning, March, and Sterling is gone, including the folders that held their résumés, their departments' evaluations, and the committee's deliberations."

"What did your committee decide about each of those people?"

"We recommended promoting Browning to full professor, and promoting March to associate professor with tenure. We agreed with Sterling's department that he should be let go and given a one-year terminal contract."

"I take it being let go isn't quite as bad as being fired?"

"Unless someone is guilty of a crime, you don't fire a professor so late in the academic year that he'd have a hard time getting another job."

"Perhaps Sterling wouldn't have appreciated your committee's generosity. Is there any chance he could have come a-hunting?"

"I don't think so. Morgan Sterling's a mild-mannered man. He evidently wasn't very surprised to learn that he wouldn't be retained. His heart is in consulting, not teaching. I hear he's joining some economic think-tank in D.C. in January."

"Can you think of anyone else who might have wanted to see those files?"

"No. The college is so small that information about who's promoted and retained—and who isn't—is no secret, particularly at this late date. President Asher and Vice-President Hamill met with everyone who was up for promotion last spring. Besides, most of what's documented is public knowledge. Or it can be for anyone who cares to find out."

"Try to remember if there was anything in those particular files that someone might want to see…or destroy. It's hard to imagine why both Brown's and March's files were taken. When and how and where they turn up may give us a clue, not only about who grabbed all three files, but why they were selected in the first place."

"But why? Won't it be almost impossible to find them now?"

"I hope not. I'll worry about locating them. You worry about what was in them." Jim paused. "Now. Your complaint?"

"I'm constantly being followed—by two men in blue. Why?"

"Out of concern for your safety."

"So you're having me spied on—and I don't like it! Next thing I suppose you'll have B.B. and Ben come to all my classes, sneak into the back row, and glare at me for an hour!"

"We won't go *that* far… Toni, wait, before you splutter and swear at me, think about what's happened. Your desk and files have been ransacked. You and Erica and your committee are looking for an elusive author. Not very successfully, I understand."

It was a good thing Jim couldn't see Toni's face or read her mind. She didn't like the fact that he must be discussing the task force's progress—or lack of it—with Walt.

Oblivious to Toni's reaction, Jim reiterated, "As I explained, I'm concerned for your safety."

"I can't believe my safety is in question. We faculty may gripe about committee work, but we consider it tedious, not dangerous. As murder mysteries go, *Academic Awards* is not very violent or filled with angry threats."

"Except for the description of the actual death blows. The first one was fatal if you remember. The next thirty-seven were vicious, the acts of a man out of control. If the writer feels the same kind of anger the young killer felt…"

"Not all writers identify with their characters, you know," interrupted Toni, immediately regretting the teacherly tone that crept into her voice. "I'm sorry to lapse into lecture mode, Jim, but I don't *like* being followed. It makes me feel as if I've done something wrong."

"Nevertheless, until we get the facts ma'am…" said Jim, imitating Sergeant Friday so well that Toni laughed in spite of herself. "Expect to see Ben or B.B. more often than you'd like the next couple of days. I hope we'll have found the missing author and the person who broke into your office by then. Until we do, you may encounter the boys in blue in unexpected places." Jim paused and then asked in a non-official voice, "You've had a long, hard day. How about letting me take you out to supper tonight?"

"Jim, you don't have to do that."

"I know I don't *have to*, but I'd like to. I promise to behave like a gentleman and not a cop."

"Thanks, that would be nice. I certainly don't feel like cooking— or doing anything that smacks of housework."

"I'll be outside your office then, in an unmarked car, at 5:30. Is that all right?"

"Could you make it 6:30? I think by then I will have restored order here. I'd like to be able to grade some papers and prepare Tuesday's classes, knowing that I won't have to return to chaos tomorrow."

"Fine. How about Ricardo's Grill? The menu is limited, but the food is quite good. While you're at work, envision yourself sitting in front of a mouth-watering steak, a baked potato with all the trimmings, a luscious salad and a thick slice of carrot cake."

"I don't think I could eat all that *and* a whole piece of cake," responded Toni. After Jim hung up, she spent the next hour and a half in a better mood than she could account for.

☉

At 6:29 Toni set the last handful of unsorted papers in a single pile on her cleared desk.

As she bent over to pick up her purse and thermos, two men appeared simultaneously in her doorway. One man, pushing a commercial sized vacuum cleaner, said, "If you're ready, Ms. Hexton, I can give your rug a good cleaning now." The other, wearing a cream-colored dress shirt, and dark olive corduroys, said nothing.

Toni thanked the custodian, and for the third time that day greeted Jim. "I was on my way out to meet you. You didn't need to come in."

"I decided I should act the part of a real gentleman and pick you up at your door." His eyes scanned the room. "Wow, you've made real headway here."

Toni pointed to the stack still on her desk. "I'd hoped to get through everything, but I didn't. Those will be waiting for me tomorrow."

As they walked to their cars, she said, "I've decided there's one good side to having my office ransacked. I've filled and emptied my wastebasket three times. I didn't realize I'd accumulated so much stuff, mostly things I don't need to keep."

Seeing Jim's car next to hers, Toni offered to follow him to Ricardo's. "No need," he said, "I'll be happy to drive you back here after dinner."

Twenty minutes later they were seated in the restaurant with a carafe of red wine and two glasses.

Toni took a sip, smiled warmly, and commented, "After today's events, a meal, produced with no effort on my part, is very welcome. Thank you."

"I'm glad to see you in a better mood than when we last talked. Other than giving your office a thorough house cleaning, did anything else good happen today?"

"Yes, as a matter of fact. My three o'clock class on editorial writing was great! I'd assigned the students a batch of editorials to analyze.

They'd read them a lot more critically than I expected so early in the term. They weren't ready to end the discussion, and on a normal day, I wouldn't have been either."

"Too bad you had to go back to your office after that high note," replied Jim, as a waiter placed steaks and salads on the table. "Incidentally, I need to apologize to you."

"Whatever for? If anyone needs to apologize, I should. There was no need for me to get so huffy with you. You were just…"

Jim interrupted. "Doing my job?"

"Yes."

"If I'd been doing my job better, I would have called you back yesterday. The trouble is I heard the whole message for the first time this afternoon. When I heard someone—I didn't recognize your voice—say there was no urgency, I didn't bother to replay it. I have an excuse, but it's not a good one. When I returned home from a quick trip to Albuquerque on Saturday, I was hot and tired. I play my messages while I shower—it's a bad habit I have—and yours must have been drowned out."

"Next time I'll shout."

"You said it wasn't urgent, but you sounded worried."

"I was and I guess I still am. Jim, did you know that Richard Frankel has guns?"

"No, I didn't *know* that. But I can't say I'm surprised."

"Oh?" Toni, who had never liked guns, sounded skeptical.

"Many westerners—and Frankel is a born and bred westerner— own guns. They hunt. They belong to gun clubs. Even professors. Does Frankel's having a gun seem especially ominous?"

"Yes. It's not just one gun. He's got a whole arsenal in his den, according to Lloyd Reasoner who interviewed Richard at home."

"Is he one of your suspects?"

"Yes, and the task force decided to talk to him even before we knew about his guns."

"Why? He seems unlikely."

"If you mean out of touch with Southwestern life, yes, he is. But he fancies himself an accomplished writer. And he knows mysteries better than anyone else on campus."

"Even you and Erica?"

"For a mere policeman you know an awful lot about the faculty."

Jim started to speak.

"Don't say it. It's your job."

Jim's laugh, deep and natural, erased the last of Toni's reserve.

"Anyway, the task force decided we needed to interview Richard. Although, if he *had* written *Academic Awards*, he would have admitted it immediately when the president questioned the faculty. And he would have bragged to anyone he could corner."

"What worried you so much about him—before you knew he had several guns?"

"By the time Sunday night rolled around, I realized I'd probably overreacted when I called you. I wouldn't have minded if you'd never heard my message."

"Do the other committee members share your concern?"

"I doubt it. I wasn't concerned myself until after our meeting was over. We all agreed that he's a long shot. If we had a more viable candidate, he wouldn't still be in the hopper. I got spooked because he seems awfully familiar with guns. And if he has some reason not to claim his contest winnings, that makes me more uneasy."

During dinner Jim and Toni talked about teaching. She learned not only that he'd studied philosophy in graduate school, but that he'd also been a T.A.—and liked teaching. They were still talking about Toni's experience working for the *Albuquerque Journal* when dessert arrived: one large piece of carrot cake with two forks.

Afterwards, she reached around her chair for her purse. Jim's hand circled her wrist. "This is my treat. Besides, we are being watched. We're not the only people from Southwestern here tonight. I think one of the women works in the accounts payable office. I'm not sure who the other one is. But they have been watching us all evening, obviously fascinated."

Toni turned just far enough to see who they were. Looking quickly back at Jim, she said, "Uh oh, they're champion gossips."

"Let them gossip. Since I'm going to be dogging your steps—along with my boys in blue—let them imagine a burgeoning romance. It'll provide a cover for my presence in your vicinity. I think your editor, Betty Frost, is already a bit suspicious about my visits to the newspaper office. But Betty, I know, doesn't gossip."

"As editor she can't afford to. Gad, news of our so-called date will have traveled all through the secretarial grapevine by tomorrow morning!"

"Not a problem, unless, of course, it embarrasses you."

"No. Why would it?"

Jim ignored her question. "Are you willing to play along then? It really will make things simpler until we've nabbed the author."

"I guess so. And thanks again for dinner. Would you drive me back to my car now? I need to grade the papers I collected today. I've found that returning graded papers immediately guarantees better work."

Jim hesitated and, not looking at Toni, said, "I'm not sure that's a good idea."

"What isn't a good idea? Your driving me to campus? Or my grading papers?"

"Neither. I don't like the idea of your driving to Ignacio at night."

"For heaven's sake, why not?"

"You know, don't you, that Asher's office has also been broken into?"

*Whoa*, thought Jim to himself. *That's not information I should be sharing.*

"I hadn't heard. That does complicate things, doesn't it?"

"Yes. Quite a bit," replied Jim.

Toni, responding to the guilty shadow that spread across Jim's face, answered a question he hadn't asked. "You don't need to ask me not to tell anyone. I won't."

Jim visibly relaxed. "Thanks. I do need, however, to convince you that there's reason for caution."

Toni looked at Jim, perplexed.

"I don't suppose I'm making a lot of sense. You see guns as inherently dangerous. I see your driving home on unlighted rural roads at night as potentially dangerous."

Jim put his elbows on the table, brought his hands together, rested his chin on his knuckles, and addressed Toni softly and seriously. "I have no leads on who might have broken into your office or the president's. And I don't know whether we're looking for one person or two. Either way, these break-ins have me worried. There may be a simple explanation for them, but until I know that there is, I have to be prepared for any number of bad scenes."

Leaning back and unclenching his fists, he smiled. "It's part of my job description." As a slow smile spread across Toni's face, he resumed. "At least being so suspicious is an antidote to boredom—one of the hazards of my new night patrols. Seriously, a week ago I thought the possibility of potential violence was ridiculous. Now I'm not so sure."

Skeptical, Toni raised her eyebrows.

"You think someone's rifling through my files, and taking off with three personnel folders, constitutes potential violence?"

"Probably not. But just on the off chance it does, I've got to be cautious. After all, it's part of my job description to worry about the college's president and his newly appointed task force."

"I think you're being paranoid."

"Maybe so, maybe not. Let me tell you about a conversation I had with an old chum on the Albuquerque police force. He's going around the state talking to school districts about the exponential increase in school violence in the last decade. He was in Farmington last Monday. We had dinner together. He convinced me I was being naïve to think of Southwestern as a calm oasis away from crime, and that was *before* anyone broke into any offices.

"After Florencio gave me a whole raft of gruesome details and statistics, I told him about Southwestern's own murder, albeit a fictional one. I waxed facetious, but my friend scared me with his questions and several equally bad scenarios. I had plenty of time today to imagine them all, and to decide how to proceed with my investigations."

"And you concluded what?"

"That you shouldn't drive home alone tonight or be home alone either."

"So?" Toni's voice rose in irritation. "Where do you expect me to spend the night? Cottonwood isn't exactly filled with motels, and I wouldn't want to spend the money for one anyway. Jim, you're being a fuss-budget. And, you promised not to play the heavy if I came to dinner with you."

"I know. Sorry. But as I said, I've spent the afternoon becoming more and more uneasy. Being stared at tonight hasn't helped, though I grant you those two ladies don't look intent on doing you bodily harm. But, their scrutiny throughout dinner reminded me that I *am* a policeman and one of my responsibilities *is* ensuring your safety."

"Well, you or B.B. or Ben can't be with me every minute. So what do you propose?"

"I propose that you spend the night at my house."

"Aren't you carrying this romantic charade a little too far? Besides, I never spend the night with a guy on the first date."

Toni laughed, but Jim didn't. "Look, you won't be spending the night with me. I'll be on patrol from ten until four in the morning. So, you can have a desk and a bed all to yourself, and I'll flop on the couch when I get home."

"Okay, okay. On one condition."

"What's that?"

"That you can loan me a toothbrush."

Toni laughed again, and this time, Jim did smile. "Agreed. I'll even give you a brand new one!"

Toni did not tell Jim that after her days as a cub reporter, she always carried an extra set of clean underwear in her briefcase or that, while cleaning out her office, she'd thrown away a very old, very grungy toothbrush.

When they arrived at his house, Jim showed Toni around. He ceremoniously unwrapped a new, plastic covered toothbrush and handed it to her. He offered to clear a space on his desk in the living room. She said she'd just as soon work at the kitchen table and dilute the effects of the wine with some tea.

Jim showed her where the teakettle and tea bags were, went back upstairs to change into his uniform and slipped out of the house without a word.

After taking a few sips of tea and putting the papers she intended to grade on the kitchen table, Toni ambled into the living room. She was restless, and curious. The living room was inviting: large, well lit, and comfortably furnished. Three big windows looked out onto the tree-lined street. The interior walls were fitted with floor-to-ceiling bookshelves.

Toni's tea was cold. She felt very tired and slightly queasy. She found a can of ginger ale in the refrigerator. Can in hand and unable to concentrate on her own work, she returned to the living room and slowly perused the titles of Jim's books. One set of shelves was filled with books on U.S. and world history. Another contained general guides to the Southwest, in addition to specific books on botany, birds, and geology, including Erica's *Landforms of Northern New Mexico.*

On the bottom shelf were books by Aristotle, Plato, Kant, and David Hume, as well as philosophy textbooks. She almost laughed aloud when she saw the wide range of biographies on the shelf behind his desk. In addition to biographies of presidents, statesmen, explorers, and baseball players, there were at least a dozen of criminals. She made a note to remember to chide Jim on his collection, surely as incriminating as Richard Frankel's guns.

Toni shook her head and thought, "Stop impersonating Kinsey

Millhone. I don't need to poke into everything just because I have the opportunity. What I need to do is read the students' news stories and editorials."

She walked back into the kitchen, made herself another cup of tea, and started in on her papers. After she finished the first one, she looked up and noticed a calendar with lovely old sepia prints of the Grand Canyon. Of course, she had to get up and thumb through all twelve months.

Before Toni was halfway through the first stack of papers, she found her eyes closing. Sleep would do her good and she could, despite what she'd said to Jim, put off her grading until tomorrow.

She climbed the stairs, showered, and put on the terry cloth robe she found hanging on the hook in the bathroom. When she went to turn off the light, she thumbed through the books sitting next to the bedside lamp: essays by Wendell Barry, a tattered copy of Pogo cartoons (with what she surmised was his father's name on the flyleaf), and Russell Baker's *Growing Up.* Full of food and drink and glimpses into someone else's life, she fell asleep.

*Killing two birds with one stone.*

Toni woke up to smells of freshly brewing coffee and frying bacon. It took her a few minutes to remember where she was. Wishing she had a clean blouse, she dressed in a hurry and went downstairs. She found Jim standing before the stove. "Good morning, Jim. I didn't expect breakfast. It smells wonderful!"

"Good morning, Toni. Sleep well? How would you like your eggs?"

"However you're having yours."

"Sunny side up and nervous."

"Hmm...would it be too much trouble to scramble mine?"

"Not at all. How about some toast?"

"Great. But let me help."

Jim, pointing to a loaf of bread on the counter and a bread knife next to it, said, "Slice as many pieces as you want for yourself—I'll take two."

"Where did you get this bread?" she asked, sniffing a hefty oblong loaf before slicing four pieces. "It doesn't look like anything I've ever seen at Ignacio's IGA.

"A new bakery just opened in Cottonwood last week," answered Jim, "and I'm doing my best to keep it in business. That's ciabatta bread. It makes great toast."

Toni sat down at a neatly set round table after putting four slices of bread in a big, elegant toaster. "Any excitement last night? Did you catch anyone breaking and entering, or sneaking into the library to write the great American novel?"

"Nope. Not only didn't I catch anyone, not a single thing out of the ordinary happened. I did stick around campus until shortly before four, came home, got a short nap, and woke up surprisingly hungry after last night's meal. How about you? Did you finish your grading?"

"No, I gave up. Yesterday was more tiring than I realized."

While Jim served eggs and bacon, Toni poured them each a cup of coffee and buttered the toast.

After a companionable silence, Jim said, "I have a suggestion. Wait, hear me out before you decide it's a stupid plan. I don't like the idea of your being home alone just now—as I told you several times last night."

Toni nodded her head vigorously, unable to speak with a mouthful of eggs.

"Why don't you stay with Erica for a few days?"

"I can't do that."

"Why not? You two are good friends, aren't you? I can't see her objecting."

"Erica's my best friend, and she wouldn't object. But I would—for two reasons. Being away from home for a night was hard—not that the accommodations at this B and B aren't first class," said Toni, between bites. "Mainly though, Erica and I couldn't keep from talking shop into the wee hours. It's hard enough to get our regular work done now that we're involved in this author hunt without being in the same house."

"Is there anyone else you could stay with until this mess gets cleared up? I'm serious; you are pretty isolated in your rural hideaway."

"That hideaway, as you call it, will make it harder for someone to find me. And how do you know where I live?"

"The usual way. I looked in the college directory and then Googled a map of Ignacio. That might have taken me a whole minute. If I could do that, so could anyone determined to get to you. You're so far out of town, you don't even have the protection of neighboring houses." Seeing Toni looking adamant, Jim changed gears. "How about staying in the college guest house for a few days? I checked; there won't be any visitors staying overnight until the end of the month so you'd have the place to yourself."

"I absolutely won't stay on campus. And I still think your idea of my needing protection is just plain silly." Toni glanced at her watch. "Yipes, it's already after eight. I told Sheila I'd swing by the hospital this morning for a visit on my way to campus."

"How's she doing?"

"Pretty well, considering. Her only complaint is with her daily P.T. sessions. She says P.T. really stands for pure torture, not physical therapy."

"In my experience, physical therapists tell you not to do anything that hurts."

"The trouble is that they have to take you over your pain threshold to find out where that threshold is! And according to Sheila, her therapist seems to delight in finding new and different contortions to test where and when she finds the pain intolerable. I told her I'd come in the morning to be sure to see her before she's moved to the hospital's assisted care center."

"Not something she's looking forward to, I'm sure. But I suppose living alone, she can't go home yet." Jim paused. "Unless…"

"Unless," said Toni, completing Jim's thought, "I agree to stay with her. Isn't that what you were going to say?"

"Yes, and you must admit it's a good suggestion. When I drove Sheila to the hospital before her operation, she told me she was dreading a long convalescence in rehabilitation more than the operation itself."

"I didn't realize you were friends," Toni said in surprise.

"Yes, we are, and have been for a long time," Jim responded with a smile. "Your staying with Sheila would solve two—no three—problems. Sheila's, and yours, and mine. Let me drive you to Farmington and see what Sheila has to say about our proposal."

"It's more *your* proposal than mine, but I suppose you know you've trapped me. I'd do anything to help Sheila. She hates the prospect of what she calls a halfway house for the injured and elderly." Toni got up and carried dishes to the sink. Jim washed them and set them in the drainer.

☙

Jim Scoop pulled into the parking lot of the San Juan Regional Medical Center a few minutes before nine. Toni headed straight for Sheila's room with Jim right behind her. Sheila, her short grey hair neatly combed, was sitting upright, with the morning paper spread over her knees.

"Good morning, Sheila. Do you really feel as cheerful as you look?" asked Toni.

"I do, especially since you brought my friend Jim with you. What a treat to have two early morning visitors. Visiting hours don't start until eleven. How did you sneak past the ogre at the nurses' station?"

"Quickly," answered Toni at the same time Jim said, "stealthily." He walked to the side of the bed and studied Sheila for a moment. "I do believe you're mending. Your color is much better than when I was here the middle of last week. And you sound like your perky self."

"You came right after my physical therapy session—and a walk. I was sore, exhausted, and bored. I was clocked on my walker. I logged a whole mile around the circumference of the hospital's minuscule gym. I swear I'll never be bored again after I get out of here!"

"Sheila," asked Toni, "are you still scheduled to move over to the rehabilitation wing of the hospital tomorrow?"

"Yes. I *should* be glad to get out of the hospital, but I'm still dreading that place. I hear you can't go outside without a full-time, fully licensed nurse." Sheila grimaced, and then shrugged her shoulders. "They've promised me, though, that if all goes well, I'll only be incarcerated for ten or twelve days."

Jim asked, "Would you like to go home tomorrow?"

"I'd love to, but my doctor says no."

"I take it he would give permission if someone were there with you?"

"But…"

Jim interrupted, looking first at Toni, who nodded, and then, with a broad smile, he looked directly at Sheila. "No buts. Toni is offering to stay at your house until you can get around by yourself. If the doctor okays it, I'll come get you tomorrow."

Sheila glanced up at Toni and noticed that her friend appeared to be mesmerized by Jim's smile. "Are you sure you're willing, Toni?" she asked. "Jim hasn't strong-armed you, has he?"

"Yes to your first question, and partly yes, partly no to your second one. I'll be happy to take you out of this place. Jim's motives are much less pure than mine. He'd like to keep me out of harm's way. He's convinced I'm in danger."

"Whatever for?" asked Sheila, peering worriedly at Toni.

"You have heard," said Jim, "about Southwestern's recent crisis, haven't you?"

"You mean about the college's biggest and latest benefactor who seems to have vanished into thin air?" asked Sheila.

"Yes, and about the task force Walt's appointed to hunt him or her down?" answered Jim. "Toni and Erica have the pleasure—or honor—of chairing it. Two new mysteries have now surfaced. Both Walt and Toni's offices have been broken into…"

"Really? Are you all right, Toni?" Sheila looked concerned.

"Yes, I'm fine. But my office was trashed and I lost most of a day putting it back to rights. Exactly what happened in Walt's office I don't know. I'm not privy to that information." Toni glanced at Jim in mock indignation.

Jim, struggling to conceal a smile, addressed Toni. "Some day all will be revealed. But not yet."

"Frankly," said Jim, turning his attention to Sheila. "I'm more worried than Toni. She's especially vulnerable, since she lives alone out in the boondocks. So you see, getting you two together solves two problems."

"I'll be more than happy to have Toni as a house guest."

Toni laughed. "Good, so long as you'll submit to a little care-taking."

Sheila beamed. "It'll be wonderful to be home. And to have your company. Thank you, Toni."

Jim left to persuade the reluctant charge nurse to put him in touch with Sheila's doctor right away. He interrupted his rounds to talk briefly with Toni and Jim and to assure his patient that yes, she could go home *if* she was doing as well tomorrow as she was today and as long as she would not be alone around the clock.

After bidding Jim and Toni good-bye, Sheila had a big grin on her face. She was happy two of her favorite people had teamed up to make it possible for her to avoid spending a week or more at Mayflower House.

## 10

*A homecoming, more office visits, another interview, and Nick at night.*

Jim delivered Sheila to her house on Wednesday afternoon.

The next morning Toni watched nervously as Sheila hobbled to the nook they had made for her in the living room.

"Don't look so worried," said Sheila. "I'm going to be fine while you're away. And it's good for me to walk around some."

"You won't try the stairs until I'm back tonight, will you?"

"No, I've got everything I need right here: books, magazines, crossword puzzles, and the TV remote. I also have my radio handy so I can catch Rockies baseball." Sheila pointed towards her lap. "Jim brought me this when he hauled me home from the hospital yesterday. I promised him to wear the thing and keep my cordless phone in one of its handy pockets. I'll holler for help if I get in trouble."

Toni leaned over to examine the carpenter's apron Sheila was wearing. "What a clever gift!"

"I've known Jim for eleven years. He has many virtues. I could tell you stories…"

Toni took the opportunity to interrupt as Sheila's voice dropped and she paused. "Is there anything we need from the grocery?"

"No, we don't *need* anything. But if you have time to stop, I am craving some chocolate chip cookies. Hospital desserts must be made out of sawdust."

"The store's right on my way and I'll be glad to stop. Anything else?"

Sheila shook her head, jumped as the phone rang in its nesting place, and then frowned. "There better be a way to turn down the sound as long as I'm *wearing* my telephone."

"Hello. Oh, hi, Erica. … Yes, it's great to be home. … Yes, Toni's here. She spoiled me by making blueberry pancakes for my first breakfast. And she's left an enormous salad in the fridge."

Sheila thrust the phone towards Toni. "Here, it's Erica for you."

"Hi, Erica, what's up? And how did you know I was here?"

"I tried your house, and then your office. When I couldn't rouse you at either place I called your secretary. She told me you were at Sheila's."

Sheila shouted from the background, "Without a little help from my friends, I wouldn't have been sprung from the hospital!"

"Could you stop by my office when you get to campus? I really need to talk to you."

"Sure, I'm on my way now."

Toni returned the phone to Sheila, gathered her purse and briefcase, and, wondering what Erica sounded so frantic about, hurried out the door. "It's my newspaper night, but I'll be here for supper—with cookies—before I go back to campus. Have a good day."

☺

Toni showed up in Erica's office fifteen minutes later.

"Okay, what was so urgent that you tracked me down at Sheila's?"

"There's been a third break-in."

"Don't tell me someone's broken into your office, too?"

"Uh huh. My damage isn't nearly as visible as yours though. It's only my papers that were tampered with. Nothing was broken and my office isn't in shambles. This morning when I looked for my task force notes, I couldn't find them."

Toni pointed at a three-tiered tray jammed with papers, files, and loose notes sitting at the back of Erica's desk. Amused, Toni looked askance at the overflowing tray.

"Toni, not everyone is as neat as you. Let me finish telling you about my search for the notes."

Erica blew out a whispered "whew," sighed, and then continued. "My first reaction when I didn't see the notes was that I might have stuffed them between other papers—though I wasn't likely to have done that—instead of placing them at the top of the stack in the top tray. *That* tray is for current stuff."

Toni smiled at her friend and nodded encouragingly.

"You may not recognize it, but I *do* have a system. Last night at supper, I realized I'd put my task force notes where anyone could see them. First thing this morning, I planned to move them where they'd be out of sight. But they weren't at the top of the heap. Nor were they *anywhere* in that stack. And they weren't in the stacks below, either. I examined every piece of paper, and everything in every file, four or five times before I called. No luck. No task force notes there, or in the drawers of my desk, or even in my spare briefcase where I keep nothing but instructions and information I need for geology labs. But in addition to the task force notes, I found something else missing."

Erica was talking so fast and so breathlessly that Toni put up a hand. "Slow down, Erica. How did you find out your notes were gone?"

"Whoever broke in mixed up all the stuff I had carefully divided. I had to decide all over again where each thing belonged: in the 'should-have-been-done-last-week' or the 'to-do-this-week,' or 'if-I-put-it-off-another-week-I-can-toss-it" stack. Seriously, Toni, don't look at me like that; have you ever seen a better system?"

Toni laughed aloud. "No, and with *that* system, you'll end up an administrator yet. Seriously, though, what *else* was missing?"

"Then I remembered I'd gotten the file containing all my old beginning geology tests out of the lockable drawer in my desk last night, and put it on top of the topmost tray. That whole file is missing, and so are my task force notes. They should have been underneath the test file. As far as the tests are concerned, I figure some poor schmuck will be out of luck, since I never ask the same questions in the same way twice. But the notes are another matter. What still bothers me most is wondering who could have them. We can't afford to have our speculations in anyone else's hands."

"You're not kidding. That would be awful," said Toni.

"And embarrassing, immoral, and maybe even illegal. After all, we've damned several of our esteemed colleagues on the basis of very slight suspicions! But before I get too worked up, let me know whether someone absconded with your task force notes also."

"No wonder you're worried," said Toni. "Have you called security?"

"No, I wanted to talk to you first."

"Why?" Toni shifted uncomfortably, wanting to urge her friend to get in touch with Jim immediately. Perhaps the break-ins were as ominous as Jim thought they were.

Without answering Toni's question, Erica asked one of her own instead. "Are you sure nothing but personnel stuff was taken from your office?"

"Almost positive. Jim made me promise to give him a list of every little thing out of place or missing in my office. "

"Will you check again and call me?" asked Erica nervously.

Toni registered how disturbed Erica was. "You sound as if you think there's a connection between what was taken from my office and yours."

"Don't you think there could be? Especially if your minutes of our task force meetings are missing. Even if they're not, I'll call security— if you insist."

"I do." Toni stood up to leave. "I'll call you immediately to let you know whether my notes are safely stashed where I think they are."

"Not so fast, my friend. You're not leaving until you tell me why Sheila said friends got her out of the hospital. I thought she was going to be transferred to the rehabilitation center."

"Jim was able to persuade the powers that be that she could go home as long as I'd be spending nights with her."

"Jim?" Erica said with suspicion. "I think you've got a confession to make. You blush every time you mention Scoop's name."

Toni, frowning, sat down again. Seeing Erica's raised eyebrows and skeptical expression, she sighed. "Listen, Erica, don't believe any gossip you may hear."

"Oh, should I expect to hear gossip? I take it it's about you and Mr. Snoopy?"

"Yes. He took me out to supper after my office break-in on Monday, and…"

Erica interrupted, "And what?"

"Well, Marty Jones and Nancy Rosen were eating in Ricardo's, too. They kept staring at us all through dinner. I'm surprised you hadn't already heard about our *date*. Those two are the biggest gossips on campus."

"Isn't gossiping one of their duties? Besides, it sounds to me as if they have gossip-worthy news! Snoopy seems to be taking a lot of interest in you."

"All in the line of his duty. He checked out my office after the break-in." Toni smiled. "That's part of *his* job description."

"Taking you out to dinner seems like strange duty if you ask me."

"Can't you accept the fact that maybe he's a nice guy? Sheila certainly thinks so—even if you don't. I was frazzled and tired by the end of the day, and I appreciated his invitation."

"If Sheila approves of the guy, he *may* be okay," Erica conceded.

Toni, doing her best to ignore Erica's comment, picked up her purse and, for the second time, headed for the door. "I hope there's no connection between what's happened in your office and mine."

"So do I," replied Erica.

℮

Toni found her notes in the locked middle drawer of her desk. She called Erica.

"That's a relief," said Erica. "I have good news to report, too. After you left I remembered something. I was going to jot down questions for a quiz while Bill reheated the supper he had waiting for me. I pulled out my batch of geology tests, thinking a couple of my previous *brilliant* questions might be an inspiration. Then I decided not to ruin a good evening at home." Erica chuckled, "My intruder must have picked up the task force notes along with the tests. I'll bet he, or *she*, only wanted to be fully prepared for Friday's quiz. I suspect students enrolled in my introductory geology class won't be able to make head nor tails of my notes. Luckily, I didn't use names, just initials."

"Erica, if *I'd* stolen tests from your office and found I'd picked up something other than the tests I wanted, I'd throw it away like poison."

"I hope you're right. I'll quit worrying—for the time being, at any rate."

℮

Erica called the security office, as she'd promised Toni she would. In answer to Jim's questions, she recounted most of what she'd already told Toni.

Erica's news bothered Jim. Too many coincidences, too many break-ins. The college seldom had three break-ins in a term, and most of those occurred in the dormitories. Three within two weeks stretched belief, unless they were linked. And if they were, how? More important, why?

℮

That same morning, President Walt Asher arrived in his office after attending Cottonwood's weekly Chamber of Commerce meeting. He didn't greet Ruby as he usually did. In fact, he didn't say anything at all to her. He planted his briefcase on the floor and stared uncertainly at his closed door.

Ruby glanced up from her computer screen. "Walt, is everything all right?"

Without looking in her direction, he mumbled, "Um, I, ah." Lowering his voice almost to a whisper, Walt lifted his hand off the doorknob, turned around, and inched his 6 foot 4 inch frame against the closed door of his office. He pulled one of the visitor's chairs up to Ruby's desk, and sat down. "Ruby, let me ask you a question."

After striking the save key, Ruby, afraid someone had broken into their offices again, gave him her full attention.

"Do you open my office when you get here, in the morning?"

"Yes, since the break-in last week, I've been checking regularly when I arrive before you do."

"And you didn't notice anything strange this morning?"

"No, but then I didn't look around carefully. I just peeked into your office and glanced at your desktop."

In response to Walt's scowl, Ruby continued, "I picked up the memo you gave me yesterday—to the faculty about holding office hours on parents' weekend. You made some corrections. Here's the new version. It's ready for your signature."

Absent-mindedly, Walt took the memo from Ruby. "Thanks, I'll sign it and get it back to you soon." Aware that he had sounded testy, he spoke more softly. "You're sure you didn't see anything unusual?"

"No. Everything looked okay to me. You seem concerned, Walt. Is there a problem?"

"I don't mean to be interrogating you, but I think somebody's been monkeying around in my office at night."

"Why didn't you tell me sooner? Especially after what happened just a week ago?"

"At first I thought I was imagining things. On Monday morning, I couldn't find my favorite pen. Not the classic Parker fountain pen my father gave me, but my old standby. I suppose I could have misplaced it. Of course, I'm sensitive about pens these days. Then on Tuesday I found the tennis trophy B.B. had brought back lying on its side. That day, the trophy was in plain sight. That struck me as possible since the floor is uneven in that corner of the room. That bookshelf has always been a little unstable. So I figured the night custodian could have jostled the shelf when he was cleaning.

"I also found one corner of my blotter loose. When I forced the blotter into place, I found a grimy sheet of paper tucked under it. It was covered with messy X's and O's in almost all the tic-tac-toe squares. I've never in my life played tic-tac-toe. If it hadn't been so obvious that somebody was sitting at my desk and that somebody has it in for my tennis trophy, I *might* attribute the misplaced pen to a poltergeist."

"Well," said Ruby, "I'm not your poltergeist. I never touch anything except letters or papers you've left for me to work on. The only reason I went into your office this morning was to see if you'd made corrections to the letters I'd written yesterday or signed them. You're usually prompt in giving drafts back to me, but you were busy yesterday canceling your trip to Flagstaff. I assumed you were preoccupied and might have forgotten them."

"Absent-minded, you mean? Sorry about that. I wouldn't be a true academic if I weren't a little absent-minded. I found my misplaced pen standing upright in a paper cup on top of my mini-fridge on Wednesday. I knew I did *not* put it there, and I certainly didn't hide a sheet of tic-tac-toe games under my blotter."

"I can see why you were upset! You're the most orderly person I've ever known."

"Even as a youngster and when I was in college, I was compulsively neat. It made my mother happy, but it drove my roommates crazy!"

"I know. I used to wonder if you were really human. By now, your neatnickery has rubbed off on me." Ruby opened her middle drawer and, laughing, pointed out the five pens and three pencils aligned in the narrow middle tray, with paper clips, rubber bands, and a staple remover each in their separate compartments, while the rest of the top drawer contained only a ruler, a paperback dictionary and Melinda Merry's most recent computer manual. "Once when my mom came to visit, I showed her this drawer. She wondered what had come over me. When I blamed you, she said she wanted to meet the man who had reformed her sloppy daughter. I told her I'd have never lasted in this job if I hadn't changed. She was really impressed that I was the president's secretary! What she doesn't know is that it's mostly a matter of sorting, and tossing, and filing."

"You do sort, toss, and file very well, thank you. And don't forget your most important duty: making nice on the telephone." Asher smiled; Ruby relaxed.

"It sounds as if your poltergeist has been at work every day." Ruby tried to sound less worried than she was. Walt sounded worried enough for the two of them.

"I wish I did believe in poltergeists. They'd be less spooky than what has been going on in here after hours. The ante goes up each day. You know my habits: I keep track of new books I haven't yet read by putting them on the shelves still in their jackets. Yesterday, I found those books piled high on the side table and all the jackets crammed into the wastebasket."

"Who on earth would bother to do that? And how did they get in anyway? I can't see anyone waltzing in here after both you and I had left. They'd have to have three separate keys, one for the building, another for my door, and a third for yours."

"What about a master key?"

"There aren't very many of those and they're *very* hard to come by. I tried to get one once and couldn't."

A few minutes later Ruby found her usually dignified, upright boss kneeling on the floor and peering under his desk. He hoisted the bronzed tennis trophy B.B. had returned a few days earlier for her view. The right arm of the statuette, now repaired, was raised for serving. The other arm, its hand once balancing a ball ready to be tossed, was badly bent.

"Finding the trophy removed from its case, dented, and lying on the floor was bad enough. This is *much* worse."

Sighing, Walt slowly stood up. He cradled the trophy as if it were a fragile, living creature. "Somebody really had it in for the poor guy this time." Unable to stop himself from his habit of quoting poetry or referring to passages from treasured books, Walt said, "Like Keats' shepherd, the server was always on the verge of winning not a girl, but a point." He shrugged. "No more delicious anticipation for this guy."

Wanting to sympathize but not having any comforting words, Ruby knelt down to search for the missing ball. She found nothing on the floor but a paper clip and a dust bunny. Then she thought to look in the wastebasket where the book jackets had ended up.

"Here's the tennis ball." She handed the bronze ball to President Asher. To keep it from rolling around, he placed it carefully in the tray for incoming mail, and laid the mangled statuette next to it.

"I'm afraid it's time to call Scoop again and tell him what's happened this week. While you're doing that I'll try to forget my battered friend and get to work. Do I need to sign all these letters before the 9:30 mail pickup?"

"Only the three on top. The rest can wait," said Ruby.

Walt stared after his secretary as she closed the door behind her. He sat absolutely still until his telephone rang, jarring him out of his reverie.

Picking up his handset, he said, "Hello. Asher here." Only after the caller had spoken for a full minute, did he recognize his wife's voice.

Annette was talking so fast he couldn't make out what she was saying.

"Slow down, hon. I can't understand you."

"Sorry. I've just had three very strange phone calls. I'm afraid they have something to do with the mess on campus."

"You mean about *Academic Awards* and the author we haven't been able to find?"

"Yes!" Annette, usually calm and collected, sounded shrill and decidedly uncollected.

"Tell me about the calls first and then explain why you think they have something to do with our search for Edith Tansley Coyle."

Annette, obviously defensive, enunciated each word—very slowly and very clearly:

"Let's see. I'll begin with call number one. The phone rang while I was finishing my coffee and reading the newspaper. The caller—I could tell it was a man—took a breath after every three or four words. He spoke loudly, but in a monotone, as if he were trying to disguise his voice. As soon as I asked who was on the line, he hung up. Almost immediately, the phone rang again. Same man, same voice. He told me to remind *my* husband to meet him in Santa Fe. I almost hung up on him, but I thought I better not."

"I wish you had," said Walt, and then wished he hadn't said anything. He knew how much Annette hated being interrupted.

"Walt, I thought you and Jim Scoop would like me to get as much information from the caller as I could."

"Of course. Sorry I interrupted you. Go on."

"Very politely I asked the caller to give me his name to pass on to my husband. There was this long silence. After a while, I heard some funny sounds. Like a glass being knocked off a table and breaking in the midst of some whooshing sounds. Finally, I heard some indistinct mumbling and then a loud click before we were disconnected.

"Gad, Annette. How weird. And frightening."

"It was. Then it occurred to me that both calls could have been from the same person dialing a wrong number, not once but twice. I would have gotten in touch with you right away, but I knew you were at the Rotary breakfast. So I washed up and went back to my newspaper."

"What do you want me to do?"

"Nothing. Just hear me out." Walt was glad to hear Annette sounding like herself—the longer she talked, the calmer she became.

"Ten minutes later the phone rang again. But this time there were no words. I could hear a radio in the background, then nothing but a slight buzz, and then nothing at all. I don't know why but I stayed on the line. After what seemed like a long time—though it probably wasn't—I heard someone saying, 'Damn, I can't get a connection.' At that point, the caller hung up, and so did I."

"All very eerie. It *could* have been someone dialing a wrong number, I suppose."

"Maybe," replied Annette, not sounding convinced. "Walt, someone's at the door. I'll call you back in a sec." Walt was relieved to hear his wife speaking in her normal voice, signaling to him that she was becoming less and less disturbed. However, waiting for Annette to call him back, he felt vulnerable. For himself, for Annette, for the college. First, another break-in in his office. And then these upsetting calls.

When his phone rang a few minutes later, Walt wasn't expecting to hear from Annette so soon. "Nobody was there," she said, "Just a UPS man delivering a package."

"Good," he replied. "You didn't by any chance check the number of any of the calls, did you?"

"No. I can read the number of the last call, though. Let's see. It's a 509 number. That's a New Mexico cell phone prefix. Walt, that makes me feel better."

"Why?"

"You're a smart man. Think about it. The most likely explanation is that someone was calling from a cell phone in his car. There are lots of dead spots where the roads around Santa Fe dip in and out of range. That would account for indistinct words, silences, my being able to hear a car radio, the guy being frustrated with poor reception, and dialing the same number so many times."

"That hardly explains the sound of tinkling glass, though," added Walt.

"Oh, yes, it does." Now Annette was laughing. "Maybe it wasn't glass breaking I heard, but a coffee cup or mug, not one of the insulated, non-breakable kind. I can imagine my phantom caller carrying his morning coffee out to his car, and instead of placing it carefully into a cup holder, letting it fall to the floor." Annette paused. "Walt, I'm sorry I bothered you with my little mystery."

"*I'm* sorry you were bothered by nuisance calls, and I can't think of anyone I'd rather be bothered by."

"I'm feeling better now. Thanks for listening. Go back to solving Southwestern's mystery and I'll forget about trying to solve mine. Unless, of course, I get a fourth call!"

Not able to shake his feeling of vulnerability and more worried about Annette's phone calls than he'd let on, Walt thumbed through yesterday's stack of interoffice memos. Finding a sealed envelope marked "confidential" from Sally Sanchez, he opened it. Attached to the transcript of an oral interview, Sally had written, "This is a statement from the freshman girl who was accosted on September fifth. As you know, she didn't choose to press charges, and the young man who attacked her has withdrawn from Southwestern and gone home. Her parents just learned about the attack. They called me this morning and they're furious. In case they call you—and I expect they will—Judy Johannson's statement may give you an insight into the young woman."

Walt read the transcript. "I felt all naked like when the guy was yanking at my blouse and pulling at the buttons. I thought the whole world was looking at me, not just that nerd, even though it was night and dark and nobody was around. I mean, I didn't know anyone was there. I was really glad to see the cop guys. It was like a really bad dream. Only like I didn't wake up, you know, cause it was real, not a nightmare. I kept wanting the last minute to go away, not, like, to have happened. But I don't want to get all legal about it. Alvin's been kicked out of school. I'm okay. He won't bother me any more." With a pang of sympathy, Walt thought he understood the poor girl's sentiments, if not her diction.

In the meantime, Ruby called the security office. Lily answered. Remembering that Jim Scoop had switched to evening hours, Ruby wondered whether it would be okay to talk to B.B. instead. Lily said, "Jim *shouldn't* be in yet, but he was here when I got to work. I'll put him on."

Speaking rapidly, Ruby said, "Mr. Scoop, please come to the president's office right away. Someone's still tampering with the president's things between the time he leaves at night and arrives the next morning— I don't know how late he's stayed this week. I usually leave before he does— No, I have no idea when the intruder broke in."

"Hang on," said Jim. "Don't tell anyone what's happened or let anyone else in to see Dr. Asher until I send someone over there. Tell him not to move anything. ...He's already moved things and cleaned up? ...That's too bad, but don't either of you touch anything else."

Ten minutes later, Scoop appeared in the doorway.

"Can you close up shop for a little while, Ruby, and come into Walt's office? He's expecting me, isn't he?"

"He had me call security, so I'm sure he's expecting someone. Not you, though, since you've changed your schedule."

Walt stood to greet Jim. "I'm beginning to feel as if I'm part of a criminal investigation."

"From what Ruby has told me, it looks like you just might be. Tell me about the damage. But first, is anything missing?"

"No, except some books are now without their jackets. I don't discard the jackets as a rule. They're colorful, sometimes informative, and I like knowing who's been paid for their praise! At least twenty jackets were wadded up, and stuffed in my wastebasket."

"I don't suppose you kept them?"

"No, of course not. They were beyond repair."

Jim turned to Ruby. "Are the wastebaskets emptied only at night?"

"Yes."

"What time?"

"I'm not exactly sure. After ten, I think."

"That'll help. I'll check with the physical plant to find out when the custodian makes his rounds in Center Hall."

Jim faced Walt again. "Has anything else I should know about made its way into the trash?"

"Yes," responded Walt. "A sheet of paper, not one belonging to me! I suppose it, along with the book covers, could provide a clue about my nightly visitor?"

Jim frowned and nodded. Walt continued, "Frankly, when I found the grubby paper under my blotter, I was so irritated that I tore it in half and threw it away."

"Anything distinctive about this sheet of paper?"

"Oh, yes, it was covered with tic-tac-toe diagrams and all the little squares were filled with O's and X's."

"I'd have liked to see it—and the book jackets."

"In retrospect, I can see why. But at the time, it simply felt, as I said to Ruby this morning, as if I were being visited by a poltergeist. The first few weeks of the school year are the busiest time for me. What's been going on in my office is a nuisance and, I must admit, I was very disturbed this morning. It's eerie, but I doubt I'm being threatened."

Jim didn't share the president's view. "Anything else moved or damaged?" he asked.

Walt opened his desk drawer and handed Scoop a black fountain pen engraved with his name. When he saw Jim unfolding a handkerchief and using it to grasp the pen before inserting it into a zip-lock bag, Walt grumbled. "Oh, come on, Jim. Is all this cloak-and-dagger stuff really necessary?"

"Probably not, but I'm taking no chances. I need to see everything that might give us a clue about who is visiting your office—uninvited."

"Here," said Walt, now serious, "This is the damage I regret most. Just look at my poor college trophy."

"Looks as if it's been brutally assaulted. Worse than last time. Put it back where you found it; I'll send someone over for it. Before I leave, tell me everything that's been tampered with this week—you don't need to describe what happened last week. If you can, review this week's damage in order."

Walt listed the recent sequence of events: on Monday, the pen he used most often was missing; on Tuesday, his tennis trophy was lying on its side but still on the shelf where he kept it; also his desk blotter was askew, presumably because the intruder had shoved a sheet of paper filled with tic-tac-toe games under it; on Wednesday, book jackets had been taken off, torn, and thrown into his wastebasket, and his missing pen turned up; today, Thursday, Ruby found his tennis trophy damaged for the second time and lying under an overturned chair.

While listening to Walt, Jim was making plans to assign an officer to the small bathroom adjacent to the president's office. He would send someone to the uncomfortable post each night. Luckily, he'd already tapped his three part-timers for extra duty.

Jim frowned in Ruby's direction. "Why didn't you tell me about all this mayhem when I called yesterday?"

"But I didn't know about *any* of this until today."

Walt corroborated Ruby's denial. "I didn't see any reason to bother Ruby. Walking back to campus this morning, I realized it was confession time."

"Even after our talk last week, Walt? Or do you think you lead a charmed life? I suppose you thought I was making a mountain out of a molehill?"

"Frankly, yes."

"From now on, let me decide what's a mountain and what's a molehill. That's my job, you know."

"Okay, you win. Ruby, you're hereby instructed to call Jim whenever you drop a paper clip, whenever anyone calls and doesn't leave a message, when…" As he was talking, Walt considered telling Jim about Annette's calls, but then quickly discarded the idea. *What could Jim do about them? If Annette was right, someone using a cell phone while driving could easily have called the same wrong number more than once. Those calls surely wouldn't even count as molehills, would they?*

"Look, Walt," said Jim apologetically, "I'm sorry for all this fuss. But yours isn't the only office that's been broken into."

Walt bombarded Jim with questions. "What offices beside mine? When? What exactly happened in each case? And why didn't you inform me?"

"Toni Hexton's and Dr. Ebenezer's offices have both been broken into within the last week. And one evening last week something happened to Steve Scott that, for the time being, my security officers and I are investigating along with the break-ins. Steve dismissed that incident as unconnected and I suspect he's right. Nevertheless, someone was in a place that should have been off-limits.

"Toni's files were ransacked and some sensitive reports are missing. It looks as if one of Erica's students was simply after test copies and picked up other papers at the same time, including some task force notes. Whoever was in the library didn't take anything. Instead, he or she wrote a letter on the library's letterhead, signed Steve's name to it, and inserted it into a stack a secretary had ready to be mailed. When I found out what was in that particular letter, I dismissed it as the work of a creative student with a sense of humor. But I still can't dismiss the fact that someone had gained access to a closed and presumably locked office."

A silent and deeply worried Walt Asher leaned forward, resting his head between his hands. "I don't like the fact that Scott, Ebenezer, and Hexton are all on the task force."

"I don't either, Walt. But don't leave yourself out of it. They're looking for the author of *Academic Awards,* but so are you. You're the only one to suffer escalating acts of vandalism." Florencio's warnings popped into Jim's mind as he spoke. They struck too close to home.

Walt's next question interrupted Jim's troubled thoughts. "Tell me more about the library's letter. What was in it?"

"A large order for books that no self-respecting college librarian would want gracing his shelves!"

"Why not?"

"Because all the books were far-out proofs of alien invasions. And the publishing house, though it does exist, has the appropriate name of Out-of-this-World, Limited."

"Egads," said Walt, laughing and showing his amusement by uttering his one and only swear word. "All right, Jim, even if we discount Steve's problem, and I think we probably can, you and I may have much more to worry about than what's happened here," he said, pointing to his damaged statue.

"I think," said Jim somberly, "we must consider the danger present and real. Until we find out otherwise, we should assume that the thefts, vandalism, and perhaps even the made-up book order could be the work of one person up to no good."

"Possibly, though the ridiculous book order is out of sync with the vandalism in any of our offices." Walt hesitated. "You're going to need more staff, aren't you? This is the kind of crisis emergency funds are for— though I'd rather support academic enterprises."

"You already approved my initial request for more security officers when we sent Johnny Burke to Albuquerque to be licensed to carry a gun. All you need to do now is authorize paying the part-timers I used last week more hours for the foreseeable future."

"Done." Walt turned to Ruby. "We'll send the request to the personnel department right away, Jim."

Ruby walked into the outer office as Jim stood up to leave.

"Wait a minute, Jim, before you go. As we've been talking, I've been thinking. I can't, in good conscience, let the task force continue to investigate what could turn out to be dangerous. The author we've asked them to locate may, as you said, have more mischief in mind than preventing the college from winning its share of NAMWA's prize. We'll have to try to locate the author of *Academic Awards* without their help. I don't want to put my people in jeopardy—no matter how much money is at stake. I'll speak to each of the task force members in person this afternoon. I'll ask them to give me their notes. And I'll get copies to you." Asher raised his eyes to the ceiling. "Knowing some of the members, I'm not sure they're going to accept marching orders gracefully."

@

At 11:30, Erica and Jeff, unaware as yet of Walt's plan to take them off the case, met to pool what they knew about Melinda Merry. In less than half an hour they'd be picking her up to take her to lunch for a circumspect grilling. Even though she'd written a very literate computer manual and was bright, she seemed a long shot.

Scott had reminded them that she was one of the few Southwestern employees with access to private records. That had led Toni to praise the clarity and fluency of her computer manuals and yearly updates. Lloyd added that while Melinda could write well, it was no secret she felt underpaid and underappreciated. Erica questioned whether Melinda had the imagination to have written anything fictional, especially since the book revealed empathetic insight into people, a quality Melinda Merry lacked. Nor had she ever shown the gentle, yet whimsical appreciation for human foibles that permeated *Academic Awards*. Despite all these reasons against Melinda Merry's candidacy, the task force members, desperately seeking possible candidates, had voted for an interview.

As PR director, Jeff had seen Melinda Merry's résumé. He reviewed it for Erica, spiced up with what he'd gleaned from the secretaries in the computer center by being a good listener—and cute. Melinda came to Southwestern right after graduating from Farmington High in 1977. She'd worked her way up from the secretarial pool to her present position. Her fellow secretaries didn't resent her rise because, with her departure, their common workspace became more relaxed and congenial. Anyway, none of them begrudged her her job: hoisting and lugging computers across campus for dismantling and then reassembling them in a dark, small workshop.

Only later did her fellow secretaries realize that the introduction of computers on the campus would create a small empire, a warren's nest of offices, a budgetary black hole, and special status for those with arcane cyber skills. They had to admit that she knew her stuff and could explain it better than the computer science professor originally assigned to train them.

At the same time, faculty members were discovering that she was willing to come to their offices to help them outsmart balky programs and retrieve lost documents. Those abilities allowed her to outlast three bosses and silenced complaints about her brusque desk-side manner.

Melinda Merry was ready and waiting for Erica and Jeff.

Looking directly at Erica but barely glancing at Jeff, Melinda said, "You haven't, I assume, invited me out for lunch because you want my company. What," she asked abruptly, "is the occasion?"

Erica opened the passenger door for Melinda while trying to ignore Jeff's down-turned mouth as he clambered into the back seat. "I'll explain when we get to Sam's Subs. It has the best sandwiches in town."

"And private booths," growled Melinda.

This didn't, Erica thought, promise to be a pleasant lunch. Never one for small talk and eager to get this interview over, Erica opted to be blunt. "We want to talk to you about your writing."

"My writing? What I do on the job, or what I do for fun?"

"Both."

"On the job, I write reports and letters for my boss, José Martinez, computer manuals for ditzy secretaries and arrogant professors who pretend to be much more computer-literate than they are, until they get in trouble and want my help—yesterday."

Melinda craned her neck around to scowl at Jeff. "You, young man, could you do your work without being adept with computers?"

"No, ma'am. Incidentally, my secretary keeps two books on her desk: a dictionary and *your* manual. It's not only well-written, it's beautifully laid out."

Erica angled into the one remaining parking space. "You said you also write for fun. When do you have time to do that?"

"Whenever I can."

"What kinds of things?"

"Mostly how-to articles." Melinda was noticeably thawing in the face of Jeff and Erica's interest. "I've had a few pieces published, so far only in little magazines."

As they entered the restaurant, Erica said, "Well, that's a start."

Soon, a waitress brought them three thick paper plates holding the overflowing sandwiches for which Sam's was famous. "I'll be back with your drinks, you know, in a minute: one iced tea, one coffee, one lemonade, righto?"

Jeff, looking the girl straight in the eye, replied, "Righto."

Melinda actually smiled at hearing Jeff echo her disapproval.

Erica returned to what she hoped might be a fruitful line of inquiry. "Have you ever tried your hand at fiction?" she asked, as Melinda struggled with her BLT.

"Yes, but it doesn't come naturally. I joined a creative writing group for a while. It was mostly young people *into*, as they said, eco-environmentalism and eco-feminism. A few earnest young women were writing religious true confessions and the only man in the class brought us another chapter of his great American novel each week."

"Sounds dreadful," said Erica.

"It was. I stuck it out for a month, but when I could see that the facilitator—that's what the instructor called himself—encouraged the navel gazing and didn't discourage drivel, I decided to work alone. Since then I've mostly been writing the kinds of articles that brought me success in the first place."

*We can cross Melinda off our list,* thought Erica, neither surprised nor disappointed.

Jeff, ever the diplomat, asked, "What *did* bring you success?"

"My big break-through came when an article I wrote on pushing the glass ceiling was published in *Women at Work*. It didn't pay much, but it did encourage me to keep writing. But you two haven't invited me to lunch to hear about my little successes, have you?"

"Frankly, we'd been hoping you had a big success," replied Jeff.

After they had asked Melinda Merry a few more questions, it was clear she had not written *Academic Awards*. She assured Erica and Jeff that she didn't have the time to write a novel, nor any inclination to write a mystery. She thanked them for lunch, and, with more grace than she'd shown at first, said she was surprised and pleased to be a suspect.

Erica drove Melinda to the back door of the computer center and then offered to drive Jeff around to his office in Center Hall.

"Oh, you don't need to do that. I'd like to walk. By the way," added Jeff, as he got out of the car, "your suggestion about Irene's taking up dance again is working miracles. I told her to sleep in last Saturday. I got the girls up and fed before she drove off to Farmington. That night—without three little girls in tow—we went out for dinner and a movie."

"That's wonderful, Jeff," responded Erica. "Even with only one child, Bill and I found it a relief to have some time to ourselves. And, Jeff, thank you. You did a lot to soften Melinda up. I think we made her day—even though she didn't make ours."

☙

After lunch, Walt told Ruby to postpone his 2:15 appointment until later in the afternoon. He had checked the schedules of the six task force members and decided he could see them all in person before 3:00. He proposed taking one of his famous campus walkabouts. If he had to have what had recently come to be known as a leadership style, he'd describe his as "management by walking around."

Responses by the task force to having their charge taken away varied. Steve Scott accepted the order with a "You know best, but I wonder if..." statement. Sarah Jennings scoffed, "Oh, pouf, how silly." Lloyd Reasoner wondered whether it was wise to "un-enlist" the help of six willing detectives. Jeff Miles looked disappointed but said nothing. Toni looked astonished, but decided to save her protests for Jim, who must, she thought, be party to the decision.

Erica argued unsuccessfully. "The book's tennis trophy is a ringer for yours, isn't it?"

"Unfortunately, yes," replied Walt.

"Then you're in as much or more danger than any of us."

"I may be," he admitted. "However, I'm willing to take responsibility for myself, but not to put others in jeopardy. The less you do, the less chance you'll provoke an incident. So far, your interviews haven't uncovered anyone who might have written the book, have they?"

"The committee is divided. Some think everyone we've interviewed can be crossed off the list. Steve, Sarah, and I don't. Wouldn't it be best to have the original interviewers follow up? Steve still has niggling suspicions about what Taylor Anderson would and wouldn't do to embarrass the school. And Sarah thinks Jane Snow is in attack mode—even though she seems too wacky to write coherently. But unbalanced people sometimes have moments of clarity. The book isn't very long, and Jane used to write well, so maybe..."

Walt cut her off, "I agree, Erica, that Taylor and Jane are possibilities. Still, if we decide to investigate them further, I want Steve and Sarah to back off. If Taylor or Jane is angry enough—and devious enough to claim innocence—then I'm afraid they might retaliate in some way."

"Even from Spain?" asked Erica, incredulous.

"The Andersons have money. They don't *have* to stay in Spain. Nothing makes sense right now, but Jim and his staff are trained and can give more attention to the search than any of you. I shouldn't have burdened you with my problem. You can be most helpful by letting go—please, without any more arguments."

Erica muttered, "Humph."

"I'll take that for agreement," said Walt. "Please convey my thanks, again, to all the task force members. You've done a good job. We may decide to sound Taylor out further and we will keep an eye on Jane Snow. Incidentally, I met Jeff on the river walk. He told me you had lunch with Melinda Merry. I don't know why I hadn't thought of her. Jeff really challenged me on her behalf. He reminded me how easy it is to ignore people who work hard and invisibly behind the scenes."

Erica's indignation at being discarded withered in the face of Walt's honesty and humility. "I've always thought," she said, "academics forget how much non-academic staff people do to keep the college going."

"I'm asking the other task force members to give me their notes. If by chance yours turn up, please send them to me. I want everything connected to this search out of your hands. Finally, re-emphasize the importance of staying cautious and remind your colleagues to get in touch with Jim if anything strange happens." Walt responded to her look of exasperation before she could protest. "Erica, let Jim be the judge of what is strange. We may be overreacting, but I'd much rather overreact than have something happen to any of you."

Erica followed President Asher's instructions—partially. By 10:00 that night, she had gotten in touch with everyone on the task force. They all agreed: they shouldn't have been dismissed. That being so, they would continue to function—even if they had to go underground. Surprisingly, it was Steve who suggested a time and place for them to meet the next day.

@

That same night, Jim Scoop was restless. Shortly after 8:00, he walked slowly to his office, appreciating the cool evening and the sun setting in the western sky. No wonder students were outside, sitting around the plaza, strolling along the river walk, or heading for the snack bar. The only discordant note was seeing so many of them talking into their cell phones. Presumably most of their calls were to friends they'd seen a few hours earlier and would soon see again.

Jim poked his head into the library. It was almost empty. He walked up to the third floor of Center Hall and found all the offices there safely locked.

Calling his night patrolmen, he heard them report that it was quiet all over campus. He flipped through the paperwork that had accumulated on his desk. He found nothing urgent—or even very interesting.

He abruptly rose, crossed the creek, and headed for the Student Union. He thought he heard a piece of pecan pie and a cup of coffee calling his name. He shouldn't have been surprised to find the door to the newspaper office, across the hall from the snack bar, standing open. His pie could wait.

Toni and Betty, the student editor and his former work/study student, were going over the layout for the front page. They both greeted him but immediately went back to work. The sports editor hailed him from a nearby table. "Hey, Mr. Scoop, what do you think of our football team? We beat Fort Lewis twenty-seven to twenty!"

"I was there. That was quite a game."

"It was great! Especially since everyone expected Fort Lewis to romp over us the way Adams State did. In Alamosa we couldn't get our running game going, and Adams picked off four of our passes. But when we went up to Durango, it was a different story completely. The guys weren't ready to be humiliated twice in a row! I've sure had a lot of fun comparing the two games for tomorrow's paper."

"You've already finished your stories? From the looks of things, you must be the only reporter who has." Jim glanced around the room at the other students, some frowning at their notes and others writing furiously.

"Yes," groaned Eddy. "I have no trouble writing sports stories. I can almost do that in my sleep."

"So why are you looking so glum?" asked Jim, laughing.

"My first philosophy paper is due Monday. I don't have a clue where to start."

"Maybe I can help. What's the assignment?"

"We're supposed to analyze a short passage of Kant's *Critique of Pure Reason*. I think I grasp Kant's ideas when we talk in class, but I'm lost when I try to follow what he's written!"

"Kant's a bear. He's dense and difficult." Jim glanced down at Eddy's open textbook, heavily highlighted, with a big "NO" scrawled in the margin by a triply underlined sentence.

"Why did you write "No" next to *that* sentence?"

"Because it goes against everything I've always believed."

Jim grinned. "I think, Eddy, you've got your topic. You should have seen your face just now. You looked interested. And when you're interested, you're more likely to make your reader interested."

"That seems obvious, but I've been afraid to base a paper on my own reactions. They're kind of vague. And how do I organize them into a paper?" Eddy paused. "You sound as if you've read Kant."

"I have—several times. I had a philosophy professor who considered Kant the most important philosopher next to Plato." Jim pulled up a spare chair and sat down by Eddy. "Let's discuss your reaction a bit, and I bet you'll find your paper structuring itself."

By the time Jim and Eddy had talked for almost half an hour, Eddy was excited. "My ideas are coming together. Thanks a lot."

Neither Jim nor Eddy noticed that Toni had come up behind them. "I expected you two to be discussing sports, not philosophy."

"Professor Hexton, I'm not goofing off. My article is all done. I just found out that Mr. Scoop is a philosopher cop. And he'd make a good teacher too. He's helped me a lot!"

Jim addressed the young man. "Thank you. You've given me what every cop needs: a good mental workout." He then turned towards Toni. "I think Eddy and I have talked enough. He understands Kant much better than he thought he did. Any chance you could break away and join me for coffee and pie?"

"Sounds good to me. Betty has everything under control here."

As they walked across the hall to the snack bar, Toni said, "I loved hearing Eddy call you a philosopher cop."

Since the snack bar was out of pecan pie, Jim had the opportunity to consider what kind of pie he wanted with his coffee, as well as time to decide how much more to tell Toni about his academic background.

Jim chose apple, Toni blueberry.

"So, Mr. Philosopher, what gives?"

"I took several philosophy courses when I was in college ages ago. I enjoyed my first one, so I took several more."

"Philosophy seems far afield for a cop."

"Why, professor, how can you say that? Isn't philosophy supposed to be the queen of all sciences?"

Shaking her head, Toni smiled and started to reply, but Jim hurried on. "At any rate, I did well on the army's entrance exam. The army sent me to American University in D.C. where I earned a B.S. in criminal justice. Anything more you want to know, professor?"

"Seriously, how did you get away with taking philosophy courses?"

"Three mornings a week when I was a freshman, I took a philosophy class. Everyone thought I was going to the shooting range, and I didn't disabuse them of that notion."

"So you lied? Isn't that considered a no-no for police?"

"I was young and unprincipled in those days. I didn't lie exactly. I just kept my mouth shut. I was already a pretty good marksman, so I managed to pass all the weekly shooting tests."

"That's a great story. A budding military policeman going AWOL to study philosophy!"

Toni looked searchingly at Jim. "I'm going to be a pushy journalist. I don't think you've told me the whole truth."

Jim cocked an eyebrow in Toni's direction. She, ignoring his reaction, spoke slowly and deliberately. "Talking with Eddy, you sounded like someone who'd written lots of philosophy papers."

"True. I did."

"Also," continued Toni, "you displayed a knowledge of Kant that you wouldn't have gotten from just one introductory course."

Jim busily tucked into his pie and avoided Toni's gaze.

"More importantly, you even *sounded* like a teacher using the Socratic method!"

"You've found me out, Toni. You must have been eavesdropping for quite a while." Jim paused. "Okay. Here's the complete version of my résumé. After twenty years in the army, I retired and took advantage of the GI Bill. My graduate work at Vanderbilt was partly paid for by the U.S. government. I paid for the rest of it working as a teaching assistant."

"I agree with Eddy. I'll wager you were a pretty good T.A."

"Being older and having seen a good bit of the world helped. Teaching I found very satisfying."

"So, Mr. Philosopher Cop, should I be calling *you* doctor?"

"No. I'm a grad school drop out. I didn't write a dissertation. I made the mistake of thinking I should read the dissertations of other graduate students. The turgid writing wasn't their fault. They were just mimicking what most of the established scholars were churning out. I was appalled. I chose not to contribute to that pile of … worthless prose. I left academia with only a master's degree, not a PhD. I looked for a job in the West in a field I had liked and was good at."

"Why the West?"

"I grew up in Montana and was ready to come back home after constant traveling for the military. I needed a job. And luckily for me,

Southwestern needed a security director at the same time. I met with Walt Asher. I liked him, *and* his attitude, *and* his expectations. So here I am—happily ensconced in this little college." *Of course*, thought Jim to himself, *I'll be happier when I know neither you nor anyone else is in danger.*

*Boy*, thought Toni to herself, *has Erica ever misjudged Jim. He's as much an academic as we are."*

℮

While Jim and Toni enjoyed their pie and coffee break, one of his officers began a new tour of duty. By 11:00, Nick was sure that he was not going to like hiding out in the president's minuscule bathroom. He was supposed to stay quiet in the dark, waiting for some nut to do what: unscrew light bulbs, deplete the president's supply of salted almonds, plow through his desk drawers? Nick alternated stretches and mini-pushups. He didn't even dare flush after taking a whiz. He'd ask—no demand—special boredom pay from Scoop, by God.

## 11

FRIDAY, SEPTEMBER 16

*Something lost is found, Walt's cease-and-desist order is ignored, and Bill Ebenezer makes a suggestion.*

Erica, to the amazement of her colleagues, usually arrived in her office before 7:00 each morning. They remained unconvinced of the great advantages of answering mail, trashing whatever garbage had miraculously accumulated on the computer overnight, disposing of administrative details, and getting one class out of the way before 9 A.M.

When she opened her office door at 6:55, Erica noticed a large envelope resting on the floor. She leaned over to pick it up and tore open the sealed flap. Attached to the top of one of Southwestern's many official forms and a batch of other papers was a note from her secretary telling her to listen to a voice-mail message. While half listening to the six messages that preceded her secretary's, Erica found the stolen tests in the envelope, along with the task force notes and a withdrawal-from-class form. To Sonia's usual fulsome, dramatized account, she listened carefully.

"While you were in lab, a scrawny, rude, unbathed kid handed me a withdrawal form and some other papers he said you'd loaned him. I told him the rules about getting signatures from all his profs in person, and he said, 'I'm outa this prison in just a few minutes.' He said he'd already spent a 'whole fricking day' getting 'fricking signatures,' he had a ride waiting to take him to the Farmington airport, and he wasn't going to miss his plane to see some 'rock-loving, hard-headed dame.' When I told him that you might not sign, he shrugged his shoulders, and yelled 'whatever' as he took off down the hall. It'll serve the kid right if you don't sign his damn form."

When she'd come to the end of the message, Erica hung up the phone, and scrutinized Form 351, trying to decipher the student's signature. It took her a minute to figure out that what looked like "Warm Stress" must be "Warren Stevens." She couldn't attach a face to the name, but this was one student she would be glad to be rid of. Then she read the heading at the top of the sheet: "Withdrawal from Southwestern College." She had to acknowledge that the kid was right: Southwestern *was* drowning in forms, all couched in bureaucratese. There must be at least 350 other forms residing in who knows how many different files in how many different offices, ready to be encountered by unsuspecting students during their sojourn at Southwestern. She sympathized with the young man.

Evidently Jonathan Gill did too, judging by the comment he'd written next to his signature: "Since I never saw him until today, I won't miss him. Let him go in peace." If Jonathan and three other professors, to say nothing of the director of housing and the vice-president of student affairs, were willing to let Warren Stevens depart, so was she. Erica was not a stickler for protocol or rules. Besides, by returning the stolen goods Warren was making her life easier. She was very glad that what had been lost was found. She'd better inform Jim Scoop. She'd call him after class.

@

Jim's secretary answered the phone. "Lily, is Jim Scoop there? …Well, let him know that he can cross me off his list. …I don't have time to explain, but he'll know what I mean."

"Okay, I'll get the message to him right away."

"You don't have to do that. It's not urgent."

Three minutes later, Erica's phone rang. It was Jim.

"Erica, are you okay?"

"Yes, Jim, I'm just fine. I thought you'd traded mornings for an evening shift."

"I have. I'm not on campus. I'm home. Until this mess blows over, I've instructed Lily to forward all messages from the president or the task force members to my house."

"You are paranoid, aren't you?"

Erica registered Jim's chuckle before he replied, "It's part of my job description." Maybe, she thought, Toni was right about the security chief. Perhaps he *did* have a sense of humor.

"Well, you have one less thing to worry about. My missing tests— and also my task force notes—are back. A student returned them. And he's left town, for good."

"Are you sure no one else saw the notes?"

"Pretty sure. I checked the attendance sheet I keep the first two weeks. Warren Stevens only came to class the first day. I'd have disenrolled him myself if he hadn't decided to save me the trouble. Jim, I refuse to consider myself in danger. Or Toni either."

"Erica, until further evidence comes in, I'm not willing to assume that there's no connection between the task force's sleuthing and several other acts of vandalism. Even Dr. Scott has had an unwanted visitor."

"Dr. Scott?" Erica asked in surprise. "Now you've got me curious. What happened to Steve?"

From the tone of his voice, Erica could tell that Jim was stifling a laugh. "An order went out for more than two thousand dollars' worth of books that neither Scott nor Becky Keen, his secretary, had seen—or signed."

"Did these extra books show up?"

"Fortunately, no. Somebody from the publishing house—Out-of-this-World something or other—called Steve to say that they had all the books he wanted except von Daniken's book on the UFO conspiracy, which wasn't one of theirs. After Steve asked for the titles of the other books, he convinced the publisher that someone had forged his name on an order and that it should be canceled."

Erica laughed aloud. "You expect me to sit on this delicious bit of nonsense."

"Yep, someday you can laugh publicly. But not yet."

"And where, may I ask, is 'Out-of-this-World' located?"

"Right here in New Mexico…"

"Roswell, I'll bet."

"Not too surprising, is it?"

"It's not only *not* surprising; it's also funny. Given how tight the library budget is, though, I guess I'm glad we're not saddled with a bunch of books on alien landings," Erica said.

"In all seriousness," Jim interjected, "I'm not willing to assume *any* task force member or Walt Asher is entirely safe. I've kept it quiet up to now, but you need to know that Walt's office has been vandalized, more than *once*. What's more, the intruder smashed his prize tennis trophy. And you may remember that a tennis trophy was the weapon used to kill the president in *Academic Awards*."

"Hmm, probably just a coincidence," said Erica.

"Maybe, but ominous if not," replied Jim. "You do see why all these things are more than laughing matters, don't you, Erica?" Jim asked. "We have no idea who's responsible for any of the break-ins except yours, let alone whether they are related or not."

"I guess you have a reason to be concerned," Erica said quietly. "I'm very sorry about Walt's tennis trophy. I know what it means to him and attacking it seems malicious, whether the attack has anything to do with the book or not."

Erica paused and then continued. "Thanks for clueing me in. I'm still hoping someone wrote *Academic Awards* for a lark. Don't worry, I'll be quiet until we figure out what's going on."

Jim heard, but didn't register, Erica say 'we' as he hung up. He turned his attention to his schedule for the day. Only later did he realize what her words implied: neither she nor her fellow task force members intended to back away from the task the president had originally assigned them.

After the phone call, Erica was glad to turn *her* attention away from mysteries and put on her hard-rock hat.

ⓒ

No one noticed five people straggling into the library's cavernous storeroom shortly before noon.

As they arrived, they untangled and assembled rickety folding chairs, opened their brown bag lunches, and began talking—simultaneously. Only Steve Scott, the sixth member of the recently disbanded task force and the host for the gathering, remained quiet as the others voiced their speculations. Neither his Eastern nor his intelligence background had prepared him for the casualness of academic society. He was still surprised to hear faculty interrupting each other and freely questioning and criticizing those at the top of the hierarchy.

"Why Walt has gotten so protective all of a sudden I don't understand."

"Together, we know the faculty better than he does. I should think he'd find us indispensable."

"Surely, Walt can't abdicate his presidential duties to hunt for the culprit himself."

"What's he going to do now, make the whole cabinet drop everything to try to solve Southwestern's very own mystery?"

"I don't think so," said Steve, entering the conversation. "President Asher isn't planning to involve the cabinet; I suspect he and Bill Hamill will take the lead from now on, with a lot of assistance from Jim Scoop. The president has made it clear that he wants as little disruption on the campus as possible."

Lloyd grumbled, "I wasn't aware that we were being disruptive. If this group can't unearth the culprit, I doubt anyone else will be able to."

Erica turned to Steve. "We've put you in an awkward position, haven't we?"

"I've put myself there. After all, I'm trained to get to the bottom of things. If we're successful, I'll be forgiven." The direct look Steve gave each of the others in turn was accompanied by a disarming smile. "I'm counting on all of you to make our search a success."

Lloyd mumbled, "I wouldn't count on it."

Steve turned towards Lloyd and asked, "What did you say?"

"Nothing. Just a philosophic sigh."

Steve continued. "It seems to me that we've got a head start and that we shouldn't quit now. Later we can worry about disobeying orders and face whatever music we have to face."

Steve's offer of a place to meet had relieved Erica's fears about his divided loyalties. What he said next was even stronger evidence that he was wearing his faculty rather than his administrative hat.

"The president's naming faculty to the task force was, I thought, a wise decision." With a glance in Jeff's direction, he continued, "Except for Mr. Miles and myself, you four have a wealth of inside information about your colleagues. You're therefore likely to think of something we cabinet members, and even Jim Scoop, might easily overlook.

"Walt's understandably worried about your safety. When I agreed with Erica and Toni to convene this secret meeting, I rationalized that anyone on the faculty the least bit curious must know who's on the task force. I suspect the danger is no greater now than it was a week ago. So we might as well proceed.

"One thing you should know. Stanley Johnson, NAMWA's CEO, has been hounding the president almost daily. At Tuesday's cabinet meeting on September fifteenth, Walt reported that he'd finally persuaded Johnson to extend the deadline from Monday, September twelfth—long gone now—to Monday, the twenty-sixth.

"I still think," inserted Sarah, "we need to be awfully careful until we prove our worth as detectives."

Toni piped up. "The cabinet should be glad we're doing *their* job."

"I'm betting someone wants to see how far he—or she—can carry a practical joke!" said Lloyd with a scowl, "and meanwhile Jim Scoop probably will turn this into a criminal investigation since Southwestern doesn't provide him with a very exciting stage. Somebody out there must be laughing."

"…and dangling the whole institution on a string," added Sarah.

"I think Walt's exaggerating the danger," continued Lloyd.

Erica held up a hand. "I don't think so, Lloyd. I just learned from Jim that Asher's office has been vandalized several times. I don't have any details but I do know that—twice *his* intruder damaged his tennis trophy."

Sarah spoke up. "No wonder Walt's worried, given how his fictional counterpart gets done in."

"Walt's concerns are understandable," said Steve, "He has reason to fear that the rash of office break-ins is ratcheting up the danger on campus."

"Then," said Lloyd, "the more of us who look for the culprit—and the author—who may be one and the same—the sooner we solve the mystery. And the sooner order will be restored, allowing Walt and the rest of us to get back to our real work."

"All agreed?" asked Erica.

Everyone nodded.

"So let's decide what we are going to do—and how we're going to keep Walt and Jim from seeing us do it. Now that we've gone underground, I think we better not risk meeting again. Or even call each other on campus. Too many ears and too many open doors. You all know, don't you, that Toni is staying with Sheila Mays? So if you need to call Toni, call Sheila's."

"Wait, *should* we call her there? What if Sheila gets a whiff of something suspicious?" asked Jeff.

"Sheila's trustworthy, and she's already in the know," responded Erica. "We had to tell her what was going on—with Scoop's blessing, incidentally. It was Jim who convinced her she'd be helping us."

"Jim's right," added Sarah. "We may find her helpful if we need someone with a good institutional memory. I'm the only one who's been around longer than she has."

Erica glanced at Steve before addressing the others. "Did you know that someone's been in Steve's office, too?"

Steve shrugged his shoulders when everyone turned in his direction. "In all likelihood what happened in the library was nothing more than a prank perpetrated by a bored student." Steve's explanation of the book order elicited laughter.

"What," asked Lloyd, "are we going to do that we haven't already done?"

"Toni made a suggestion that at first I thought was crazy. But she finally convinced me that approaching our task from a different angle might work. Toni, why don't you explain your idea?"

"Okay." Toni shoved her half-eaten sandwich aside. "So far we've looked at people who can write, who are familiar with Southwestern, or who might enjoy seeing the school forfeit its share of the award. It occurred to me that we should spend our time looking *inside* the book. I think we should all read *Academic Awards* again. Only this time, instead of looking for parallels with Southwestern, we should be looking at style."

"Style?" asked Lloyd.

"Characteristic words and sentence structures. That sort of thing."

Lloyd groaned. "You're expecting us to become literary analysts?"

"I guess in a small way I am," replied Toni. "I suggest we pay attention to some stylistic features readers are aware of but don't ordinarily notice."

Jeff spoke up. "In college, I had a lit professor who argued we should be able to identify the author of any quotation that was more than a couple of sentences long. Even if we didn't remember the quote, he said, the style should be a dead giveaway."

"On the principle that 'style doth make the man'?" asked Steve.

"Exactly," responded Toni. "Without seeing their bylines, I could pick out a Thomas Friedman or Froma Harrop editorial from a batch of editorials all on the same subject. And I bet you can do the same thing."

"Toni is right," said Sarah. "One of the things I teach my music students is to listen for stylistic markers separating one composer from another."

"Surely that doesn't apply to rock 'n' roll." Steve groaned. "Rock bands all make the same kind of noise."

"Not according to the younger generation. They can tell the difference," replied Toni. "Seriously, what Sarah calls stylistic markers I call stylistic features. They are as distinct as fingerprints."

Sarah said, "It's like recognizing a Beethoven overture or a Debussy nocturne."

Toni continued, "If we compare stylistic features in *Academic Awards* with something else a faculty member has written, there's a good chance we'll have identified our writer."

"I could start," said Jeff "making a list of what our suspects have published if that would be helpful. My publicity files already have that information."

"Great," answered Erica. "That *would* be helpful." She paused and then asked, "So where should we start? Taylor Anderson and Jane Snow, definitely. Frankel? Gill? Merry?" Erica looked at Jeff before asking, "Should we exclude Roanhorse?"

Jeff replied, "I think we can safely dismiss him. Charlie would've had no reason to lie to me. But since I'm doing a story on him for the alumni magazine and have samples of his writing, I can make a quick comparison."

"Good," replied Erica. "At this stage we might as well be thorough."

"Send me your list, Jeff," said Steve. "The timing is perfect. Next week the library will be showcasing the works of campus authors. I'll send out excerpts from our current possibilities, and I can easily copy passages if we decide to add to our list of suspects."

"Then let's divvy up the people we've already interviewed," said Erica.

"Before we do that," said Steve, "I'd like Toni to give us some concrete examples of what we should be looking for." The others nodded.

"For a starter, repetitive words and phrases. For instance, Andrew Greeley sprinkles his detective's conversation with 'patently,' 'arguably' and 'doubtlessly.' I say 'doubtless' on occasion, but not nearly as often as Bishop Blackie. And while 'patently' and 'arguably' are part of Blackie's conversational repertoire, they're not part of mine. Before I called Erica with my crazy idea, I skimmed through several pages of *Academic Awards*. And I noticed that the author's characters do an awful lot of *peering at each other* and *furrowing their brows*. We should be looking for other repeated phrases like that."

"I don't think I'll have trouble picking out characteristic words or repetitive descriptions," said Steve. "Examining sentence construction is another matter. You're talking about something more complex than sentence length, aren't you?"

"Right, although sentence length is an element of style, too. Compare almost any twentieth century writer with someone writing in the nineteenth or eighteenth centuries. Hemingway versus Dickens, for example." Toni paused. "Would it help if I gave you sample sentences from *Academic Awards*?"

"Yes," came a chorus of replies.

"I won't get too technical. I'll bring samples around to your offices later this afternoon."

"Wonderful," said Sarah. "But will you have time?"

"Actually, I did my search last night. I couldn't go to sleep after Erica and I talked. I finally got up at two and jotted down more examples. I'll select the ones that occur most frequently and type them up for you."

While the others were thanking Toni, Steve spoke up. "I foresee a hitch. What if the president wants our manuscript copies back now that he's disbanded the task force?"

"I could stay later than my secretary" said Jeff, "and secretly make another copy of *my* copy."

"So that, if necessary, we could each make copies of your copy of the original copy?" asked Erica, standing up and throwing her hands into the air.

Lloyd looked skeptical. "That seems like a lot of work for something that may turn out to be insignificant."

"Not so insignificant, Lloyd," said Sarah. "For years the debate about who wrote Shakespeare's plays has been fierce. And I know of literary scholars who've been promoted for demonstrating that Shakespeare's vocabulary was three times larger than the vocabulary in the King James Version of the Bible. Other people claim that the *real* playwright had to have been an aristocrat or at least someone who had a university education."

"Whew," said Lloyd, "And that counts as scholarship in English?"

"Except for a few holdouts, most English professors believe that Shakespeare was in fact Shakespeare, rather than Bacon or Marlowe or Lord Somebody or Other. Oh, dear," said Sarah, "I've lapsed into my lecturing style. Sorry."

With a half-smile, Toni turned to Lloyd and said, "Who knows, we may just prove that you wrote *Academic Awards* and are sitting here laughing up your sleeve at all of us!"

Signaling the end of the meeting, Erica stood up. "It's getting late. Let's hope Toni's fingerprint analogy gives us the missing clue: as Toni explained, it's not just one line or swirl that's diagnostic, but the total combination. If we're lucky, style may unmask the guilty party. And Steve, I'll examine Merry's computer manual and compare it with *Academic Awards,* although I think she's as much out of the running as Charlie Roanhorse. Hah, Jane Snow is all yours, Sarah. I don't envy you. Poor Lloyd, I hope you enjoy reading Richard's book reviews. I hear he's written hundreds. And, Toni, you get Gill."

"Luckily," answered Toni, standing up. "Gill hasn't written as much as Frankel and I'm sure he's more organized than Jane. His stuff should be interesting."

℗

Later that afternoon, Toni made a tour of the campus, depositing her memo on style for the task force members.

### Interoffice Memo: Confidential

**To**: My Fellow Characters in Search of an Author
**From**: Toni, heretofore Clueless in Cottonwood
**Subject**: Possible Verbal Clues

1) Note how author X handles compounds.

   X prefers triplets to doublets—"tall, dark, and handsome"—rather than "tall and dark."
   For example, X describes Geoffrey Thomas as
"short, uncoordinated, & non-descript."
   *1*            *2*                        *3*

2) Look for frequently used words and phrases. For example:

   • X's characters *nod, squirm, chuckle,* and *raise their eyebrows* a lot.
   • Geoffrey repeatedly "*taps his foot impatiently.*"
   • Many sentences begin with either "*it was clear* ..." or "*it seemed obvious...*"

(*It* isn't the real subject in these sentences; *it* is a place-holder, standing for a subject occurring later. *Something* was clear, or *something* seemed obvious.)

3) Often our author inserts an unnecessary "that."

         "Judge Begay thought *that* Geoffrey was naïve."
         "Judge Begay thought Geoffrey was naïve."
   In each case, Judge Begay thought *something*.

4) Author X introduces many sentences with negative words and phrases:
         • *Unfortunately*, President Frank Burns...
         • *Not one to gloat*, Mary...
         • *Despite his fears*, Geoffrey...

5) Our author works hard to avoid using *said*, substituting a raft of variations—a trap many writers fall into. Repeating *said* is less intrusive than using lots of substitutions.

      *explained*
      *groaned*
      *commented*
      *reported*
      *whispered*
      *insisted*

ⓒ

Toni returned to her office after distributing the memos, pulled out her desk chair and sank into it. She'd been on campus until after ten the previous night, thanks to Jim Scoop. She tried not to think about him. She knew she ought to resent his protectiveness, but she didn't. She ought to write off her growing interest in *him* as part of the let's pretend game they'd agreed to play, but if she were honest with herself, she couldn't.

Damn it, the phone. Who could be calling at 5:56 on a Friday afternoon? She looked at caller ID. She would have gone out the door without picking up the receiver if it had been anyone but Erica calling.

"Toni, I hoped I would catch you before you left for Sheila's."

"You've caught me," Toni said, slumping wearily in her chair. "Haven't we talked enough for one day?"

"You sound as if my voice is the last one you want to hear. Hold on, I have an offer you won't want to refuse. Bill is making barbecue and potato salad. Come eat with us."

Hearing no answer, Erica continued. "When you brought the memo by, you did tell me that Sheila's niece and her five noisy kids were driving down from Pagosa Springs and bringing the Colonel's best, didn't you? I can guarantee Bill's supper will be preferable to greasy fried chicken, limp coleslaw, and mounds of barely warm mashed potatoes and gravy, but…"

"Okay, okay," Toni interrupted. "I'll come, if you'll call Sheila and make my apologies. You're right, I certainly won't miss the clamoring hordes. Also, I'll be counting on you to ply me with a large gin and tonic and the opportunity just to sit and scritch Aaron Burrhound."

"Fine. Just wait until you hear Bill's suggestion. He phoned me about half an hour ago saying he thinks we've overlooked a possible candidate. We shouldn't have, but it's understandable. After all, out of sight is out of mind. …No, I want Bill to tell you. I don't want to steal his thunder. …Yes, I'll call Sheila and have that gin and tonic—and the world's best dog—ready for you. If they can't bring you out of the dumps, nothing will. See you soon."

An hour later, Toni was feeling much better. Visiting the Ebenezers was always enjoyable. She was too tired to be truly excited about an-

didate. But believing that she should earn her dinner, she ad-
ll with a show of anticipation. "And who, pray tell, have you
thought of that we didn't?"

Erica, hastily shoving dirty dishes into the dishwasher, turned to
watch Toni's reaction as Bill answered, "Jake Henderson."

"Didn't he leave Southwestern several years ago?" asked Toni.

"Um hum, and that's why I didn't think of him," replied Erica.

"I didn't know Jake well," replied Toni, "but I can't see him writing
a mystery novel. Go on, Bill, explain your reasons for suspecting him."

Bill tugged on the lapels of the shirt showing beneath his nubbly,
well-worn Lands End sweater and then began speaking softly. "Jake's
life changed dramatically a few years after he came to Southwestern.
He was involved in lots of campus activities when he first arrived. He
and his wife never missed a concert or a play. He wrote a hilarious
spoof of Southwestern, a tongue-in-cheek history of the college of
'cows, rodeos, and contentment.' He even chaired the faculty senate."

"More than once," murmured Erica.

"He wasn't very visible by the time I came to Southwestern," said
Toni.

"That's because his wife, Dayna, went into a deep depression after
their third child was born," said Erica. "It was one of the worst cases
of postpartum depression I ever heard of. It lasted for years, not the
usual weeks or months."

Bill continued. "Jake began spending most of his time at home
when he wasn't actually teaching or holding office hours. He took care
of Dayna—which I gather wasn't easy. She slept a lot. And even when
she was awake she was absent. He had his hands full keeping the children from feeling totally rejected, being his wife's nurse, and being
chief cook and bottle washer. For fun or relief—I was never sure
which—he wrote. In addition to the articles he managed to get out
each year, he produced two popular history books."

"If he was such a hermit, how did you get to know him so well?"
asked Toni.

"I was developing a proposal for a book on Aaron Burr." Bill absentmindedly patted his loyal dog that had abandoned Toni to curl up
under his feet. "I went to talk to him after I came across several articles
he'd written on Burr. I decided I wasn't likely to find a better source of
information than Jake Henderson right here in River City."

"Jake," added Erica, "appreciated having someone to share his interest in history. Bill started dropping in at the Hendersons' house regularly and was warmly welcomed."

Bill looked both sad and excited. "I really liked Jake, and hated to see him go. Incidentally, Burrhound's mother belonged to the Hendersons. That's part of the story I need to tell you to explain why I think Jake might be your culprit.

"Dayna seemed to be coming out of her depression in the summer of—let me see—it must have been '96. She convinced Jake that if she could have some time alone, she could recover. So Jake took the three children to stay with Dayna's parents in D.C. while he was off at a conference in Maine. Jolene Gonzales, the Hendersons' nearest neighbor, agreed to check in on Dayna before and after work. I promised to water and mow the lawn. Both Jolene and I were able to report that Dayna did seem to be coming out of her shell. She was sociable, the house was neat, and she was eating regularly.

"But one day when I went over, I found the mama dog in the shed too weak to nurse her four pups. A few days later, the mother and two of the pups died."

"How did Dayna react?"

"That was the odd thing. She didn't. She'd forgotten the dog. Jolene came by when I was trying to figure out what to do. She said she'd take one of the pups, and I took Aaron Burrhound. When Dayna saw us holding the poor little things, she went to pieces and started screaming at us. Jolene, who was the only person Dayna would talk to during her long period of hibernation, couldn't calm her down. It was awful. We left her standing in the middle of the half-mowed yard, holding on to a lawn chair, weaving back and forth, and cursing the world and us. I stayed with Dayna while Jolene ran to her house and called Dayna's doctor. He called the hospital where she'd been institutionalized for a few weeks right after Loren's birth and was able to arrange for Dayna to be readmitted immediately. Luckily, the doctor made a house call, and got her sedated enough so that Jolene and her son Roberto could drive Dayna down to the hospital in Albuquerque.

"I reached Jake in Maine. He left his conference, picked up the children in Washington, leaving them here in Jolene's care—she was already a substitute mother—and then drove straight to the hospital. He never talked about what happened there, but he was devastated."

"And you think he'd have had time to write a novel with all that going on?" asked Toni.

"Not then, but later. Jake hated to leave teaching and living out here, but Dayna's family in D.C. thought she'd be better off there near them. Jake agreed. So the Hendersons moved to Washington. Jake found a house close to her parents and her sister. And by October the Smithsonian had hired Jake. It was an eight-to-five job. Between those hours and her family helping out with Dayna and the children, he had more time than he'd had as a professor. After he got the kids to bed, he wrote. We talk on the phone often, and I always stay with them when I go east..."

"Which he does way too often," interrupted Erica. "Not only do his editors want to see him in New York, but he's also become quite the darling on the lecture circuit back East."

"*Darling* is overstating it a little. In the last decade, I've talked once at Columbia, twice at William and Mary, and conducted three workshops in the D.C. area for writers' groups. But what I'm trying to say is that I've spent enough time with Jake and read enough of what he's written to think he could be the author of *Academic Awards.*"

"Especially," said Erica to Toni, "after Bill read the memo you gave me as I was leaving my office."

"Well," said Bill, "if you didn't want me to read it, you shouldn't have left it in plain sight. Furthermore, Toni, I was intrigued by the way you addressed your fellow committee members—*Six Characters In Search of an Author,* indeed. That made me curious, and the memo was staring me in the face. What was I to do? I read your list. For the last day or two, I'd been wondering if I should suggest Jake. I read your memo again. And then I read the first two pages of one of Jake's books. Bingo. Not only does he use lots of negative words, but he also puts them in little introductory phrases rather than in his main clauses— just like the examples you'd used. That was enough to convince me that your task force had missed a bet. I'm surprised neither Sarah nor Lloyd thought of Jake."

"I'm not. We were looking for slightly villainous people," said Erica. "Jake doesn't fit that category. But he is someone who wouldn't have heard about the reward."

Toni, perking up, commented, "You know, it's struck me that our search has become increasingly tame. In all the mysteries we read, Erica, the suspense and tension increase as the story develops. South-western's real-life mystery won't be very exciting if Jake turns out to be our missing author."

"Why ever not?" asked Erica. "I don't know about you, but I for one will be very excited to return to a normal life." As soon as she'd spoken, she leaned back and interlaced her fingers behind her head. Toni recognized the characteristic pose as a signal that she was ready to relinquish a pet idea. "Okay, Toni, you may be right. Anyhow, part of the mystery won't be solved if Jake's our man. *He* hasn't broken into any offices or threatened anyone on the task force or Walt Asher either."

"Just in case, I think we ought to follow through on Bill's promising suggestion."

Toni turned towards Bill. "Jake would be happy to find out about the prize if he wrote *Academic Awards*, wouldn't he? He'd have no reason to say he hadn't written the book if you asked him straight out, would he, Bill?"

"No, I'm sure he wouldn't."

"It's not too late to call him right now, is it?"

"It's only ten-thirty in Washington. He's a night-owl, I'm sure he'll still be up."

As Bill dialed Jake's number, Toni gave him a thumbs up signal and said good-bye to Erica. "Call me if Bill gets through to Jake, especially if he has good news for us."

While driving the short distance to Sheila's, Toni's doubts about Jake's being the missing author of *Academic Awards* resurfaced.

Her cell phone was ringing as she stepped through Sheila's front door. She was not surprised to hear Erica say, "Unfortunately, Jake's innocent."

☺

Friday night was Nick Delmari's second tour of duty hiding in the president's private bathroom. Again, it had been a long, boring night. He'd been tempted to leave his hiding place. He'd have been much more comfortable sitting in one of President Asher's chairs, but Jim Scoop had given strict orders to stay where he wouldn't be seen by an intruder.

# 12

*A quiet morning at Sheila's; Nick's third night on duty.*

On Saturday morning Ben checked the Math and Science Building. Except for a laboratory where a few students were working with a faculty member, he found every door that was supposed to be locked, locked.

He started to walk through the science parking lot on his way to his next building when Jim drove up and called to him. "I thought I'd find you here."

"What are *you* doing on campus so early?"

"I stopped by the office before going to visit Sheila."

"Nice lady. I heard she had to have hip surgery. How's she doing?"

"Toni Hexton is staying with her while she recuperates, and Toni reports that she's doing better."

With a knowing grin, Ben responded, "Ms. Hexton is there, too? You have yourself a good time."

"I'll be back about noon," said Jim as he left the parking lot for the short drive to Sheila's. Cresting a rise a few minutes later, he thought he saw Erica's truck ahead of him. She must be going to visit Sheila also. Not wanting to arrive on her heels, he slowed down and pulled to a curb.

When he rang Sheila's bell, Toni opened the door. "Jim. Sheila will be delighted to see you. Erica's here too."

"I know. I recognized her truck."

Jim entered the living room and went straight to Sheila, taking both her hands in his. She shoved aside the newspaper that was spread out across her lap.

Sheila pointed to the walker next to her chair. "I *can* walk on my own, but I'm doing physical therapy three days a week. Yesterday's session still has me zonked. The walker is only for insurance—in case I get wobbly when I stand."

"You might get less wobbly if you didn't hop up and down all day long!" said Toni.

"You sound like your feisty self, perhaps a bit difficult but completely normal," said Jim, bending over to kiss her cheek.

"I *am* myself. And I'm looking forward to discussing Southwestern's novel with my friends. It is such a *nice* little mystery trying to figure out who wrote *Academic Awards*. You're a professional detective, Jim. You're not going to let these two figure out who wrote it before you do, are you?"

"Sheila," said Erica, trying not to look guilty, "I'm afraid Jim and the president will have to proceed without our help. Didn't Toni tell you we've been called off?"

Sheila, quick on the uptake, noticed Erica's frown and Toni drawing a hand across her throat. "By the time Toni arrived home, I was ready for her to shepherd me up the stairs and into bed. This morning over breakfast, we chatted about other things."

"I'm sure," said Erica, "Jim wouldn't approve of our talking about *the book*."

"Now, Erica," said Jim facetiously, "how could I possibly disapprove of a ladies' literary discussion group?"

Jim pretended he hadn't noticed Toni and Erica both sighing with relief when Sheila told what he was sure was a white lie. They hoped he would believe they were only curious, not that they were ignoring President Asher's marching orders.

Sheila's next comment muddied the waters again. "I haven't gotten very far, but I'm sure enjoying the book. Comparing it to other mysteries I started reading after retirement—encouraged by my two friends here—I can see why it won a prize. It's clearly written. I had no problem recognizing our little school. I even see some resemblance between Walt and the book's impeccably-dressed fictional president," said Sheila, laughing.

Toni gulped, noticing Jim's suspicious expression and wondering what had prompted it. "When the whole task force agreed that Sheila would be discreet and might be a good source of historical insights, I lent her my copy of the manuscript. Now I don't see any reason not to let her finish the book."

Sheila laughed. "I've had to swear on a whole stack of crossword puzzles not to breathe a word to any visitor that I've found something more engrossing than watching my beloved Rockies' games or tackling the latest *New York Times* puzzles you supplied me with, Jim."

Toni quickly turned the conversation away from *Academic Awards* to the fiendishness of Sunday's crosswords. While Jim admitted he hadn't advanced past Monday or Tuesday, Erica disparaged the crossword mania and predicted that Sudoku would soon render crossword puzzles obsolete. No one else having tried it, she pulled a three-by-five tattered booklet filled with the new cross-numbers out of her pocket and demonstrated how she'd solved the first puzzle. She offered to tear a page out for Toni, Jim, and Sheila. All three shook their heads.

"I think," said Sheila, "I'll stick to my crosswords, thank you, Erica. Those puzzles must be specifically designed for the mathematically inclined."

"Not so," responded Erica. "I've got a friend who teaches fifth grade. She says she regularly confiscates these puzzles from her students during class time."

"What a wonderful way to get kids to like math," said Jim, standing up. "I'll leave you ladies to it. I've got a week's shopping to do this morning, so I must decline your invitation to join you. Sheila, take care of yourself."

As the door closed behind Jim, Erica grumbled, "I'll bet ole Snoopy Scoopy will be on the phone to Walt as soon as he gets back to campus. Unless he has his cell phone with him, in which case he'll be dialing as we speak."

"I'll take that bet," said Sheila immediately. "He wouldn't have teased us if he meant to tattle on us."

Erica, somewhat less leery of Jim than she had been, still hesitated to relinquish all her suspicions about him. "Both of you really like that glorified dog catcher! Well, you may be right. I withdraw my bet. Sheila, I didn't realize that you knew Scoop well enough to merit a kiss."

"Erica," said Sheila, "I can see by your face, that you don't appreciate Jim as you should. And I'm not quite sure why. Aside from his uniform, what have you got against him?"

"He doesn't appreciate my dog. That's my litmus test for judging people."

"A security chief can't ignore the college's rules, can he? If I remember, the faculty voted to keep dogs off campus."

Erica sighed. "I know, I know. But of course I have a double standard when it comes to dogs."

"Erica, you were here when we hired Jim. Everyone agreed he was a great find. I chaired the search committee that hired him. Even the students who attended his interviews were as excited as we were. He had exceptional credentials, including a criminal justice degree from American University. He was everything we could have hoped for in a security chief. In his twenty-year army career he was stationed all over the place. He retired with the rank of lieutenant colonel. Then, he attended graduate school at Vanderbilt."

"He went to graduate school! I can't believe it! Toni, did you know that?"

Toni nodded sheepishly.

Sheila continued. "Jim came to us with outstanding recommendations from his commanding officer *and* from Vanderbilt. The most impressive endorsement, however, came from his former top sergeant, Florencio Ordoñez.

"Mr. Ordoñez called me from Albuquerque to set up an appointment with the search committee. Florencio had served under Jim for fifteen years, starting as a corporal. Jim took a personal interest in him, saw that he got police training, and pushed him for promotion. Florencio talked to the committee for over an hour, by which time I was ready to hire Jim Scoop sight unseen. When he came in for an interview, the whole committee was charmed as well as impressed."

Toni, head down, was glad that Erica couldn't see her blush. Luckily, Erica was looking at Sheila rather than her.

"Let me give you some more reasons why I've long been a fan of Jim Scoop's and why I think it's time you changed your mind about him.

"When Jim arrived in Cottonwood," continued Sheila enthusiastically, "I showed him around town to look at homes for sale. He bought the little house he now lives in. He spent the next two weeks familiarizing himself with the campus, meeting his staff, and visiting with administrators. We lunched together several times and he always asked good questions about the college. That was a rather long answer to your question, Erica, but we go back a-ways. And if I were twenty years younger..."

"Okay, you've made your case. *Maybe* Jim is a good cop," said Erica, "but answer one more question. Since when has Vanderbilt offered graduate degrees in criminal justice?"

Toni was silent. Sheila answered Erica's question. "They don't."

"Well, what *did* he study?"

This time it was Toni who, unable to suppress a grin, responded. "Philosophy. But he found he couldn't imagine writing the kind of dissertation churned out by his fellow graduates, so he left before getting a PhD."

Erica shouted. "Oh, my gawd! Scoop's a philosophy ABD."

"Yes," said Sheila, "All But Dissertation."

"He's not keen on having that information spread around. He *likes* being a cop."

"I certainly give him points for balking at writing about philosophy," Erica said, laughing. "I prefer rocks, myself."

"By the way," said Toni. "Thanks for calling last night with the news that Jake isn't our man."

Sheila looked up, astonished. "Jake Henderson? He isn't even here anymore."

"That's why Bill thought he was such a good possibility. Off in D.C., he couldn't have heard about the prize."

"And if it had been Jake," added Toni, "that would give all of us on the task force a good excuse for overlooking him."

Sheila, with an amused gleam in her eye, glanced over at Erica. "You look dejected," she said. "Are you sad because the case isn't solved, or because learning so many good things about Jim Scoop is hard to swallow?"

Erica shook her head and shrugged. "Ahhumm. Let's get back to what Jim called our literary discussion. Sheila, you may be able to help us out. If you'd been on the task force, what would you have done to narrow down the list of our suspects?"

"As I said to Jim, the book is clearly written," said Sheila, "Perhaps from a stylistic perspective you should be looking at the clearest writers among your suspects and colleagues."

"That's exactly the tack the task force has taken. Even though she's not a faculty member, I believe the clearest writer among our candidates is Melinda Merry, but she denied writing the book," said Toni.

"Jeff and I talked with her, and we believed her denials," said Erica. "So did the task force. We eliminated her."

"We did consider Frankel," said Toni to Sheila. "His book reviews are simplistic, and repetitive, but I have to admit, they're *clear*."

"But not very imaginative, I suspect. What about Lois Pidgin?" asked Sheila.

"Why on earth would *she* write a mystery book?" asked Erica.

"Because she's chair of the faculty. She seems to enjoy baiting administrators. When I was on campus, I saw her take on President Asher at least once a week. If it's clarity you're looking for, *her* memos to the faculty were always clear—albeit frequently annoying."

"But she's never vindictive."

"She's usually not. But something happened years ago between Walt and Lois that she may not have ever forgiven him for."

"Oh?" asked Toni.

"You weren't on board yet, Toni. Erica, do you remember when Walt and Vice-President Hamill announced that Southwestern could finance adding a full-time faculty member to our permanent teaching staff?"

Erica nodded. "Yeah, I do. I've seldom seen—or heard—so much fierce competition among the faculty. Toni, each department was invited to make a case for why they thought *they* deserved the additional faculty line."

"Who got to decide?" asked Toni.

"Ultimately, the president and his administrative cabinet," answered Sheila. "But the curriculum committee, which both Lois and I were on at the time, was given the job of determining the three most deserving departments. Not a pleasant assignment, believe me."

"I take it Sociology was one of the finalists?" asked Toni again.

"Not only were they one of the finalists, but their number of majors and the size of their classes justified their claim to be the most deserving," explained Sheila.

"I thought they got the position!" said Erica.

"They did," replied Sheila. "However, the president was not happy about it! When our committee reported that we unanimously recommended the position go to Sociology, Walt, who was new that year, made the mistake of saying what he thought of the field of sociology."

"What on earth did he say?" asked Erica.

"I don't remember *exactly* what he said. Something about the field being a 'lightweight Johnny-come-lately.' He surmised that students flocked to sociology because the content of its courses was based on either 'common sense' or 'nonsense.' You could hear a pin drop after Walt's unfortunate remarks. Everyone sitting around that conference table could tell that as soon as the words were out of his mouth, Walt knew they were inflammatory and wished he could withdraw them. But of course it was too late."

"What about Lois? How did she respond?" asked Toni.

"With barely reined in fury. Slowly and very deliberately, she stood up, and, looking Walt right in the eyes, told him his prejudices were unprofessional and unfounded. And then she stomped out of the conference room."

"I never heard even a whisper about this," said Erica. "Why not?" Before Sheila had a chance to answer her question, Erica jumped in with another one, "What happened next?"

"First, President Asher had the grace to look chagrined. And then he apologized to us. He said he didn't know why he'd given voice to a long-standing rivalry and competition between anthropologists and sociologists. He said he *thought* he'd abandoned his suspicions when he was in graduate school, and was mortified that he evidently hadn't. He informed the cabinet members that he planned to tell the sociology department they could start their search for an additional faculty member. They all agreed, the sooner the better. He got up to leave the room. Looking sorrowful and still embarrassed, he turned around in the doorway and said he'd do what he could to mend his fences with Dr. Pidgin.

"The reason that interchange was never reported, Erica, was that we all agreed that we wouldn't say a word outside the room where we were meeting. I think everyone reacted as I did: I admired Walt's quickly taking the blame for what had happened and not trying to pass off what he'd said as a joke. I'm sure he tracked Lois down immediately, but I have no idea what he might have said or how she might have responded. In public, they're both polite but when they're in the same room. I never see her showing the warmth to him he shows to her. So—that's my reason for thinking the book *might* be her revenge if she's harbored a grudge ever since."

"Ouch," said Erica. "Knowing that, I think we *should* look at her."

Toni nodded her agreement.

And, thus, Frankel remained on the suspect list, and Lois Pidgin was added.

ℰ

On Saturday night, Nick came better prepared. The padded stadium seat he'd purchased to watch his son's junior high football games made him comfortable, but he was no less bored. He repeatedly looked at his illuminated watch. An hour before his shift would finally be over at 2 A.M., he stood up and stretched lazily.

He heard the faint but unmistakable click of a key turning in a lock. That must be the door to the outside office. Holding his body rigid, he reached for his flashlight with one hand and his gun with the other. Then he heard a second, slightly louder click. He crept towards the door. A thin sliver of light reached the toes of his shoes. Flinging the door open, he came face to face with Lance Lopez, the night custodian.

As he told his wife later, Lance's confession gave him a good idea. Lance wasn't the person breaking into Dr. Asher's office, but what he did there gave Nick an antidote to future boredom.

Lance confessed only to sneaking into the president's office for his weekend coffee breaks. "Here," he'd said, pulling an issue of *American Archaeology* out of a row of plastic magazine holders. "Take a look at this." Lance opened it to a two-page spread of rock art in Canyonlands.

"I've been there," said Nick. "That's one of the places my brother and I go biking."

"President Asher has a collection going back decades. At first I didn't know why anyone would want to keep old magazines," said Lance, "until I started looking at the pictures. Most of them showed me things I'd never noticed when my friends and I went jeeping and exploring. There's stuff under the ground, hidden in overhangs, and sometimes just scattered about." Lance reached for a book on the top shelf. "The gal who wrote this book claims that many of the ruins in the Southwest resemble those in Chile and Argentina, and…"

Seeing Nick's interest wane, Lance reshelved the magazine and book. "Anyway, the president's library has been a godsend for me. No one else is around when I take my breaks. I bring a thermos of coffee. Want to join me? I'd welcome having someone to talk to."

"No thanks," Nick answered. He figured he'd better pretend to be making his rounds. He'd return to his post later, after Lance had left. He didn't want Lance to start asking him questions since Jim Scoop had enjoined the security staff to silence and he didn't want to have to explain what he was doing in the president's private john.

# 13

*Nick and Jane.*

Officer Nick Delmari hadn't looked forward to returning to his post on Monday night. But, with Lance's example in mind, he brought a Stephen King thriller to his cramped quarters. The book helped. By 11:30 he was so lost in King's world that he didn't notice the noise of footsteps in the hall outside Asher's office.

Hearing the door to Ruby's office open with a bang, Nick jerked upright, clicked off his flashlight, and laid *The Shining* on the floor. He heard the intruder clomping past Ruby's desk. From inside the president's office, Nick held his breath as he reached for the doorknob. At precisely that moment, the late night visitor inserted a key into the lock and pushed the door open. The intruder would have ended up on the floor if Nick hadn't blocked her fall.

He was as surprised to be facing a woman as she was to see him. She spoke first.

"Young man, what are you doing here in the middle of the night?"

"What, Ma'am, are *you* doing here?"

"Oh, I come here often—to work."

Not knowing what to say in response to her matter-of-fact reply, Nick switched on the overhead light. Facing him was a frowzy woman dressed in gray sweats, carrying a large, worn, brown briefcase, her hair tousled, and her lips smeared unevenly with a heavy layer of bright orange lipstick.

Nick was trying to figure out how to usher her out of the office, when she harrumphed and said, "I have every right to be here. I'll have you know I'm *still* an employee of this school."

"But it's close to midnight."

"So? *You're* the one who shouldn't be here. Please leave. You're keeping me from my work!"

"You're working *here*? In the middle of the night? In the president's office?"

The woman tightened her hand on the back of one of the four upholstered chairs positioned neatly around a highly polished walnut table. Nick attempted to nudge the chair she was gripping back in place. Angrily, she shoved Nick's hand aside, pulled the chair out of his reach, and plunked her briefcase down on the table. Calmly, she inched out of the grungy parka she was wearing, folded it neatly into a square, and laid it on the table.

"I have important work to do, and you're interfering with it."

Nick didn't budge. He simply stared.

She glared back. "What, pray tell, is your name, young man?"

Without waiting for an answer, the woman began laying out paper and pens on the table. She barreled ahead. "I've got a good mind to report you to security. Their extension is 6100. You see, I have it memorized. I'm often on campus alone, so I know who to call if I need help."

"I *am* security, ma'am."

"Oh, good. Then I won't call. You may check back in an hour. In the meantime, will you please see that I'm not disturbed again?"

"Who are you?" Nick asked. At the same time he reached into his pocket, pressing the button that he hoped would bring someone to his aid—soon.

Nick did not get a direct answer from the woman, but he did get a long one. "Oh, I guess you don't recognize me in this getup. I don't dress like this in the daytime, you know, when I teach. I'm not as informal as some of the new young women on the faculty who wear jeans or those long, most unbecoming shapeless dresses. For my evening runs, though, this is comfy. Look at these wonderful, ridiculous shoes. They've got reflective inserts. Very bright. They keep me from being run over. And I think they scare off the dogs that roam around at night. Whatever, these shoes make me laugh every time I put them on. Who'd have ever thought I'd wear neon orange and lime green tennis shoes?"

At the end of this speech, she moved towards the offending chair and dropped onto it, shoulders leaning against the backrest, the base of her spine precariously resting against the front edge of the seat. She waggled her feet in Nick's direction.

By this time, Nick was completely befuddled. He could only think to ask, "What is your *name?*"

"Dr. Snow. Dr. Jane O'Connell Snow. Professor. Of Psychology."

Nick, unable to think of anything more to say, was cautiously backing out of the inner office when Dr. Snow said, "Thank you, young man. I really appreciate knowing you're in the building. A woman working alone late at night can't be too careful, you know."

Nick waited in Ruby's office for backup.

Finally, he thought he heard footsteps in the hallway. Jim Scoop arrived more quietly than Jane had. Jim, breathless, whispered, "Sorry it took me so long. I was clear across campus." Jim pointed at the closed door. "You've cornered our intruder?"

"Yeah," whispered Nick. "It's one of the profs. A dame. She's totally batty."

"I take it since you're out here, she's not violent?"

"No, maybe drunk—or on something. She acts like what she's doing is perfectly normal. She even thanked me for guarding her while she works!"

"Do you know who she is?" asked Jim.

"A Dr. Snow. Teaches psychology she says."

"What's she been doing since you sent your alert?"

"Messing with some papers, but mostly, from what I can tell, admiring her ghastly shoes!"

Jim and Nick entered the president's office and found Jane Snow sitting upright, the heels of her shoes resting atop a pile of blank paper, pens and pencils pushed aside. She seemed mesmerized by the sight of her shoes.

Jim pulled out a second chair, seating himself on the opposite side of the table for all the world as if he were the lady's dinner companion. He waved Nick into the shadows.

"You're Dr. Jane Snow, aren't you?"

"I recognize you. You're wearing the same uniform as that young man standing behind you," she replied, ignoring Jim's question.

"Yes, I'm James Scoop, chief of security at Southwestern."

"How nice of you to come. When I do my runs at night..." Jane paused, apparently drifting off into her private world. Nick looked at Jim, expecting him to say something.

After a long silence, Jane continued. Responding to a signal from Jim, Nick pulled a small pad out of his back pocket. "Nights can be dark and scary, you know," she said. "I've always had a hard time getting to sleep. Going for a run always helps. I get up early too. I worry about crashing sometimes, but so far, I never have. Not needing much sleep gives me time to be productive."

"Productive." Jim pulled his chair closer to the table and asked, "How?"

Jane lowered her feet, leaned forward, and whispered confidentially. "Classes, first, of course. And my own writing projects."

"May I ask what you're writing?"

Jane didn't answer immediately. Lifting her shoulders and oozing indignation, she said, "I never tell *anybody* about work in progress."

Abruptly shifting her eyes away from Jim, Jane stood up. "You'll have to excuse me for a minute." She looked around until she spotted the door to Nick's earlier hiding place.

Nick moved forward, ready to escort Jane to the bathroom. Jim shook his head, then stretched, and arched his back. He appeared more relaxed than he must be feeling. Jim, Nick realized, was simply going to wait for Jane Snow to talk herself into a corner.

Shortly, she emerged from the bathroom. She was smirking and disdainfully holding Nick's novel between thumb and forefinger.

"Hah, look what I found. Not only does Walter Asher still revel in games he played as a child, he reads juvenile trash." Nick winced. Jane dropped her voice conspiratorially. "What an ego. He displays his diplomas on his wall and silly trophies in his bookcase. Who can respect such a man? He's not fit to be president. A book by Stephen King, for god's sake. At least he has the good sense to be embarrassed or he wouldn't hide it in the bathroom. And look at this," she screamed, holding up the padded stadium seat emblazoned with the Denver Broncos logo that Nick had been sitting on. "The next time I see our *dignified* chief administrator, I'm going to laugh in his face. He claims *I'm* not fit to teach. Well, *he's* not fit to preside."

Nick supposed he'd have to explain the book as well as the portable cushion to his boss later. He hoped Jim would understand that he had had to do *something* to keep from going crazy during his long night watches.

As Jim reached for the book, he said, "Thank you, Dr. Snow, I'll put this on the counter behind the president's desk. I suspect he needs some light reading now and then."

"That man doesn't appreciate the people who do the most for this institution. I'll give you an earful if you'll just wait a sec," muttered Jane as she retreated into the bathroom, grabbing the door, and slamming it. While she was out of the room, Jim peered into her open briefcase and pulled out a small metal mallet.

"What the hell is that?" whispered Nick.

"Shh. It's a meat tenderizer, I think. Undoubtedly the hammer we've been looking for." Jim placed the weapon on the table.

Jane Snow rejoined them. She was completely occupied in tugging at the waistband of her gray sweats and then wiping her hands on her pants.

*This dame is no lady*, thought Nick. *She might be drunk, she might be high, or she might just be wacky.*

At any rate, it was clear to Nick that Dr. Jane Snow was ranting and raving about the president.

Jim steered Jane back to the chair she'd left, changed tactics and began to barrage her with questions.

Jim pointed to the mallet. "Yours?"

"Yes, it is." She pulled the handles of her briefcase as far apart as she could, and bent over until her face was almost inside the case, apparently searching for the mallet she'd just identified. She looked at Jim accusingly. "How did you get my meat tenderizer?"

"It fell out of your briefcase." Jim lied, smiling encouragingly. "Why do you keep a meat tenderizer in your briefcase?"

"I didn't have any mace." Looking thoughtful, Jane immediately replaced her glare with a look of teacherly forbearance. She looked first at Jim, then at Nick, and back at Jim again. "I never knew what mace was until I started reading detective stories. Did you know mace is made from nutmeg?"

Jim, with a wave of his hand, signaled that Nick could stop taking notes during Jane's lengthy, and surprisingly interesting, lecture on nutmeg and how it became a key ingredient in mace.

Ignoring her own interruption, she answered Jim's question. "I picked up the first handy thing I could find in my kitchen. Good protection, don't you think?"

"What are you protecting yourself *from*?"

"You're a policeman. You ought to know. When a lady makes a practice of taking solitary runs late at night, she needs all the protection she can get. See," righting the briefcase and opening it again, "I have other things too. A can of Raid, hair spray, spare light bulbs, a water pistol…"

Nick resisted the impulse to laugh as Jim said, "You're certainly well prepared for any contingency. You could deflect your attackers… but why the light bulbs?"

"Sometimes, this office is pretty dark. And I work here at night, you know," said Jane as if that made everything clear. Swiveling her head, she stared at each of the four walls in succession. "That man sent me his horrid letter. President Walter Asher himself is responsible for my insomnia. He hath murdered sleep." She peered almost flirtatiously up at Jim. "That's from *MacBeth*, you know."

"Yes, I know the quotation," replied Jim soothingly. Nick raised his eyebrows. He couldn't figure out why Jim, normally direct and to the point, was letting this woman beat around the bush.

"Nothing lets me sleep," she continued. "Not Tylenol PM, not the milk toast my mother used to give me when I was little, not wrapping a hot towel around my neck, nothing. So I run. I've got a sure-fire routine now: two Xanax, a double Scotch, and an hour's prowl. Being out late at night is special. Places have night vibes and they are quite different from daytime auras. It's not only people who have auras. Places do too. You can learn a lot about people from the auras in their rooms."

Nick wasn't sure how to spell 'auras.' He had a vague idea of what they were, though. Related to 'vibes' and 'ghosts,' he guessed. But he didn't expect a college professor to be taking them seriously. Only the likes of his gullible sister-in-law saw auras, felt vibes, and smelled, she insisted, traces of ghosts.

"What," asked Jim, "is the night-time aura in President Asher's office?"

"That's just what I was going to tell you. It's been fascinating to find out. Last week, I started, as I said, my prowls. I don't know what impelled me at first. It was as if I were circling nearer and nearer to some target. This room," she said, slowly surveying each of its four walls in turn, "is both my destiny and my destination."

Jane Snow began a long finger-pointing tirade that featured the parka she'd placed on the table. Nick sighed audibly, shrugged his shoulders, and quit trying to follow the lady's incoherent ramblings. Absentmindedly, he stuck his pen back in his pocket. Jim frowned at him, and, pointing to the pen Nick had just pocketed, indicated that he should start taking notes again.

Jim turned his full attention to Jane. He asked, "Is there something especially significant about your parka?"

"Yes, yes, yes. When I put my hands in the pockets, what did I find amidst the crumbs and candy wrappers but a very old key?"

"Was that key by any chance a master key to this building?" asked Jim.

Jane chortled. "It is! And luckily it opens all the doors in Center Hall. It's coming in handy since I prefer not to use my regular office at night any more."

"I'm not sure," said Jim, "President Asher would be too pleased to find you using *his* office. He certainly wouldn't expect to find you here late at night."

Jane smirked and smiled coquettishly. "He doesn't have to know, does he?"

At this, Nick looked up, astonished. Jim glanced at him sympathetically, raised his hands and stretched his fingers out in a "I-don't-know-where-all-this-is-going-either" motion.

Jane Snow became silent as if there were nothing more to say. She rose and picked up her briefcase. "It's been nice talking to you. I'm really grateful for your protection, and that of the young man over there. It's nice to feel safe when I'm out late. Again, thank you, but I must be going now. I'll just take this." She reached for the mallet.

"I'm sorry," said Jim, "I can't return it to you just now."

"Why not? It's mine."

"Yes, and we *will* return it to you. But first, we need to examine it. It's been used to hit something—you can see the flakes here," said Jim, pointing to several bronze bits visible between the raised knobs. "I think it's been used as a hammer. We need to find out what it hit."

"I only use it in self-defense."

A look of fear clouded Jane's eyes. Her head began shaking rapidly from left to right. Even when she looked at Jim, she didn't seem to see him. She grabbed her briefcase, stuffing papers into it.

*Poor lady,* thought Jim, *thinking she needed to attack a tennis figurine.* Aloud he said, "You talked about the aura of this office. You met with Dr. Asher in here, didn't you?" When, instead of an answer, she fixed her eyes on a distant point in the ceiling, Jim rephrased his question. "I suspect those meetings were very disturbing."

"You'd have been disturbed too," Jane barked, "if you were suddenly told you couldn't do what you'd been trained to do and had spent your whole life doing!"

Nick, aware of the sadness and a note of defeat in her voice, felt a moment of compassion for the woman. Jim obviously felt the same.

Jane Snow tried to scoop up the pens that were rolling across the table. Gently, Jim gathered them together and ceremoniously handed them to her. Unceremoniously, she shoved them into the pockets of her parka, turned on her heel and said, "Good-night."

"I'll walk you home," said Jim, rising and signaling Nick to lock up.

"Why thank you. I've always liked having an escort."

*Getting out of Dodge.*

The next morning, Jim Scoop summed up his late-night encounter for the president. He explained what he'd gleaned from Jane Snow's rambling non-sequiturs, leaving out her harangues about Walt's reading habits and unfairness. Although she hadn't admitted to moving or damaging anything, she had admitted coming into the office during the first weeks of school. She was surely responsible for the misplaced pen, the crumpled dust jackets, the tic-tac-toe sheet, the spilled tea, and the two separate attacks on his tennis trophy. After their late-night conversation he'd relieved her of a meat tenderizer and a master key to Center Hall. At the moment, Billy Bob was comparing the tenderizer with the damaged trophy. There was no doubt it would prove to be the weapon used to hammer the statuette.

The report was a relief to Walt—for several reasons. Not least of which was being able to enter his office each morning without trepidation. More important, though, was that he wouldn't be dreading a long, acrimonious year. Jane's final year could legitimately be cut short.

"One final question, Jim. Do you think there's the remotest chance she *could* have written *Academic Awards?*"

"No. Not unless her mental state began deteriorating only during the last few months. I can't see *any* sustained effort coming from a woman who wears psychedelic running shoes, hoists up her sweatpants in front of a young male officer and me, carries a meat tenderizer along with light bulbs for your office in her briefcase, admits to regular late night doses of Scotch and Xanax, and calmly gives me a midnight lecture on the ingredients of mace.

Knowing that Jane Snow's nightly visits to the president's office would come to an end was a great relief to Jim. He was convinced that Jane, insulted and hurt, was guilty of breaking and entering. Whether her criminal trespass was more than a sign of her unraveling, and what she might do next, still had him worried.

℮

Much later that morning Jim sat at his desk and went through yesterday's mail. He was having trouble concentrating on memos about dining hall hours and the minutes of the last faculty meeting. He was distracted by his frustration about not finding the mystery book's author. With few leads, all of them tenuous, he was still worried about the other office break-ins. Mostly he was concerned about those high-profile individuals, Walt Asher, Erica Ebenezer, and Toni Hexton. Jim was relieved that Walt was scheduled to depart on Wednesday for a Rocky Mountain College Presidents' conference in Flagstaff.

He began nervously drumming his fingers on the desk. Better to do something, anything, rather than fruitlessly replaying the same tapes. Jim decided he'd be a little less worried if he knew when Walt would be leaving Cottonwood.

Ruby answered Jim's call. "President's office. How may I help you?"

"Jim Scoop here."

"I assume you want the president. Let me put you through."

"Thanks, Ruby."

"Sorry to disturb you, Walt, I'm checking to find out when you're leaving for Northern Arizona University…."

"I've cancelled my trip, Jim. I'm not going to NAU."

"What do you mean, you're not going? You can't do anything here! Furthermore, if you are *here* I have to try to protect you! …"

"Isn't that part of your job description? To protect everyone here at Southwestern?"

Jim was glad to hear the playfulness in Walt's voice. It made him hope he could convince Walt he'd be more help out of town than in. "It was bad enough seeing your poor battered trophy. I don't want *you* battered in the same way!"

"Jim, if you feel it necessary to banish me, what about other members of the task force? Even though I've disbanded the group, they may still be in as much danger as I am."

"Granted. And since Ms. Hexton and Dr. Ebenezer were the most visible members of the task force—I heard the faculty were calling your task force the Toni and Erica show—I'll get them out of town. With your permission, that is, and only if you'll go to Flagstaff as planned."

Walt sighed. "All right, Jim. I'll be at Little America Wednesday night through Saturday. I'll expect to hear from you just as soon as you connect Jane's strange weapon with the wounds inflicted on my trophy. The best time to reach me will be before eight in the morning. Call, too, if there are any other new developments. In an emergency, I can always be paged. Ruby will have phone numbers."

"I'll report in each morning. I'll inform Erica and Toni that you want them out of town. Hopefully, Erica won't argue too much."

"I wouldn't be too sure of that."

"She won't be able to protest *too* much if I tell her it's your order, not mine. Try to have a good time at the conference. I'll see you when you return."

Jim hung up. He was glad he'd called. He had no idea that Walt had cancelled his trip. Luckily, the president had caved in quickly and was willing to reschedule.

Jim hoped he could be as persuasive with Erica and Toni. He reached for the phone, and dialed Toni's number. With her schedule etched in his mind, he knew she'd still be in her office.

"Good morning, Toni. It's Jim. I'm calling to invite you and Erica to lunch. I'll serve pizza and salad at my place at noon. I need to confer with you both about your hunt for the mysterious author."

"President Asher disbanded the task force, Jim," Toni said. "He took us off the case."

"But you're still looking, aren't you?" Jim asked.

"How did you know?" Toni sputtered.

"You told me—just now. But even before that, I had my suspicions after the awkward conversation at Sheila's place. You thought I wouldn't notice the silences or the signals being passed around the room. Now that you know that I know, I need to talk to you both. Away from campus. I'll order pizza, with your choice of toppings."

"Well, that'll be a change from the snack bar. Erica and I were planning to have a quick lunch together today."

"You can come for a quick lunch at my house instead. It won't take you more than five minutes to get here. I'll see you shortly before noon."

At 11:45 A.M. Toni walked to the science building and intercepted Erica as she was leaving.

"What're you doing on this side of campus?" asked Erica, surprised to see her friend.

Toni concocted an excuse about a meeting that had just ended.

"Good, we can walk to the snack bar together. I'm starved. I want something humongous and tasty. I wonder what the special is today."

"How about deep dish pizza, loaded with everything?"

"Great, as long as there are no anchovies."

"There won't be," said Toni, steering Erica away from the plaza and towards the side street where Jim lived. "We're not going to the snack bar. We're going to Jim's."

"Why on earth are we going to his house?"

"He called a little while ago saying he wants to talk with us. *He* sounds willing to work with us even though Walt fired us."

"Toni," Erica objected, "if Jim thinks that our hunting season is over, why would he want to talk to us?" Before her friend could answer, she added accusingly, "Unless you broke the task force's pact and revealed our secret sleuthing!"

"C'mon, Erica. You were at Sheila's the morning she almost spilled the beans in front of Jim. You may fault him for being a dumb policeman, but he's too intelligent and too observant not to have noticed how quickly we changed the subject. I suspect until we acted like the proverbial cat on a hot tin roof, he'd planned for a longer visit. If you remember, he skedaddled—fast."

Erica reached out to give Toni a gentle punch on the arm and softened her statement with a smile and a quiet laugh. "You've made your case. Both you and Jim are *entirely* without fault. By the way, has Jim said what in particular is so important that he needs to talk to us *now*? Or does he just want to show off his pizza-making skills?"

"I don't know about his agenda. As for the pizza, he's getting a take 'n bake from the Cottonwood Grocery. I mentioned my stylistic analysis idea to him when he called this morning. And I must say he was lots easier to convince that it was a good idea than the task force was!"

"It's the *only* avenue we have left," grumped Erica as they approached Jim's house.

Toni was silent for a moment. "It's going to be a lot of work reading the samples Steve collected for us."

"*When* are we going to have time?"

"I guess it'll have to be this weekend," replied Toni, knocking on Jim's door.

"Come in. Welcome. Pizza will be out of the oven in precisely two and half minutes," said Jim making a show of looking at his watch. "The salads are on the table. What would you like to drink? I can offer water, iced tea, or Coke."

As they selected their drinks and dressed their salads, Scoop explained, "I wanted you both to join me for lunch to share information about our elusive author."

"Fine, Jim, you start. I hope you have better leads than we do," said Erica.

The timer beeped. Jim shut it off and took the pizza out of the oven. He replied, while cutting the pizza, "First, I must tell you that Walt had cancelled his Flagstaff trip, but I've persuaded him to go to his college presidents' conference after all. He leaves tomorrow morning early and won't return until Sunday night."

"I thought he was all set to go," said Toni.

"He felt he couldn't leave campus with the mystery unsolved," Jim said as he turned towards Erica. "You asked whether I have any good leads. I don't. I have a few very slender leads. I doubt they're as good as yours. I have my guys checking them. I'm worried about Walt's safety; that's why I'm sending him away. I don't want the elusive author lurking around, waiting to attack Asher, or you folks who are looking for the writer. I doubt anyone on campus knows that the president disbanded—or," said Jim smiling, "at least *tried* to disband the task force. Next to Walt, you two are at the top of my worry list."

Erica reached for a slice of pizza, "Oh, Jim. Don't worry about us. My only worry is that this pizza has those nasty, salty little fish on it!"

"Erica, the anchovies are only on one half, and that half is for Toni and me. The rest is all for you!"

Jim continued, "What I want you to do is to take your writing samples and your copies of *Academic Awards* and go to the Cozy Cabins in Dolores, Colorado. I've already made reservations for you. You can work there without interruption. I think you have a better chance than I do of finding clues that point to the author. I want you to leave tomorrow."

"Jim, this is very highhanded of you!" said Toni. "Who's going to look after Sheila if I'm in Dolores? It was you who arranged for me to stay with her."

"Toni, don't worry. I'll see that Sheila is taken care of."

"Well I still don't like you making arrangements without talking with us first," Toni said.

"I agree," Erica said as she pushed her chair away from the table and stood up abruptly. "It's bad enough when students cut classes. But for professors to play hooky is totally irresponsible."

"It's not irresponsible when it's for a very good cause," Jim replied. "Besides, you're not playing hooky and you're certainly not the first faculty members to cancel classes. You're creative. You can make up convincing reasons why you have to be gone."

They both envisioned all the people on their list and the stack of pages they had to read. The more they thought of the task they faced, the more overwhelmed they felt, and the more willing they were to accede to Jim's orders.

"I guess so," admitted Erica. "Some of our colleagues don't even bother coming up with reasons." She shrugged her shoulders resignedly while Toni's glare was gradually replaced with a rueful smile.

"Hmm," Erica said as a sly grin spread across her face. "You know that Lloyd Reasoner is on our list."

"No, I didn't! Even though he's on the task force?"

"Toni and I have begun to think he might be a dark horse candidate. He seems to be having too much fun looking for an author who can't be found. And he seems amused by the committee's proceedings. Lloyd is a philosopher, and that's my problem." Erica leaned toward Jim. "How about a deal? I don't read philosophy and you do. Now that I know about your secret past, I figure you're the perfect person to read Lloyd's book, *A Discussion of Derida's Deconstructionism. You* can hunt for Lloyd's stylistic markers!"

"Oh, no." Jim shook his head.

It was Toni's turn to grin. "We'll go to Dolores on one condition. You take Lloyd and we'll take all our other potential authors."

"I'm not particularly fond of either Derida or Deconstructionism. I won't enjoy reading Lloyd's book one tiny bit. As you well know, I do have a copy of *Academic Awards*." Jim smiled conspiratorially at Erica. "I *might* be able to compare the styles of the two books. That is, if Toni would give me a quick lesson in stylistic analysis."

"Okay, you win. We'll get out of Dodge. That'll give us more time to read all the stuff we've got to read," said Erica. "I'm sure I can get a geology colleague to cover my Thursday labs, and I'll cancel my Friday classes. The students won't mind at all. But I can't leave before noon on Wednesday."

"Wait a minute," interjected Toni, "*I* haven't agreed to this yet! I still think it's high-handed of you, Jim, to have made reservations before talking with us. And what is this place called Cozy Cabins? It sounds to me like an upscale version of a no-tell-motel."

"Toni, relax," said Jim. "It's a nice little place on the Dolores River. I've stayed there myself on hunting trips. The cabins have microwaves and small refrigerators, and if you don't want to cook, the motel is less than a quarter of a mile north of the town of Dolores, easy walking distance. As Erica says, you'll need the uninterrupted time to read everyone's deathless prose. I've charged the reservations to the college. After all, you'll be on important college business."

"Okay, Jim, it seems a reasonable way to proceed," admitted Toni grudgingly.

"Would you mind telling me who your other suspects are?" questioned Jim.

Erica started down the list. "Becky Keen, Steve Scott's secretary, who writes short stories; Jean Abernathy, the wife of the anthropology professor, who writes occasional columns for the *Albuquerque Journal*; and, even though it seems unlikely, Jane Snow."

"I think you can leave Jane out; she's a fruitcake," interjected Jim.

"She can, or could, write clearly, particularly if she wrote the book several years ago," responded Toni. "Jim, I'm surprised that you'd let us dismiss Jane so quickly. Aren't police investigators trained to leave no stone unturned?"

Jim shrugged, sorry that Walt had forbidden him to tell anyone about last night's encounter.

"We'll have to examine an article Jane wrote entitled *Finger-painting: Beyond Rorschach*. It'll be filled with a lot of jargon. There's nothing more painful than reading the jargon of someone else's discipline. Oh well, it'll serve our purposes. Even though she wrote it a decade ago, people's styles change very little over time."

"We've reduced the number of suspects," said Erica. "For a while, we considered Jake Henderson, but we had to eliminate him. Too bad, since his *Santa Fe Under the Spanish Governors* is the only thing I looked forward to reading. But Jake didn't write our mystery. Bill called and asked him. He denied having done it."

"Jake Henderson would've been a really good candidate!" said Jim. "I've read a couple of his history books. I wish the guy were still here. I'd sure like to tell him how much I've enjoyed his work. The two books I read were scholarly *and* down to earth."

"Besides Melinda Merry, Taylor Anderson, Lois Pidgin, and Richard Frankel," said Erica, "we feel obligated to reexamine some of our earlier suspects. And to peruse the work of some people we don't suspect at all. Steve's given us excerpts from books and articles written by faculty members going back a decade or more!"

"You have your work cut out for you. You're going to thank me for forcing you to take a long weekend away from campus. Are you sure you can't make your task easier by eliminating anyone else?"

"I wish we could," replied Erica. "But as Toni said, at this stage, we're not going to leave any stones unturned. Becky Kean, Melinda Merry, and Jean Abernathy are all long shots."

"We'll put their stuff at the bottom of our stack and read them only if no one else's style matches up with the style in *Academic Awards*," said Toni.

Erica, grinning broadly, faced Jim. "Enjoy your weekend with Reasoner and Derida. And thanks for the anchovy-less pizza."

"Thanks for your help, Jim," said Toni.

As the two women walked towards the front door, Jim, looking solemn, said, "I hope you'll drive Toni's nondescript car rather than Erica's truck; it's too easily identifiable."

Toni cringed as she heard Erica say, "Paranoia speaks again!" But then she turned to see her friend put a hand on Jim's arm and smile warmly at him. The gentle gesture belied the spoken words.

*Jim's ducks fall in line.*

At 7 A.M. on Wednesday, September 21, President and Mrs. Asher began their five and a half hour drive to Flagstaff, Arizona, for the annual regional meeting of the Association of Presidents of Small Colleges.

At 7:45 A.M. Jim Scoop rolled over and looked at his alarm clock. Knowing that it was too early to get up after his late duty the previous night, he tried to go back to sleep. He couldn't. He was tempted to call Toni, asking her to notify him when she and Erica were on their way out of town. But he didn't. He could imagine various retorts she'd make to his "unreasonable" request. She'd accuse him of interfering, call him a fussbudget, or worse yet, complain that she did not want or need an Orwellian "big brother" to "watch" over her.

At 9:30 A.M. there was a disturbance on campus. Several dogs, illegally on the loose, were chasing each other around the college guesthouse. A security officer had been making his rounds at the north end of campus when the three dogs—a stray mutt, a student's German shepherd, and an unleashed golden lab he recognized as belonging to one of the sociology professors—gleefully discovered each other. The officer advised the student to put his dog back in his truck, and leave him home in the future. He wrote out a ticket for a very indignant Dr. Lois Pidgin. She, having ignored two previous warnings, tried unsuccessfully to refuse this one. The officer shooed the stray up the Waterfall Trail away from campus.

At the start of her eight o'clock geology lecture, and again at her ten o'clock class, Erica Ebenezer announced the two classes would not meet on Friday. She handed out special assignments—due Monday—to substitute for missed class time. None of the students objected.

At 11:55 A.M. Toni Hexton posted a note on her office door. She conveniently—and quite out of character—forgot to tell the department secretary how to get in touch with her during her absence. Nor did she mention that Chief Officer Jim Scoop would be checking in at the newspaper office in her stead.

At 5:15 P.M. Jim called the Cozy Cabins Motel in Dolores and asked to be connected to Miss Hexton's room. The phone must have rung at least ten times before Erica answered gruffly. "Yes? Who is it?"

"Jim Scoop."

"You scared me, Jim. Nobody except you, Sheila, and Bill is supposed to know we're here. The phone kept ringing and ringing. Damn it, Jim, I only answered because Toni and I figured it had to be one of you and that you'd only call if there was an emergency. You're not calling to tell us about a new crisis at Southwestern, are you? Or to let us know we can come home because the author of *Academic Awards* has come forward and confessed, saving Toni and me the task of reading thousands of words?"

"Neither. My apologies. I just wanted to make sure you got in okay."

"Yeah, we did. The room is fine, Jim. The bedspreads don't match, but there's a table with two chairs, an old scruffy recliner, and a refrigerator that works. The hideaway that you picked out for us will be a *cozy* place to read late into the night."

Erica sounded sarcastic. "Thanks for your concern. We *did* have a little excitement on the way here. Two guys pulled in behind us a mile or two past Durango and then tailgated us all the way from there to Mancos. When we turned right, so did they. When we came to the place where Highway 184 comes to an end at the T intersection, we stopped at the stop sign. They almost rear-ended us."

Not sure he liked the sound of this, Jim tried to eliminate any hint of concern from his voice. "Did they follow you into Dolores?"

"No," Erica started to giggle, "but they did accost us. The guy in the passenger seat jumped out of the car and knocked frantically on my window."

"Now you're scaring me!" said Jim, torn between laughter and worry.

"Serves you right, but you don't need to be scared," responded Erica, her giggle descending into a low chuckle. "He held up a grimy, wrinkled map in his hand. He kept tapping the map, and then pointing his left hand at his chest, and his right hand in my general direction."

"What did you do?" asked Jim.

"Well, I didn't feel at all threatened. The kid looked about sixteen. And *he* was obviously scared." Erica paused. "Here, I'll let Toni tell you the rest of the story."

Toni did not call Jim a fussbudget. With amusement, he heard her echo what he'd imagined her saying early this morning. "So, big brother *is* watching me."

"Maybe you need watching if someone's going to follow you for forty-some miles."

"The tailgaters were perfectly innocent of harboring bad intentions towards us. We decided they were bad drivers, not bad guys. Turns out, they just wanted directions. The trouble was, they had a New Mexico map—useless, of course, in Colorado! Seeing another car with plates like theirs, they weren't about to let us out of their sight.

"I'll try to describe our encounter briefly, Jim, but I guarantee you it won't satisfy your policeman's instinct to see a criminal behind every steering wheel."

*That's fine with me,* thought Jim to himself. Convinced now that he had not sent Toni and Erica into danger while trying to keep them from it, he relaxed, letting go of the sense of uneasiness that he hadn't been able to shake off all day.

"Our pursuers," continued Toni, "must have been happy to see the road sign at the intersection pointing left to Cortez and right to Dolores. When they saw my turn signal pointing right, going *away* from Cortez—their destination—they evidently panicked. The driver began to honk and the passenger stuck his head out the window. Erica told me to drive off the road. She signaled for them to follow us. All four of us got out of our cars. Amazingly, between my limited Spanish and their limited English, we managed to communicate.

"I learned that they're brothers working for a brother-in-law, or an uncle, or a cousin—my Spanish isn't fresh enough for me to be sure which—somewhere north of Aztec and south of Bondad. They showed us a scrap of paper with an address for some kind of shop in Cortez that repairs tools. Luckily, the shop was on Main Street and I could tell them how to get there."

"Did you believe their story?"

"Why ever not? Erica's right. You *are* paranoid, Jim. Their car was muddy. I could barely make out a Preston Excavating sign on the passenger door. Jim, they had no reason to pretend to be anything they weren't. They might have been working in this country illegally, but they had no designs on us. We sent them on their way, suggesting they cruise Main Street once they reach Cortez. They'd be sure to see the shop they're looking for. We waved good-bye and drove on into Dolores. And here we are, safe and sound."

@

Shortly after 7:00 the next morning Jim's alarm went off. He yawned, sat up, and pulled his bedside phone onto his lap. As instructed, he put in his call to the president well before Walt would be leaving for a day of meetings.

Waiting—endlessly it seemed—for the motel clerk to connect him to Walt's room, Jim's mind wandered. If only he were calling Toni instead of Asher, he thought with some surprise.

So engrossed was Jim in his own thoughts that he was startled when Walt's voice came through the receiver, "Asher here."

"Walt, it's Jim. I hope you appreciate my getting up early to keep you posted about what's going on. It's been years since I took evening patrols and on the first day I felt like sleeping in, I have orders to report to you."

"Only fair, since you were the one who said I wouldn't be welcome on campus." Asher sounded hopeful. "*Is* something going on?"

"Unfortunately, not much. One of my officers gave Lois Pidgin a ticket for having her dog on campus, unleashed—again. And Joe Blake thinks he has a good idea on who broke into Toni Hexton's office. If he's right, it doesn't look as if the vandal is our author and benefactor."

"In some ways I'm sorry to hear that. It would have been nice to kill two birds with one stone."

"I'll fill you in on Toni's, er, Ms. Hexton's intruder when I know more. Joe Blake is meeting with me this afternoon to tell us that one of the custodians may have a lead we'll want to follow."

"Good," said Walt. "Speaking of Lois Pidgin, wasn't she on the task force's list of suspects at one time?"

"Yes. Personally, I don't think there's a chance she's our author, though. The lady is too serious," said Jim.

"And too fair. She wears her indignation on her sleeve. You wouldn't have needed to send me or Toni and Erica away on her account—even if she *had* written the book."

"I don't have much to report on the missing author front. I'll fill you in on what's happened quickly and then I'll let you go to breakfast."

"No hurry. My wife just began her morning ritual. Why it takes a naturally beautiful woman a half hour to put on make-up that she hopes no one will notice I've never been able to figure out. So take your time. As long as you're calling on the presidential dime."

"I am."

"Good. Remind me about damage done in Toni's office. As you know, I'm sensitive about office vandalism these days. What makes you think the person who broke into Ms. Hexton's office *isn't* E.T.C.?"

"The book is orderly. The break-in was decidedly not. We have narrowed the field of possible authors though. And by tonight if Joe's right I may know who broke into Toni Hexton's office." Worrying that he'd slipped up by saying 'we,' Jim almost didn't hear Walt's next question.

"Sounds as if you're making progress. Are you prepared to take a guess at who might have written *Academic Awards?*"

"Taking Toni's intruder out of the running is a sign we're making some progress. I'd really rather not name any names just now. No point in spreading suspicions."

"I suppose that's wise. No use tainting the innocent—even though I've been president long enough to have lost any illusions I might once have had about the innocence of faculty. Sorry to have sidetracked you. Back to the Hexton break-in: you described it as disorderly. It sounded as if the damage was widespread."

"Very. The break-in occurred nine days ago. All the desk drawers were pulled out, the lock on a filing cabinet had been forcibly opened, and the contents of several files were scattered about. Even the telephone on Toni's desk had been dumped on the floor."

"Was anything stolen? Any computer damage?"

"No computer damage. If the intruder had tried to get into it, he—or she—wouldn't have been able to get past Toni's password. And yes, there was something stolen. But she's pretty sure that nothing was taken other than a few copies of recommendations from last year's promotion and tenure committee."

"Hmm. Sounds like the work of someone with a grudge—especially someone denied promotion or tenure. But tell me again why you're exempting Toni's thief as our author?"

"Bill Hamill says there's no way the filched files belong to people mad enough to do you in—in either real life or fiction! I don't blame you for being spooked, Walt. There are lots of parallels between you and Frederick Burns, the book's president. What still bothers me is that faculty files were stolen. That's more of a coincidence than I like."

"I'll be waiting to have you tell me tomorrow morning—or better yet, tonight—what makes Bill so sure we have separate *crimes* on our hands: the vandalism in my office and personnel files stolen from Toni's. Jim, I don't know that I can forgive you for wanting me *here* instead of *there*. I don't expect my conference to be half as exciting as your two pursuits."

"I'm meeting the vice-president and after I talk with him I'll go over to the physical plant office. One of Joe's custodians encountered a student in the journalism hall late at night, evidently going back to the scene of his crime. Enrique got a good look at him, though, and was able to supply an excellent description of him. He thinks the fellow will cave in pretty easily when we confront him."

"I'm looking forward to hearing all the details tomorrow. Happy hunting!"

☺

Ten minutes later Jim was in Bill Hamill's office.

Twenty-five minutes later he left—convinced that Toni's intruder couldn't be the author.

Of the three professors whose files had been taken from Toni's office, only one had complained about being wrongfully denied promotion. His complaint evaporated when he accepted a position that was, he said, "more to his liking and lots better paid than academia."

"I do have one suggestion, though," Vice-President Hamill said hesitantly, "but only if you're truly desperate."

"Who?" Jim asked.

"George Rankin," Hamill replied.

"The physics professor?"

"Yes. He applied last spring for early promotion and tenure. That's very unusual. He didn't get it, and he was threatening all kinds of bad publicity and maybe even a lawsuit. In talking with him, I quickly learned he has such a grandiose view of himself and is so little attuned to campus politics that he saw nothing unusual in expecting to skip the associate level altogether and be anointed a full professor before he turned thirty and after only two years at Southwestern. He had deigned to come West after earning a PhD from MIT. There he'd been engaged in 'cutting-edge' research with one of the shining lights in the field. And since Rankin was a name to be reckoned with in Boston, he expected the family fame to garner him special privileges everywhere.

"But," concluded Bill, "I'm convinced Rankin is too busy bolstering his own reputation to take time to write a book his colleagues back East would deem frivolous.

"Besides, Rankin probably didn't pay enough attention to the campus to find his way from one building to another. He didn't know that his request had been sent to the faculty promotion and tenure committee, who immediately passed it on to me because he didn't have his department's endorsement. It never did register on him that a review by his peers mattered."

Figuring that Rankin was too much of a long shot to be taken at all seriously, Jim decided he should at least talk with the physics professor. Reluctantly making his way to Rankin's office, Jim was relieved to find a note on the door announcing that George would be off campus for the whole week—with no explanation given for his absence.

@

As promised, Jim "happened" to drop in on Betty Frost and her newspaper staff Thursday evening. He found the student editor talking with one of the reporters. They both looked unhappy. Jim walked over to join them.

Betty looked up as he approached. "Mr. Scoop, I'm really glad to see you. Professor Hexton is out of town. Jody," said Betty giving a tentative pat to the girl's shoulder, "is a new member of our reporting staff." The girl, appearing embarrassed and uncomfortable, examined her feet while pulling away from Betty. "Jody wrote two really good stories for last week's edition, but the lead story I assigned her for this week has some problems. Maybe you could help me explain what's wrong."

Jim smiled at Jody, hoping to put her at ease. "That's what I'm here for. I told Ms. Hexton that I would fill in for her as best I could."

"Jody, the problem with your story about Southwestern's mysterious mystery book," explained Betty, shifting her glance from Jim to the young reporter, "is that too much of your information is based on hearsay and speculation. You don't have any official information."

Jody looked down at the floor. "Well, I couldn't get anyone *official* to talk to me. The president's secretary wouldn't even make an appointment for me, and the vice-presidents didn't really answer my questions. The two faculty members I went to, Dr. Frankel and Dr. Pidgin, really didn't know anything or wouldn't tell me much. Dr. Frankel just gave me a knowing grin, and refused to comment. Dr. Pidgin could only tell me that a mystery book set at SWC had won an award. And I already knew *that*. So I talked with students. They're bursting with curiosity, especially about how all the money will be spent!"

"And no wonder," said Jim, kindly. "Half a million dollars is nothing to sneeze at."

For the first time, Jody lifted her head and smiled. "Yeah, the students are really excited. They have all sorts of ideas about what Southwestern should do with the money, from expanding the stables to remodeling the student union building."

"Your quotes from students are just fine, Jody," said Betty. "But the rest of the story is filled with rumors treated as if they were facts. This piece is too much like a *National Enquirer* story."

While Betty was talking to Jody, Jim was skimming her article. He said, "As a journalist, if you can't get people who know what's going on to talk with you, make sure you haven't included unsubstantiated rumors."

"But then," pouted Jody, "I don't really have any story at all!"

"Maybe by next week, you'll be able to get more information." Betty turned to Jody and suggested that she hold her article on the campus mystery and work on her story about Monday night's Student Senate meeting instead.

"That is so totally boring," Jody replied, stalking off.

Betty looked gratefully at Jim. "Thanks. I don't like telling my reporters that I won't accept their articles." She paused. "Would you like a cup of coffee?"

"Yes, I'd welcome the coffee *and* the chance to sit down."

Betty led Jim first to the coffee pot, then to a chair beside her desk. She sat and peppered him with questions. "What do you know about the mysterious mystery writer? Do you think the author has heard about the award? If so, why not come forward to claim the prize and let the college celebrate?" Betty raised an eyebrow and wagged a finger at Jim. "And just why have you taken to dropping in to the newspaper office so often? I have a suspicion you want to see Professor Hexton?"

"Whoa, Betty, one question at a time."

"Okay, I'll start with my first one. It was the question Jody *should* have asked you."

Jim shrugged. "I imagine she sees my uniform and doesn't see me as a source of information."

"But you're in a position to know about most things happening on campus. I couldn't have worked for you for three years without learning that! What *is* the story on this mystery book?"

Jim hesitated a long moment, "I can't speak for publication."

"So 'No comment,' huh? That means you *do* know something. So, tell! The editor can write stories, too. Maybe I'll take the story I assigned to Jody back. I'd love to write it! It'll be the biggest news to hit Southwestern in years!"

Jim hesitated again, and then spoke slowly, "Betty, you are right on both counts. I do know some things, and the story probably will be big news. But I can't talk now. The best I can do is to promise you an exclusive interview when it's all over."

Eddy knocked on the frame of the open door to Betty's cubicle. "What do you need, Eddy?"

"Nothing from you, Betty. I just wanted to tell Mr. Scoop that I got my paper back. I got a B plus, thanks to *Professor* Scoop here."

As Eddy returned to the sports desk, Betty continued, "So what about my last question?"

"Toni Hexton's a fine lady and a friend. I think I would like her to become a better friend. That isn't for publication either."

Betty laughed, "I'm not a gossip columnist. I'm just curious. Toni *is* a fine lady," she said, looking up with a sly smile, "And you're a fine gentleman, and quite *attractive*—for an older man."

Jim laughed to himself at the reference to his age, but said nothing. To someone like Betty, he was old.

Getting back to business and unaware of his reaction, Betty looked around the newsroom. "Things are under control here. I've approved all the articles. There's nothing left to complete except the final layout."

"You're doing a great job, Betty. I'll report to Ms. Hexton that all is well." Jim hastened out the door. He mentally breathed a sigh of relief. Betty had the makings of a tenacious reporter and he was glad to escape with no more questions. He did trust her to keep his answers to herself.

When he found it hard to go to sleep that night, he replayed their conversation. Perhaps he should have been less open with Betty. Not only about the mystery book, but also about his regard for Toni Hexton. Having worked with Betty closely for three years, he tended to forget that she was still an undergraduate. Ah, what the heck, she seemed more mature than many people twice her age and he could count on her discretion. *Who am I fooling?* he thought to himself. "*Regard*" *is a pretty tame word for what I'm feeling. And from the look Betty gave me, she's on to me.*

*Narrowing the field.*

"Hey, Jim, come in here," Joe Blake called out as Jim walked by his open door a few minutes before noon on Friday. "Sorry I wasn't here to see you yesterday."

"I hear you had to rush off to take care of a crisis in one of the dorms."

"What a mess. The lower floor of Tanner Hall was completely flooded. There must have been two inches of water soaking the rug in the hall and an inch or more in most of the student rooms. We had a helluva time getting the students who were in their rooms to go outside, and keeping those who were out from coming in. It took us hours to find the source of the leak, meanwhile persuading the students that we couldn't turn the electricity on until we did. They were frantic to check their computers, stereos, hair dryers, popcorn poppers, and even television sets. Now all we have to do is keep them from tripping over the cords of all the fans we've got going full blast.

"But," continued Joe, shuffling through a pile of pink slips, "that's my problem, not yours. Some of these reports are from Enrique Moriego. They may help you solve one of the campus's many mysteries."

"It's about time one of our mysteries got solved," grumbled Jim.

Joe found the slip he was looking for and began slowly reading from it. "When I was vakyouming in the hall in the jernalism wing, I saw a student lerkin round Miss Hexton's ofice. He was walkin back an forth, staring at her door. He lookt closer to 30 than 20. When he saw me come tords him he ran.

"This is a little hard to read. The guy hasn't mastered English spelling, but once I get the hang of it, his misspellings are sensible. Look at the wonderful way he spells vacuuming," said Joe, passing the report over to Jim. "It's a kick."

Jim perused Enrique's report. "You're right, Joe. v-a-k-you-ming is much better than 'v-a-c-u-u-m-ing!' Incidentally, when did he send in this report?"

"Let's see," said Joe. "Wednesday, September seventh. Here's another one dated Friday, September ninth. Take a look."

Jim's smile broadened as he read. "I saw the same guy agin. At leest I gesst it was the same guy—cuz of his hite. The second time I saw him, it lookt like he was trying to get into Miss Hexton's ofice. He was huncht over mesing with her dorenob. I was at the other end of the hall. He musta herd me, cuz he ran a ways agin."

As soon as Jim returned Enrique's reports, Joe became serious. "Sherry Littlefield is pretty sure she knows who was outside Toni's office."

"Oh?" said Jim. "Littlefield's chairman of English and journalism, isn't she?"

"Yeah. I showed Moriego's reports to Littlefield. By the way, she's okay. She's not like my high school English teachers. She said Enrique's description was wonderfully detailed and accurate, and didn't say a damn thing about his misspelled words. As a matter of fact, Jim, what most impresses me, is not Enrique's spellings, but his excellent observations. Professor Littlefield said she was going to recommend moving Enrique from my staff to yours!"

"I'll take him—gladly. And thanks, Joe. I'll call Sherry."

Sherry told Jim what she'd told Joe: from Enrique's descriptions, she could come up with a name to match. "I'm almost positive the custodian saw Neal O'Donald. He's a perennial malcontent with a big grudge against Toni Hexton *and* the whole department. Once outside my office door, he yelled over and over that Ms. Hexton had no business chairing the department's scholarship selection committee.

Jim's hopes that Toni's intruder could have written *Academic Awards* evaporated when he remembered what she'd said about Neal. A topnotch photographer who believed he was a budding Ansel Adams, he was not nearly as good with words as with pictures. Fruitlessly, Toni had tried to explain to him why one of the department's top scholarships would *not* be given to a student with a C-minus average.

After listening to Sherry and remembering Toni's words, Jim revisited a scene in the newspaper office. He saw someone, undoubtedly Neal, dumping a stack of photos on the layout table while Jim was talking to Eddy. He recollected Betty thumbing through the photographs and starting to thank Neal, but the young man left without a response or even a nod in her direction.

Jim next called Sally Sanchez's office to get Neal's class schedule.

*If I don't cool down before I find him,* he said to himself, *I'll be likely to shake Neal by the scruff of his unshorn neck before I start questioning him.*

Jim waited in the corridor outside Neal's afternoon class. Neal was the first one exiting the classroom. Figures, thought Jim, the scumbag must have been sitting in the back by the door. Neal, wearing what must be a habitual frown, looked around vacantly at hearing his name called. At first he raised his eyebrows and shook his head in disbelief that Southwestern's security chief had any reason to talk to him. Sullenly, he accompanied Jim across campus. After an hour of relentless questioning, Neal shrugged and confessed. He maintained that he had every right to see what had been said about him. "Why," he yelled, rising out of his chair beside Jim's desk, had "the damn committee given my scholarship to some snot-nosed kid?"

Neal, shaking a dirty finger at Jim, barked, "You'd a done the same thing I did!"

He ignored Jim's muted "probably not."

"C'mon, man, what I did was no big deal. Listen, I couldn't nab the prof. She's never in her office." Jim doubted that.

"So," drawled Neal, "I downed a six pack in the parking lot. Boy, was I getting hot under the collar."

"What time was this?" asked Jim.

"Oh, I don't know. All I know is I hadn't eaten and I was getting hungry—and angry. It was Friday night. Nobody much was around."

As Neal got caught up in his self-pitying, self-justifying story, he began talking more and more rapidly. "I figured if the bitch wouldn't show me why her frigging committee dissed me, I'd find out for myself. I tried to get into her office twice. The second time, I had no trouble forcing the lock, but after I'd been in there for a few minutes I heard someone running a vacuum cleaner down at the other end of the hall."

"What did you do then?" asked Jim, trying to sound more civil than he felt.

"I guess I threw some stuff around, and then, when it sounded as if the janitor was coming towards Ms. Hexton's office, I grabbed a couple file folders and some papers. By then, I hadn't found anything labeled scholarships."

Neal ignored Jim's next question. "Wouldn't Ms. Hexton have given scholarship files to Dr. Littlefield?"

"Huh?" Neal slumped back into his chair.

Jim insisted that Neal go with him to Sally Sanchez's office right away, even if he had to miss his next class. Neal slouched along beside him. Jim was glad to turn another problem over to the vice-president of student affairs. He'd call her at the end of the day to find out how she'd dealt with Neal.

Silently, he asked himself, "One down, how many more to go?" He decided *not* to call Toni at the Cozy Cabins Motel with the news. Her least favorite student was guilty of ransacking her office, but the break-in had nothing to do with *Academic Awards*.

At 6 P.M., Jim drove to Aztec and knocked on Sheila's door.

"I'm sorry it's taken me so long to get here, Sheila," Jim said as she opened the door. "I promised Toni I would look after you. Thank heavens for your neighbor."

"She's been very helpful!" Sheila said. "Stop fretting about me and come on in."

"Well at least I could bring you dinner tonight," he said, showing Sheila a take-out box from her favorite Mexican restaurant.

"Rubio's enchiladas, I'll bet," she replied, savoring the aroma. "They'll be a big improvement over my half-baked tuna casserole. I hope you can help me eat them. I want to hear the latest about Toni—and Erica."

## 17

*Tea and Sympathy.*

Toni and Erica left their motel room at 7:30 A.M. and walked to the Ponderosa Restaurant, next to the Ponderosa Craft Store. They were bored with the healthy breakfast that came with their lodging. And they were bored with poring over stacks of their colleagues' writings while they searched for words, phrases, and patterns that matched the style of *Academic Awards*.

Walking into the restaurant, they found themselves surrounded by large, colorful posters of fish.

"Two for breakfast?" asked the hostess who greeted them.

"Yes," replied Toni.

Lagging behind the waitress and looking around the half-empty dining room, Erica asked, "Could we sit over there by the window?"

The waitress abruptly turned away from the table next to the kitchen door where she was plunking down two menus. She nodded curtly and led them to another table. "This okay?" Without looking at them or waiting for an answer, she asked, "Coffee?"

Erica frowned. Toni, to deflect the snide reply she saw forming in Erica's mind, spoke up quickly. "The table's fine and coffee would be lovely."

Erica pushed the menus aside and leaned across the table. "You know, Toni, once we've had a long, leisurely, thoroughly greasy breakfast, I may be able to face reading Abernathy's, Keen's, and Merry's stuff."

"Of those three, Erica, I think Merry is the only possibility."

"I don't know. I'll lay odds on Becky Keen. After all, she's had a couple of short stories published. I think Melinda Merry would have told Jeff and me if she'd been our author. However, right now I'm not eager to read another word written by anyone!"

"Not even J.A. Jance?"

"We-ll, I might be tempted by a new Joanna Brady book. But Jance's Seattle detective stories are too violent for me."

Toni laughed and shrugged. She and Erica, having made their choices from the menu, began inspecting their surroundings. There was a great deal to inspect. In addition to the fish posters, every inch of wall space was covered with samplers in knotty pine frames and mounted trophy-sized fish. As they contemplated the luxuriant but out-of-season poinsettia on the table, the hostess returned with coffee in thick brown mugs.

Erica squinted as she tried to read the names on the nearest "Fish of Colorado" poster. Toni surveyed the hand-painted plates displayed on a high, narrow shelf encircling the room. Not surprisingly, fishing scenes adorned each one.

"I'm glad I decided not to order the trout special," said Toni.

"And did you notice, there wasn't any granola and yogurt on the menu?" laughed Erica. "I'll bet even the trout is fried. Everything looked marvelously unhealthy!"

A new young waitress appeared, with a smile on her face, and pen and pad in hand. "Are you ready to order?"

"I'll have the ham and eggs, hash browns, biscuits and gravy," said Erica.

"Bacon, two scrambled eggs, toast, and a glass of orange juice for me," said Toni.

The restaurant was rapidly filling up. Toni and Erica took no notice of the people coming into the dining room until someone stopped at their table.

Erica was surprised to see the president's secretary looking down at them. "Ruby, what are *you* doing here?" she asked.

Ruby, as surprised to see Erica and Toni as they were to see her, explained, "I'm meeting Jolene Gonzales in a few minutes. She took the first three weeks of September off to move her family's sheep out of the high country and back to their ranch near Cottonwood. She ran into a problem, though. She and her sheep tangled with some guy from California who couldn't believe that animals were allowed on the road and that he didn't have the right-of-way. A few days ago Jolene received a summons to appear in small claims court in Dove Creek at eleven-thirty this morning. Can you believe it? Dunbar—I think that's what Jolene said his name is—is taking her to court to collect damages for a broken headlight and a couple of dents caused when *his* vehicle collided with her sheep. What gall!"

Again, Toni looked surprised. "The court is meeting on a *Saturday*?"

Before Ruby could answer, Erica jumped in with an explanation. "It's not surprising. Way out here in the rural West the judges as well as ministers are still circuit riders, and Saturday is their busiest day."

Acknowledging what Erica had said with a slight nod, Toni turned to Ruby and asked, "When did this collision between Dunbar's car and Jolene's sheep occur?"

"I'm not sure. About ten days ago."

"I've never heard of a court scheduling a small claims case so quickly."

"Oh. I didn't know that was unusual. Anyway, Jolene was contacted by the county clerk. She implied that Dunbar managed to bully his way onto this Saturday's docket. He evidently said he'd be *inconvenienced* if he had to appear in November when his case was scheduled. The clerk felt so pressured by his demands that she apologized to Jolene and ensured *she* wouldn't be inconvenienced."

"Hmm," said Toni, "giving Jolene so much information could get that clerk in trouble. Oh well, I suspect she has the courthouse in Dove Creek all to herself for hours on end and looks forward to talking with someone." Toni paused before asking, "How's Jolene doing?"

"She's worried. She thinks Dunbar is the one at fault. At least, she's really glad to be facing him in court today. She wants to get this behind her before she has to go back to work on campus. Besides, she says having to wait until November would spoil the next six weeks."

Erica grumbled indignantly, "I can't believe she'll owe this Dunbar anything!"

Toni spoke up. "Poor Jolene. I hope the judge sees her side of it."

"I'm sure he will," responded Ruby, taking the chair that Erica pulled out for her. "But Jolene's awfully nervous. That gal can do anything with her hands, but she has a phobia about speaking in public. Sounds like her adversary is a big shot and a bully. Anyone driving in the Four Corners in the fall should expect to meet livestock on the roads."

Ruby laughed, and then continued. "She seemed so worried when she called yesterday that I told her I'd meet her here for breakfast if that would help her stay calm waiting for her day in court."

"What a story!" Erica beamed. "Mind if we wait with you? Now that you've made us curious I hope Jolene will tell us the whole story over breakfast."

"I'll be glad to have your company," replied Ruby. "Jolene wasn't quite sure when she'd get here. While we're waiting, I've got some news you'll be interested in, Toni."

"Oh?"

"Jim Scoop stopped by yesterday. He's discovered who broke into your office."

"Really? Who?"

"Some older student who's been grousing all over the place about how unfair you and your whole department are. I don't remember his name."

"Sounds like Neal O'Donald."

"Yes, that's it."

"What on earth did he expect to find in my office?"

"Something about student scholarships. I think that's what Jim told Walt." Ruby looked down, embarrassed. "I confess. I can look busy when I'm eavesdropping."

Erica laughed. "An admirable skill."

"No matter how hard he pawed through my files," said Toni, "Mr. O'Donald wouldn't have had any luck. The chairman kept all the scholarship information, not me. Besides, we didn't even consider Neal O'Donald, so he wouldn't have found anything about himself! Did Jim learn why Neal took off with some of my personnel committee files, and not others?"

"He hadn't intended to take anything out of your office, or so he said. He'd broken into your office before the building was locked up for the night. Then he heard footsteps down the hall and panicked. He grabbed a number of folders, then ran past the security officer and out of the building. The night patrolman reported the incident."

"You have to give it to our students; they're very resourceful, especially when it comes to cadging keys," said Erica.

"I heard Jim Scoop tell the president," continued Ruby, "that Neal admitted to having had a few too many beers and that he had to find out why everyone in the department passed him over for a scholarship he thought *he* deserved."

"But why would he be interested in faculty folders?"

"Carelessness. He said he didn't even know *what* he'd grabbed. He just ran out of your office clutching something. He tossed the whole kit and kaboodle into the nearest dumpster."

"Did you listen long enough to find out what's going to happen to him?" asked Erica, smiling.

"He's not going to get a degree, for one thing. You should have heard Jim imitating this Neal guy saying he couldn't learn anything more in this place anyway." It was Toni's turn to smile. She *could* hear Jim.

As Ruby finished telling them about Scoop's getting a confession from Neal O'Donald, Jolene walked into the restaurant. She looked around the room twice before she saw Ruby sitting with Erica and Toni.

She approached their table. "When I called you, Ruby, I just needed to vent. I was glad when you said you'd meet me this morning." Jolene looked puzzled. "Hello, Erica, Toni."

"We're here," said Erica, "to lend our support and sympathy too."

"Sounds as if you could use it," added Toni, motioning to the fourth chair.

"But I don't think I need *this* much support," said Jolene, sitting down.

Toni said, "We corralled Ruby. She told us that you and your sheep had a nasty confrontation with a California city slicker. What happened?"

Jolene started to answer when the waitress appeared with coffee and two more menus. She placed heaping plates in front of Erica and Toni, all the while mumbling in the direction of the newcomers, "Everyone want coffee?"

Ruby nodded. Jolene answered, "Just black tea and rye toast for me."

The waitress leaned over and patted Jolene on the shoulder. Her sympathy engaged, the waitress crooned, "Why honey, you're not feeling well, are you? All's you ordered is toast. Lemme poach a coupla eggs for you. There's nothing like poached eggs to make a body feel better. My mother always said…"

Jolene interrupted. "My mother said the same thing, but I really don't want any poached eggs, thank you. I'll just stick to toast and tea."

When the waitress was out of hearing, Jolene said, "I've usually got a good appetite. But I'm scared to death. I'm not sure I'll be able to eat anything, even though the Ponderosa's marbled rye is scrumptious."

"You don't have any reason to be scared," said Ruby soothingly. "From what you told me on the phone, it doesn't sound as if you were at fault at all. Maybe if you tell us what happened, that'll help you get over the jitters."

"The old tea and sympathy cure?" asked Jolene, relaxing a little.

"Okay, I'll tell you the story. And I hope it's good. I have to tell it again to the judge in a couple of hours."

Jolene's self-consciousness dissolved as she warmed to her tale. "It had taken several days to round up the family sheep. My nephews and I were taking the flock to the highway south of Rico. Leonard and Lionel were riding in front. The sheep dogs moved through the flock, keeping them all together and nudging the stragglers and loiterers to move along. We had sixty-two ewes, sixty big lambs, and my beautiful magnificent ram, Buster. As usual, all the lambs looked remarkably like their dad.

"It was my last day out on the trail. It was a gorgeous fall day and I was enjoying it thoroughly. Leonard and Lionel would be trucking the sheep back home in a few hours. I planned to visit some friends in Cortez for a few days since I still had more vacation time. I was looking forward to a shower, a meal that wasn't cooked over a campfire, and a real bed instead of a sleeping bag."

The waitress returned, precariously balancing two plates in one hand and holding a coffee pot in the other. She refilled three cups. "I'll be back in a jiff with a pot of tea."

"We topped a ridge," resumed Jolene, "and could see the highway. We were really making good time. We only had to herd the sheep for about a mile on the road, something I never look forward to.

"When we reached the pavement, we let the dogs circle the sheep while we got out our red flags to warn drivers coming from either direction. Leonard took the lead, Lionel rode near the middle of the flock, and I followed in the rear. The highway wasn't very busy at eleven on a weekday morning. It was ten minutes later when the first car approached from the south. It stopped and waited as the dogs moved the sheep onto the left shoulder. The couple in the car waved at us as they drove slowly by.

"Suddenly another car came up behind us. I waved my red flag but the man driving an enormous Excursion ignored my warning signal and kept going—fast. He wove his way through the flock. Despite Leonard and Lionel gesturing wildly and waving their flags at him, he only slowed down a little bit. Pretty soon most of the flock was behind him. My nephews veered aside several times, to avoid a collision. Finally, he braked and then kept going ahead at a crawl."

"The guy sounds like a real jerk," interjected Erica.

"Wait—the story isn't over—it gets worse, much worse. The sheep behind his car kept gaining on him. And when they did, his car's automatic warning sensor started beeping. I don't think the four star idiot had any idea that his fancy new SUV was designed to alert him whenever he was tailgated. The closer the sheep got, the louder and faster the beeping got. The dummy speeded up. And when he did, he clipped two sheep. They were stunned, but not seriously hurt. Out of all the sheep he could have hit hard, he hit just one, Buster. That brute killed the best ram we Silvas ever had.

"He hit Buster so hard that the ram was flipped up onto the hood of his car. Finally, his motor stalled. Dunbar just sat there. The boys hauled Buster off the hood and laid him on the shoulder of the road. I checked the other injured sheep, glad to find that they were only scared and bruised. Lionel stood up, turned around, and pulled Dunbar's keys out of the ignition. In the meantime, Leonard was calling the state patrol on his cell phone.

"Dunbar could have hit you or your nephews!" said Toni.

"He ought to be hung," added Erica.

"Or maybe tarred and feathered," said Ruby.

"Unfortunately, there's no chance he'll get hanged, or tarred and feathered, either," said Toni, "but he should be charged with reckless endangerment, destruction of property, and sheer stupidity. Although stupidity isn't against the law."

Jolene paused and took a deep breath, then resumed her tale. "While we were waiting for the patrolman, Dunbar claimed it was *our* fault for having sheep on the road. He couldn't believe we didn't see it that way. In less than five minutes, a Colorado state patrol car pulled up. The patrolman walked over to where I was standing. Dunbar was sitting sideways in the driver's seat, with the door open. The patrolman asked me what had happened. That made Dunbar mad. I'm sure he expected to get to tell his version first. It didn't seem to occur to him that he wouldn't be allowed a good man-to-man talk before the 'little lady'—that's what he kept calling me—got her two cents worth in.

"I told the same story I've just told you. While I was talking, Dunbar impatiently drew circles in the dirt with his feet. As soon as I finished, he stood up and yelled, 'This little lady should never have had all those animals on the roadway. They caused a serious traffic hazard. Luckily, I wasn't injured. One animal hit my car so hard he smashed one of my headlights and put a big dent in my hood. She needs to pay for those damages!'

"The patrolman ignored the outburst. All business, he asked to see Dunbar's license and registration.

"Faking politeness, Dunbar drawled, 'Certainly, officer.' He turned his back to me and asked the patrolman ever so smoothly, 'What are you going to do about this unfortunate accident?'

"The patrolman told him he was going to write a report and issue him a citation for reckless endangerment."

"Dunbar looked utterly astonished. He yelled, 'You can't cite me! What about her? She has to pay for the damage to my vehicle!' Dunbar got red in the face and shook his fist at the policeman, all the while talking faster and faster and louder and louder. He said he had the right-of-way since *he* was driving on a public highway, a highway designed for motor vehicle traffic, not a bunch of unleashed animals. He looked from my nephews to me as he spat out his final argument. 'I was driving my motor vehicle. This little lady, her helpers, and *her* sheep blocked my way!'

"The patrolman was wonderful. The angrier Dunbar got, the calmer and more soft-spoken he got. He told Dunbar that ranchers moving livestock *do* have the right-of-way as long as their warning flags are clearly visible, as ours were. He wrote out his citation and handed it to Dunbar.

"It looked as if Dunbar was going to tear it up.

" 'I wouldn't do that if I was you,' the patrolman said.

"Dunbar stuffed the citation into a pocket, glared at all four of us, and then delivered his final threat to the sky: 'Buddy, this may be the last mistake you'll ever make in uniform. If I've broken any law, it's a law no civilized state honors. I'll take my case to court and then you'll regret you ever handed me your ridiculous citation. You and your lady friend here haven't heard the end of this.' "

As soon as Jolene finished her story, she choked up. Wanting to comfort her, Erica said, "You're quite a story teller, Jolene. I can't believe the guy can say anything in court that'll convince a judge you'll have to pay damages. *He* should have to pay *you!*"

"Thanks. But that may not happen. At least, he's not asking for much—not by his lights anyway. I checked. The legal limit allowed in small claims courts in Colorado is seven thousand dollars. I know, I know. That's a lot—it will keep me eating cereal for months if he wins his case, but when I remembered all the expensive extras I saw, leather seats, a padded steering wheel, designer hubcaps, etcetera, I figured he'd think he deserves the full amount." Unnoticed, Toni and Erica both grinned when they heard Jolene say "etcetera."

"Humpf," snorted Erica. "I doubt your accuser cares about the money. But I suspect he needs to massage his ego by strutting his stuff in court," said Erica, "and seeing you squirm. Although a court as little as Dove Creek's," she added, "won't give him much room to strut."

A shadow of a smile crossed Jolene's face as Erica waxed ferocious. "Thanks for listening. It was easy to talk to you, but I'll get tongue-tied if I have to talk extemporaneously in a courtroom. Especially with Mr. Dunbar there. I've written a statement I'm hoping the judge will let me read."

"What a story," exclaimed Erica. "I can't believe it won't hold up in court. No matter what kind of case this jerk thinks he has."

Erica glanced over at Toni for confirmation, "We'd like to hear you make your case. Would it be okay if we come to watch the court proceedings?" Toni smiled and nodded her agreement.

Before Jolene could protest, Erica said, "I've always loved old courthouses—even before my husband started photographing them in little towns all over the Southwest."

Ruby leaned forward. "Whatever for?" she asked.

"Mostly for fun, I suspect. He claims it's for a second coffee-table book. His first one, on arborglyphs, has done so well he wants to try his hand on another book with lots of pictures and few words. Anyway, we've had fun poking into old courthouses. But I have another reason for wanting to see you in court, Jolene," said Erica. "I want to see this Dunbar get egg all over his face."

Later, as the four women walked out of the restaurant, Toni said, "I want to hear what the judge has to say to him. I hope he puts him in his place."

"See you in Dove Creek in a couple of hours if you're sure you want to take the time. Thanks again for being such a good audience," said Jolene.

@

Toni and Erica spent the next hour and a half in their room, trying to stay awake while wading through the last of their colleagues' soporific prose.

Suddenly Erica threw a copy of the article she was reading on the nearest bed, jumped up from her chair, and shouted, "Time to go!"

"Boy, am I ever looking forward to getting out of this *cozy* cabin," said Toni, wearily lining up her stack of papers and stretching her shoulders. She grabbed her purse and keys from the top of the microwave, and trudged outside. "Looking for stylistic clues was *not* one of my best ideas!"

"Don't blame yourself; none of us came up with a better one!" said Erica, as they locked the door of their motel room and climbed into Toni's car.

Toni still hadn't gotten over her fatigue and frustration from the night before. She'd hoped the drive would clear her mind of last night's tedium. But it couldn't. Examining assorted memos, letters, and committee reports as well as excerpts from articles and books *had* been a fruitless endeavor. After Erica announced she'd had enough at 10 P.M., Toni had kept reading for another hour. But when she climbed into bed, sleep escaped her. She cursed herself for suggesting the hunt for stylistic clues. She tossed and turned. Finally, she got up, made herself a pot of strong coffee, and plowed on. At 3 A.M. only a small stack of the material remained unread. By then she didn't expect she *or* Erica would come across anything resembling her list of stylistic markers. Exhausted, she had crawled into bed.

When she woke Saturday morning, Toni realized she didn't look forward to reporting back to Jim. But shouldn't she tell him he'd be wasting his time examining Lloyd's book? The more she thought about it, she realized they shouldn't have included Lloyd Reasoner in their list of suspects. He wasn't mean-spirited enough to carry on a joke for such a long time. And he respected the president too much to let him stew needlessly. Nor would he consign his colleagues to hours of tedious work.

Oh well, since she and Erica had agreed to wait until Sunday night to return to Cottonwood, she might as well be on her way to Dove Creek. She hadn't watched court proceedings since her reporting days. Most were boring, but a couple had been exciting.

Interrupting Toni's reminiscences, Erica announced, "I'll have bragging rights when I get home. Bill and I *never* saw any action in the rural courthouses when we visited them in the summer."

"While you're making Bill jealous, this member of Walt's erstwhile task force is ready for a diversion. At least, we won't have to pull another late nighter. I only have a few more pages to read. What about you?"

"Well, I didn't count them, but I'm becoming a whiz at speed reading. We'll be done before dark. We can have a long, leisurely dinner, and then drag Dolores's Main Street before vegging out in front of the TV."

"Yeah. Saturday night's inane offerings may send us early to bed, but none the wiser!"

For the rest of the journey, both women remained silent.

Slowing down to obey Dove Creek's speed limit—reputed all over the Four Corners to swell the town's budget—Toni saw Ruby turning into a parallel parking place in front of the courthouse. They pulled in next to her, and Erica jumped out to join Ruby and Jolene. They walked three abreast towards the courthouse's imposing double doors. Toni took a moment to lean back against her headrest, trying to ignore her itching eyes and aching back. Then she climbed out and hurried to catch up with the other three.

A woman neatly dressed in a navy blue skirt and matching blazer met Jolene in the hallway. "You're Jolene Gonzales? Yours is the fourth case Judge Chitwood will be hearing. I'll be recording the proceedings. Let me take you down to your seat."

Jolene handed the recorder a note addressed to Judge Chitwood as she fell in step beside her escort. Toni, Erica, and Ruby took seats several rows behind two teenaged boys, a couple of stolid farm couples, a young man in a crumpled khaki suit holding a stenographer's pad in his lap, and a few assorted parents, friends, and witnesses. Jolene was ushered to a front row seat behind a long narrow table. Across the aisle from her sat a large, flashily dressed man whose stomach came perilously close to the table in front of him.

A fly buzzed irritatingly around Toni's head as the proceedings began. She dozed through the first three cases. Erica jabbed her awake when Judge Chitwood announced "Next, Dunbar vs. Gonzales." The large man rose and stomped toward the bench.

"That's undoubtedly our villain," whispered Erica.

"I presume, sir, you're Mr. Dunbar," said the judge.

Dunbar scowled. "Yes, and I'm prepared to explain exactly what happened." He stepped closer to the bench, tilted his head, leaned slightly forward, and spoke in a confidential tone. "As I wrote when I asked your court to consider my claim for…"

Judge Chitwood raised his hand, with fingers splayed as a signal for Dunbar to stop talking. "Mr. Dunbar, speak up so that you can be heard by everyone in the courtroom."

Dunbar blinked, feigning surprise at this attack. He slowly swiveled his head several times, to keep both the judge and his larger audience in his line of vision. His voice boomed out over the hushed courtroom.

"On September thirteenth," he said, giving a sideways glance in Jolene's direction, "I began my drive home from Telluride to Los Angeles. Incidentally," he growled, turning towards the judge again, "*I was obeying the speed limit.*"

Once again he turned to look at Jolene. He spoke slowly, as if talking to a small child. "Coming around a corner, I saw *hundreds* of sheep entirely blocking *both* lanes of the highway. I honked my horn *several times*, but the cowboys on horseback were *obviously* unable to control their animals. As I proceeded, they did manage to push a few of them to the sides of the road. But the buckaroos *rudely* waved some flags at me as if I were a bull in some damn bullring."

When he became aware that the judge was about to raise his hand again, Dunbar shrugged. "Sorry, sir, but as you can imagine, I am still very upset by the disrespectful treatment I received.

"The dumb cowpokes kept waving their silly flags. All of a sudden the biggest sheep in the whole bunch leapt from the edge of the road and landed square in front of my car. The other sheep were all crowded together. When this happened they began to move about in all directions. I slammed on my brakes—hard, but of course I couldn't stop completely. That d…arn sheep ended up on the hood of my car and the rest of the animals started making a godawful noise."

Dunbar's eyes swept the room, as if to demand everyone's attention. After a long pause, he lowered his voice and resumed his tale. "I got an estimate for repairing the damage to my vehicle. Six thousand, seven hundred and seventy-five dollars! And that was a *conservative* estimate. I immediately called your county clerk and she said I could bring a claim to recover my expenses to your small claims court. And then she told me the next available opening would be in November. I wasn't about to drive back to Podunksville at that time of year. You'll probably be buried in four feet of snow by then. Besides, come November, I'll be out of the country on *important* business."

Dunbar looked at the judge, expecting some sort of reaction.

Judge Chitwood remained impassive. He finally broke the silence. "Now, Ms. Gonzales, I'd like to hear what you have to say about Mr. Dunbar's claim."

The minute Dunbar sat down, the shrill sound of a cell phone pierced the courtroom. He reached into a shiny new, gilt-edged leather briefcase prominently embossed with *P.U.D.* He pulled out a small cell phone, palming it in his beefy hand.

Erica poked Toni. "I wonder what the 'U' can possibly stand for— ugly, uppity, unlikable…" Toni grinned as she shushed her friend.

Dunbar turned away from the judge and cradled the phone next to his ear.

Peremptorily, the judge said, "Mr. Dunbar, turn that thing off." The ringing continued. The judge, looking exasperated, pointed to a sign behind the court reporter. "Cell phones are prohibited in this courtroom."

"Your Honor, I'm in the midst of several important business transactions."

"Mr. Dunbar," said the judge, leaning forward over the bench and glaring at the man, "This morning, your business is with this court. So stash that phone. And *silence* it."

The judge turned towards Jolene and smiled encouragingly. "Ma'am, you may step forward. Jolene rose, and grasping her statement, looked from it to Judge Chitwood.

"Oh, for heavens sake," blurted Dunbar. "Can't she just tell what happened? After all, it's not very complicated. She and her sheep and her young chums impeded…"

"Mr. Dunbar, you are again out of order. This court has adjusted its schedule to accommodate you. Do not take advantage of our consideration, and do *not* interrupt these proceedings again."

Dunbar glared as the judge switched his attention from him to Jolene. "Ms. Gonzales, I've read your request and you have my permission to read your statement."

Jolene stood stiffly and began to read from the first of several yellow hand-written sheets.

"On the fifth of September, my two nephews, Lionel and Leonard Martinez, joined me in the high country above Rico where our family pastures our sheep each summer. Eight days later, having rounded up the whole flock, we broke camp, corralled the sheep dogs, and headed for highway 146.

"As we made our way onto the paved road, Lionel was riding at the head of the flock as first flagger, I was riding at the rear with the second warning flag, while Leonard stayed in the middle.

"Our positions, as well as the positions of the flags, clearly signaled that we were moving our sheep down the road."

Mr. Dunbar jumped up and shouted, "Good God, roads are for cars…"

The judge struck his gavel on the bench. "Mr. Dunbar, for the last time, you are out of order."

As Dunbar retreated to his seat, Erica whispered in Toni's ear, "This is getting better by the minute. You should reassert your reportorial skills." Erica handed Toni a small notebook and gestured in the direction of the khaki-clad young man, who was leaning over to retrieve a steno pad that had slipped to the floor. "Your competition is dozing. I can't wait to see your byline in all the important papers!"

Toni, nudging Erica, whispered, "Such as Dove Creek's daily or Pleasant View's weekly newspaper?"

"Ms. Gonzales," said the judge, "I'm sorry about the interruptions. Please start again at the beginning."

Jolene did so. Toni found her attention drifting. Despite the hardness of the seat and her struggle to keep them open, her eyelids closed and she became vaguely aware of the rhythm but not the sense of Jolene's words. The heat of the courtroom and hearing the story for a second time, along with Jolene's soft delivery, were hypnotizing.

"To make sure we wouldn't miss the sheep hauler, whom we were scheduled to meet at noon, I checked my watch when we made it to the highway. No more than ten minutes later, I saw a car approaching from the south. Lionel waved his flag, the car stopped completely, and the dogs moved the sheep onto the right shoulder."

Toni blinked her eyes and stared at Jolene. The written version was not an exact replica of this morning's account. Toni noticed each of the words and phrases distinctly, not just as part of a rhythmic pattern. She listened intently, trying to figure out what had niggled her out of her torpor. Was her mind playing tricks on her?

"That first car passed the sheep, my nephews, and me. It was clear that the couple in the car understood the rules of the road, what a sheep drive was, and what they needed to do to get past us."

Toni straightened, suddenly alert.

Jolene continued. "The driver of the next car was coming from the north. He looked furious. He either ignored the rules, felt exempt from them, or couldn't see the flags in front of his face. Whatever the reason, it became clear to me that Mr. Dunbar expected us to move over for him, and not vice versa."

At this, Dunbar spluttered and would have risen if the judge hadn't frowned, and repeatedly raised and lowered one arm, fingers splayed and palm downward.

Toni flipped open the note pad Erica had given her and quickly wrote: 1...2...3...

Erica looked at her quizzically. This time Toni whispered, "Triplets…" Still uncomprehending, Erica raised her eyebrows. "What?"

Toni tore off a sheet of paper and put it into Erica's lap, "Listen carefully," she whispered. "Count how often Jolene says 'it was clear' and 'it was equally clear.' I'll start counting the *that*'s and the three-part compounds."

Light dawned. Excited, Erica foraged for a pen in the depths of her purse. Then, resting her right ankle on her left knee, and balancing her purse along the edge of her raised leg, she created an unsteady but usable writing surface.

Erica and Toni listened intently, ignoring the familiar narrative and instead jotting down examples of the words and phrases they'd been hunting for in vain the last three days.

Next to the opening phrase, "Despite the flag I was waving," Toni nudged Erica. She pointed to her marginal note, 'Neg intro,' under which she wrote, 'despite…waving,' followed by a row of exclamation marks.

Jolene kept reading. "The second car, a big Ford SUV, didn't slow up at all." As soon as she'd read, "Not hearing the sound of brakes," Toni scribbled the whole phrase as another example of a negative introduction and underlined the word *not*.

In the meantime, Erica was drawing a wide smiley face around the sentence she had written: "It quickly became clear to me."

"Since a few of the sheep were spread out all across the highway, Leonard, with the dogs' help, was working the strays back onto the shoulder of the road. The Ford pulled around me." When Jolene read, "It was obvious that the driver expected to push or scare the sheep out of his way," Erica was scribbling frantically while Toni put another slash mark under a column labeled "*that* - not necessary."

Oblivious to the excitement she was causing, Jolene continued, eyes glued to her prepared text. "Most of the flock were behind the car by now. Only then did the driver stop."

During the next few minutes, Toni and Erica were too busy tallying telltale words and phrases to look up at Jolene.

"As the sheep were gaining on Mr. Dunbar, his car began to beep.

The closer the sheep got, the louder and faster the beeping got. It was clear to me that the driver was starting to panic, since he sharply accelerated. His right bumper struck two lambs. Then he hit the ram, hard enough to flip him up on the hood. By this time, both of my nephews had reached the car and dismounted from their horses. Leonard went around to the driver's side of the car, Lionel opened the passenger door, and I memorized the license number. It was clear that the driver was furious with us, and with the situation. The patrolman didn't get flustered. The angrier Mr. Dunbar got, the calmer and more soft-spoken he got. He told Mr. Dunbar that ranchers moving livestock do have the right-of-way in Colorado as long as their warning flags are clearly visible, as ours were."

Jolene, shaking her head angrily, looked up from her notes and spoke directly to the judge. "Mr. Dunbar's damages are a result of his failure to heed the warning signs and flags. *My* damages are a result of *his* failure. It will cost me at least three thousand dollars to replace my ram, plus another thousand for vet bills to care for the injured sheep. And that doesn't include all my time and travel expenses to deal with the results of his carelessness."

Dunbar, looking ready to spring out of his seat, exploded, "That's impossible!"

The judge remained impassive. He ignored Dunbar and gestured for Jolene to go on.

"That's all I have to say, judge. Thank you for listening to me," she said.

Jolene folded her notes lengthwise and tucked the four sheets under her left arm. The judge nodded twice and addressed her quietly. "Thank you, Ms. Gonzales. You may return to your seat." Raising his voice, he said, "The court declares a short recess. If you leave the courtroom come back promptly. I will deliver my decision on Mr. Dunbar's claim in ten minutes."

Jolene remained seated while Paul Dunbar, clutching his cell phone, dashed from the courtroom. Seeing that Jolene was sitting immobile, Toni and Erica took the opportunity to stretch their legs and go in search of a drinking fountain.

℮

When Erica re-entered the courtroom she noticed that Dunbar

looked confident and impatient. Jolene, on the other hand, looked anxious.

Judge Chitwood addressed his remarks to the plaintiff and defendant as if no one else were in the room. He adjusted his glasses, squinted at a small index card, carefully placed it on the bench in front of him, and then spoke solemnly. "Paul Dunbar, this court rejects your claim."

His jaw dropping, Dunbar clenched his right fist into a ball, and started to rise.

"Sit down, Mr. Dunbar. You had your chance to speak. I have weighed your account against Ms. Gonzales's account. During the recess, I re-examined the patrolman's complete report. Frankly, I wonder why you bothered to waste your time bringing such a frivolous claim to this court's attention. You were duly informed of Colorado's law giving the right-of-way to cattle and sheep drives as long as flags are clearly displayed at the head and rear of the drive. Unless your eyesight is very bad, you must have noticed three flags, not just two, indicating the extent of Ms. Gonzales's flock. Ms. Gonzales exceeded the statutory requirement for notifying drivers that she was moving sheep on a public highway. It was your responsibility to heed those warnings."

Dunbar huffed and puffed, then took a deep breath that could be heard by everyone in the courtroom. Glaring at the judge, he sputtered, "How do you expect me to follow some quaint Colorado law I've never even heard of."

"You've heard of it now. And you should have been aware of it when you were driving south from Telluride on the thirteenth of September. Warnings were posted all along Highway 146 that day."

The judge faced Jolene. "Ms. Gonzales, I have some advice for you. You have incurred a substantial loss. You have the right to claim damages against Mr. Dunbar."

Hearing this, Dunbar's face became red as he clenched his left fist and repeatedly slammed it into the palm of his right hand. Facing Jolene, he pulled out his wallet, and extracted five one thousand dollar bills and threw them at her.

"I'm not coming back to this Podunk town again! I trust this will more than cover your costs," he shouted as he turned and stormed out of the courtroom.

℗

At the ensuing victory lunch in Dove Creek's only open cafe, Ruby couldn't stop smiling while Jolene answered Toni and Erica's questions. Yes, she had written a mystery and, yes, she had sent her manuscript to NAMWA. August 20, a date she'd circled in her calendar, passed without her having heard from the North American Mystery Writers Association. The last two weeks in August were always the busiest time of year for her maintenance crew, and consequently, she'd given no more thought to her chances of becoming the recipient of a prize for the best first mystery novel set on a college campus. Entering the contest had been a long shot anyway.

"Jolene, how could you possibly have time to write a whole book?" asked Ruby. "And why didn't you tell me?"

Jolene smiled. "I *did* tell you I took some creative writing classes a couple of years back. I'd already completed a first draft of *Academic Awards* by the time I took Matt Leslie's creative writing class. What I learned from him really helped me improve my book. I wrote shorter things for his class—stories, some articles, a few old-fashioned essays, and even some poetry. Writing poems was the hardest."

Ruby, frowning, shook her head at Jolene. A slight smile replaced the frown as she turned towards Toni and Erica. "Yeah, during our lunch break. I was mad at Jolene for letting me down. We'd always eaten together at noon. If I'd known," she said, beaming at Jolene, "you were going to win fifty thousand dollars, I wouldn't have minded nearly so much that you skipped out on me!"

Jolene was all smiles as she turned toward Ruby. "This morning, I thought I was lucky to get five thousand dollars instead of having to pay an obnoxious jerk for the damage *my* innocent sheep had done to *his* precious vehicle. And now I discover I've earned ten times that amount!"

"When *did* you find time to write *Academic Awards?*" asked Toni.

"I started it when Roberto and Ricardo flew the nest and went off to college." Jolene paused. What she didn't confess was that Jake Henderson's simultaneously moving to Washington left an equally big hole. "If I hadn't met you at breakfast, I guess I wouldn't have learned about the prize until I got home and picked up my mail."

Toni laughed. "Trouble is, NAMWA hasn't written you. You didn't receive any letter from them."

Jolene looked puzzled.

"A harebrained secretary dutifully separated all the manuscripts from the submission letters," said Erica.

Ruby grumbled, "Wouldn't you know, a secretary would turn out to be the villain?"

Toni ignored the interruption. "What's worse, she then managed to misplace your letter."

Erica picked up the story, reveling in her description of the resulting fuss on campus. "President Asher was fit to be tied, and Jim Scoop has been a nervous Nelly."

Erica looked pointedly at Toni when she said, "Jim's been acting like a knight in slightly tarnished armor." Toni was either too tired or too lost in her own thoughts to react. Erica continued, "Our Jim was worried that someone might be out to sabotage the campus or planning to murder some undeserving faculty member or administrator!"

Jolene laughed. "I wish I'd been around to watch all that."

"Well, if you had been," said Toni, "the mystery of the unknown author would have been solved promptly. Southwestern would have been off to its usual humdrum start. Seriously though, we should have thought of you. Especially you, Erica. You and Jolene have been playing softball together for years." Toni didn't quote Erica's oft-repeated praise of Jolene as being twice as intelligent and three times more articulate than most of their colleagues. Toni did say, "I can't tell you how often I've heard my colleagues in the English and history departments praise you for being the best maintenance chief Southwestern has ever had as well as the best writer who ever showed up in their classes."

"Not only that," added Erica, "but you probably know more of what goes on at Southwestern than anyone else on campus."

"Yeah," said Ruby. "You get to eavesdrop even more than I do. Think of how many offices and labs you go in and out of every day. People kind of watch what they say in the president's office."

"I'm curious," asked Erica, "how did you choose your pseudonym?"

"Oh," laughed Jolene. "Edith Tansley Coyle? Miss Coyle was my fifth grade teacher. She liked my stories. She encouraged me to write. Edith was my best friend all through school and Chip Tansley was the boy I had a secret crush on in junior high."

Ruby frowned. "I still can't believe you never told me you were writing a book."

"I never told *anyone*."

"Why not use your own name?"

Jolene looked down and blushed. "I suppose I thought my made-up self wouldn't mind losing as much as I would."

℮

After their late lunch, Erica and Toni high-fived Jolene and waved good-bye to her and Ruby. They began their return drive to Dolores to collect their belongings and the less than immortal words of their suspects. They reviewed Jolene's admission, their own failure to envision her as an author, but mostly, their delight in anticipating how Walt, Bill, and the other members of the task force, to say nothing of the rest of the faculty, would react to learning that a non-academic had pulled such a coup.

Erica handed Toni her cell phone. "Call Jim. Right now."

Toni was glad Jim Scoop picked up his phone after only two rings. "Jim, mission accomplished! You can quit trying to wade through Reasoner's tome."

"Wonderful. I'm only on page four and I'm already bogged down. Who is the author? And how did you find him?"

"*Her*, not him. And it was, as I thought it might be, an element of style that led us to her. But we were sure off track. We didn't look in the right place. Our writer is not any of the people Erica and I spent the last few days reading…"

"And being infinitely bored by," shouted Erica in the direction of the phone.

## 18

*It's all over but the shouting.*

Toni and Erica had called Sheila Mays on Saturday afternoon. From their chaotic, ecstatic account, Sheila finally figured out they were trying to tell her about Jolene's triumph and theirs. They'd discovered that Jolene Gonzales was E.T.C. just in the nick of time. If Edith Tansley Coyle hadn't been identified by Monday morning, the prize money would have gone to the runner-up in the mystery-writing contest. President Walt Asher would have been sick. Sheila would not have offered to host a celebratory party.

At 2:30 Sunday afternoon, Sheila surveyed her yard and pronounced it ready for guests. Toni, Erica, Jim, and the college caterers had laid out enough food to feed a small horde.

Annette Asher had orchestrated a celebration and Sheila had readily agreed to host it. With orders from the president, delivered by phone as Walt hurried home from Flagstaff, Annette commandeered the food service staff to stay on the job until midnight Saturday and the facilities people to deliver folding tables and chairs and even a portable college podium early Sunday morning. Annette herself had dropped by at noon with packages of balloons, and a second-hand banner saying "Congratulations! You did it" retrieved from some ancient horsemanship contest.

"Thanks for making me look like the ultimate hostess, Annette," Sheila said with a smile as the two sat together. "And congratulations on pulling all this together in such short order."

"Arranging this party has been easy," Annette said. "The last few weeks were not. As the days went by, I have to confess, I couldn't imagine *any* good outcome. Walt would have been deeply disappointed to have missed out on the windfall from NAMWA, and I would have been a nervous wreck. We have a lot to celebrate."

Erica ambled over to where Sheila and Annette were sitting, plunked down in the chair next to them, and handed each woman a large iced tea. Erica sighed contently. "I think everything is ready."

Sheila beamed at Erica, and then glanced over to the corner of her yard where Toni and Jim were attaching the last balloons to the lowest branches of a heavily laden apple tree. "You three are wonderfully efficient, and I haven't had to do a thing," she said. "We've even got half an hour to spare."

As Toni and Jim joined them, Sheila asked, "Would you mind going over the whole story again? I'd like to know all the details before Jolene and the president and the other guests arrive. The version shouted at me yesterday over your cell phone was rather garbled."

"Sorry about that," said Erica.

Toni chimed in, "We were too excited to be clear."

"Sheila," said Jim, "I think it took Toni and Erica four or five tries before I had the remotest idea they were telling me the search was *over*."

"Jim," said Erica, "absolutely refused to let us call Walt."

"Why?" Sheila asked, turning towards Jim. "I'm sure Walt would have wanted to hear the good news."

"Officer Scoop said he was afraid we'd run off the road if he *allowed* us to continue using our cell phone while driving." Anyone hearing the mock indignation and affection in Erica's voice, thought Sheila, wouldn't have believed that only a few days ago Erica had been suspicious and snippy about "Toni's policeman."

Toni summarized yesterday's events, starting with meeting Ruby and Jolene in Dolores, and ending with Jolene's statement in court.

"And that statement provided the proof you were looking for?" asked Sheila.

Jim broke into a wide smile. To Sheila, he sounded like a teacher proud of a star pupil. "Did Toni tell you how she proposed to solve Southwestern's mystery of the missing author?"

"You mean catching the perpetrator by matching styles in the book and another piece of writing?" asked Sheila.

"Yes, and Toni was right, although I was ready to give up. As soon as we started listening to Jolene in the courtroom, *it was obvious*," said Erica, winking at Toni, "we knew our search was over."

"Boy," said Toni, "Were we impatient for the hearing to end so we could accuse Jolene—and thank her all at once."

"She was astounded when we told her that *her* book had won two awards, one for her and one for the college." said Erica. "She admitted to writing *Academic Awards,* even before Erica and I finished explaining why she was the most sought after person at Southwestern College."

Jim and Sheila looked at each other with amusement as Toni and

Erica tripped over each other's sentences in their eagerness to continue their tale. Today's account, especially in response to some targeted questions put by Jim and Sheila, was considerably easier to follow than yesterday's telephone calls.

"Jolene said she'd seen NAMWA's ad last winter. The guidelines happened to describe a novel she'd written…" said Toni.

"…and put aside…" interrupted Erica, before she herself was interrupted.

"…a novel she'd started five years earlier," resumed Toni, "when Roberto and Ricky went off to college and she found herself in an empty nest."

At the end of their joint tale, Erica shook her head and frowned. "I'm still kicking myself for overlooking Jolene."

"You weren't alone," said Toni. "All of us on the task force, to say nothing of President Asher and his cabinet, couldn't see beyond faculty—and several staff members who only seemed possible when we were desperate…"

Erica frowned at her friend. "We did consider Charlie Roanhorse, though, so why not Jolene?"

Jim leaned forward, "It's not surprising that you all thought the author would turn out to be a faculty member." Chagrined, he silently acknowledged that *he* should have thought of Jolene. But his biggest blind spot had been not recognizing Jolene's descriptions of so many places she knew and loved, places he'd come to appreciate through her eyes.

Erica interrupted Jim's rueful reflections, jumping up from her chair, and spilling the last of her iced tea as she did so. "Our academic bias *is* the point. We take people like Jolene for granted. We see them as their jobs. Blue-collar jobs. Lesser jobs than ours! We professors pride ourselves on our lack of class-consciousness and our open-mindedness. And so what did we do? We included Charlie and a few others who crossed our *academic* paths. Year after year, Melinda Merry's manuals sat by our computers. And during the last several years, Charlie sat in our classes. We gave him a diploma and our academic stamp of approval. We even considered Richard Frankel, for god's sake."

Sheila wagged a finger in Erica's direction. "Don't be so hard on yourself, Erica. Jolene will be very visible to everyone on this campus by tomorrow morning. I suspect that many a bona fide academic would like to be in her shoes just now."

Erica, laughing, sat back down. "You're right, Sheila. Jolene Gonzales, with fifty grand, to say nothing about a published book and the president's eternal gratitude, will no longer be invisible to *anyone* at Southwestern College. She'll get money and fame, and we'll all have to eat a little humble pie."

Just then, pouring through Sheila's back gate came the college president, his wife, his secretary, and Jolene Gonzales, followed by deans, vice-presidents, security officers, the entire physical plant staff, Jolene's twin sons who'd driven up from Albuquerque, and the remaining four task force members. The innocent suspects they'd interviewed were happy to attend and garner some reflected fame. Three suspects were not there: Charlie Roanhorse, who couldn't be reached; Taylor Anderson, who had not been sent an invitation in Spain; and Jane Snow, who had been invited but who had unrespectfully declined.

Sheila stood to greet her guests. Walt rushed over to her, pecked her on the cheek, and insisted that she sit back down before making his way to the refreshment table and signaling for silence. He held up a sheaf of papers—instead of the usual book without which he was never known to speak.

Waving his copy of the prize-winning manuscript, the president launched into what he promised would be a brief speech. "We're gathered here today to say thank you to Jolene—for being not just the author of *Academic Awards* but also the author of the largest single gift ever received by Southwestern College. We're also here to thank the six characters who successfully searched for an author—and found her."

Erica whispered to Toni, "Walt Asher should be thanking *seven* characters, not just six. Jim Scoop's been as involved as any of us on the task force. Don't frown at me, Toni. I've come to like your cop!"

Sheila tuned out the president's words. She doubted they'd be brief. Trying not to stare too noticeably, she watched Jim move his chair closer to Toni's and quietly take her hand. Happiness, she thought, is seeing people she loved looking pleased to have found each other.

# ACKNOWLEDGMENTS

My biggest thanks of course go to Doreen Mehs, my collaborator. My thanks also go to our husbands, Mark Coburn and John Sanders, as well as friends who read early drafts and said they enjoyed the book.

Several readers pointed out problems with clarity, phrasing or facts, and a few of them even urged me to publish, for which I've both thanked and cursed them: Sally Bellerue, Marylaine Block, Lynn Coburn, Will Coe, Jim Cross, Ann Flatten, Anne Fuller, Joel Jones, Reece Kelly, Lisa Lenard-Cook, Colleen Lyon, Shelley Mann, Sandra Mapel, Aggie Owens, Faith Peeples, Ingrid Ryan, Evelyn Wagner, and especially Judith Reynolds, who gave the manuscript a wonderfully close reading and commented on various passages that rang true of academia and academics as she experienced them.

Doreen and I were grateful to the waitresses at the Edgewater Grill, where we met over lunch for several years. Stephanie, Heidi, Angela, and Iresa cheered us on and supplied us with many cups of coffee way past the normal lunch hour. Doreen was as pleased as I was when Mary Jean Moseley joined us as an appreciative and probing audience during the last months of our joint revising sessions.

Beth Green, the encouraging editor I've been privileged to work with over the last year, taught this teacher many things I wish I'd known when I was teaching. Her good eye and good ear made this a tighter, better book. Also, I want to thank Lisa Atchison for preparing the book for publication and designing the cover.

# ABOUT THE AUTHORS

Doreen Mehs earned chemistry degrees from Harpur College, SUNY Binghamton, and the University of New Mexico. Shaila Van Sickle earned philosophy and English degrees from Carleton College, Occidental College, and the University of Denver.

Both Westerners by choice, Mehs and Van Sickle met in the early 1970s when they joined the faculty of Fort Lewis College in Durango, Colorado. Though their offices and fields of study were far apart, they wanted their students to see the humanities and sciences as liberating arts. To that end, they team taught several courses and created a freshman program requiring students to analyze, do research in, and appreciate areas of study aside from their chosen majors.

They liked collaborating and welcomed the opportunity to continue doing so after retirement.

Like the characters in their book, both served on various committees and task forces and chaired their departments. They were honored for their teaching at Fort Lewis. For her encouragement of women science students, as well as her teaching, Doreen was named Colorado's Professor of the Year in 1991.